THE BURIAL PLACE

Stig Abell believes that discovering a crime fiction series to enjoy is one of the great pleasures in life. His first novel, *Death Under a Little Sky*, introduced Jake Jackson and his attempt to get away from his former life, in the beautiful area around Little Sky. This book is the third in the series, and Stig is absolutely delighted that there are more on the way.

Away from books, he co-presents the breakfast show on Times Radio, a station he helped to launch in 2020. Before that he was a regular presenter on Radio 4's *Front Row* and was the editor and publisher of the *Times Literary Supplement*. He lives in London with his wife, three children and two independent-minded cats called Boo and Ninja (his children named them, obviously).

𝕏 @StigAbell
◉ @TheStigAbell

Also by Stig Abell

Death Under a Little Sky
Death in a Lonely Place

THE BURIAL PLACE

STIG ABELL

A Jake Jackson Mystery

Hemlock Press,
an imprint of HarperCollins*Publishers* Ltd
1 London Bridge Street,
London SE1 9GF

www.harpercollins.co.uk

HarperCollins*Publishers*
Macken House, 39/40 Mayor Street Upper
Dublin 1, D01 C9W8, Ireland

First published by HarperCollins*Publishers* Ltd 2025
25 26 27 28 29 LBC 6 5 4 3 2

Copyright © Stig Abell 2025

Map by Liane Payne © 2025

Epigraph from *Autobiography of an Historian* (1949) by G. M. Trevelyan, used with the agreement of the heirs of G. M. Trevelyan

Stig Abell asserts the moral right to be identified as the author of this work.

A catalogue record for this book is available from the British Library.

ISBN: 978-0-00-864366-9 (HB)
ISBN: 978-0-00-864367-6 (TPB)

This novel is entirely a work of fiction. The names, characters and incidents portrayed in it are the work of the author's imagination. Any resemblance to actual persons, living or dead, events or localities is entirely coincidental.

Set in Sabon LT Std by HarperCollins*Publishers* India

Printed and bound in the United States of America

All rights reserved. No part of this publication may be reproduced, stored in a retrieval system, or transmitted, in any form or by any means, electronic, mechanical, photocopying, recording or otherwise, without the prior written permission of the publishers.

Without limiting the author's and publisher's exclusive rights, any unauthorised use of this publication to train generative artificial intelligence (AI) technologies is expressly prohibited. HarperCollins also exercise their rights under Article 4(3) of the Digital Single Market Directive 2019/790 and expressly reserve this publication from the text and data mining exception.

For Nadine – who likes new pottery, rather than old

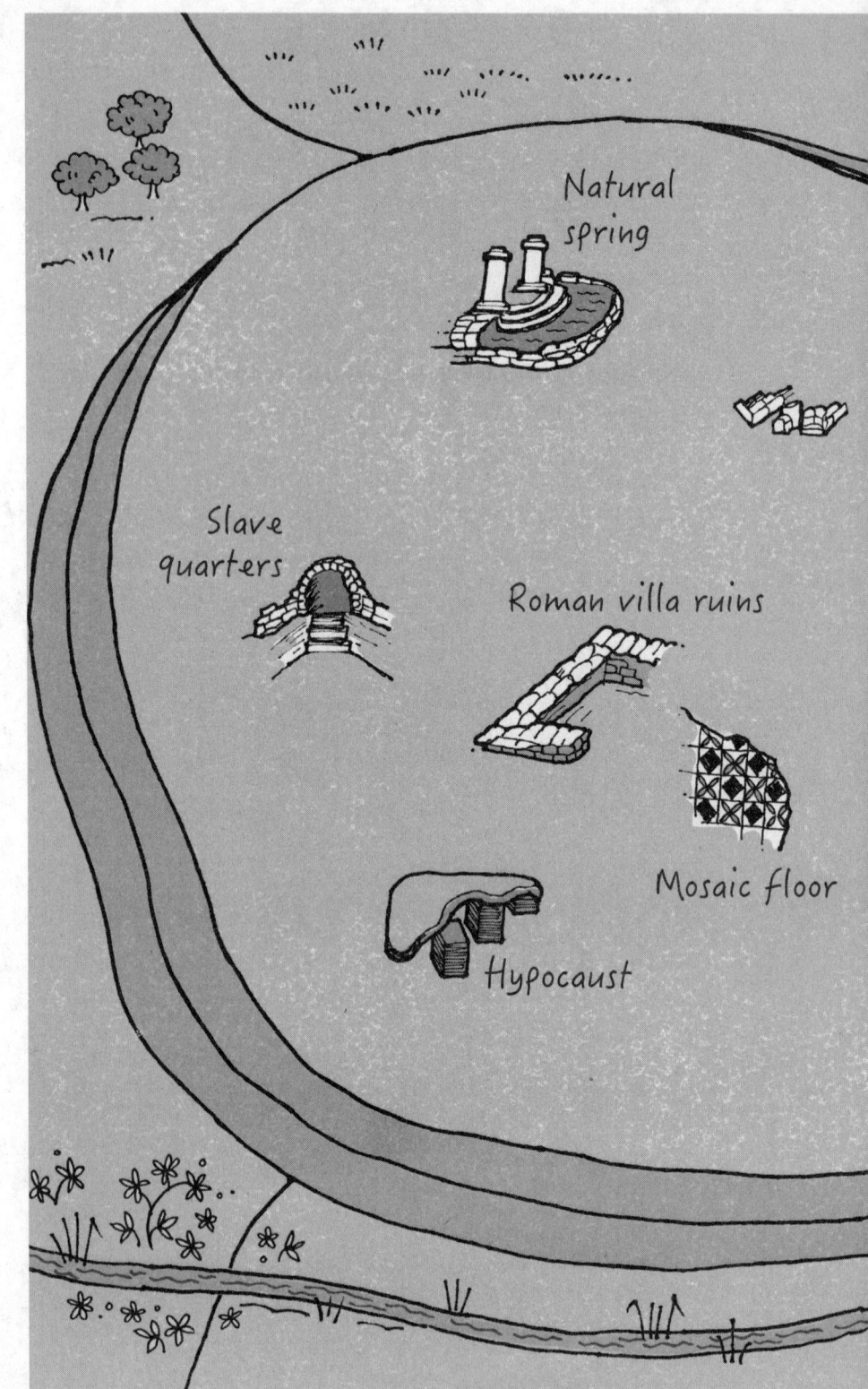

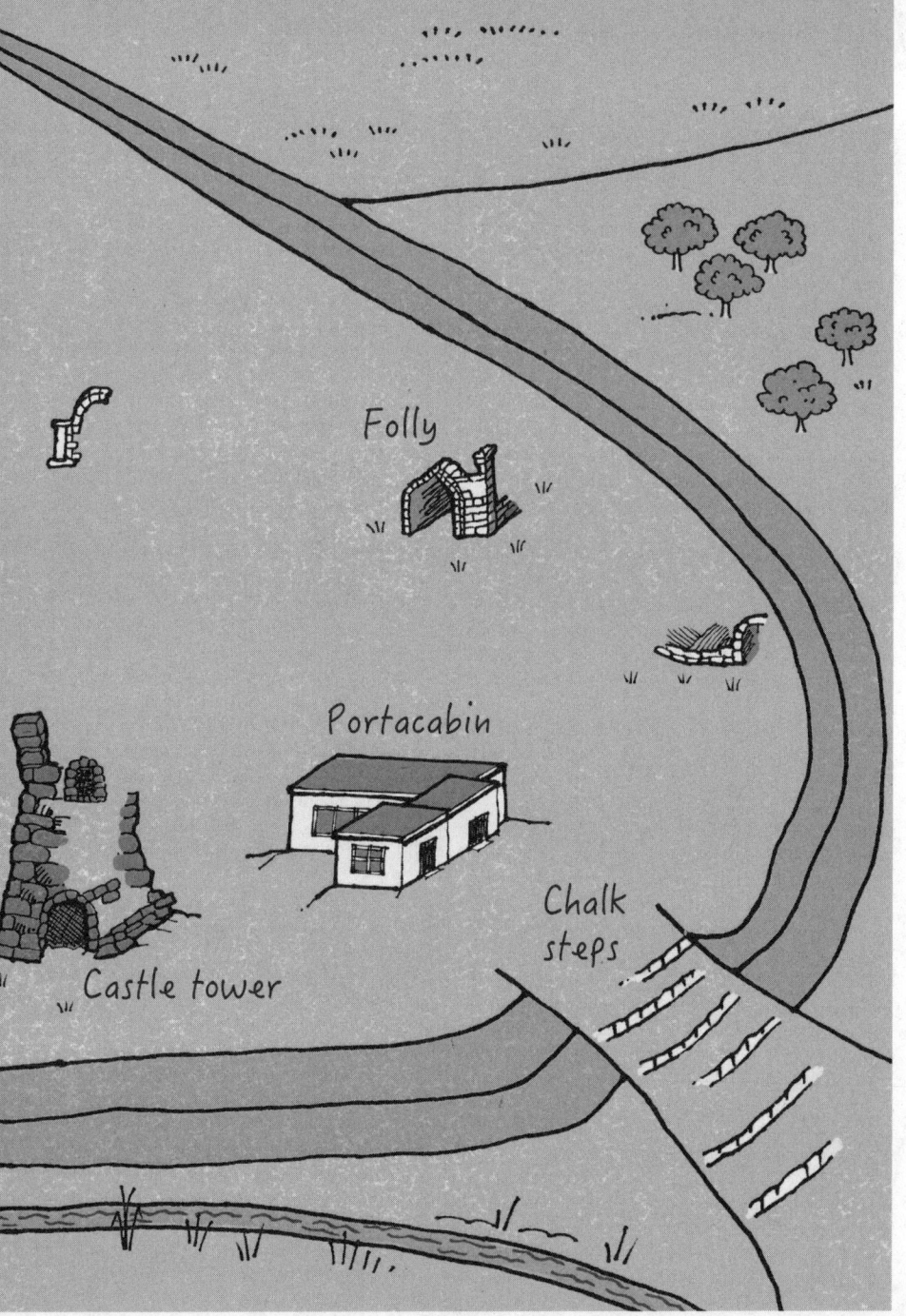

The poetry of history lies in the quasi-miraculous fact that once, on this earth, once, on this familiar spot of ground, walked other men and women, as actual as we are today, thinking their own thoughts, swayed by their own passions, but now all gone, one generation vanishing after another, gone as utterly as we ourselves shall shortly be gone, like ghosts at cock-crow.

    G. M. Trevelyan, *Autobiography of an Historian* (1949)

Prologue

Outside, the hillside is buffeted by an unseasonable wind, the brackeny undergrowth shifting and flattening, patternless. The sky is a pool of gloom, purpling towards night, the sun absent and concealed. If you climbed the nearby tower, you would see a huge expanse of land, stretching out towards where the horizon should be, a raised flatness studded with marks of history. These marks have been painstakingly uncovered, but they had been there all along, just waiting to be returned to the light. Temples and shrines, buildings of peace and violence. This is, above all else, an old place.

Underground is where some of the treasures are kept. Two people creep down to see them. They stare uneasily at one another. Their eyes gleaming coals in the dusky half-light. Mistrust etched on their faces. Behind one is a stone tomb, a cold block of grey; behind the other a display of bones, white and stark and sterile. A notebook lies on the table in the corner, beneath a lamp. On it a drawing of the hillside, a demarcation of disputed boundaries.

Time passes. Then, familiar violence returns to the place. All is quiet once more.

Two of them walked down into the underground room. As night finally falls, the squalling black, only one of them climbs the steps back onto the hillside, back into the present.

The First Letter

To the desecrators

The land does not want you here. History does not want you here. Blood has been spilled in this cold, dark soil once, and it shall be spilled again.

What once was built high and proud has been lost to the tides of the past. Buried deep by the mounting earth. It should not be disturbed.

You should leave this land, before the land rises up and drives you forth. I will drive you forth. I will take the revenge of the unquiet land and the people and the past.

'Wherefore is light given to him that is in misery, and life unto the bitter in soul; which long for death, but it cometh not; and dig for it more than for hid treasures; which rejoice exceedingly and are glad, when they can find the grave?' Job 3:21

You are digging for death. I am death come alive once more.

I shall not be silenced. The treasure shall stay hid.
You have been warned.
Wulfnoth

Chapter One

Chandler Lake, Little Sky

Dawn always comes before the sun. Light glimmers and glows and grows. It swells up, formless, from somewhere hidden beneath the horizon, paling the sky upwards. Minutes pass, faint hues spread like a stain before you actually see the sun itself, a ball of bolder colour. If you always sleep late, Jake thinks, you would reckon dawn breaks like a peal or a shout, immediate, when instead it seeps in, quiet and unannounced.

He doesn't need to get up with the first light, which is perhaps why he does it so easily. When he lived in the city, amid the tyranny of alarm clocks and train times and work deadlines, he hated the mornings. Their insistent demands, their refusal to brook tired excuses; the artificial light that made you squint as it struck, false and yellowing against your bleary eyes. A bed is a comfortable refuge when you are being dragged from it.

Now he lives, if not free from all pressure, free at

least from that sort of pressure. He imagines looking at himself from above, how he appears at this moment, so lazily and joyfully free. He is lying on a rowboat in the middle of his own lake, his body long and lean, pale skin already slightly varnished by the season. Spring reaching out and handing the baton over to summer. His thick brown hair is pooled against the old wood, which is roughened by time and use and water; his long beard is dense and scratchy. A pair of old black shorts hanging slightly off his hip bones.

The boat is his, as is the water that surrounds it, and the land – stretching out beyond sight – beyond that. If Jake were to rise up on one elbow he could make out his home behind him, a big L-shaped farmhouse nestled in the ground. To his right a wooded area, dense with purpling limbs and thick green foliage, looming up right to the edge of the water. To his left, a small land mass in the middle of the lake, a tangle of trees in its own right, with a new pier jutting out, bright white and still bearing the marks of his own recent labour.

He calls it Reacher Island, set within Chandler Lake. It is Agatha Wood he can also see, each of its inharmonious outlines familiar as a pattern to him. When Jake was given the house, he named all of the landmarks after characters or writers of detective fiction. A fitting conceit in lots of ways: he was a retired detective; his uncle had bequeathed him the place, Little Sky, along with a library of thrillers. Arthur's love of books, passed on to him as a child, had sent Jake on the path towards the police force; his bequest had enabled him to leave the job and the city and a failed marriage. The names honoured his past and the whimsy of his new, mostly idle present. They also reminded him that, so far, he had never quite managed to get away from the perils of crime or the need for detection.

It is still too cool to be completely idle this morning. He sits up, breathes in deep, and grips the oars loosely in his calloused hands. The day promises warmth, light blue skies and soft scurrying clouds, but it is not warm yet. Jake's body still holds the heat from his morning run, but he doesn't want to let himself get too stiff. Rolling his shoulders, he pushes hard against the water, the faint splash of the rowing stroke muted against the hissing noise of the nearby reeds, riffled insistently by the wind.

Jake had been checking the paint job of the island pier, which is why he had come this way in the first place, and sees he will have to come back to do another coat. Now he decides to stretch his muscles and loop long around the island, before taking the boat back home. He has no plans for the rest of the morning beyond the happy, puttering effort of chores that never end.

Later that day Livia would return, the woman he loves and almost lives with. She is the vet based in the nearby village of Caelum Parvum, and she splits her time between her cottage there and Little Sky. Her daughter Diana is a contented inhabitant of both homes, though is a regular and noisy advocate too of them all living more simply together in these vast, welcoming spaces. Jake and Livia have almost agreed on the point, but are awaiting – needlessly, he often thinks – a big change in their circumstances before finally making a commitment: the baby they are trying for. It is his superstition that is really stopping them: if you change your life for the idea of a baby, what happens if the baby never comes? He'd done it before, and it had brought him pain and sorrow.

Jake's shoulders crackle as he shrugs the thought away. He is past the island now in the middle of the open water, the sunlight scattering gems upon the waves. A family of ducks bob together, mottled browns and creams and newborn yellows, neatly aligned as if in a miniature squadron. He starts the turn, his left arm taut with effort, when he looks over his shoulder at the beach that marks the far border of the lake, soft pale sand, strewn with old branches and stubborn plants.

Set against the canvas of living greens, faded like old watercolours, is a line of black, police black: a figure watching him, standing as if to attention.

Chapter Two

The beach, Little Sky

As Jake sculls nearer, the line becomes a man, clad somewhat incongruously, given the promise of heat, in a dark jacket, open-necked shirt, black trousers with a pronounced crease in the middle. He offers a wave when Jake comes within hailing distance, and makes no movement to shift his ground.

Jake lets the boat bump against the shingles, slick with flattened weeds, and leaps into the splashy shallows. He grabs an old cloth shirt from the bow, red faded into pink by the sun and rough washing, and pulls it on. He smiles into the sky's glare, eyes thinned into a wince, and holds out his hand.

'Morning. Though a policeman up this early is never good news.'

His hand is grasped firmly. The voice when it comes back to him is confident, a firm Scottish lilt. 'I didn't think my appearance screamed copper quite as loudly as that. But guilty as charged, your honour. My name's David McAllister. Chief Inspector McAllister.'

Jake shifts to one side so he can see him more clearly. He is of middling height, dark cropped hair lightening faintly at the temples, stubbled face that looks too young for the role, grey eyes that have a touch of irony lurking within them. Jake had heard the name before: McAllister was the man sent in from another force to replace his former friend Watson, who had been recently found guilty of corruption. Watson also had ironical eyes, he recalls, so it would be as well not to read too much into them.

Jake gives a cautious smile. 'Welcome to the neighbourhood. What brings you here this morning?' He can hear the faint edge in his own voice, the hint of suspicion. He had been bruised by the discovery of Watson's treachery; it had pushed him further inward, more keen for isolation and peace, away from his past and the workings of the state.

McAllister's face doesn't change. He pats Jake's arm equably. 'No need to worry about anything. I was on a walk and thought I'd introduce myself. I'm not long down from Glasgow and all of this rural quiet is killing my sleep. So I've been spending my early mornings before work, wandering about the place, not getting up to much.'

'And stumbled across my bit of the countryside specifically?'

A mild chuckle. 'Ach, I'll not pretend I didn't want to introduce myself too. You're a bit of a legend in law enforcement around here, and I wanted to look you in the eye, especially after that unfortunate business with your man Watson. You know right enough that dodgy cops will always be around, but they leave a bad atmosphere, do they not, a lingering stink. So why not clear it up from the get-go?'

Jake finds himself charmed by the frankness, the open face. 'Would you like to come up to the house for a coffee?'

McAllister bends his knees in an extravagant stretch. 'You're a gent, but I've overstopped too long. My legs aren't yet used to all this walking and I need to get myself back to the car and get on to work. I'm pleased to meet you, though. Mebbe we might have a coffee or a pint at some point. Mebbe at that cricket game folk keep telling me about. A Scotsman at the cricket, it's a first step to going native, I tell you.' He grins. 'It unsettles me.'

They shake hands again. Jake notices the thick black hair that spills out from his sleeves, coiled and wiry, feels the strength once more in his grip. Their eyes lock amicably, before McAllister gives a vigorous nod, and plunges back into the field behind, arms waving as he walks.

Jake watches him depart, and spends a few minutes wandering aimlessly, breathing deep, pulling up dandelion clocks and letting their greybeard fluff scatter and shimmy in the wind. There are swifts dancing in the air above him, recent migrants, restlessly alive, refusing to pause in their acrobatics. Whistles and shrieks, tuneless as a milkman. He likes the feel of the still-cold grass on his feet, the ground soft and plumped like a pillow. Out of habit, he walks up the ridge, which gives him an extended view of the land down to the river. There, in a large, proud beech tree – a mass of vivid green leaves shooting forth – a pendant of pink is fluttering in the morning breeze.

Chapter Three

Livia's cottage, Caelum Parvum

'Are you really going to play cricket then?'

Livia is lying nude on the bed, her feet raised high in the air, thigh muscles faint curls under her smooth brown skin. Her eyes are wide, feline green, her auburn hair a sprawled mess across the pillow. The covers beneath her are rumpled, and the early afternoon light pours through the windows, dappling all it touches. Jake is pulling on his shorts in a corner, ungainly as a stork.

'I'll answer that if you tell me why you're sticking your legs up like that.'

Livia doesn't move, her fingers drumming upon her stomach, which is flat and solid, if a little soft around the edges according to her own occasional complaint. 'You know why. It's what those wretched websites recommend. If you weren't here, I'd have them all the way up over my shoulders, but I want to keep a bit of the mystery alive between us.'

Jake leans over and kisses the film of perspiration on her forehead, as she huffs her fringe away for a second. The fabric in the tree – Sherlock Beech, as he calls it – had summoned him immediately. One of the central joys of Little Sky is its electronic isolation: no phones or internet function there at all. He and Livia cope by the permanent regularity of their arrangements to meet, by embracing the serendipity of arriving casually upon one another, and finally by this old-fashioned signalling system. At the moment, the signs normally mean an urgent call by Livia for sex to meet her biological timetable, her careful monitorings of cycles and temperatures.

'Does it work? It seems like an oddly literal way to encourage the little sperm to reach the egg.'

'Nobody knows what really works. That's why it's important to enjoy all the attempts, isn't it?'

He shrugs on his shirt and opens the bedroom door. 'You certainly sounded like you were enjoying it at least. Though maybe vets always make the best animal noises.' He looks back over his shoulder. 'And I can't complain about the view from here either.'

A pillow flies out and catches him on the chest. Livia swings her legs down, and stands, gloriously unselfconscious, the rosy flush seeping from her chest. She bustles past him and heads towards the bathroom, twitching her hips. The thunderous outpour from the bath taps immediately follows.

Jake pads down through the house and pours himself a coffee from the pot bubbling gently on the stove. He knows that he and Livia are speaking cautiously, lightly of their attempts for a baby. It's an act of self-protection, shielding the true sense of importance even from themselves. He had never been able to have children with his first wife, Faye, their life eventually blighted by the unforgiving rhythm of repeated exertion and failure. Their marriage shunted towards inevitable collapse. So now he jokes, as does Livia, and they don't discuss what it might mean if no joyful outcome is ever reached. He blows on the coffee. They have only been trying for a couple of months after all.

Jake opens the back door, and a gentle breeze alights on his exposed body, clutching at each of the still-damp patches there. It is the perfect late spring afternoon, as predicted that morning: the turquoise sky fluffed with cloud, the sun hazy and warming, scents of black earth and opening flowers. Woodsmoke spiralling somewhere in the distance. Livia has followed him down, now clad in an old black bathrobe.

'You never told me about the cricket after all that.'

He stretches his legs out on the step, watching the brightness turn his dark hairs the colour of fired copper. 'I should've said no, but Rose wanted me to do it, despite me warning him I wasn't much good. Apparently his team is two men down, and the opposition have some ringers from the dig nearby, so they're desperate to make a game of it.'

Livia traces patterns on the velveting of her robe, fingernails etching pale against black. 'I keep meaning to take Di to have a look at that dig. They found all that treasure there, didn't they? She did a project on it at school.'

'Come along to the match and you can meet Rose's sister. She's helping out there for the whole of the summer. I bet she'd give you a tour.'

'I'd quite like to meet the female version of Rose. Although she already sounds a bit too conscientious to be related to him.' Rose was their friend, a man of dubious means, who earned a proportion of his income by selling locally produced cannabis. The criminal and the former policeman had managed to find enough in common since they first met three years ago, not least because Jake smoked a little recreational weed himself. Rose had also helped Jake tackle a serial rapist, and they had been close ever since.

Livia remembers the bath running and skips off, her dark hair now filigreed with summer gold, thick coils springing against her shoulders. Jake sees a copy of the *Shire Gazette* by the door, and idly picks it up. There is a story about the dig he sees as he flicks through the pages, pausing wryly on other headlines that make him even fonder of the paper: 'Woman finds hat in a tree', 'Warning over dangerous cupcakes', 'I'll shoot dogs if I want to, says farmer'.

The dig intrigues him because of his new-found love of land and place and history. The idea that a way of life had been pursued on these soft hills and fertile valleys for countless ages before him, for the ages beyond memory; the sensation of following generations of footsteps every time you trod upon an old farm's threshold, or stood and stared at the rough-hewn masonry of a church. The reassuring sight of a stream trickling ever onwards, before joining up to the river that has ebbed and surged across the landscape forever. The history of geography.

The site in question is atop a hill a few miles away, the location – as is now being established – of an Iron Age fort, which became a Roman villa, an Anglo-Saxon settlement and a medieval castle of sorts. Human continuity in one place preserved in the measurable strata of the earth. And all this is interesting to the local paper because the excavation is being filmed for a television programme, whose crew had returned annually there for the last five years. Even more so because a year ago, four people from the dig had wandered down from the hill, fossicking without great intent, and uncovered what was probably the largest horde in the country's history. It was a store of treasure, coins and weaponry, engraved and gilded, the product of countless hours of effort and unimaginable expense. And worth a fortune in the modern world, millions probably, once the government had approved the find and a museum been identified to pay for it.

The story he is reading is a recap of the excitement with a short update that the TV crew are back filming once more, taking advantage of the mild weather. Jake tosses the paper aside as he finishes his coffee. He'd like to see what was being unearthed at the dig as well.

Chapter Four

The Green, near St Giles

Not everyone is wearing white or the image would be too picturesque, Jake thinks. Everyone has made some sort of effort, at least, so that when you look from a distance, there is some harmony of hues, flecks of cream, pale blue, even the occasional splash of pink. Muted tones, modest flutters against the expanse of land. He is not formally dressed himself, inevitably: he is in a white cotton shirt, open at the neck, and some beige shorts he uses for gardening.

The scene is certainly picturesque enough: the large swatch of mowed grass, with the straw-coloured wicket, precise and angular, just off centre; an oasis of order against the wilderness that threatens to overcome it. Sheep cropping the heather at one end, a brook trickling winsomely at the other, one big oak tree that stands forlorn but proud in the outfield, the target no doubt of a thousand hoicked shots over the years. The pavilion is old and thatched, the wood varnished chocolate, a black-and-white scoreboard to one side, and two old privies at the back.

Jake's team, the Wanderers (so called because they had no home and were painstakingly put together week-by-week by core enthusiasts), are batting, so he lounges behind the boundary to the left of the pavilion. His teammates are similarly stretched out, a hodgepodge of ungainly bodies and strewn equipment. McAllister is there, as promised, though it appears to be under some sufferance: he is wearing a Scotland rugby shirt and blue tracksuit bottoms, and looks uncomfortable in public without his suit.

Further around the green Jake can see Livia, seated on a picnic blanket, brown legs against violent pink. She is talking to a woman in her twenties with dark hair in a tiny pair of shorts and a long thin gauzy jumper. Behind them are more blankets, individuals in clusters of repose, half-engrossed in the game: a middle-aged man alone, brow reddening under the sun; a couple whose legs are intertwined companionably; two women seated on chairs, occasionally directing a remark to one another.

Jake is next to a man who bears some resemblance to Livia's companion. Rose snorts gently as he fastens his pads. 'Even at the cricket, she can't help getting almost everything out. But she won't listen to her brother, I can tell you that. She never has.'

Jake yawns. 'As soon as you of all people start giving moral advice to anyone, you've already lost. And no brother in history has ever convinced their sister about what she should wear.'

'You've never had a sister, so how would you know?'

Jake nods silently at the wisdom of this. Rose stands, and is adjusting his box liberally when the subject of their conversation wanders across. 'Please stop thrusting your privates about, Rose; it's embarrassing for your relatives in the area.' She gives a beaming smile to Jake, who sits up to accept her proffered hand.

'Hi, I'm Lily. Yes Lily Rose. One too many flowers for a serious name.' A fake grimace. 'I've met your lovely missus. I'm taking her around the dig tomorrow if you're interested. You look like a hippy, so you'll fit right in: we're all artsy types over there.'

Jake looks her in the eye 'You don't seem exactly like my image of an archaeologist, if you don't mind me saying?' Rose snorts to himself.

Lily leans forward. 'You don't look much like a copper either, for that matter. Come along anyway. I know you're good with corpses, even if ours are more than a thousand years old.'

'Thank you. I'll make sure I can make it.'

'From what I hear, you're not exactly overworked.' She holds her hands up. 'That's not a criticism, by the way. I'm no striver myself. I'm only doing this job so I can finish my MA next year. This one here refuses to support me.'

Rose is doing lunges, twisting his torso and breathing effortfully. He doesn't move his attention from the game. 'I support you more than I should do. It's good to see you grafting a bit.' There is the distant click of ball on stump, and a muted cheer is raised around the field. 'That's me in,' says Rose, looking around happily. 'Get ready for some fireworks.'

He strides to the middle. Lily is rolling a cigarette in one hand, a mannerism she shares with her brother. Up close, Jake can see the family similarity more clearly: the olive skin that absorbs the sun, the thick brown hair, the prominent nose that gives her a faintly owlish expression. She lights up and inhales pensively. 'I shouldn't moan about Rose, really. He's letting me live with him this summer and he's not a bad sort.'

'I know that. So you're Lily Rose – what's his first name?'

She smacks his arm playfully. 'Oh you'll need to know me a lot better before you make me betray him like that. Everyone calls him by his last name, and I've fallen into the habit too.' Her eyes are pale and mischievous, but her tone is studiously neutral. Jake is fleetingly conscious he is getting too old to be flirted with. Probably for the best.

He busies himself with his own kit. He'll have to bat at some point soon. A cheer goes up around him, as Rose has lustily knocked the ball into the stream. Some local children hare in after it. Splashes and high-pitched cries. 'Are you here with the dig lot?' he asks, as they watch the flurry of motion.

Smoke emerges dragon-like from her nostrils as she speaks. 'Everyone seems to have made it, yes. We're a pretty close team already. Some of us have been here on and off for the last few years. Let me point them out to you.'

She settles down next to him, cross-legged, stubbing her cigarette against the sole of her sandal. Faint whiff of apricot perfume mingled with smoke. She motions towards various figures in sight, her fingers slender, her nails the colour of the pavilion's varnished wood.

'The two women sitting on the chairs are the most important, probably. The one on the left is Amy Johnson, she's in charge of the dig itself.' Jake sees someone in her mid-forties, curling thatch of strawberry blond hair falling across her exposed shoulders. Her skin is pale and creamy, pinking in the sun, and freckled, especially under her eyes.

She looks a little stout, but strong, weathered, someone who spends her life healthily out in the open.

'She's talking to Daisy Sharma.' The woman she gestures towards is probably a couple of years younger, brown skin and black hair, slender, and over-dressed for the weather in a dark shirt that covers her top entirely. Expensive sunglasses glint on the top of her head. 'I think Daisy's an anglicized version of her birth name. Her family is Indian originally, but she's lived around here forever. Her parents owned some land not too far away, and she went to boarding school the other side of Meryton. That's why she got interested in the project in the first place: she's the director of the film crew, makes sure they get the TV show recorded properly. I like her, I guess. She takes no nonsense.'

The two women are together, conversing politely, but Jake senses no great warmth there; no expansive gestures, or infectious laughter. They are both drinking Pimm's from a watercooler next to them.

Lily carries on her commentary, her voice a disinterested drawl. She is rolling another cigarette. 'The couple on the floor just about avoiding heavy petting in public are Matt and Elaine. They're grad students like me, do a lot of the scut work. Moan a lot about the bosses. A couple, obviously. He's French.' As if that explained everything.

As they speak, a third figure joins the lovers on the blanket, fastidiously sticking to the edges at the furthest point from them. He is pencil thin, mop of black hair, a moustache that is barely visible from the distance, a Hamlet all in sombre clothes. 'That's Zach. He's a grad, but also Amy's assistant. Thinks he's a bit above us. In love with her, of course. Would love to have all that creamy womanhood pressed down on top of him, and I'm not saying he doesn't get it.' Lily laughs gleefully. 'It's all a bit Mrs Robinson, if you know what I mean.'

Jake watches Zach ignore his colleagues and cast occasional glances at his boss, pawing at the ground with one hand, scattering the plucked grass over his trousers.

'Is that everyone?' This is Jake, enjoying the acerbic commentary.

'Only a couple more to tell you about, we're quite the gang. Out playing that ridiculous sport is Brian. He's the chief archaeologist.' She gestures towards the wicket keeper, a middle-aged man, stomach straining against a faded rugby shirt, a shock of orange hair, bursting from his old school cap down to his shoulders. He is chirping away, at the centre of events, gesturing wildly at Rose, who is taking strike. When Rose swings at a ball and misses, Jake can hear the thud into Brian's gloves and his sing-song voice in mild mockery.

'Life and soul that one.' Lily exhales, wriggling her toes experimentally. 'OK, two more. The tall drink of water over yonder.' She points to a young man fielding in the deep, who looks faintly confused. 'He's Brad. American. Probably has no more idea of what the fuck is going on with the cricket than I do. Nice chap, though. Big Christian but I'm trying not to hold that against him. And . . . lucky last, and speaking of Christians, is the Reverend.' She points to the old man to the right of the picnic blanket. 'Local vicar, John Jordan, bit of an odd'un, wouldn't want to be stuck in a room with him.' She enacts a caricature of groping. 'But he loves history, the ancient past of it all, never out of our trenches. He was one of the people who found the horde, so he could become quite a catch in a few months' time when he gets paid, but that's a tale for another day, Jake.'

She stands. He can see the wriggly outlines of grass impressed into her upper thigh, tactile indentations. Her hand reaches down and clasps his shoulder, as Livia walks up to them. 'I'll see you both tomorrow, I guess.'

As Lily swishes away, Livia watches her appraisingly. 'Don't get too charmed by that one, lovey.'

Jake fastens his trainers tightly. 'The funny thing is that as I get older, I'm more attracted to older women. She can be trouble for some young lad somewhere, and leave me with you.' He grabs Livia and pulls her down to him. She collapses gratefully, and he feels the welcome heat from her skin against his. The joyful clasp of connection. She tweaks his ear. 'Who's calling me an older woman? I'm well within child-bearing age, you know.'

Before he can formulate an answer, another soft cheer goes up. Rose's partner is returning to the pavilion, mournfully practising his failed forward defensive. Livia pats Jake on the behind as he stands up to go out to play. 'I'm attracted to older men still, as well, so you've got nothing to worry about. But show me a bit of youthful prowess if you can.'

Jake lifts his bat in martial salute. He feels enthused, the sun tingling his body. Fun and games in the bright light, with no clouds or shadows looming near.

Chapter Five

The fort's entrance, the bottom of the hill outside St Giles

It is still early morning, damp and warm, the mapless depths of the countryside. They are a day late, and excited about the prospect of exploring this place of historical drama.

Clouds had come from nowhere late on the afternoon of the cricket, and a sodden downpour brought the game to a hasty conclusion. Jake had been relieved, fielding in the deep, watching the other team masterfully chase down their smallish score. His own innings had been enthusiastic, satisfying and short-lived.

As they stood under the eaves of the old pavilion, the smell of the rain redolent somehow of both renewal and decay, Livia and Lily had agreed to postpone the next day's site visit. The old barometer nailed to the wall by the door was pointing to a day-long wet spell, and you could sense the weather settling in, the clouds clustering around the hills and refusing to shift.

Jake had stayed at Livia's that night and returned home

the next morning, his clothes given a fresh soaking as he walked. It was mild, so he shucked them off and dived into the lake, letting the cool velvet of the water enshroud him. After his shower, it was a day designed for indoor idling. Weeding in the greenhouses. Reading in the library. His new workshop project of building a guitar, something slow and difficult, where each painful step was an act of quiet deliberation. Jake was playing guitar concertos by Vivaldi on his record player to inspire him as he planed and carved, his face sculpted into its own lines of concentration.

Livia and Diana had arrived for dinner just as the rain stopped and a stiff breeze had driven the cloud away. They agreed to drop by the dig in the morning, and had all been up early, excited and cheerful. Straight after breakfast, they had parked in the shadow of St Giles church and tramped a while across the fields towards the looming hill.

It is bright but cool, the sun a faded presence in the sky, chill winds singing around them. They are standing looking up at the chalky path that meanders and circles up to the summit when Lily comes up behind them.

'I know this good-looking family. Lovely to see you all. Do you want me to show you where the treasure was found? I bet you do. Diana, isn't it?'

Diana's face beams, and she clasps Lily's hand as they skirt the side of the hill, long grass swishing against their bare legs. A thin stream trickles alongside them. The land dips as they walk and they see down into the long trench that has been scored into the ground, at right angles to the bank of the water course, its floor and walls brown and smooth. A dark scar against the green.

Jake listens abstractedly while Lily talks of what had been found. 'The stream was probably much bigger back in the post-Roman period, and the treasure was buried deep into one of its banks. It was hidden away for more than a thousand years, this huge stash of stuff, rich stuff, still preserved in this big wet sack that had been sitting in the earth.'

'Actual treasure?' Diana is almost breathless.

Lily nods, pony-tail bouncing. 'Actual real-life, swear-to-God treasure. Money, weapons, golden bits that used to cover old books.'

'Why was it hidden?'

'Ah, excellent question. Excellent question.' The voice barrels forth behind them, from an elderly man striding up, dressed blandly in tweeds. The vicar from the cricket, John Jordan. He is accompanied by the woman Jake recognizes as Daisy, the TV director. She smiles warmly.

They shake hands as Lily introduces them. Jordan leaps extravagantly into the trench, brown boots scuffing the still-soft earth. Jake catches Daisy rolling her eyes. Jordan is unruffled, if he even notices.

'Yes, found here, well away from the fort itself, so not part of the dig.' He winks at Jake. 'Which is important, because it means it can be classed as treasure. If it'd been discovered in the dig itself, it wouldn't be treasure and the wretched government'd get their hands on it. And this is probably the biggest haul of treasure seen in this country ever, or at least since the Dark Ages when it was buried.'

'So why was it buried?' Diana is unshakeable.

'You rightly persist in your excellent question; I see we have a future historian on our hands. The answer is that nobody knows. Maybe because the Romans were leaving to go back to defend their failing empire and the very rich family who lived in the big house up top thought they were going to be robbed. Maybe because they wanted to make a sacrifice, a ritual donation, to some god or gods. This whole area is filled with old bits of temples, and priestly pools, hot springs and the like. My church over yonder is probably built on a shrine that came before Jesus ever lived. Exciting, isn't it?'

Diana nods enthusiastically. She is excited by it all.

'So who found it, apart from you?' Jake can't help asking questions.

'My companion Daisy, up there. Along with Amy, the big boss, and her assistant, close assistant you mark me, Zach. We were messing around with metal detectors, and whoomp there it was. We couldn't believe it when it appeared.'

'You were messing around, John. We were keeping you from mischief.' This is Daisy, pushing her black hair back from her face where it has been whipped by the breeze.

'Nothing wrong with mischief in my experience.' Jordan nudges Diana, who smiles.

'And you all are sharing the reward?' Livia asks what they are all thinking.

Daisy picks up a shard of stone, thumbs it idly, her nails manicured and polished, a contrast against the muddy, thick-grained material. 'We hope to. There's a very long process, and the owner of the land should get half of it, but we're not sure who it is. The church owns the hilltop, but this bit's ownership is shrouded in mystery. Either way, we'll do all right.'

'All right, she says.' Jordan's face breaks into a snaggle-toothed grin. 'The horde is worth at least three million. Not that I'm desperate for the cash, you understand, but it certainly will pay for my retirement.'

'Maybe you should take your money and bury it.' Diana is thoughtful.

'A fine idea. And then someone in a millennium's time can stand here and wonder why we did it. Magnificent.'

They have started walking back round to the front of the fort. Jordan's airy blather, as he points out various landmarks to Livia and Diana, is being whisked by the breeze away from Jake's ears. Lily is staring at her phone. Jake falls in companionably with Daisy.

'Congratulations then, this must be good for the telly too.'

She shrugs, diffident. 'Of course. Have you seen the show?'

'I don't want to be one of those "I don't have a television" guys, but I honestly don't. I think I saw one of the earlier ones back in the day.'

'We got lucky. Back then we didn't know what we were working with, and were only in it to show off the idea of archaeology. A sort of educational programme. Then the finds kept coming and we realized we had uncovered something big in terms of the scale of the site, then along came the treasure as well. The audience loved it. Not that everyone is thrilled about it, mind.'

They are climbing now, boots scraping against the chalk, as the path moves slowly towards the summit. Jake looks up and sees a ruined tower, falling in on itself, skeletal, almost black against the blue sky. A bird of prey circling above it soundlessly. He can feel the pleasant tingle of exertion in his thighs.

'Who isn't thrilled?'

'You know what it's like in places like this. Small-minded, resentful of change. Not everyone wants things to be disturbed. They think we're modern-day despoilers, tomb raiders, desecrators. We've even had letters.'

'Threats?'

'More or less. They're signed "Wulfnoth", which is the name of a prominent figure here in the Anglo-Saxon period, the local thegn – you know, the bigwig of the area. He died rebelling against the Normans in the second half of the eleventh century. Became a symbol of local resistance. Anyway the letters warn us of the peril of disturbing the place. They're rather creepy. You know, I'd actually like your thoughts on them, you being a former cop and all.'

Jake looks sharply across at her, but she is staring ahead, hair swirling, chest heaving slightly. She turns back to catch his eye. 'Come now, don't be modest. You might not have a TV, but your name has cropped up once or twice on mine. Would you mind? I'd be grateful.' She reaches across and squeezes his wrist. Her hands are cold, bloodless.

'Happy to help, of course.'

They have all reached the summit and can look across the full sweep of the site. It is huge, surprisingly so. Not so much a hilltop, which might suggest a scrubby patch perched in the air, small and defensible, but a broad plateau that descends gently down from its peak where they are standing, so that its final undulations merge with the land below, like an estuary surging into a green sea.

Scattered across the area, like toys in a child's bedroom, are bits of stone wall, half-formed buildings that had once been toppled and never rebuilt; also ditches and trenches, bitten into the soft turf, concentrated in the area immediately proximate to them, but then sporadically occurring as far as the eye can see.

Lily turns to look at all of them. 'Welcome to our hill-fort. Amazing, isn't it?' For all her cool, studied charm, Jake can see that she is genuinely proud of it, thrilled by the prospect before them. It is beguiling enough. The grand horizons, the windswept views, the figures out of earshot, crouched in their trenches, furtive burrowing creatures. That overwhelming sense of the immortality of history again: things had happened here for thousands of years, and you could almost breathe it in the cold, clean air.

Chapter Six

Inside the tower, St Giles site

Lily seems to have adopted Diana for the morning, and takes her down onto the plain, pointing out the submerged walls and the protruding ruins, explaining the continued history of occupation from the Iron Age enclosure through to the late castle-like structure to the West. Jordan follows them, puppy-eager, interjecting his theories, just about tolerated by Lily.

Daisy has disappeared so Jake and Livia wander the plateau, hands clasped and swinging. The sky is huge above them, paler now, bone-white, filled with clouds that feel almost within reach. Jake is wearing a thick blue jumper and his gardening shorts; Livia jeans tucked into her work boots and an outsized cardigan. She shivers as the wind gusts. They can make out Brian directing operations in a trench some distance away, hear his enthusiastic words, as energetic as he had been on the cricket field. He gives a jaunty wave, but makes no effort to approach them.

The largest surviving structure is the castle tower, mossed and spotted stones piled high and tight, bleached grey for the most part, the product of strenuous manual labour beginning at some point around the first millennium. Inside, out of the wind, it is quiet. A papery scrap of light above them through the roofless opening. The ground had been dug out here too, and they have to step down into it. There is a church-like hush. Jake traces his fingers over the rock, which is cool and rough-hewn and hard.

A shadow looms in the doorway. Daisy, clutching a letter, encased in cellophane.

'This is what I was talking about. Livia, I hope you don't mind me showing him this during your visit.'

Livia's face is hard to read, but she is quietly courteous. 'I know what happens when you get close to a sleuth. You can't stop him sleuthing away sometimes.' There is mockery here, concealing a certain flintiness. They had argued in the past about Jake's involvement in solving other people's problems, but had reached a certain peace a few months earlier when they had both tackled a conspiracy together. Livia stays close to Jake, and reads over his shoulder.

'This is the fifth letter. The police still have the first, which had the same tone and sentiment. They started coming, what, two or three years ago.' Daisy hands it to him. The words are printed in black ink, orderly lines from a computer screen.

> Grave-robbers and desecrators, beware what you do. This land has been sanctified by your forebears, who lived and loved and fought and died here. It is not a trove to be trampled over, a field to be ploughed up, or a piece of cheap drama to be gawped at.

Treasure is not for the finder, but for the nation, the great English nation that provided it. Do not claim what is not yours. Do not dig up what has been decently buried.

'Better is little with the fear of the Lord than great treasure and trouble therewith.' Proverbs 15:16

Look to your souls and your conscience. Leave here before you are driven away. The land rejects you. History rejects you.

Wulfnoth

The paper is otherwise unmarked. He gives it back. 'I presume this came after your big horde find?'

'A month later, but, as I say, we'd had a few before. When the letters come, they get wedged into one of the stones at the gate on the top of the hill. Sometimes addressed to Amy, sometimes to me.'

'What do the police say?'

Daisy gives a mirthless grin. 'Look around you, Jake. There's not a police station in ten miles. They've looked, they asked around a bit, but got nothing. And the threats are a little elliptical, haven't been backed up by any action. Nobody's been threatened in person. Maybe it's just the rantings of some local eccentric.'

'Who knows your name.'

'I try not to let that worry me too much; we've been here for a good while now and nothing has happened.'

Livia wrinkles her nose. 'The reference to the Bible as well as the love of local history – have you asked Reverend Jordan?'

'I showed him the first one, and he was happy to talk about the biblical quotation but had little else to say. It's generally known we get letters like this occasionally, but we don't show the texts to absolutely everyone.'

They step out of the gloom of the building back into the light, Livia's restless eyes searching out Diana, who has been given a trowel and is scraping away in a far-off trench. Jake hands the letter back.

'And you say nothing's escalated with these, no mysterious events, or acts of vandalism?'

Daisy shakes her head. 'Not that I've been told about. I'm here only a few months a year; Amy's the real spirit of the place. She'd be very reluctant to cede authority to me in any way. Though I think she'd have at least told me if there was anything else going on. Do you think it's nothing then?'

They wander down towards Diana, over the tussocky mounds, speckled with dandelions and thistles, a forgiving bounce for their feet. 'Looks like a crank, definitely. If you'd like me to take a look at all of them, though, see if anything leaps out, then get someone to send me copies and I'll see.'

Daisy checks him with her arm as Livia marches on. She looks at him carefully. Her eyes are brown, almost black, deep and uncompromising. 'I would like that a lot. I always appreciate hard-earned expertise. It's an attractive characteristic, and one important thing you really welcome in making TV. I'll get some copies sent. Thank you so much.'

'Don't thank me yet. Send them to the Jolly Nook in Caelum Parvum. My place isn't on the postal route.'

'Jake, I lived around here all my childhood. I know the joys and the pains of isolation, believe you me. Now, I'll leave you with Lils.' She mouths the casual abbreviation oddly, like it is learned and not natural. 'We're doing some shooting this afternoon and I need to get ready.' She shakes his hand once more, her touch austere, and turns away.

He watches her walk towards the portacabin, feet high, stepping like a colt, hair wild in the wind. Livia meanwhile has scooped up Diana and come back with her and Lily.

Jake points towards the building where Daisy is heading. 'Is that the base then for everything?'

Lily nods. 'Yep, it's got the office, the loos and a rec room. Behind it – you can't quite see from here – is the folly. It's half underground, a sort of cave thing built by a mad antiquarian in the eighteenth century who was annoyed that all this history had disappeared and wanted to create some of his own. Beautifully constructed: it's where we keep all the non-precious finds from the dig, the cleaned-up pottery, the bones. There's whole skeletons in there, inside the stone coffins we dug up, waiting to get homed in a museum.'

'Can we see it? Sounds exciting.'

'Yes, yes, I want to see the bones!' This is Diana, earwigging and enthusiastic.

Lily shakes her head, emerald earrings bouncing against her shoulders. 'I'll need to introduce you to Amy for that. If you come back one day, I can sort it.'

'I'm going to take a look at those crazy letters you've been getting, so maybe we'll come back after that.'

Lily has an insouciant expression. 'Ah yes, the weirdo writer. He'd love to get inside there, I'm sure, but we keep it locked up away from the locals. Funny thing, though, do you know what the old guy called his little building back in the day?'

'Surprise me.'

'Wulfnoth's Keep.'

Chapter Seven

Livia's cottage, Caelum Parvum

Three days after their site visit, the hour late. Jake is at the old oak table in the corner of the living room, which has been remodelled since the events of the previous winter, when Livia had driven a car almost through the street-facing wall. They had rebuilt using reclaimed bricks from the same period as the cottage's original construction, and left them unplastered, thick-grained and burnt orange, a reminder of what had happened that morning and how they had come through triumphant.

The new big windows are open and the cool spring air enters, hedgerow scents. The night is silent but brightened by a pearly moon, imperious and aloof. Jake is smoking a small joint, which adds to the room's herby flavour, while he uses Livia's computer to speak to Martha, one of the people who had helped him so much a few months before.

Livia is stretched out on the sofa to his right, clad in a muted blue and purple jumpsuit, which seems to merge in the gloom into the cushions themselves. She has the hood up, but when he looks across he can see the wry flash of her green eyes. She is listening to music with invisible headphones on. Her ginger cat, Cyprian, is coiled bonelessly on her stomach, nose buried under its paws.

Martha and Jake are discussing detective books. They had discovered a shared love of the genre (of which she was also a practitioner herself) and found they enjoyed their spirited arguments about it. Livia called their monthly calls 'The Irascible Loners' Book Club' and enjoyed dipping in and out of their conversations. She had to play the host anyway, as Jake couldn't use a phone at Little Sky and Martha seldom left her own property.

Martha is herself smoking cannabis from a small pipe, which she periodically relights. She is, as ever, in her chair in her own library, a gloriously chaotic room of tottering piles, sporadically lit, a temple of reading. She is a small woman, but visibly strong, her arms curved and muscled, faint veins bisected by the dark lines of her tattoos. Her hair is light, currently pinkish, and spiked aggressively. She had worked in the intelligence services before she suffered a devastating injury – her legs shot off below the knee – and had been pensioned off, understandably bitter and cynical, to spend her days writing books. After the events of last winter, she was back doing some consultancy work for her old employers, shadowy and uncompromising, or at least as far as Jake imagines it.

She exhales a creamy puff of smoke. 'The point about Nero Wolfe is that he's not a bad copy, but a deliberate answer to Sherlock Holmes. He is Holmes made fleshier, the detective that puts his own physical needs first.'

'Why's that entertaining though?' Jake had agreed to

give Rex Stout another go on her suggestion, and they were currently discussing *Some Buried Caesar*, a novel of murder and prize cattle written back in 1939.

'Because the books are all a constant reinforcement of mood and place and sensation. The food he eats, the endless beers he drinks, the smell of the orchids, the furniture of the brownstone. Or, in this one, what it feels like to be at a country fair in the middle of nowhere.'

'I like Archie Goodwin.'

'Of course you do, he's Watson with brains and sarcasm.' There is a pause. She grins ruefully. 'Fucking Watson. I can't believe as well as nearly getting us killed, he almost ruined Sherlock Holmes for us. Every time we mention the name I think of him coming through that door behind you. I wish he'd been called Smith or whatever.' She is talking about the former chief inspector whose corruption they had uncovered together.

'I wish you'd stop mentioning him too, it cuts right through my music.' This is Livia, half-serious. Jake reaches back and rubs her toes. Her feet are in old Pilates socks, hole-ridden, and he can see the pinkish flash of her soles. He faces Martha once more.

'It'll fade over time. Did I tell you, Martha, I met the new bloke? A Scotsman called McAllister. Showed up one morning on the beach by the lake. Seemed nice enough.'

'I'm always keeping my eye on you over there, you know that. As soon as he was transferred, I did a check on him. Off the books, as it were. He seems straight enough. Good arrest record. Regular home life: wife and daughters. No obvious deviancy. Why'd he call round in the end?'

Jake stands, keeping Martha in vision, and pads across to the sofa to hand the joint to Livia. She inhales, the end flaring tangerine, and smoke curls within her hood. It unsettles Cyprian, who glares and stretches, before jumping to the floor and stiffly walking off to an unlit corner. Livia takes one more hit, then kills it on a plate on the floor.

Jake settles back down. He is in shorts, honey-coloured legs glinting in the half-light, and a dark hooded top. 'He was introducing himself. Said he'd heard of me, wanted to be upfront. Should I be suspicious?'

Martha is sipping from a martini glass. 'Only that you're now a marked man, despite all your protective wilderness, so any tricky case is going to come your way for a consult. I know how wifey feels about that.'

Livia rolls over languorously, puts her headphones on the table. Her hair has fallen forward, her fringe quivers. 'You can't rile me, Martha. I'm warm, a bit spacey, and at peace with the idea that Jake may occasionally want to exercise those law enforcement urges you both can't shake. I don't pretend to understand. If I were you, I'd just write your mild and quirky caper books, but no – you have to meddle in serious things once in a while.' It is an irony that she and Jake both enjoy: Martha is one of the toughest people they know, whose life has been a catalogue of violent excitement, who wears cynicism like a shield, but who also writes cosy crime fiction where almost nothing bad ever seems to happen.

'Was that a literary opinion, Livia darling? You're joining the loner book club now?'

'I'm too well-rounded a character, and I think three might be too much of a crowd. Although Aletheia's coming down for a visit next week; she could always join you sad loners.'

Aletheia was a former colleague of Jake and Martha,

and a friend of them all. She worked as a Searcher, an investigator of online information, a tracer of people and data, representing both the police and some intelligence agencies. She had written to Jake and Livia earlier in the month, asking if she could stay for a week's holiday, away from the job and the city. Having been in Little Sky in the winter, she had a craving to see it in the full flowering of spring.

'I trust Aletheia on crime, but not crime fiction.' A swaggering puff of smoke follows the statement. Jake intervenes gently to bring the conversation back to the matters in hand. 'I did get a consult from another source actually, M. About crank letters at the dig I mentioned. Some local, semi-mythical figure called Wulfnoth warning people to stop interfering with history. I'll send them across if you're interested.'

'Sure, why not? I only have boring old national security stuff to do, you know the kind of cases where people get blown up, or water supplies get poisoned, or wars get started. I'll drop all that and take a look at your village poisoned pen.'

'Was that a yes?'

'Go on then. What was the strange name again?'

'Wulfnoth.'

As he says it, there is a pounding at the door. Jake and Livia jump, startled, the drugs in their system instantly taking their mood from mellow to panicked. Jake stands, breathes deeply to calm himself, feels the weight of his bare feet on the old polished wooden floor.

He opens the door, and Rose and Lily walk in. Rose's normally playful face a mask of seriousness, Lily – behind him – more circumspect. His voice is soft still, though his black eyes flash warning signs of anger.

'Sorry to disturb you folks this late at night.' He walks over to the table and gives a friendly salute to Martha. 'I'm glad you're on the line, actually, Martha. I could use your brand of cynical wisdom tonight.' Martha inclines her glass towards him. She liked Rose, admired his loyalty: modest crooks were always the most charming characters, she liked to say. 'Lils, this is Martha, who's a sort of spy, tough as an old boot.' Lily smiles awkwardly. 'Martha, this is my baby sister.'

Livia is sitting upright, the colour returned to her face, her hood down. 'What's going on, Rose? Not like you to visit at this hour.'

He and Lily join Livia on the sofa, Jake takes the soft armchair and manoeuvres the computer so Martha can see and hear everything. Lily is rolling a cigarette in one hand. Rose pulls out a letter from his jacket.

'I know you guys were at the dig the other day, and they mentioned that nutjob writing crank letters.'

Jake reaches forward to take it. 'I was telling Martha about it.'

'Well, Lily got one. And it says somebody's going to die on that hill in the next week.'

Chapter Eight

The rolling fields around Little Sky

The next day, Jake is running, his eyes red and tired, his body complaining. The late morning is brisk, the chill breeze a constant accompaniment, the sun a merest suspicion in the sky.

Jake exercises every day. It is a source of comfort to him, a ritual addiction. He has run the five-mile circuit around his home so often that the landscape can simply blur, unheralded, into a soft, green background. But today he makes himself concentrate, his eyes dart, his restive senses sharpen towards his surroundings: the feel of the downtrodden turf, bruised and muddied; the colours in the fields that surround the track, wide and wild, full of fluttering grass, stippled with the new flowers of the season; the dense smell of all that earth, thick with life, heavy with new decay; the chirruping of songbirds and scuffling of invisible creatures; the watchful swoop of larger birds of prey, hovering, priestly, in the sightless draughts of air above him.

He is in a sunken hollow behind Agatha Wood, his legs strong, heading towards the river, a merest hint of reflected light in the distance.

They had stayed late at Livia's discussing the threat. The letter from Wulfnoth was different in tone, more strident, shorter, but still written in the same orderly font.

> My warnings have gone unheeded. My rage is being stoked. Those in charge of the desecration ignore me, but they will not ignore this: my promise of bloody intervention.
>
> If you do not stop your despoiling, someone will be sacrificed before the week is out.
>
> Warn everyone. The wages of their sinning may be their death.
>
> Vengeance is mine, I will repay, saith the Lord.
>
> Wulfnoth

Lily had found it in her backpack, stuffed into a pocket. She'd only noticed late that evening, and Rose had insisted they came around right away. Jake lifted it carefully and placed it into one of Diana's plastic folders, and told her take it to the police the next day.

Rose was antsy, rubbing his fingers on the material of his jeans, appealing to Martha for reassurance. She was calm as ever, but unable to promise that the danger was not real. She did agree to review copies of all the letters, see if there was anything useful in her system, any other relevant cases. 'I'm not going to lie, Rose, this sort of psycho nonsense is always nothing to worry about, right up until the point you wished you'd taken it more seriously. I mean, how much can you trust someone who rants in biblical and calls himself Wulfnoth?' She shook her head sadly.

As they left, Rose turned to Jake, gripping his bicep. 'You'll look into this too, won't you, Jake? I know it might all be nonsense, but it worries me. And she may be annoying as hell, but she's my sister, you know.' Jake had nodded, understanding.

And now as he runs, lungs expanding, brain clear, he realizes he does want to help. The best advice, he knows, would be for Lily to walk away, get a different job, but she has her brother's disdain for orthodoxy, and her own disinclination to be pushed around. She'd made it clear she was staying at the dig, and would brook no alternative.

Jake turns at the river, which is still faintly misty, so it looks like the water is steaming, some witchy potion spilled across a tabletop. Livia had wanted to help too; she liked Lily, admired her youthful zest and offhand beauty, appreciated how she had behaved around Diana. As they had lain in bed after their guests' departure, the late night pushed out even later, the scent of sex clinging in the damp air, she had urged him on, with caution, her feet raised high in the gloom like a salute.

He makes it home, and swims the full length of the lake and back, the water cold enough to soothe his muscles. Now he stretches in the sauna he'd built for himself two years before. It's silent bar the whispering of the coals, the wood inside pale in the muted light, hot enough to bring his breath up short. He ponders his possible approaches. The police would take the note seriously, perhaps even sending it up to the new man, McAllister. But if it was all clean forensically, even he would be able to do very little.

Unless Amy decided to shut the dig down, this spoken threat would loom over everybody.

Jake showers outdoors in the courtyard, his body a mottled red, writhing in the alternating hot and cold jets. He runs his hands down his torso, touches the firm flesh, the lack of excess weight. He feels light on his feet, active, able to take on the occasional challenge like this. He eats quickly, standing up at the breakfast bar, cheese and ham, bread and thick local butter. The coffee is hot and strong. He dresses against the chill in cotton trousers and a thick wool shirt, and decides to walk up to St Giles.

It is no modest journey without a car, four miles or so over uneven ground, but his legs have not stiffened since the run and he still has wind in his lungs. He follows the river round, leaving Parvum behind. There is still plenty of daytime left, the landscape a mess of pastels, washed through in the afternoon pallor. As he approaches the hill, he appreciates afresh the sheer scale of the dig site. The vast earthworks reach all the way around the plateau, three channels delved at some distant point in history, encompassing a vast spread of land, rising and falling, the size of maybe fifty football fields. From a distance – framed by a bank of dark grey clouds that seem to billow from its summit – the whole place looks unreal, manufactured somehow, like a giant thumb has made indentations around the rim, the work of some sort of divine potter shaping the ground.

The archaeological team are on a break when he eventually enters through the gate. They are sitting a hundred yards in front of the portacabin, sipping steaming mugs of tea, trying to garner warmth from the fugitive glimpses of the sun. Daisy waves at him, and gestures for him to go inside. He knocks, and Amy rises from behind her messy desk to greet him.

She looks tired and distracted, strawberry hair falling in front of her eyes. She is wearing dark jeans and a green vest-top, hardly concealing an expanse of milky skin. Around her neck she has a small Celtic cross of pale gold and green.

'Jake, isn't it? Lily mentioned she'd spoken to you. Are you here to offer us your security services?'

Jake slides into the old armchair in front of her. The whole place is furnished with what look like cast-off items from other rooms, a mismatched medley: old wooden table here, sagging sofa there, orphan chairs from various dining sets placed higgledy-piggledy all around.

He scratches his head thoughtfully. 'I'm the wrong person to do anything like that. Lily wanted me to come back, look over the lie of the land, speak to you, see if anything jumps out.'

'We should take this seriously then?'

'Who knows? But any time someone makes threats and seems a little eccentric or out-of-control, I think it always pays to be a bit concerned. Tell me, how do you think the letter got in her bag?'

Amy sips her outsized mug of coffee, which has a nude male statue as its logo. 'I've wondered about that. Lily came and left on the bus, and it could have been slipped in then, I guess. She says she was none too careful about it. But the bag was also left all day in that room there.' She points to a small kitchen containing a fridge and microwave, and a much stained tabletop. Rucksacks and coats are piled in the corner, all looking old and scuffed and forlorn.

'So there's a chance, a better than good chance perhaps,

that it happened in here. Which might make one of your team the author.'

Her smile is thin, weary. 'It might. But you've got to remember this is an open site. We keep people out of the folly, the spring, and most of the trenches, but it's free for people to wander over. Indeed, we kind of encourage it, you know, bringing archaeology to life. It's why we agreed to let Daisy do the filming. The day Lily got the letter – and it could've even been put in her bag the day before, for all we know – we'd had the whole film crew, plus at least three hikers I saw, plus Reverend Jordan and a few folk from his historical society. And it's not as if we signed everyone in and out again. We are a bit amateurish here, you know.'

Her hands, strong and weathered, the knuckles damaged like scratched porcelain, cling to her mug. 'I'm not even sorry for that, Jake. We all got into this to uncover history, make the land speak, find fellow travellers who loved that world as much as we did.' She leans back, touches the cross on her neck. Jake keeps his eyes studiously no lower than that. 'You must think I'm a terrible hippy. And I suppose I am.'

'Not at all. I can appreciate a vocation.'

'Yes, of course, the art of detection, the call of policing. I can see the similarity. Along with a love of making sense of bones, I guess.' A liquid trickle of laughter. 'Well, I'm not sure we're going to make the job easier for you, if you do actually want to help us out of love. An amateur detective. The word amateur means that, you know? Someone who loves things. I don't know if you did Latin at school: amo, amas, amat, amamus, amatis, amant, and so on.' Her voice is soft, soothing, almost mystical.

Jake looks through the window and sees people heading back out to the various digs. Jumpers and bobble hats and bare legs and wellies. 'Tell me about the place, what you're doing here.'

She smiles instantly, pale blue eyes alight, friendly lines across her skin. 'I'm superbly qualified for that. Come here, Jake, and I'll show you the plan.' She pushes papers and pens to one side of the table, heedless of their disorder, and pulls out of a drawer a large sheet of paper, which she unfolds carefully. It is a schematic of the full site, beautifully sketched in grey ink. Jake once more marvels at the size of it all.

Amy's voice has deepened slightly, become more authoritative. She leans forward, pendant swinging over the drawing, like incense in an ancient church. 'This hill has been continuously occupied by high status individuals and figures of worship for thousands of years. It began as a fort in the Iron Age, but by fort we really mean enclosed settlement, wooden fences built behind those giant earthworks you can see as soon as you arrive. Within that was a natural spring, which you can still see here.' She points with a pen, which she then tucks behind her ear, dislodging a stray hair. 'That led to some sort of temple structure, a place of ritual anyway for centuries. Then the Romans came along, appropriated the religious bit, and built a villa with baths on the north side. We've dug down a long way, and you can see a mosaic floor, beautifully preserved, as well as some hypocausts, which is the Roman term for central heating.'

They lock eyes. She smiles again. 'Let me know if I'm being too schoolmistressy.'

Jake shrugs. 'I'm enjoying the lesson.'

'Anyway, the Romans and their army eventually bugger

off back to Rome to try to rescue the dying empire, and the big house probably collapses. Most of the stone and wood is then scavenged and used to build another, more military structure. We're in the Anglo-Saxon period more or less now, and that left us the tower on one side, and some ruined walls beneath the surface. And a whole stretch of land used for burials. We've uncovered not only complete skeletons, but even stone tombs – sarcophagi, we say – with bones within them, very rare for the period. Suggestive of a very high status site in the pre-Norman years.'

'And that's the time of our friend Wulfnoth?'

'Confusingly enough there were several Wulfnoths over the centuries, but yes, someone of that name would have been a central figure here at about the time of the Conquest. A local lord, perhaps *the* local lord. Then along came the dratted Normans and besmirched our proud Anglo-Saxon heritage, or that's what some of the more patriotic locals have always thought. With the Normans came a change in size and use for the nearest towns, and eventually a whole new castle was built twenty miles away. This place fell to ruin, plundered by everybody, ruined once and for all in the Civil War when some unruly Roundheads camped here, and then not much happened until we came along.'

'Apart from the folly?'

'Yes, we're in the mid-eighteenth century there. A local eccentric, rather brilliant actually, Sir Patrick Dalziel. He made lots of correct assumptions about the place, but didn't have the wherewithal, or maybe the patience, to dig properly. So he dipped around the edges, traced some of the walls, and decided it was all too buried and invisible. He built the grotto in a cutesy medieval style and named it after Wulfnoth, who he rather fancied, I think. It's a pain, because it ruins the integrity of the site, but it's all history now, and we use it for storing the finds. Would you like to see it?'

Jake nods. She looks at her watch. 'Bugger, I have to go and supervise a planning meeting at Trench 4. I'm basically a glorified referee here most of the time.' She sweeps out of the door and shouts for Zach. She turns back to Jake. 'He's my assistant – bright boy. Come on, he can take you.'

She pulls Jake gently by the arm, and they stand outside upon the austere plain. The sun is now completely hidden behind the grey clouds, plump and menacing, and the light has dimmed almost to gloaming. Zach walks up, buttoning his cardigan, black hair like a cowl covering his eyes.

'Can you open the folly for Jake? Get him a torch and then make sure you lock up after him when he goes. Thank you, my love.'

He smiles nervously at her, and nods, his glance lingering as she bustles off towards one of the outer trenches. With Jake he is immediately rather stiff and formal, handing him an outsized torch and then marching off, making him hasten to keep up. Jake soon matches him stride for stride, starts asking questions, his usual instincts kicking in.

'What do you make of the threatening letters, Zach. Are you worried?'

Zach's mouth is small and in permanent pout, his moustache thin as a caterpillar. His voice is quiet, reluctant. 'I only know what Amy's told me. She doesn't seem concerned.'

'Really? If someone was saying he'd kill people who are disturbing the earth around here and my job was, you know, disturbing the earth, I'd be a bit worried.'

Zach continues walking. 'I leave that to Amy really. There's always cranks about.'

'Anyone in particular who might be Wulfnoth?'

Zach turns quickly, so Jake almost collides with him. 'Here we are, the folly. Let me open the door, and then you can shout when you're done.'

'You don't want to guide me?'

'I've got a lot of work on, I'm afraid.' Zach pulls out an ornate key, almost preposterously large, and pushes it into the lock of the big blackened oak doorway. It turns with an effortful creak, and the door swings open. It is gloomy within, the air surprisingly cold and dry, the lingering scent of earth, and something else, medicinal or chemical.

When Jake turns to ask Zach what it is, he realizes he is alone. He switches on the torch, and presses on down into the darkness.

Chapter Nine

Wulfnoth's Keep, the St Giles site

It feels old, as if submerged for countless aeons in the earth, and Jake feels a little cheated when he thinks of when it had been built. Clearly this Dalziel character wanted a bespoke ancient experience and had succeeded in creating one. The walls are rough-hewn, misshapen rocks expertly joined. They form a downward sloping corridor that heads beneath an enormous lintel.

Jake's steps echo faintly, but the bright light ahead of him is reassuring. Through the gap at the end of the passage, the path widens into a large cave-like room, mostly beneath ground level, the size probably of the church interior at Parvum. The walls and floor are dry but comfortless, thick with weathered stone. Light comes from various lamps that also give off a faint hiss and heat, the only sound Jake can hear.

Boxes, immaculately labelled, are piled across much of the room, but the centre seems to be designated as a display area. Two giant stone coffins, blocky and rectangular, the size and heft of churchyard tombs, are lined up end-on-end, horizontal. Their lids are shut, their contents unknown. Behind them are tables for cleaning and filing, and Jake stands over the bones there, dry and smooth as driftwood, solid, symbols of the perdurable nature of existence. The flesh might seep away, the walls might tumble, but this was a shrine to obstinacy, to life's sheer lastingness.

At another table lies a sword, the golden patina of its hilt worn away, but the beautiful encumbrances of its decoration still visible, its tip gleaming sharp in the light. Jake feels like he is in a museum or even a temple. The quiet is thick, laden somehow with history. He thinks that Dalziel would have relished the use to which his foolish building was being put. He spends a happy, footling hour, looking through boxes, staring at artefacts taken from the ground that were once simply practical – boring even, discarded by the people who walked these hills – but now had been sanctified by the arbitrary process of historical survival.

He also sees how considerable and professional an operation is at work at the dig itself. There is a passion for order and meticulousness. It must come from Amy, despite the clutter of her desk and the casual nature of her appearance.

He walks across to the sword, running his fingers along the edge of the blade and is surprised when a thin line of blood wells from their tips. A tiny sting that reminds him of the weapon's original purpose and the probable tale of its use.

'Sharp as a killer would want, eh?'

Jake leaps, and the sword clatters onto its side. He spins around, to be met with a beaming smile from Reverend Jordan.

'Unforgivable of me to surprise you like that, Mr Jackson. And I am delighted to find in you a fellow potterer of this place. It's such a marvellous sanctuary, isn't it? It reminds me of a church somehow.' He carefully returns the sword to its stand, his touch delicate and assured.

Jake wipes his fingers on his trousers. 'I know what you mean. Do you get free run of the site then, Mr Jordan?'

'John, please. We fellow alliteratives must stick together. I always think that having "J" in our names makes us a bit special too. Didn't exist in the Latin alphabet you know.'

'I'd never thought of it.'

'No? How odd. Well, you were asking about my role here. Totally unofficial, but I think Amy would concede not without use. The church had to give initial approval for the excavation, it technically being our land, and I've personally given all the support I can ever since. Plus, I'm an amateur historian myself, so enjoy getting my hands dirty.'

'Amy told me how much she valued amateur assistance.'

'A little joke perhaps, but a germ of truth there. No, I'm afraid I'm a part of the landscape, like the old tower or this not quite as old thing. And then I helped discover the horde, and so got involved even more.'

'Which may or may not make you a millionaire.'

'We found it as a foursome, as I told you: Daisy, Amy, young Zach and me. We'll share with the landowner if he can be tracked down. And nothing's certain – they haven't even valued it properly yet. But nobody's going to lose out. Ah, you seem to have finished the tour here. Can I escort you back to the surface?'

They are treading back up the corridor towards the door. When they emerge, an early dusk has fallen, the wind rising, the smell of rain in the air. They look across the half-light, as the team across the plateau start to cover up trenches, tarpaulin billowing, bright colours against the green and brown, their work brought to an early conclusion.

Jordan is pushing a tattered wide-brimmed hat down on his head, buttoning up his jacket. 'A bit of weather coming in, I think. Rain about to stop play. Can I offer you a cup of tea at St Giles? It's a shortish hike to the south, there.'

'That's kind of you, but I better be getting back before I get drenched. One thing before I go. Have you ever received a letter from this Wulfnoth character? He seems to have some religious leanings, I can imagine him directing his anger towards you.'

Jordan's chest swells, face tightens. 'It's all nonsense. I did get one, addressed to me personally, and burned it in the furnace right away. Using the Bible to stand in the way of legitimate archaeology. Disgraceful. And he can bluster all he wants, nothing would stop me doing this.'

'So you didn't keep the evidence?'

'The rantings of a sub-literate philistine are not "evidence", Jake. I didn't even know he'd sent other letters till the last one. No, I'll not waste my energy and power of thought on Mr Wulfnoth, whoever he is.'

He strides off down the hill, calling back over his shoulder. 'Come and see my splendid church someday. A treat for a real lover of history like you.' With that he is lost in the spreading shadow. Jake looks around to say goodbye to Amy or Lily, but he can't see them anywhere. He sets his chin against the wind, beats his arms against his chest for warmth, and heads back homeward.

Chapter Ten

The cellar of the Jolly Nook, Parvum

The rain holds off for most of Jake's journey home, but he can do nothing about the early encroachment of evening's dark. It gets colder quick. He takes a woollen hat from his pocket and pulls it down over his hair, feeling a sense of separation from the elements. The moon is invisible in the cloud-streaked sky, which shifts from bruised purple to muddied brown to impenetrable black. Fortunately, he knows his way without any silvering of night-time light, and steers himself by the presence of the river, which will always take him to a corner of home.

At Parvum, he passes Livia's cottage, but sees that she and Diana are out on some after-school venture. The place looks chill and aloof. He stops off at the Jolly Nook, still warm with peachy light, to pick up his post. It is closing time for the shop, but his friend Sarah is in her usual place, perched on a pile of old newspapers behind her counter.

She was one of his first acquaintances in the village, and now one of his closest connections there. A widow of indeterminate years, her small body hardy, her face resolute and kind, she has run the local shop for an age. In the evenings, the cellar below serves as an unofficial pub, with barrels of local beer and cider, and no closing time. Everyone in the area has an account with her, settled in a largely incomprehensible fashion on a monthly basis.

'Jake, how nice to see you. I've some post for you, my old duck. And Rose is down below, having a quiet one. Would you like to look in?'

'For a bit. I've been out all day, and I want to get back while my legs still work.'

She pats him on the hand. 'Have the cider then, it'll put a spring in your step – there's a little scritch of apple brandy mixed into it.'

'You're a dangerous woman.'

'So they've always said.'

Jake walks down the whitewashed steps into the cellar's cool exterior. Candles flutter, making extravagant, ghostly figures on the walls. The scent of orchard, the cloy of spilled drink. Rose is sitting with a pewter tankard, smiling.

'Good to see you, Jake. Grab a seat.' He waves a pickled onion at him vaguely, before biting into it. Jake fills his own tankard and takes a draught, which is appley and spicy and strong. He sits beside Rose, on an old barrel.

'I've been up at the dig, nosing around. And I've got the letters Daisy provided; I'm going to go home and see what I can see. How's Lily?'

Rose drinks deeply, wipes his mouth on his sleeve. 'She's fine. It's her brother who's worrying.' He stretches his legs out, belching softly. 'I'm going to spend a bit of tomorrow there, keeping an eye, and wouldn't mind you nipping back at some point, if that's OK with you.'

Jake is rubbing his aching thighs. 'That's fine with me. I like the place, I can see why people would spend their time digging up the past there. I really can. But neither one of us can stop a determined person just by hanging out. You know that.'

'I do, but I know I'll feel better if we're both looking out for Lils. We can't do much more.'

'Well, if you're on duty tomorrow, I'll go on Wednesday and we can think again after that.'

Rose chinks his mug. 'Deal. Fancy another?'

'One more and I'll be asleep. You make sure you get home safely. I used to be a cop, you know.'

'I'll keep an eye on him, officer.' This is Sarah, coming down the stairs and wiping her hands. People drink and drive around here, Jake knows, and it has always been tolerated in moderation. The police, such as there are any, largely look away. But there also seems to be some sort of tacit agreement as to what constitutes irresponsible drinking, and people are largely protected from themselves by their peers. It works, too. There hasn't been a notable prang in Jake's time, and it wasn't uncommon to see someone stumbling out of the Nook on a chilly early morning, eyes red and breath steaming, rubbing the small of their back after an uncomfortable night on a bench in the cellar corner.

It starts to rain as Jake turns off the road towards his own land. Mithering drizzle to begin with, then something steadier, a constant thrum on the ground, a rising whisper in the hedgerows. The lake is a dark presence to his right, a slumbering creature shifting endlessly in its repose. He squelches the last mile, and is happy to be inside.

He throws his clothes in the basket in the kitchen, and pulls on a velvety robe, wet hair clinging to the fabric on the back. He heats up a warming drink of thick cream with dark chocolate melted into it. Then he lights a fire in the library, the tongues of yellowy flame clutching at the kindling, and collapses onto his sofa. He puts on one of his favourite late-night records, *The Blue Notebooks* by Max Richter, haunting and maudlin, a minor-key soundtrack to the dismal mediocrity of the hour.

He has five letters from Wulfnoth, all longer, more measured than the latest. He reads them carefully, trying to sense their purpose and threat. They all quote scripture with a heavy, hedge-preacher hand. The early letters tend to cite the Book of Job, that gloomy inquiry into the justice of the divine: 'O that thou wouldst hide me in the grave, that thou wouldst keep me secret, until thy wrath be past, that thou wouldst appoint me a set time, and remember me!' reads one. Ideas of anger and retribution and the impermanency of death.

The references, like the surrounding words, are bold and grandiloquent, flirting with the ridiculous. Jake can sense the author's enjoyment in the sententiousness of it all, the schoolmasterly way it chastens and warns. It doesn't feel like a prelude to action, but satisfying action in its own right.

So why does he feel a shiver, a presentiment of dread? He shakes his head at his nerviness, and lumbers off to get some sleep, which eventually comes, but fraught and non-renewing.

The next morning is brisk and clear, the spring light a tonic to his tired body, liquid and mellow glimmers bouncing forth from a pale blue sky. After he has exercised and showered, he sits on a bench by his vegetable garden, sanding the front panel of the guitar he is making. He is aiming for a piece of wood thin and level, which involves a process of endless attrition. There is the scent of his steaming mug of coffee, which mingles with the flowery sweetness that lies heavy in the air. He has left the kitchen door open, with the record player on loud enough that he can hear the softly meandering piano. Schumann and his *Papillons*, flitting around like the butterflies he can see at the dance all around him.

Life is certainly bursting forth. When the music dips, he can hear, in the distance, the soft croonings and fussings of his chickens from their luxury apartments in a lower field. In front of him, the black, fertile earth is home to various sprouting plants. He's come to find that, while spring brings random largesse to the surrounding wild places, it is less generous to the gardener, who has to work hard to get a harvest much before the summer. He has had some success with lettuces, which are now emerging, compact and bright, alongside cabbages and parsley and broad beans. He had started the latter in his greenhouses, and they came early, budding up against their supporting canes, already sweet to eat.

Movement catches his eye, and he sees McAllister, the policeman, warily treading the path by the lake. Jake hails him in a friendly fashion, and goes to the kitchen to pour another coffee from the pot. He hands it over when McAllister arrives, his suit jacket over one arm, perspiring gently.

'That's kind of you, Jake. I parked in one of those fields a way away, but it's still a fair old trek to get here. And when I do, what do I find but you sitting among your vegetables with music and nature and a brew. It's enough to make me want to retire.'

'I can see it in your eyes that you don't mean that.'

'From what I hear, I might say the same about you. No, I'm here for business not pleasure. I thought we might talk about the dig, and what you make of these letters.'

McAllister sits awkwardly on the corner of the bench, until Jake goes back to the house to bring him out a chair. They sip their coffee for a moment, and discuss their impressions of the site and the people who work there. Jake marshals his thoughts from the night before about the letters themselves.

'Their progression worries me a little. On the surface, I think they come from a crank, who likes the sound of his own sentences. But then the last one is punchier, less ornate, and I wonder whether it might betray a desire for action. I'm no psychologist, mind.'

'A similar notion occurred to me. There's a few prints on the old letters, but hard to say when they were put there, and none of them pop up on the system. This latest one is completely clean. Another difference to worry us.'

Jake lets the 'us' pass without comment. 'I've been on the site. Can you work out when and where the letters could've been planted?'

McAllister purses his lips, pensive. 'This is the first one to be left in someone's bag. The others appeared overnight at the gate, could've been put there by anyone. There's no meaningful security anyplace, except in that storage room, the folly thing.'

'Do you think they come from someone regularly on site?'

'Could do, but why work there if you object to it so much? From what I can tell, there's nothing sinister going on. Just people digging very slowly in very boring holes, and then gabbing about it a lot.'

'Not an archaeology fan, then?'

'Ah, but don't tell that director – Daisy, isn't it? – or any of them for that matter. I'm a city boy, born in Bearsden, but a Glaswegian through and through for most of my life. I can't be doing with all this footering about in the soil.'

'What can you do about the threats?'

'I've sent a local copper down each morning for an hour or so, which I'll keep doing. And I'll not be that far away when I can. Do you think you might hover about the place a bit?'

'I'm due there tomorrow. But if someone wants to make trouble, what's there really to be done to stop them?'

'That's as true here as it's always been elsewhere.' He sighs expansively, gripping his thighs. 'We can but do our best; we can't stop evil in its tracks.'

'A philosophical chief. You'll go far.'

'I thank you. Now, speaking of which, I best be on my way. You'll report in if you find anything?'

'Of course. I'll walk down with you.'

The damp ground clings to their boots as they pass the lake, the strands of grass easily broken and mulched. It is warming up a little more, and it feels peaceful. Above them in the sky – white clouds like spilt milk on a blue tablecloth – a falcon hovers. McAllister talks more about the contrast of the new job with his old, the countryside with the city. He tells stories of bloody crimes solved and not solved back in Glasgow. Jake reciprocates with his own tales, and feels a sense of communion with him, senses goodness in the man's open face, then remembers once more the trust betrayed by Watson.

McAllister seems to notice. 'Jake, I know you've been burned by my predecessor, but I reckon I'm going to value your advice while I'm here. You never leave the brotherhood of policing, you know. You can't escape entirely from what you are. And I know enough about you to see you as a pal, a consultant, if you like. Even on this, I'm glad to have someone on the ground I can trust. I hope you don't mind that.'

'You're worried about what might happen then?'

'Put it this way, I'd rather be surprised by the peace than caught out by a calamity. I don't have a feel for these folk like I did back home, I don't know what's merely local eccentricity and what isn't.'

'I'm not much better; I've only been here three years. And I'm definitely a local eccentric. But I'm as uneasy as you, for what it's worth.'

McAllister pauses before he cuts across Bosch field towards his car. 'I don't find that reassuring, that's for very sure.' The sunlight dips as he says it, a shadow across the sun. The bird in the air bobs, sullen. Then the light washes over them once more, as he strides off.

Jake shakes off the portent. Light and gloom are always alternating. Birds of prey always look like they might signify a thing beyond, but they always are indifferent observers of human fate as well.

Chapter Eleven

The uncovered mosaic, St Giles site

The next day, trouble. From a distance, raised up on the land that overlooked the site to the south, Jake can see the aftermath to an incident, people running hither and thither like ants. No sound reaches him, but he can sense the panic. He slips his backpack over both shoulders, feels the corner of his book pushing into his spine, and starts to run forwards, the immediate dip taking everything out of his sight.

It's a considerable trek, even running, his feet sticking into the soft ground, sweat-shod, as he cuts on and off the track. Flattened bracken, hidden humps of ground make him stumble. It's a warm day and he can feel his T-shirt cling to him as he approaches the hill. There's the mark of a four-by-four's departure at the base, where someone has spun the tyres fast, sending up a spray of mud that has fallen back as giant worm-casts.

At the top of the incline stands Daisy. She is smoking

a cigarette, holding it away from her body, like she is not used to the habit. She smiles bleakly as he puffs up.

'No need to hurry, Jake, not now. Our little drama's come and gone.'

'What happened?' His chest is throbbing, but he keeps his voice calm, letting the bag fall to the ground.

'Reverend Jordan's had an accident.'

'Accident?'

She inhales, her face distorted as the smoke enters her lungs hot. 'I don't know what to call it really.' She is about to continue when Lily rushes up, a damp blur of soft hair and concern.

She throws her arms around Jake. 'Thank God you're here. Did Daisy tell you?'

'She was about to. I'm glad you're OK too. So what happened?'

Lily looks up to Daisy, seems to get tacit approval to resume the narration herself. 'Jordan was helping clean mosaic tiles, when he must've taken a drink, and then starts writhing on the ground, clutching his throat, shrieking like I don't know what. I was maybe twenty yards away, and when I got to him, he was gurgling, tongue sort of bubbly, his body all stiff. He couldn't breathe.' Her voice subsides for a second, and she buries her head in Jake's shoulder.

'Acid – we think he'd drunk acid.' Daisy's voice is oddly calm, numb with shock. She manoeuvres Jake and Lily through the fortifications and onto the main plateau. 'My crew weren't far off, and we happened to have the Land Rover nearby, so he's gone to hospital. He was still breathing when he left, but he didn't look good.'

The plateau is a flurry of fraught activity, the same confusion, the same aimless activity he had seen from a distance, though people have slowed down a little. There is milling about, some tears, people packing up and heading towards them by the exit. He thinks quickly.

'Get Amy here now. We need to close off the site. Daisy, can you bring her?'

He walks forward, holds his hands upwards, his voice strident, carried long by the wind. 'Everybody please stay where they are. Nobody can leave the site until the police have come.'

Amy comes running up, face blanched. 'Jake, thank God you're here.'

'Have you called the cops?'

She nods. The top of her chest is pinked, an ebbing flush. 'I did that as soon as they took him, but then I wasn't sure what to do next.'

A crowd has gathered around them. Mostly young-ish, knees stained, weathered clothes, workers on the dig. Behind them is a middle-aged couple, clutching thermos flasks as if for protection, and some others he can't quite make out at the back. He keeps his voice raised, projecting confidence.

'I know there's been a terrible accident, and we don't know exactly how it happened. But until we do, we have to treat it like it could be a crime. So can everyone please go and sit in front of the office and wait for the police. Nobody can leave until they say so.'

'A crime? Really? I was told it was an accident with acid. What are you talking about?' This from one of the thermos carriers, a bosomy woman with the piercing eye of an oystercatcher.

'I'm afraid a crime is possible. I don't want anybody to be alarmed, but we must take precautions.'

His voice drops. 'Lily, can you move everybody back to the office, and get a list of names, addresses and contact details? Daisy can let you know who took Jordan to the hospital. The cops will want that first of all.'

There is a moment of hush, of stasis, no noise other than the buffeting of the breeze, and then a babble of questions starts to emerge. Jake is resolute, pacific. 'Please, I'm a retired policeman. We need to protect the scene. The cleaner we are about it, the less the actual cops will have to do when they get here, which'll be in the next few minutes.' It might be a little longer. As he surveys the panorama, beginning behind him, he can see no movement: hills and valleys, greens and browns, a solitary road like a discarded bootlace, the steeple of a distant church pointing forlornly into the greying sky. 'That means the sooner you all can get home.'

'He doesn't look a retired policeman.' That plangent voice again.

Amy claps her hands, suddenly resolute. 'OK, you heard Jake, who I can vouch for. And he's right. I'm sure this is nothing more than an accident, but we should listen to the expert. Daisy, can you go along with them?'

Daisy is clearly the other figure of acknowledged authority here, and her philosophic acquiescence seems to spread calm among the group, who turn and head back into the site ahead of her. Murmurs and questions and sidelong glances at Jake. He is not necessarily a reassuring vision of order, he concedes: long hair fluffed wide by the wind, some strands plastered to his face, beard dampened with exertion, his exposed arms and legs weathered and humped with muscle. He takes Amy softly by the arm. 'You better show me where this happened.' Then, to Daisy, 'Once Lily has taken their name, pick someone you trust, and station them here to fill the police in and bring them across.'

'I'll do it myself once everything is sorted. I can work on my smoking skills a bit more.' Nervous laugh, a bray of disquiet. She looks ruffled, clearly an unusual experience for her.

Amy and Jake make for the centre of the dig, past various now deserted trenches. The sun has reappeared from behind the clouds, casting a bleaching light upon everything. Amy clasps her cardigan around her, as if for reassurance. After a few minutes, they get to an area where a large square has been taken out of the ground, a hole almost six-foot deep, perhaps thirty feet broad.

Jake leans over and sees half of the floor is a mosaic, a recognizably Roman artwork, the colours dulled by the passage of time, but the intricate patterns still visible: swirls and diamonds, triangles and flowers, brilliantly isometric. The product of precision and skill and a demanding patron. It is an easy skip of the imagination to place a Romano-British family here, sandal-clad, standing on this spot a millennia or two ago. Easy, but still dizzying.

Amy takes Jake down some rough steps cut into the turf and into the trench. She points, her hand trembling faintly. 'We're still excavating the edges where the mosaic has crumbled over time, which means we dig up hundreds of tiles, chipped mostly, but some still whole. They're taken to that table there.'

A trestle has been set up in the corner, resting on the smooth dark soil. It is covered with brushes and sieves, the clutter of work. On the floor is a water bottle, which must have fallen.

'So where was Jordan?'

'He was by himself, doing some cleaning. It's pretty unskilled work. There's a whole bag of tiles, and look, a washbasin there filled with water. The clean ones go in those trays, sorted by quality.'

'Lily mentioned acid.'

'I know. We do use it, very dilute, but not normally in the trench like this. There might be a bottle in the equipment box there.' She moves towards it, but Jake checks her.

'Don't go any further into the trench, don't touch anything. We should get out from here, and then wait for the police. This whole area will need looking at. He was alone, you say?'

Amy swallows and nods, and they clutch hands awkwardly as they heave each other up to the surface. Jake looks back towards the entrance and can see two uniformed police officers at the gate talking to Daisy. A third has already stepped to the side and is speaking into his radio, presumably seeing who else can come to help. And then behind them, in shirtsleeves, his bearish pelt visible even at this distance, McAllister is climbing the path, his movements sprightly and tireless.

A few minutes later, Jake watches him stride towards them. He and Amy had made desultory conversation about the notes, about Jordan, about the chances that this was deliberate. She is now wringing her hands, clearly distressed, the quiet sound of sandpapery rasps. McAllister has a cynical expression as he reaches them. He looks Jake in the eye. 'Thanks for securing the scene for us, Jake. It's a good job you did. Jordan died not long after he got to hospital, I'm sorry to say. Heart attack brought on by exposure to hydrochloric acid. There's a goodish chance he might have been murdered.'

Chapter Twelve

The sauna, Little Sky

Black night outside, the moon up, a coin of nacre. Inside the crackle and hiss of the coals, the faintly orange light casting shadows against the walls. Heat enough to make your heart flutter. Diana is in bed, safe and secure.

Jake and Livia lie outstretched beside each other on hot towels, their familiar bodies naked and glistening, controlling their breaths with care.

'So how did it happen then, do you reckon?' This is Livia, eyes closed, pensive, trying to will the stress from within her body.

Jake had stayed until the light ebbed away, closing down the scene until the morning. He stood with McAllister and watched crime scene technicians sweep the trench, picking up various utensils and bagging them, paying particular care to secure the ceramic drinking bottle that had fallen to the floor. As they had carried it up the steps, Jake had pushed his nose near and smelled it, an unmistakably vinegary, vomit-like scent. There was a small amount left undrained in the bottom, which could at least be tested. But it seemed like strong acid, placed there to harm.

Lily had come to stand with them, hands in her windcheater pockets, her bare legs apparently impervious to the stiff breeze.

McAllister nodded towards the bottle, his eyes sleepy, his voice measured. 'Do you recognize the bottle?'

'We all got given them, they're branded with the name of the TV show. You know, like merchandise. I've got one at home, and we kept a few around for people to fill up when they needed to.'

'Someone seems to have done that, certainly.' This was Jake, running through scenarios in his mind. Lily nodded silently, for once at a loss for words.

After that, it was a matter of ensuring everyone's names had been gathered before they were all allowed to disperse. Amy had decided to close the site for the next day, and McAllister posted a watch to deter any sightseers. He had asked Jake to meet him the next morning in Parvum, and then been driven off in the final car. Jake had been left alone in the vast and heedless space, and trudged off to meet Livia to take her home.

Livia rolls over to her front, and Jake notes with pleasure the raised ridge of her spine, almost saurian, a bony oddness that terminated in the pillowy softness below. He traces his finger along it, a connoisseur, feels the cool slipperiness of the skin.

He has paused to answer her, as he is still a little uncertain of a clear-cut theory. He leans on his side, lets the sweat slide into the towel, runnelling along the lines of his stomach muscles.

'An accident is just about possible, I guess. Someone fills the bottle with acid to use in the trench, Jordan, a bit of a dodderer, mistakes it for water, downs a load, and it kills him.'

Livia shifts in the heat. 'Unlikely, I'd say. Didn't someone say that they don't use acid much in the trenches? And anyway, we can't ignore the Wulfnoth stuff: we worried about a death, and then a death happened. That can't be a coincidence.'

'I agree. So it could be whoever calls themselves Wulfnoth, going after either anybody on the dig indiscriminately, or targeting Jordan specifically. It's a strange method, though. Acid can kill you, but you need to know the person is going to drink a big mouthful, and even then the damage isn't always fatal, unless the victim has underlying issues.'

'Did Jordan?'

'Heart trouble over the last few years. Made no secret of it. And it was a heart attack that finished him off.'

Livia moves down a level, where it is slightly cooler, and sits, hands resting on the pale wood, damp prints. 'Perhaps he was targeted then?'

Jake runs his hands through his hair, hot and damp and smelling faintly singed by the heat. 'But why him? He didn't run the dig, or make the decisions.'

'He let the dig happen on the church land, he was the most blasphemous in that sense, as Wulfnoth might see it. And presumably any death is enough to strike a blow. The site's closed, isn't it.'

'For now. I don't think it will be forever though. They can't leave it half-finished.' He wrinkles his nose. 'And maybe there's stuff we don't know about Jordan, too. Lily told me more than once he had a bit of a reputation for perviness. He was also about to strike it rich with that horde. There could be all sorts of motives to go after him.'

Livia bites her lip. 'True, but that makes Wulfnoth a coincidence again.'

'Or a blind.'

She reaches across and pats his leg. 'I can see the cogs whirring; you don't like things straightforward, do you?'

He clasps her hand. 'I'll see what McAllister says tomorrow and let you know.' A pause. The coals stutter. 'Are we done here?'

Livia is angling her foot this way and that, making the shadow shift and hover. She looks up at the giant egg-timer in the corner, the sand pouring inexorably forth. 'A few more minutes and we'll have earned our dip. Though maybe all this heat isn't good, you know, for the baby-making.' She slips a lascivious hand between his thighs, pinching gently. 'This area needs to be as cool as possible, apparently.'

He grips her wrist, gives a nervous laugh. 'We're not taking it that seriously, are we?' A pause holds. Immediately he knows he has struck the wrong note. Her hand recoils, her spine stiffens.

'I think I am. I thought *we* were. We want this baby, don't we? We want to have it now, don't we?' Her voice is cold, austere.

He strokes her arm, and she flinches. 'Liv, of course we do. Of course I do.' The silence builds. 'I . . . I don't know. I worry about placing too much pressure, too much weight on it. I've seen this go wrong before.' As he speaks, he knows he is identifying what has been at the back of his mind for the last month, a coil of concern that he has tried not to acknowledge, but has persisted, a painful stubbornness. He puts his head in his hands, scratch of damp beard on his wrists. When he lifts it, Livia is beside him, her face trickled with moisture, her eyes now warm with compassion.

She kisses his forehead, a benediction, a sign of an argument nullified. 'It's too fucking hot to talk seriously. Come on, we'll cool all the bits of you off in the lake, and then speak calmly when I can actually think.'

Hand in hand, they leave the sauna, perch on the edge of the pier, their bodies the merest outline in the dark, their hearts racing. He hears her gasp as they leap, wait for gravity to pull them down. As they hit the water, the cold drives the air and their thoughts and their fears out of them for the lingering instant, the lake a healthful, overwhelming abyss.

Ten minutes later, they are wrapped in their robes, their faces tingling, the night air a welcome caress. The bench by the lake is uplit, so they can see each other clearly, damp hair, glowing skin. Livia holds Jake's hand, a cherishing gesture. And he talks, more than he has done in the past, of what it was like when Faye kept miscarrying, his sense of failure, her relentless pain. The blood on the floor, red so dark it seemed like black. The terror reflected in their eyes. The misery, the compounding misery that accumulated like a poison in their relationship.

His voice is thick. 'And maybe I'm the failure, the danger, the one who can't have children. I was checked out, we both were, and all looked fine, but all never was. I don't know, Liv. I want this so much, and yet I don't want to not give you what you want. I don't want things ruined.'

A tear trickles down her cheek. 'It breaks my heart to hear you talk like this. Not because I'm frightened of the future, but because I want you to know that the only thing that matters is me and you. And Di, of course. If we add to it, we get even more joy, but this joy is enough, more than enough for me. I'm sorry, Jake. I've been a bit thoughtless. I was enjoying the game: you know, summoning you for sex like some sort of queen with my flags in the tree. I didn't take it that seriously, and didn't think what might have been going on in that quiet brain of yours. You should've said.'

He feels the choke in his voice, his own eyes damp. 'So we carry on?'

A pause. Across the water, the trees in Agatha Wood sway and whisper. From out of the dark, a heron swoops over them, landing with an unruffled splash in the lake, its angular body, the muted greys and blues of its feathers, barely picked out by the outer glare of their light. A heron, their heron, a sort of mascot of their relationship. It stands aloof, glaring into the gloom of the water.

Livia grins, small white teeth. 'Of course we carry on, you old worrier. We carry on doing it for fun, and we'll see what happens. Come on, you can start now if you're not too tired.'

And, hand in hand, they head back to the house to do just that.

Chapter Thirteen

The garden of the Jolly Nook, Caelum Parvum

The two men sit by the stream on an old bench, clutching mugs of coffee. It is 11.30 in the morning, warm enough for shirtsleeves, though the air holding enough of a chill so the sun feels like a gift. McAllister is running through the first cut of the police's forensic work.

'The acid was strong, barely diluted at all. It would have been sour to the taste, but think on this.' He mimes a lusty swig from an imaginary bottle. 'You're thirsty, you're not suspicious, and you go for a big drink. By the time you know what you're drinking, a good amount's gone down.' He swills his coffee around his mouth in contemplation, and shivers. 'The damage done to Jordan was pretty major right enough: mouth, tongue, throat and the lining of the stomach, all affected. But the shock seems to have killed him; his heart gave out as they were dealing with him in A&E.'

'And you're treating it as murder?'

'I'm treating it as suspicious, let's call it that. I spoke to Amy this morning, and she thinks the acid may have come from the communal store, though she couldn't be sure. Jordan could've brought it into the trench to use for cleaning, and then picked up the wrong container.'

'You buy that?'

'Nope. But I can't rule it out. There were no fingerprints on the bottle other than his. Nobody saw anybody with it, nobody saw anyone pouring the acid. If it hadn't been for the Wulfnoth notes, I would've been interested, but not, you know, over-excited. We need to get into that side of things more. Finding out who this Wulfnoth is would be a grand start. Plus, as you've said, old man surrounded by young students, rumours of sexual shenanigans if I can put it that strongly, there might be something there.'

'What's happening to the dig?'

McAllister stretches his legs, looks across the empty patch of ground, which has been mown ahead of the summer, and smells fresh and meadowy and salutary. Tiny purple flowers poking out of the stubble. 'Amy's not closing it permanently, at least not now. If it is Wulfnoth, whoever the sodding hell that might be, she doesn't want to be driven from the field by a crank. She's having a meeting about it later with everyone, telling them they can leave if they want, but she'll be staying.' He grins. 'I thought you might wander over and be part of it. It's happening at four.'

Jake has been thinking about his involvement, his commitment to Rose and Lily, his own natural instincts perking up at the prospect of a mystery, the quiet relish of being asked to be of use. 'I can do that. I said I'd keep an eye out for Lily, and was already helping Amy a little, I guess. I'll let you know anything I turn up. I should also say that I've got a visitor coming next week who's in the force. She's looking for a break from the city, but might have a few thoughts.'

McAllister's smile widens. His teeth are grey, crooked as old graves. 'That'd be the woman who worked with you last winter. What was her name?'

'Aletheia Campbell. On holiday, as I've said.'

'Holidays are made to be broken. I'm not proud, you know; I'll take the help wherever I can get it. You're more or less an honorary policeman around here, and so I'm more open with you and yours than I mebbe otherwise would be. But either way I don't want stuff going unsolved on my new patch.'

'If there's anything to solve in the first place.'

'Aye, we need to solve that question first: is there a question to solve? That's part of the game, though, isn't it? Let's catch up at the end of the week, or sooner if you get a bite. Here's my number, give it to Livia to keep hold of, and call me if you want. I'll leave a note here if I need you.'

Jake stays for a few more minutes, breathing the still air. There is a cuckoo in the old oak tree by the corner of the field: stripy, pyjama-like plumage, beady yellow eye, its familiar warble a soothing accompaniment to the scene. A sign of the seasons, the straddling of spring with summer.

He thinks for a moment about McAllister, who he finds himself liking, and trusting. There is a warmth about him, but also the feeling you get with police officers who have walked the streets in big cities, who have gone into the darkest and rankest tower blocks, been surrounded by the sour ache of deprivation: a firmness, a steel, a sense of being hardened by the too-regular sight of violence and pain. McAllister may speak affably, his voice may soothe and slide into its gentle brogue, the odd and welcome Celtic mannerism here and there, but there is always bristling beneath. Jake finds that reassuring. He is quietly spoken himself, he prides himself on it, and he knows that in the end it is a sign of strength, not of weakness.

Jake carries the cups inside, and washes them meditatively at the sink. He leans forward and drinks some water from the tap, letting it bead upon his beard, numbingly cold. He has time to walk to St Giles, have a prod around Jordan's church, before getting to the meeting.

It is yet another beautiful old building in a landscape abounding in them. And an extraordinary-looking one, small and uncanny, a mingling of periods and styles. The chancel is rough stone, a hodgepodge of greys and browns and pale blues, and must have been built early, probably the time of one of the Wulfnoths. Attached to it is a timber structure – the nave, Jake guesses, which looks like a Tudor building, not dissimilar to Livia's cottage. The church is at once fragile, overwhelmed by the surrounding humps and dips of the land, yet sturdy in its mongrel nature, the product of things being adapted and mended and made to carry imperturbably on.

Standing outside are the hikers Jake had seen at the dig. They are clearly engaged in some sort of tombstone inspection, reading out inscriptions with the tell-tale pitch and volume of a couple who stopped listening to one another many years before.

The man's eyes light up when he sees Jake approaching. 'Ah, the detective who doesn't look like a detective. What can you tell us, sir?'

Jake smiles as the wife sidles up alongside him, her jaw working soundlessly, her eyes gimcrack black. He shakes hands with them both. 'I was hoping you might have something to tell me. Did you know Reverend Jordan?'

She glares at her husband, determined to speak first. 'We did. We were part of a historical society with him, touring the local churches in the area.'

'He was the leader of it,' her husband points out gently.

'Well, not that he did much leading.'

Jake senses a futile squall building between them and asks about their visit to the dig. They try to compete in their recollection of events, but do not add much to Jake's understanding. One thing sticks out: they had seen Jordan in heated dispute with Zach, Amy's assistant, about an hour before. Raised voices and gesticulation. Jake stores it for future use.

After a few minutes, the couple depart, off to another historic landmark, evidently the preoccupation of their waning years. Jake stands in the comparative peace, watches the light break through the branches of the yew tree by the church gate. His concentration is interrupted by an elderly man, broom in hand, clearing some fallen leaves from the path.

He tips an imaginary cap. 'Good day to you, captain.' He gestures to his chest. 'Dudley, one of the churchwardens. I heard you asking about the Reverend.' He makes a half-hearted crossing gesture in his memory. 'Do you think he was offed by someone then?'

Jake gives his name and shakes the proffered hand. 'It's a chance, I suppose. I'm helping the police, used to be one myself.'

'You won't get much sense out of them two, though. Always carping and complaining, chattery as magpies. They didn't know the Reverend much.'

'But you did?'

'I saw him most days, passed the time, helped out with the services. These churches are empty most of the time, you know. It's not like it was in the fifties. No, hardly any demand for God now.'

This is evidently a favoured subject. 'Do you know anyone who wanted to harm Jordan?'

A lingering pause. Dudley is looking at Jake intently, as if deciding whether to trust him or not. After a moment, he gestures with one finger, the nail purple and torn, blotchy with blood, in the direction of the church. Inside, it is gloomy, the wooden beams black, a spill of light making one patch of timber brazen. Dudley goes to the pew furthest to the rear and lifts it. Beneath is a cracked piece of slate, concealing a small depression, from which he extracts a sheaf of letters.

He hands them to Jake, whispers conspiratorially. 'I saw the Reverend hide these once. They're from his old parish. The father of a girl he paid too much attention too. Have a look, see what you think.'

Jake folds them and puts them into his pocket. 'Can I take them?'

'Don't see as he'll have much use for them.' Dudley looks intently at the altar, then surveys Jake critically once more. 'And jes because someone accuses someone, don't make it true.'

'Roger that. That's why we investigate things.'

Dudley nods, as if satisfied, and heads back out into the churchyard. He waves mutely when Jake emerges a minute later – having briefly scanned the letters, enough to see they look genuine – and heads off towards the hill, the church clock reminding him that he needs to get moving.

He is early for all that. People are thronging near the gate, a bit shiftless, concern etched on their faces. They acknowledge Jake with slight nods and narrowed eyes, apart from Lily, who waves exuberantly. He walks up to the portacabin and turns the handle of the door, which opens without noise. Inside he sees Amy and Zach in the kitchen, pressed together, his hands white-knuckling on her back, she grasping a clump of his black mop of hair. An intimate moment, two people seeking succour from one another.

They spring apart when the floor creaks. Zach looks daggers at Jake, Amy a little flushed, but unperturbed, smoothing down her top and offering a reassuring smile. She pats Zach's arm and ushers him to the door.

'You better start gathering the troops.'

Jake stays him with a gesture. 'Before you do. I hear you had words with Jordan a bit before he died. Can you remember why you argued?'

Zach's face twists sharply in disdain. 'I don't suppose you can tell me who's been badmouthing me?'

Jake advances a step, to within a foot or so, an old copper trick to assert physical dominance. His voice remains calm, his expression placid. 'You don't suppose right. So what was the problem?'

Zach glances towards Amy, who nods gently. He turns back to Jake. 'We disagreed about the future strategy of the dig. He thought we needed to put more focus on the Roman remains. I didn't.'

Jake exhales thoughtfully. 'But he's not in charge, is he? Why does his opinion matter?'

Zach's voice is thick, syrupy with bitterness. 'His opinion didn't matter. But the way he spoke about Amy and her management of the site did matter. To me. I told him to take care how he spoke about a successful and respected woman.'

'You were angry?'

'I was sharp, and with good reason. But to be clear, it didn't make me tempted to watch the poor old bastard choke to death on acid. In case you were wondering. Now I'd better gather the troops.'

A final scowl and he departs. Jake retreats and leans against the back of an old armchair, brown scuffed leather, much mended and patched.

'Nice to have someone to take your side,' he ventures carefully.

'Yes, it actually is. I trust Zach totally.'

She goes to the chair behind her desk, and sags into it.

'Does that mean there's folk here you don't?'

'Of course. I don't know that I trust you, for example, Jake, though I'm glad that you seem to want to help. I didn't trust Jordan, not to speak ill of the dead. I was always worrying he might make an embarrassing pass at someone and cause a stink.'

'Was he like that?'

She sips some water from her mug. 'You hear rumours. He never struck me as a predator, but perhaps I'm too old to notice now, or be the object. He never showed me much deference at least.' A mirthless chuckle. She looks down at herself reflectively. 'I doubt very much he ever could or would do anything, but who knows?'

'What about Brian, and Daisy? They're senior folk around here.'

She purses her lips; Jake can hear her breathe out, sees the moisture at her temples, the fluttering of the reddish tips of her hair. 'Daisy is an added benefit to our operation.

She's an asset, and is one of the reasons we get the money from the university to keep digging – she guarantees publicity and interest. Brian is, well, more or less as cheery as he looks, though I presume he has his moments of disloyalty to me. He'd like to run this dig, I'm sure, and he might even have support from his acolytes, especially the youngsters. Why are you asking? Do you think Brian could be a killer?'

'If Jordan was killed, it's likely it was someone who knew that you had acid and how it was used, and knew the rhythm of the site and how you worked. It takes a pretty cool hand to slip someone a bottle like this, walk away and let them choke on it. Hard to imagine a stranger doing it.'

'Maybe. But we've had probably fifty folk here over the last couple of days, we've had hundreds over the years, all of whom could wander around without arousing comment.'

'We're back to finding a motive, then.'

'That's your area, Jake, while you're still interested. The mysteries I'm good at solving are all rather older.'

Knock at the door. Zach's head pops around, flush with authority. 'Amy, everyone's waiting for you.'

She stands. 'I'd better get this over and done with.'

'What are you going to say?'

She brushes past his shoulder. 'Come outside and find out.'

Chapter Fourteen

The natural spring, St Giles site

Jake lingers after the meeting wraps up, a solitary statue amid the scurry for the exit. Amy had been forthright, acknowledging the existence of the threats, that Jordan's death was suspicious, and that she understood if people felt they wanted to leave. Daisy had then spoken, her voice clear and cultivated, unhurried. She said she wasn't worried about events, but that filming had nearly finished in any case. They would be on site for only a few more days; the fate of this series of the show would be decided in the edit. They would do some reflections on Jordan's death, the odd vox pop perhaps with them if they were willing, though she couldn't be sure it would ever be broadcast. She thought he would have wanted them all to continue on, but others would have to decide. She sat down, pushing her hair behind her ears.

After that there was quiet. Two crows fussing noisily near a tumbledown wall, croaks and cackles. The American, Brad, finally raised himself to his feet, pushing his baseball cap down self-consciously. He wanted to know if their safety could be guaranteed. Amy was kind but firm: no guarantees were possible; this was a tragedy, and she understood how unsettling it was. But she did not propose to let it deter her.

Jake had been asked about the letters, the chance of their author being caught, the likelihood that Wulfnoth was responsible for Jordan's death. He was non-committal, searching the crowd of faces for a sign of any untoward reaction. But they had behaved as he expected they would: a bit grumbly, tense and concerned, conscious of their rights, but also not entirely believing that a threat would ever encompass them. Most would stick around, he reckoned.

He stands alongside Brian as the crowd thins around them. Plenty of friendly nods in their direction; occasionally a more searching or suspicious glance as well. Brian seems oblivious, hands thrust deep in his pockets. When he speaks, he lifts them free, gesticulates helplessly, and Jake can't help but notice his fingernails, long and thick and greying, gnarly as talons. Guitar player's hands, Jake thinks, remembering an old folk singer he used to watch. They must be an impediment of sorts as he digs, but he seems entirely unselfconscious about them.

Jake half flinches when Brian pats his shoulder. 'I'll be heading off shortly. This is another mess we don't need on top of everything else.'

Brian's face is blank, cheeks windblown and coarsened. Jake keeps his voice neutral. 'What else is there?'

'Oh, this may look like a well-organized festival of archaeology, Jake, but we're hopelessly behind schedule, and I'm not sure the university will keep its support for us next year. If that treasure hadn't shown up, we'd have been closed down already.'

'Amy seems to think the telly programme will be enough to keep everything going.'

'Aye, she does think that. But some of us think that our priority shouldn't be cheap television but doing the right job by the land, by the history. That's what we're here for.'

'Wulfnoth would agree with the first bit.'

'You've seen the letters then? Yes, I suppose I might agree with him when it comes to the sanctity of ancient lands, if not what should be done with them.'

There is quiet all around them as the plateau empties of people. A breeze flutters their hair, cools the sweat on their brows, fleeting damp.

Jake turns more closely towards Brian, who is now scratching his thigh gently, those claws leaving thin red lines on his pinkish skin. 'Didn't Reverend Jordan have a similar idea about how the dig was going?'

Brian's face doesn't change, retains that sort of beatific blankness that he seems to use to shield himself against the world. 'Jordan was a fool, and a pain in the old arse, but he did have a sense of history. He thought the best thing to happen to this place would be for it to be shut down and started up again. Done properly.'

'That must have made you angry?'

The facade slips, and a wry grin cracks the blank. 'Oh, Jake, I'm as soft as a bunny, me. He wasn't wrong in some respects about how bad things have got, and maybe we do need a break, but he had no more power to stop this dig than I do to flap around above it like a bullfinch. No, I'll not pretend a grief I don't feel. He was a pain and an old woman, but all in all I'd rather the old bugger hadn't kicked it. Especially in my trench, of all places.' A pause lingers. 'And on that positive thought, I'll bid you good evening, Jake.'

With a wink, Brian turns away and walks back towards the office, hands thrust in his pockets, shoulders hunched against nothing.

Left alone, gloriously alone, Jake takes the chance to explore the whole site for the first time. He finds he can lose himself in this vast elevated plain, flat and largely without feature, the evidence of life buried beneath the heathery ground, the grass swaying rhythmically as if the land were the sea. The only signs of mankind's presence, the dark blots upon the pastel, are the tower back on the raised ridge behind him, the curved roof of Wulfnoth's Keep, and the occasional walls that rise and fall all around, imposing for a few feet, before time and the wind and depredation must have collapsed the rest.

He skirts one set of walls, sees eroded mortar, big, roughly-shaped stones resting on one another like child's bricks. But when he shoves them, they do not shift in his grip, fused as they are into position by age and their ponderous weight. The sun is slowly dipping beneath the horizon, tracing out the same colours as the crocuses in his greenhouse, a deep yellow that threatens to bleed into bronze, soft pink turning to angry purple. He nearly falls into another trench, eyes so transfixed by the many-hued horizon, and sees he has come to the area marked on Amy's map as the natural spring. The area has been partially excavated, a line of pillars visible, their rough marble yellowing with age. He can see the word 'FONS' traced in the stone, Latin for 'fountain', as even he knows. Between the pillars are three steps that take you yet lower, where there is a stone-rimmed pool, faintly sulphuric-smelling, steam visible in the evening light. He can hear the running flow of water, feel the heat against his face. There is an unseen channel somewhere, taking the overflow down from the hill, presumably running into the stream there, carried off towards the river in the distance.

Jake stares into the water, his reflection fractured and shimmering, sees the debris at the bottom, bits of plaster and ceramic and metal, detritus that has come inevitably with age, or maybe evidence of long-past offerings, votive demands for divine intervention by generations of believers. How long had humans connected wishes with water, he wonders. How often had they shared the same ritual of placing their hopes upon the unprovable and unlikely? Had someone stood here two millennia ago, wife at home, despairing and questioning, both desperate for a child, perhaps, demanding fate's malign curse to be lifted, beseeching some unseen spirit to help? It is somehow heartening to think so.

The rilling of the water soothes, holds him in rigid pause, as the dusk descends around him. He doesn't know how long he lingers without moving, an hour maybe, the chill creeping upon him, only partially dispelled by the natural warmth of the spring. The steam thickens as it is claimed by the dark. He places his hands on the edge of the pool, feels the stone at his fingertips, its firmness but also its fragility, as a little crumbles away in his grip, falls away, pockmarking the surface below. After a few more minutes he can no longer make out his own image before him, can feel the water rather than see it. He sighs, sends his mind back to Livia, pictures the smooth contours of her face, those grass-coloured eyes, the warmth of her body, thinks of his and her desire to extend their family. He feels inside his pocket, and grips a hard stone, a piece of flint he had found while walking, and kept with him, smooth and reassuring, a sort of charm. It had been chipped and sharpened by someone in the distant past, and represented another connection between him and the land he called home. Maybe it is a fitting sacrifice, he thinks, good for a pagan prayer in the night. Maybe that is ridiculous. He pulls it out and tosses it in the air anyway. Faint splash in the black. Make a wish, hope it counts.

    He breathes in deep, and perhaps some part of his subconscious mind hears a noise behind him. His conscious mind is too preoccupied to care, but he must have shifted an inch or two, away from the blow that he has somehow sensed falling, the merest flash at the corner of his eye before the heavy impact smashes into the back of his head, sending him toppling into the water.

Chapter Fifteen

The darkened area outside the spring, St Giles site

There is a moment of absence, the world on pause, before sensations teem back in upon him: the water all around, tepid and enveloping and soupy, rank in his nose, and caustic in his throat, his clothes weighing him down, his feet kicking at the bottom but finding nothing in reach. He sinks and chokes again, shucking off his thick woollen shirt, prising off one shoe then the other. He can feel the sting of the cut at the back of his head, wonders if the wetness is blood or water, or some commingling of both.

His movements slow as he takes control of the situation, treading water, realizing he has escaped serious injury, his eyes flashing around, looking for his assailant. But there is nobody there in the departing dusk, no looming presence, no silhouette to remember or pursue. No sound but retreating footsteps into the emptiness of the plain, and the gurgling water that follows the course lain down for it over the centuries.

Softly cursing, he drags himself from the pool, skin scratching against ancient stone. As he stands, a faint lick of moonlight offering the merest hint of the landscape, he feels almost completely alone. He calls out, gets nothing in response, his voice eerie and brassy in the night. The office in the distance is unlit; it feels like no life exists within miles, bar the person who had tried to bash his head in, who must still be somewhere nearby.

He squelches clear of the spring, then crouches behind a wall, biting down to stall his shivers, each one of his senses alive. He wants to make sure another attack is not looming in the night. Nothing stirs. It feels safe enough to make a move out of there, so he heads for the most direct line off the hill, away from the main gate, up and over the earthworks, slow and cautious, letting the contours guide his pace. Every few moments he pauses, sinks down like a wild animal, eyes straining for shapes in the abyss-like darkness. With each passing second, he becomes more confident his assailant has departed. Soon the hill is a giant swatch of added darkness behind him, then lost completely.

The walk back is long and cold, Jake shuddering at every breath of wind, his shirt and shoes lost somewhere in the bubbling depths, his head throbbing. The ground he walks upon is soft, tussocky and yielding, each step an oddly soothing sensation. He feels his strength returning, despite the pain in his head. He knows he can go for miles, is a hard target in this environment for anyone to pursue. He decides to make for Livia's cottage, where he can use the phone, report what happened.

She answers at his first knock, her face falling at his bedraggled appearance. He must look wild, he thinks, even by his own standards: topless in the night, scarecrow hair, skin goosebumped, his chest a little scratched by his efforts clambering out of the pool, trousers still damp and clinging. When she grasps the back of his head appraisingly, her fingers come back sticky with blood.

'Jesus Christ, Jake. What's happened? Are you OK?'

She leads him in. Her living room is warm, with a small fire puttering in the corner. Livia, alone, always has a fire, even this late in the season; she is salamander-like, Jake has often said, a glutton for flame like she is for the searing summer sun, as if drawing life from the heat. Diana is in bed, though only just. For all the darkness of the night, and all that has happened, the grandfather clock is about to chime ten. Jake crouches before the blaze, arms open in welcome, while Livia clucks, concerned, around him.

She has been listening to music, and she heads into a corner to turn it down. It is one of the records she has borrowed from him, a César Franck Violin Sonata, lush and soft and romantic to linger alone with. Even quiet it seems to fill some of the spaces around them.

De-thawed now, Jake peels off his trousers, taking his underwear with them. Livia gives a lubricious chuckle. 'I can't believe you didn't even give me the chance to say, "Let me get you out of those wet things."' It is a private joke between them, and always makes him smile. Livia reaches into a linen cupboard and tosses over a towel, thick and crimson, which he wraps around his waist. Then she pours some brandy from the bottle by the fire, and hands it over: the glass is thick and square, heavy as lead, reassuring in his grasp. He takes a sip and revels in the muted burn in his throat, taking the pondy taste away.

Livia sits him down on the rug and perches next to him, hands in his lap. 'Now tell me what you've been doing, swimming in your clothes.' As he explains, she twists and looks at the back of his head, pushing the strands of hair aside to assess the extent of the wound. While he is talking, she goes to get her vet's bag, starts pulling out small vials and cloths and swabs. He finishes up, and she kneels back down, eyes glinting.

He raises his hands, half-joking. 'Hey, remember I'm one of those two-legged things, not some bit of livestock you can stitch up and slap on the rump when you're done.'

'That's exactly how I treat you, and you love it, you big dirty beast.' She takes a sip of his brandy. 'Now don't be silly. We could go to the hospital, but I'm not sure it'll need stitches. It does need a good clean, God knows what germs live in warm outdoor springs, and the stuff I have works as well on human beasts as animal ones. Stop being such a worrier, and lean forward.'

She pours some clear liquid onto a piece of cloth, and pushes it against the cut. It stings, a tingle that becomes a burn. He grits his teeth, and exhales noisily.

'There's a brave boy. Now, serious point coming. I'm not worried about the cut, but the knock on the head could have been much nastier. You might be concussed, and the effects are being delayed by the adrenaline. I'm going to run a bath, and then you'll need to stay up a bit to make sure you're all right. No more brandy either.'

She heads off, and the rumbling of water soon follows. He feels stiff and tired all of a sudden. But he takes the opportunity to borrow Livia's phone, sending messages to McAllister, Rose and to Martha. McAllister texts back immediately, and arranges to come over in the morning. Jake agrees, and heads off to the bathroom, where steam is curling out of the doorway.

When he emerges half an hour later, he is wobbly, pinked by the heat of the water, wearing one of Livia's robes, also pink, which comes down only to his upper thighs. Livia is at her computer, on a video call. Jake sits down beside her, the hem rising dangerously as he does so.

'Put it all away, JJ. You look like a camp medieval peasant, and I can see far more tangled hair up there than I want to, thank you very much. It's all a bit goaty for my tastes. I'm glad you're all right, obviously.'

'Evening, Martha. Just to say I can't be a goat and a peasant.'

'You are OK, Jake, aren't you?' This voice is quieter, more caring.

'Al, what are you doing there?'

'I'll have you know my company is winning. Why shouldn't she be here?' Martha sounds happy. Aletheia is sitting behind Martha at her desk, and is in every way a more muted, more controlled presence. She is in her early forties, a little stooped, but elegant in a thick roll-neck jumper, her black skin smooth and clear, her face warm and open. She had worked with Jake when he was a policeman, and since, as a Searcher, someone who traces the lives of targets by following their behaviour online: where they shop, who they talk to, where they appear on cameras, where their lives snag upon the electronic web that is spun around everyone all the time without most people troubling to notice.

She rolls her eyes at Martha, with whom she used to work. 'My holiday already started, and I thought I'd come see Martha before I get to you. You know how cranky she gets when left to moulder.'

Jake has been thinking in the bath. 'I was probably

going to call you tomorrow, Al. Are you sure you want to come? It seems that our quiet life is getting messy again.'

'You try and keep me away. I need to get out from the city, and Mum, and the politics of the job, but I can do all that whether you're battling a medieval ghost or not.' Aletheia lived with her mother, an invalid whose well-being tended to dominate her existence outside of the office.

Jake winces. 'Martha has told you then.'

'She's not the soul of discretion, as you know.' Martha is puffing away at her pipe and billows forth a twisty plume of smoke, which Aletheia tolerantly waves away. 'I think you could use some help, now more than ever. Clearly something's going on, and we need to find out what. Count me very much in.'

Livia beams. 'I had a feeling you'd say that. It makes us both feel better I'm sure.'

'Plus, I got a bit fond of Rose last time I was down there, so I want to help his sister too. He's mentioned her when he's been in town.'

Livia's eyes widen. 'Have you being *seeing* him, Al?'

'Not like that, just the odd dinner. He's far too much of a minor criminal for me. He'd get my security clearance revoked in a moment. This one's smoking is bad enough.' Martha smirks. Aletheia ignores her and continues. 'About your problem, I'm going to take a look at those letters, and also the other mystery in this whole affair.'

Jake sips some cold water, trying to keep fuzziness at bay. 'What's that?'

'The owner of the land where the treasure was found. I don't like open ends, and that's a weird one. Probably innocent, but why is there no obvious claimant to that money?

Worth a gander. And finally there's the background to Reverend Jordan too.'

Jake suddenly feels foolish, realizes he has forgotten about the letters from the church. He gets up and retrieves his trousers, the robe flapping slightly.

'Come on, Jake, my eyes, my eyes!' Martha smirking again.

He brings them back to the table, extracting the sodden pulpy substance between two fingers. He fills everyone in on his conversation with Dudley.

'Can you make much out from the remains there, Jake?' This is Aletheia, immediately practical.

'Not really. I can remember the name of the father, though: Alan Williams. The parish was a city one too. It was a formal thing in a way, the first one setting out his concerns in a letter so that Jordan would note them officially, the second one confirming that he would take steps if needed.'

'What was being alleged?'

'That Jordan was too close to his daughter, spending too much time with her; reference to some gossip about them sharing what he called an "intimate moment", denied by her. And that's all I got from the skim read.'

Aletheia is writing notes on a pad, ornate gold pen in her slender fingers. 'That'll be enough. Leave it with me, and I'll share thoughts on Saturday.' That is two days away. 'Meanwhile, watch your collective backs, and stay off that site in the dark.'

Jake nods painfully. After a few more pleasantries, they hang up. Livia leads Jake tenderly to the bedroom, sees that he is comfortable. The ceiling sways faintly, but then his eyes close and he is unmoored in his subconscious, blissful oblivion. She wakes him once in the night to check he is not concussed, her face a sudden presence above him in the greying pre-dawn, her hand a caress on his bristly cheek. And then he sleeps once more until the sun is high in the sky, the birds outside insistent that he wake up for good.

Chapter Sixteen

On the bank of the river, outside Parvum

McAllister is prompt to his proposed hour, and raps smartly on Livia's front door an hour or so after Jake gets up. Diana is long at school, and Livia out on her rounds, so Jake has eased into the day quietly. His head is sore, but he seems to have no other lingering after-effects of the blow. If anything his senses feel unduly sharp: the late dew on the grass standing out like pearly beads, the smell of coffee dense and biscuity, the birds an orchestral accompaniment to his shuffling and pottering. It is a warm clear day, summery, the sky a deep and mesmerizing blue, the cloud high and fading, a gauzy hint at canvas edge.

Jake and McAllister take their coffees down the empty road to the river, which glints like silver plate, each ripple a reflection of the metallic light of the sun. There is a bench where the river bends as it lumbers off into the distance, framed by a huge blackthorn tree that is now losing its spring blossom. It was late to flower this year, but then it came profusely, clouds of white petals, concealing their tiny golden hearts, a big, cushiony candyfloss swirl set against the dark green surrounds. Jake can see more of its leaves now, the beginnings of the purpling fruit, the hint of gin sweetness in the breeze.

McAllister is laconic, but it seems to conceal genuine concern for Jake, and the situation. 'I think this definitely means we have a problem, though I suppose we knew that already. Are you free to come with me to see Amy? I wonder whether the best thing to do's to shut the place down for a bit, let things calm down. We can't have someone this violent wandering about there. If he got you, think what more damage he could do.'

Jake sips his coffee, which is black and sweet with brown sugar. 'I was an easy target, I reckon, staring into a lonely pool in the dark. But it does suggest that the attacker isn't stopping at Jordan.'

'Which means it is most probably this medieval role-playing character who wants you all off the land.'

'In that case, I wonder if we'll get another letter.'

'Speaking of which, you better give me those soggy bits of paper you got from the church before I go. Though it hardly makes sense to come after you if a sex-pest vicar was the target all along.'

'Unless there's more than one person involved, for more than one reason.'

'That did occur to me, but it's a pain in the backside I'm not over-eager to experience.' A boat passes containing a young couple: the man, cropped hair, sun-pinked neck, rowing effortlessly, over-conscious of his form, T-shirt sleeves rolled up to expose the soft bulge of his triceps; the woman, blond hair high on her head, trailing a hand in the water, drinking through a straw. She waves at them happily, and they wave back.

'Young love.' This is McAllister with a note of cynicism in his voice. He slaps his thighs, energetic. 'Now why don't you come with me to the station, and we'll get a proper statement, and then I'll drive up with you to the hill site? In the meantime, I don't suppose you saw anybody hanging around the place before you got whacked?'

'I was talking to Brian for a while, and he was explaining why there was some tension at the dig. But he was well gone by the time I got hit.'

'Did you see him go?'

'Not really. I saw him head off towards the office, and then I assumed I was alone.'

'Though clearly you weren't.'

Jake rubs his head, rueful. 'Clearly.'

'I'll try and talk some more to Brian, I think. He was the feller more or less running the trench where Jordan died, after all.' McAllister lets the thought linger a beat, then gives Jake a nudge. 'Let's be having you then.'

'I don't suppose I can say I'd rather sit here, enjoying the weather and the river, can I?'

'No you cannot. There's too much idling in this whole place for my liking. Too much stopping and sniffing the flowers, digging about in the ground. It's decadent.'

'Especially to a puritan Scot.'

'You ask my wife, I'm as puritan as all hell.'

Later that afternoon, they are back at the hill, which is now fairly unpeopled. Word must have got out about what had happened to him, Jake thinks. Lily is there, small denim shorts and an oversized jumper, her gleaming legs coiled beneath her as she kneels over a shallow trench, trowel in hand, raking the earth with a practised, repetitive motion. Next to her are the two other graduate students, Matt and Elaine, who both look up at his arrival. Their expressions are not exactly friendly, not exactly neutral. In fact, he senses near-hostility, as if he is encroaching into their personal space, upon their sacred turf. They do not hold his gaze, instead bowing their heads back to their task, the soil thinning and crumbling before them, the tinny sound of metal on partially-clad stone.

Lily waves and leaps to her feet before almost barrelling into him, her strong arms wrapping him in a hug, her hair – warmed and fragrant with the sun – pressed against his face.

She steps back, beaming. 'Jake, I'm so glad you're all right. Rose filled me in, of course, and now Amy's putting everything on hold. Leaving a skeleton staff to maintain the integrity of the site, and only if we want to.'

'And do you want to?'

'I certainly do. A bit of mystery, fewer hairy-arsed diggers around to get in my way, the prospects of an interesting summer. It'll be a handful of us in the end, including those two lovebirds.' She gestures with her glinting trowel. 'They're impossible to shift. But Brad is already making plans to get back to the safer surroundings of urban America, would you believe it?'

McAllister has detached himself and is heading to the office. Jake drops his voice, examines Lily's face. Her eyes are tar-black and shiny, her hair pulled back, which opens up her expression even more. 'Are you sure you want to stay? This guy seems pretty serious. I'm not sure your brother would approve.'

'My brother, Jake' – she grips his arm, her fingers are

strong, the nails scuffed and shabby – 'is a drug dealer and a general, even if basically decent, degenerate. He's not my guardian or any moral authority for that matter. He cares, and I'm grateful, but the decision's mine.' Her lips pucker in forthright fashion. 'Plus, I'm fairly sure the security on this place will get better and – who knows? – maybe Wulfnoth's made his point, and will be content that the big show is shutting down.'

It's possible, Jake concedes, warily touching the still-stiff cut on the back of his head.

'Anyway, you look after that old head of yours. Will you be back again, or are you being driven off as well?'

He grimaces, having posed a similar question to himself. The answer is clear in his mind. 'I'll be around. I'm unofficially helping the police, and now I have a score to settle too. I'd like to find out whoever is doing this, maybe knock them into some water somewhere.'

Lily nods and pivots gaily back to her work. 'Glad to hear it.' She waves her trowel in distracted farewell. He turns back towards the gate, nearly bumping into Daisy who is walking towards him. She is dressed in austere black, jeans that follow the hard contours of her legs, a long cardigan over a ribbed vest.

She is clutching a letter, holding it carefully by the corner, her fingers wrapped up in her sleeves. 'You must've expected this.' She is brisk, almost angry. 'It's another letter from our madman.'

Chapter Seventeen

The thriller library, Little Sky

Jake likes being surrounded by paper, the reassuring, crackling, tangible power of words all around him. It helps him concentrate, he thinks, makes his mind more agile somehow. Lamplight flickers against the impassive ranks of bookshelves, the titles part-concealed by the gleam, their contents both reassuring and tantalizing. He has a large glass of red wine in one hand, his copy of the latest Wulfnoth letter in the other. More documents – the earlier letters, old newspaper articles, some information about the site he has taken from Amy's office – lie carpeted at his feet.

The most recent letter is as short as the last – punchy even.

> My warnings have gone unheeded, and now you have paid.
> The land is not yours to plough up and ruin and

plunder. The man of God was ungodly in his vanity, his greed. He had to pay too.

And the man of the law, abetting lawlessness: he was lucky to escape with his life. The next trespasser will not be so lucky.

'Arise, O Lord, and may your enemies be torn apart and those who hate you will flee from your face.' Numbers 10:35

You must make reparation, fleeing is not enough.

Wulfnoth

The style feels familiar, full of pomp and portent, the same black ink, the same unremarkable paper. Jake has a nagging feeling he has seen that quote somewhere before, but cannot quite recall where. He underlines it to remind himself to give it further thought later. With his spare hand he takes a bite of his sandwich, local cheese on the whitest loaf he could find, thick slabs of sharp, gnarly creaminess softened by the dough, the layer of butter beneath flecked with salt.

He wonders again why Wulfnoth is behaving this way, what he is plausibly seeking to gain from his actions. Does he really want the land preserved untouched, and why? Is it a sort of paranoia, a mania? If so, Jake reasons, it would not have emerged, fully formed like this, from nowhere. There would have been other signs, surely, in his social behaviour, visible manifestations of his inner turmoil, either around the dig or his personal life. He looks again through the files – brief and basic – he had cajoled from Amy, the professional biographies and qualifications of those connected with the site.

Nothing leaps out at all. Brian is oldish, perhaps, to be

working underneath Amy, who is actually ten years younger than him. The file of the graduate student Matt is almost entirely blank, as if his French background has deprived them of any possible paperwork. All Jake learns is that he came from a religious school outside of Paris, founded in the pre-Revolutionary period and still connected to a monastic foundation. His girlfriend Elaine also had a background in a faith school, also originally monastic. Of course any one of them, however they were originally educated, would have enough practical knowledge to quote scripture and concoct these hymns to history, but equally none of them would obviously benefit from doing so.

So Jake goes back to the idea of Wulfnoth as a blind. What if Jordan was the real target and everything else – including his own attack – was a way of obscuring that, of covering tracks? It isn't impossible, just unhelpful, because it means the field has not been narrowed at all. The letters are either revealing or concealing a secret, and he can't be sure which.

He is listening to a strange album by the jazz saxophonist Jan Garbarek, recorded – according to the sleeve notes also now lying on the floor – in an Austrian monastery: high, wincing wails of brass accompanied by medieval plainchant, religious music made yet eerier, more disembodied, appropriate for the hour and the subject matter. Jake rests his head on the back of the sofa, closes his eyes, feels the muted sting from the cut, tries to think through the next possible moves. He wants to get a file ready for Aletheia, so they can work through it together, see if anything leaps.

The next day he is up early with the rising sun, the cold air a salve to his skin, the ground damp and giving, saturated with life. The hedgerow feels restless with rustlings and scurryings, the sky full of birds proud in flight. He runs hard, spends half an hour boxing, hands pummelling the home-made bag he hangs from the beech tree that stands sentinel outside his house, and then swims, naked and free, in the lake.

He spends the morning getting his house ready for Aletheia's visit, his first proper guest there other than Livia and Diana. There are several bedrooms he never uses, and he picks the largest and airiest, with a view down to the lake. He puts new sheets on the bed, opens the window so the breeze can flutter through, and picks some tulips and crocuses from the borders of the vegetable garden to go in a vase on the dressing table. He is arranging them as best he can, mindlessly shifting the stems in the water, when a voice makes him start in turn. Livia in the doorway, amused and wry.

'There's nothing I find sexier than a man who knows how to arrange flowers. It's pure filth.' She advances theatrically, half-lifting her vest, smooth brown stomach beneath.

'Don't distract me, I've got pillows to plump, food to prepare. A man's work is never done.'

Livia pats him mischievously on the bottom. 'Ordinarily, I'd throw you down and make you impregnate me on those erotically crisp linen sheets. But I'm on my way to pick up Al, she's due in an hour. Do you want to join me, or do you want to peel me from these trousers and make me late?' Her face shows she is half in jest, but only half. She runs her hand up his arm, he feels his hairs rising, faint goosebumps. Amazing she still has that bodily, instinctive effect on him.

'Don't tempt me. You go, I'll finish cooking. Come, look at this.'

He takes her by the hand out of the bedroom and through the side door to the firepit, dug carefully a few metres outside the library. He's augmented it over the years, surrounding it with two benches, a ramshackle table he has built from offcuts, an improvised arbour that keeps the rain off, which trails early roses, their petals tight and cream-coloured. The fire is smouldering, high flames now waning, adding a smoky richness to the surrounding woodland scents. Spitted to one side is the carcass of a whole young goat, the flesh purple-pink, bulging under the skin where he has put herb-studded balls of butter. Sarah got it for him from a farm a few miles away.

'I'm going to roast this all afternoon, then I thought we'd have the dinner for Aletheia we talked about. I've invited Rose and Lily too, so with you and Di, it will be a feast of sorts. Does that sound good?'

Livia feigns haughtiness. 'And when were you going to tell me we were having more than one guest?' She lets her chest deflate. 'No, I knew you were being all social, and that's why I invited Jo too. So it will be a real party. Oh, think of it.' She raises her hands camply. 'Our first dinner party!'

'I wouldn't go that far. It's a phrase that sends shudders down my spine.' He is pleased Jo is coming though. She is the news editor of the *Shire Gazette*, a cantankerous, cigarette-smoking ally, who has occasionally covered Jake's detecting exploits in the area. She always brings some gravelly levity to any proceedings, and Diana adores her.

Livia is nibbling a mint leaf from a bush that is growing wild by her knees, little rabbit bites, teeth white. 'Well, it's definitely dinner, there'll be a party of people, so I don't know what else to call it. But will our poor little goat cook in time?'

'I reckon so, and if not we can always have cheese sandwiches.'

'I think Diana would prefer that, actually. It looks good, so I'll leave you to it. I'll drop Al by the river and point her in your direction, then see you back here after school.' She reaches over and kisses his lips. Hers are soft, her eyes like smoked green glass. 'Maybe we'll mess up another bed later, if you're lucky.'

She heads off to her old car, and Jake busies himself with the meat, positioning it high above the coals, which are soon sizzling and spitting. He prongs some vegetables on whittled applewood sticks to cook later, peppers and tomatoes and courgettes and onions from his greenhouse. He leaves some potatoes next to them to cook in the embers at the same time, makes some rudimentary kebabs with venison sausages, lets them sit in some garlic-flavoured oil. He rotates the goat, admires the char on the outside, and makes sure it is out of range of the direct flame.

Happily preoccupied with his preparations, he sees how house-proud he has become over the last two years. It's not as if he wants a constant parade of guests intruding into his solitude, taking up time and space, wandering about to admire the furnishings, but he feels oddly content in expecting company, perhaps because of its rarity. The last time Aletheia was here, they had been in a fight for their lives, so this is really the first time he has made the place nice for a guest.

From the corner of his workshop he manhandles a barrel of cider, which had been delivered by a friendly farmer and then painstakingly rolled over the undulating fields. It sits nicely in the corner of the arbour, by one of the benches. He puts some pewter tankards on the grass in front of it.

He is stretching his smarting arm muscles when he sees movement down below, by the side of the lake. The day is mild enough, but still bright, the sun with a lemony quality to make your eyes ache. A man is striding purposefully, head hooded, with a self-confident, almost prancing gait. It is Rose, holding a fishing rod.

Jake walks to intercept him, face wreathed in a cynical grin. 'Rose, what brings you here so early. Surely not the chance to spend some time with Aletheia?'

Rose grasps Jake's proffered hand, then lights a small, hand-rolled cigarette. 'She mentioned that I'd been to the city once or twice then, did she? Nothing serious. I like her, she's interesting to talk to, and you know how much I admire effective and brilliant servants of the law.'

'Foundation of our friendship.'

'But I'm not visiting to get an early shot at your friend. I came because I wanted to check on your head, and also I thought I'd try the fishing we talked about. See if I can catch whatever is lurking down there. Tench, you reckon?'

'Nobody's ever told me. Whatever it is, we're not eating it, to be clear as well.'

'You're such an urban softie. I'll see what I get, but I'm not bothered what we do with it. I fancied a quiet afternoon, that's all. Lily is getting tired of me huffing around after her. She more or less kicked me out the house. I wouldn't mind, but it's my fucking house. She'll be along later.'

Jake and Rose fished together regularly throughout the year, but always in the river, or the lagoons off it, backwaters created by the shifting course of the water, quiet and tucked away, little pools of peacefulness. They had not tried the lake, for reasons that had never been clear, and Rose had always threatened to arrive unannounced for a proper go at it. Today is clearly the day.

'Well, you can knock yourself out. Al is on her way so I can look after her while you splash about here.'

'Jake!' He is hailed from a distance. Aletheia herself, in jeans and a jumper and big brown boots supple around her calves, a heavy bag in one hand, striding towards them. Rose gives a fleeting smile. They watch her for a few moments as she pauses to look across towards Chicken City, where the birds are out in their usual preening display. Flutters and flurries of feathers. When she reaches the two of them, she is faintly out of breath, patina of sweat on her brow.

'God, I'm getting unfit. Give me a hug anyway, old man.' Jake does, with affection, noting the familiar sweet, cakey smell coming from her body. He'd sat next to her for many hours in many nook-filled offices, and recognizes the scent with pleasure. She hugs Rose too; he faintly flustered for once. She drops the bag onto the ground with a flourish.

They talk of her journey, her mother, Rose's sister. Jake brings down some elderflower cordial he has made, an experiment which had been almost successful. Aletheia twists a face as she swallows; it probably could have done with a bit more sugar.

'I'm keen to have a look at the old fort, Jake, get my bearings on this mystery. Do you fancy an afternoon wander, while Rose here does his fishing?'

Rose fails to avoid looking disconsolate.

Jake is enjoying the tension. 'Why not? I was going to take you there tomorrow anyway. Rose can fish, and keep his eye on the goat for us. Needs turning every half hour.'

Aletheia rolls her eyes. 'Last time I was here it was venison. Do you think you're some sort of medieval baron?'

Jake takes her by the hand, and they head off towards the river, leaving Rose to scuff the ground and set up his fishing position. 'Medieval characters,' says Jake ruefully, 'are a bit of a sore spot for us at the moment.'

Chapter Eighteen

The Roman villa behind the spring, St Giles site

It is quite the hike back to St Giles, and Aletheia pauses once or twice to get her breath. The sun has hidden behind a fugitive cloud, so it is not too warm for them at least. They stop to drink from a stream, which heads out of a watercress farm, the water ice-cold and peppery and restorative.

As they walk, they talk. Aletheia has some ideas for avenues of investigation, questions she wants answered. 'Here's the big one, Jake: how for real is Wulfnoth?' Jake nods; his mind had been tending this way itself.

'I reckon that if he's willing to move to murder, to attack someone like you, there must be some history of violence or aggression before this. It's not plausible that he goes from nothing to slipping someone acid to gag on.'

They are cresting a hill. The wind tugs at them, breathes cool against their hot skin. Down beneath them, the land falls, only to rise again, a patchwork of fields, some bursting forth with late spring life, some scrubby and fallow.

The occasional tree, thick-trunked and rangy, its branches teeming green, stands like an observer on the sidelines. The sky is almost entirely clouded over now, the colour of soapy water.

Jake points to the next hill, which he feels he could almost touch, a painted backdrop, beautiful and intricate. 'We get over yonder one, then we're there.' He'd started using 'yonder' like many in Parvum, initially as a way of annoying Rose and Sarah, but it has stuck as a useful word and he now doesn't notice it in his vocabulary. They start the walk down, the gradient increasing their pace, thighs aching with the strain of keeping themselves upright. 'But aren't the letters themselves the history, Al, the warning signs?'

Her nose wrinkles. 'Maybe, but they seem too pat to me, they're not quite convincing, how they start and how they end up. That sudden shift from platitude to actual bodily harm. I could be wrong, but even if I am, I still think our killer will have revealed themselves before, been caught acting in an antisocial or unacceptable fashion. So I think we look at crime data in the area, including unsolveds for the last few years. I've got the files coming by email.'

They step over a stile, the wood soft and fungal and foot-scuffed, nearly overwhelmed by the bank of stinging nettles they take care to avoid. 'Now, next big thing. The treasure. That's got to be a big part of where we look.'

'How come? Wasn't it settled a while back?' He is asking simply to enable her to make her case; he has seen where this is going.

'It's the biggest event connected with all this, so we have to at least rule out that it's not important. You know that. And it's not been settled in that the government has not paid out, and the owner of the land has not come forward. Not come forward to claim a share of maybe three or four million quid, maybe more. Now that is suspicious.'

'So Jordan could have been killed for his share of the treasure?'

'It's an obvious motive for either of the other three who found it with him, or – more likely – this figure who's not making themselves known yet.'

'I think you might keep all that under your hat for the afternoon, though. We're probably going to meet some, if not all, of those three who found the treasure.'

'Yes, thank you, I'm not a total moron. Final thing: was Jordan some sort of perv, some sort of predator? If so, we could be looking at an angry family member from the past, or maybe even a new victim from around here who we don't know about. He touched someone, they killed him in revenge. Didn't like you snooping, so gave you a shove to warn you off. It means that Wulfnoth is a dodge, a diversion, which is complicated but possible. All worth checking.'

They climb the hill into the fort, which is oddly busy, but it is the bustle of a place being packed up, shut down. Trenches are being covered with tarpaulin, tools are being packed away. A thin line of volunteers are already on the way out, backpacks high, faces glum, snaking past them in the other direction.

Jake ushers Aletheia towards the office, where Amy is sitting, chin resting contemplatively on her outstretched hand. She gives a wan smile and waves them to the chairs in front of her desk. 'I'm glad you're OK, Jake. I wish some of us had been around to see who did it.'

Jake nods in acknowledgement, and introduces Aletheia

as a senior police figure. Amy shakes her hand, wrist limp, dangling bracelets.

'I'm hoping there'll be not much more for anybody to investigate, because whoever did this will see there's no point carrying on. We're shutting down the whole dig, postponing all of the proposed excavations for the year. None of this will happen now.' She flicks a piece of paper in the air, and it falls sadly to the floor. 'I had such big ideas too, you know. We were really going to go after the full extent of the Roman villa. Our geo-phys studies show that we might be able to dig out a whole room, maybe two connected rooms, with floors, maybe plastered walls. Hard reality you don't need to imagine, real history brought to the surface.'

Aletheia leans forward. 'And you can't do that now?'

'No, most of our staff and money come from the university, and they want a full safety check done before they let their folk back here. And we can't do that with someone roaming around threatening people. No, we'll run a small team, clean our finds, maintain the site, maybe get some cataloguing done, but it's a lost year.'

'How will you keep the small team safe?' This is Jake, not volunteering but curious.

'We all know what we're getting into, and we'll be off site before dark, stay out in the open. Daisy's team will only be here for a couple more days, and then it's me and Brian, and a few grads.'

'Including Lily.'

'She's pretty unbudgeable, and that's a quality I like in an archaeologist.'

'How about the others?'

'Zach is loyal to me. Matt and Elaine like the lifestyle of

being together on the dig. And they passionately believe in this place – at least, I think they do. I know they and Brian were keen we became more focused on the Roman side of things. I think they'll want to bide their time until we can get back to it.'

Aletheia is scanning the room, noting, no doubt, its scruffiness, its distinctly lived-in quality, the echoes of all the activity there must have been here each summer, people eating and drinking and arguing, mopping their brows and tramping their dirt into the floors. She makes to stand. 'We'll leave you to it. But I take it you'd still welcome us clearing this up, finding out who did it, give you a chance to get back on schedule.'

'Of course. But you'd have to convince my bosses that you've got the right man.'

'Even if it's someone we know here already.' Jake is interested in her reaction.

Amy is unperturbed. 'The thought crosses your mind, of course it does. But I can't think of anyone who'd do anything so vile as to kill Jordan, or even attack you, Jake.'

Aletheia and Jake go to the door. 'Do you mind if I show Al around, so she can get her bearings?'

'Please do, you know most people, so shout if you need anything. I'll go back to my wretched form-filling. Who knew stopping a dig was as laborious as getting it started in the first place?' She picks up a pen and absent-mindedly scratches behind her ear.

Outside, the exodus is half-complete as Jake leads Aletheia around the plateau. They can see one or two shapes in the distance, people moving in and out of trenches, but visibility is quickly getting worse. They discuss the possibility of the violence being motivated by nothing more complicated than professional resentment, a protest against how Amy is managing things. It seems unlikely, but not impossible. Matt and Elaine stalk past them at a distance, hand in hand, talking intently. They do not respond to Jake's half-hearted wave.

Soon a damp mist starts to blow in, wispy and ethereal, moisture beading on Aletheia's jumper. Scraps of smoke you feel you could reach out and touch. The sun is now a dimmed lamp above them, its light pale and watery.

'This is weird, all of a sudden,' says Aletheia, shuddering.

'It happens on these hills outside of high summer. The mist descends, and it all gets a bit uncanny, but it'll blow across in an hour or so.'

Jake shows her the spring where he was attacked, and she is transfixed – as he was – by its bubbling presence, the steam and mist mingling, the sense of the primordial and mystical, the earth a living, gurgling creature in front of them.

Jake is turning to lead her away when the thick quiet is rent by a shriek, a wail that becomes a recognizable shape in the air: 'Help! Help!' It comes from behind the spring, more than a hundred yards away, where fragments of the villa can be glimpsed in the gloom. They both run towards it, taking care where they put their feet, slipping on the damp grass.

Ahead of them is a wall of reddish brick, more than waist height, which acts as a border to a deep trench. There are some steps leading down below, which they follow, Jake ahead by no more than an instant, the footing all of a sudden treacherous. There they see a flat patch of ground, surrounded on all sides by brick walls. Scattered across the floor are pillars, two hand-widths across, made from fired clay, a burnt umber colour, brown in the faded light, some a few inches, some several feet high. They look bizarre, pointless, columns in support of nothing. The mist hangs cobwebby between them even at this low level.

Jake knows what they are, because he has been round here before and spoken to one of the many at the dig keen – to the point of desperation – to share their knowledge. They have come into the middle of a Roman central heating system, beneath the old floor level in the section designed to let hot air circulate. These pillars, these *hypocausts*, he remembers, when fully built, were designed to hold up the floor. They were integral to the functional stability of the building. Now they stand, asymmetric and forlorn, like limbless statuary.

He has little time to think these thoughts, though, as he searches for the person who had shouted for help. They hear a moan, softer now. Across the way, he spots a dark tangle of clothes strewn beneath the far wall. There is a slab of masonry balanced precariously on top of it. Aletheia and he run over, and move it together, it is cold and damp and friable in his hands. As they heave it, the shape beneath shifts, rolls over, and he sees black hair against the sandy ground, then a face, pained and alive, one cheek an angry red flush upon pale, brown skin. 'Thank God it's you,' Daisy says, and tries to sit up.

Chapter Nineteen

The arbour by the firepit, Little Sky

'So how badly hurt was she?'

Jake is telling the story a few hours later. It is a warm evening now back at Little Sky, as if those earlier events had taken place in a different country, in a different season. The shadows are long, the light warm and generous, colours of saffron and turmeric. The goat has been cooked and is resting, prostrate like a sacrificial victim on a large chopping board, the skin brown-black, rich steam rising. Jake is finishing off the potatoes, which have broiled in the ashes. He takes out their flesh from the burnt outsides and mixes it with oil and vinegar and capers. The vegetables have been grilled, the sausages cooked. Everything is almost ready to eat. Diana is racing around the edge of the lake on a bike, exultant in the sheer novelty of having late-stopping guests. Those guests are seated, soaking in the final, sleepy hour of serious sun, their glasses half-empty, their expressions captivated. The kitchen door is open, and the record player is on low, Gershwin's 'Rhapsody in Blue', whimsical and flighty as the birds in the trees above them.

Livia had asked the question. She is perched next to Jake on a bench, sideways to him, both legs over his lap. She is wearing a pale green jumpsuit, with thick turn-ups at the base, exposing the little knitted bones of her ankles. Jake traces a finger against the knuckled hardness there beneath the soft skin. On the other bench Rose and Aletheia sit, a few inches apart, Rose's feet on the old tree stump that serves as a table. Lily is flat on the mossy floor, her long hair splayed out like willow roots, her tankard of cider bobbing on her stomach as she breathes. Jo has her own chair, a thick cushion beneath her, and is smoking a cigarette with typically amused expression.

'Daisy was fine, didn't need a doctor or anything. She'd been alone in the trench, taking a final look around there, apparently it was one of her favourite spots. She heard a scraping sound, then looked up, and suddenly saw the big slab, a bit of plinth, coming down. She shrieked, which is what we heard, and then half-caught it, half-pushed it away. It landed more softly than it otherwise would have done, and on her legs not her head. She had a big bruise on her thigh, cuts on her hands, a mark on her face where she fell.'

'Lucky escape for her. She was taking a risk, wandering off on her own, given what happened to you, lovey.' This is Livia, who stands to pour herself and Jake another drink, twisting the tap at the bottom of the barrel, watching the golden liquid fall.

He takes the proffered tankard. 'I thought that. But the weather was being weird. When she'd gone there a few minutes before, all was bright, and it probably felt like everyone could see her, and it was totally safe. When the mist came, it came quick and made everything enclosed and strange; easy for someone to sneak up on her.'

Aletheia isn't much of a drinker, is nursing hers carefully. 'So do we think the person who did it was lucky with that mist, was waiting for a chance and then took it? How could they have predicted sudden weather that would conveniently hide them from view?'

Jo stubs out her cigarette on a little offcut of wood Jake had given her. She has cut her hair into a bob, which frames her face neatly, makes her look a little younger; she is wearing a pair of dark jeans and a sky-blue jumper. 'Gosh this is exciting. So can you rule in or out anybody from the dig?'

Aletheia smiles brightly. 'That's a great question. And I think the answer is no. Jake and I were on our own, and the visibility was pretty poor. By the time we'd shifted the stone, helped Daisy up and checked she was OK, a whole crowd had run up: Amy and Zach, Brian, Matt and Elaine, a few others, all looking concerned, all could have come from anywhere, near or far.'

'So only Lils has an alibi, because she was lazing around in my house.' Rose looks down at his sister.

'Awkwardly enough, older brother, I'm not in the clear. I realized I'd left my phone on site and had come to get it; I bumped into these two when they were walking out.' She takes a deep drink. 'Though I didn't kill anyone or try to kill anyone, if that makes folk feel better before dinner.'

Aletheia picks up the tale from Jake. 'We had a look around before we left, and you could see where the slab had come from. There was some frayed twine, blue stuff, left nearby, but that could have been blown by the wind. You certainly didn't need rope to push the thing. We reckoned somebody had walked around quietly in the gloom, waited until Daisy was underneath and heaved away.'

'And what about footprints or anything like that?' asks Jo. 'Please don't disappoint the romantic in me. I hope you went full Sherlock and got your magnifying glasses out.'

'Ha, there was nothing. Jake and I aren't forensic people, but we had a good enough look. It was heavy, the slab, and would have taken shifting, but I think a reasonably fit man or woman could've done it.'

'That rules me out,' giggles Lily softly. 'Physical fitness has never much appealed to me.' And yet, thinks Jake, there is clearly power and poise in her body: she is slender, but not slight at all.

'Did anybody call the cops?' asks Jo.

'Amy did, and they came out to prod around a bit. But they didn't find anything much. Stone doesn't take fingerprints easily, and so there was nothing really to get hold of for them. They'll report back to McAllister, the new chief, and he'll add it to whatever he thinks about the case.' Jake is processing as he is talking, trying to establish in his own mind a narrative that binds it all together.

Livia, as ever, is way ahead of him. 'So we now have two of the four people who discovered the treasure attacked. Do we think one of Zach or Amy is a killer, or are they the next victims?'

Aletheia sets down her drink, leans forward and grabs a charred bit of pepper. 'You've got the detective mindset, Liv. I think that's a very reasonable line of thought to pursue. So is the idea that some of the staff have it in for how the dig's being run, don't like Amy's approach, want to ruin things. And that opens up the suspect pool even more. The last people we saw before the mist came in were Matt and Elaine, marching off with some purpose.'

'Well what do you reck, Lils? You know these people.'

Rose is now rolling a cigarette for Jo, and then another for himself. Their smoke is carried off into the evening, joined by the wispy emanations of the fire. A chill is seeping in from the edges, furtive and thievish, as the sun dips, the sky pinking around it, night now on its way.

'I know people moan about Amy's approach, but the idea of killing anybody for it, to get the dig cancelled, is more or less ridiculous. Matt and Elaine have this mystical, monastic zeal about archaeology, but they're a fairly normal couple, so far as I know them. The most scandalous thing about Zach and Amy is that they're screwing, though the idea of her clambering aboard that mop-haired creature is a bit beyond me. I guess either of them, or both, could be interested in money, but they don't strike me as desperate for the stuff. I mean, you don't get into archaeology to be rich, you do it because you love it, the land, the history, the drama of exploring the past.' She raises herself up on her elbows as she talks, her eyes suddenly agleam.

'Do you feel like that?' Jake's interest is genuine.

The gleam winks out. 'I guess so, I mean why not? You need to have a purpose, right? Or maybe you've found a calling as a student and never want to grow out of it.' She puts her drink on the ground. 'No, Zach and Amy don't feel like killers to me.'

'Are they definitely bonking, though?' Jo, the journalist, can't help herself.

'I did see them in what your profession might call a passionate embrace,' says Jake, remembering that time in the office.

'Ah yes, technical journalistic term there, a little short of a clinch, and nowhere near a steamy romp.'

Lily is grinning, eyes half-shut. 'I did see a full romp

once. Last year, a very warm evening, site shutting down for the day. It was in the Roman villa, she was leaning over what we think was the stone base for an old bed, he was behind her, both had trousers around their ankles, lots of jiggly buttocks, slip-slap of skin. She looked good for her age, I'll tell you, something very – I don't know – cushiony and welcoming about her.'

'As someone probably of her age, like many of us here, I'll be the first to say that's enough of that. I shudder to think of being called "cushiony".' Livia walks to the path, which drops down towards the lake, a shimmering, now clementine-tinted presence in the setting sun. 'Di, Di, dinner!' She turns back. 'Did they see you, Lily, watching them?'

'I wasn't watching them, I stumbled across them. Stayed for a little out of curiosity and then left. They had their eyes shut mostly. I think they were getting off on the idea of being the first people to fuck in that bedroom in two thousand years. They were screwing history as much as each other.' She sighs. 'That's archaeologists for you.'

Livia helps Jake put platters out on the big table, a thick slab of old wood, dark with age and varnish, its surface scored and pitted. She speaks as Diana tears up, pausing only to park her bike. 'And let's keep the conversation away from these current cases and sordid recollections, while we have a child present, thank you very much.' A new subject is selected, but you can tell that several of those around the fire are thinking of matters dark and not yet explicable. Passion and digging do not seem in particular opposition.

Chapter Twenty

The thriller library, Little Sky

The evening proceeds pleasantly. Jake stokes the fire up once more, orange sparks fluttering, jittery as lightning bugs, as the wood roars and hisses. The lamps go on, pooling gentle light that shows enough but no more, people merely animated shadows to one another, greyed presences apart from the flickering reflections trapped in their eyes.

There is much laughter and joshing. Diana, with artful pleas, manages to linger until past her bedtime, gorged on the company and the ice cream that Jake brings out once most of the other food has disappeared. By the time she goes to bed, reluctant, under Livia's martial escort, black night has come, the moon an indistinct white disc in the ripples of the lake.

'We must all have a sauna!' declares Jo, a little rambunctiously. She is not too drunk, as she is intending to drive home later, but merry enough to relish some mild adventure. Jake lumbers off to light the coals. It will take an hour to get to temperature, so action is postponed, and the party relaxes into itself, breaking up into small groups. Livia and Lily are seated on the cool, soft floor, wrapped in blankets and giggling, the glare of a small reefer sometimes visible as it is passed hand to hand. Rose is probably the drunkest, sitting restful and beatific on his chair, head moving to the music. Jake has put an old jazz record on, and 'The Girl from Ipanema' is making everyone subconsciously sway.

Aletheia stretches and looks across at Jake. 'Are you too tired to talk business, old man?'

Jake has had the stress of hosting – mild though it might be – to keep him sober, so is quite willing to turn his mind to matters more serious and active. Jo's ears prick up too, and she slides an arm into his. 'I like business too, remember.'

Aletheia grins in the gloom. 'I hoped you'd say that. I was going to go through the unsolved crimes in the area, and you might remember them and fill out some pictures for us.'

'This sounds like a final-drink type conversation to me.' Jo goes to one of the tables and pours a generous slosh of whisky into a tumbler. 'Ready and reporting for duty.' The three of them step carefully over the evening's debris, Jake pausing to kiss Livia's head as he goes, scents of fruit and smoke and booze. He switches on the lights in the library when they get there, lights the pre-laid fire.

'Whoa, too much, Jakey.' Jo screws her eyes almost shut. 'It's too late, and I am too old for full naked lighting.' He dims them to a more forgiving glimmer and they sink into the soft furnishings. Aletheia picks up her tablet device, logs into it carefully.

Jo looks quizzically at Jake. 'I thought this place was off the grid. No internet or anything, and that's your excuse for looking and acting like some sort of moonshine-slurping hillbilly.'

Jake is sipping from a ceramic tumbler of water. 'Al is high enough in the government to have special kit that gets connected anywhere. It's best not to inquire too closely.'

Jo snuggles deeper into her cushion. 'Colour me impressed. I knew I needed to keep my eye on you, Aletheia.'

Aletheia has been concentrating, ignoring their conversation. 'One line of thought has this as an inside job, which makes all of the people on the dig potential suspects. We covered that earlier. But what about external candidates, or evidence that comes from elsewhere, away from the plateau? I think there are three cases worth chasing down, though to be honest they all could have nothing to do with what's happening at St Giles.'

'What's the theory here again, Aletheia?' Jo waves a pack of cigarettes at Jake, who nods reluctantly. He can air the place out tomorrow. She lights up and exhales a cloud of smoke that lingers below the ceiling.

'At the moment it looks as though Wulfnoth has moved quickly to murder and assault. It's more plausible that such behaviour would have a precedent somewhere, so I've looked up crimes in a twenty-mile radius that involved violent assault or murder or kidnapping, where the guilty parties were never found or were found and are now out of prison.'

Jake is thoughtful. 'Not to be that guy, but . . . One: people do crack and act without prior experience – in fact the first time someone does anything, it by definition comes out of the blue. And two, who's to say our killer is from this area, or has lived here all his life?' He counts the points out on his fingers as he speaks.

Aletheia mimics his gesture in response, leaving her two middle fingers raised, a smile on her face. 'One, that's statistically less true of *serial* assault or murder, which tends to be arrived at by progression not impulse. Two, these crimes seem peculiarly rooted in the local soil and a weird love of it, which suggests somebody with a connection to the area. And three, nobody likes people who throw stones rather than build houses.' The third option is not accompanied by a third finger.

'Keeping you honest, Al. It's never good to leave a theory unchallenged, even at the beginning.'

'Fair point, but now shut up.' They are kidding each other, Jake thinks, as they used to when they were both actual colleagues. The thought pleases him enormously. Aletheia continues talking.

'Case number one involved a spate of vandalism of old churches five or so years ago. Graves pushed over, windows smashed. All sounds a bit boring, but then a churchwarden – this is in a place called St Frideswide's, about thirty-five miles away – must have stumbled across them in the act. He got his head caved in, and died two days later. No witnesses. The murder weapon looked improvised: a shovel left in the churchyard, one big heavy blow across the front.'

Jo is trying to place the story. She sits forward and throws her cigarette butt into the fire, where it flares and is consumed. 'It's a bit outside of my catchment area, but we'd have covered it, I'm sure. And it never got solved?'

Aletheia shakes her head. 'Apparently not. The working assumption is that it was some kids who got unlucky, and were as shocked as hell that it led to murder, never did anything again.'

'Possible. But it would be good to know if anything connected the churches together in the first place, was there a reason other than convenience that made them targets, was it a protest of some sort?' This is Jake, scratching his beard as he watches the flames writhe and hiss and caper.

'I thought you might say that. But I don't know the answer. It's one we should find out.'

Jo nods. 'On this one, and any of the others, I'll do a cuttings job and send them to you. See if there is anything in the coverage. Plus, I know all the old regional journos in the area. Ten years ago we probably had an actual real-life reporter who knew the place well, had St FridayWhatever in his patch. There may have been unprintable stuff about the case they knew about.' She sighs. 'Don't get me started about the decline in local journalism, Al.'

Aletheia is making notes on the screen. 'And one of us should maybe go to the churches, see what if anything leaps out. It's all a longshot, Jake, and we should keep our eye on the main prize too.'

'Agreed. Who's next?'

'Contestant number two was a man wanted for assaulting professional women in two towns across the county. Seems he had a hatred for female empowerment, three violent attacks, the victims a solicitor, a doctor and a *history* teacher. All attacked outside their place of work, punched pretty bad. This is fifteen years ago.'

Jake wrinkles his nose. 'That sounds like a reach. Our first victim was an old man.'

Jo nods, rubbing her hands against her jeans, the thrill of the chase visible in her face, hectic in her blood. 'I do know this one. Remember, Jakey, the dossier I put together about rural violence against women?' He does indeed: it was partially due to Jo's diligence that he had identified a local man called Mack as a serial predator, the first case he had been involved with – reluctantly enough – since his retirement.

'Anyway, this one was grim because it seemed like straightforward misogyny and envy towards successful women. Everyone I knew talked about it, worried about it. Now I was a junior hack, so nobody in their right mind would've had a go at me because of my conspicuous success.' She snorts reflectively, and downs the dregs of her whisky. 'But it still was a big thing for me at the time. I seem to remember that there was a suspect, a good one, and he died, run over by a car and so could never be prosecuted. I'll check but I think this is a no.'

'Good enough. Which leaves our final candidate, a woman who simply disappeared a year or so ago.' Aletheia checks her screen. 'Her name was Janet Sanders, had a main place in the city, but lived increasingly out here.'

Jo stands, excited, and possibly a little drunk, and starts pacing. 'Now I do know her. She was a media bigwig, used to work in papers and TV, some sort of CEO figure. You know, a glass-ceiling cracker. I think I even met her once or twice. But she retired, did some interviews about getting out of the rat race, started running a watercress farm – with help, of course – not that far from here. Then one day, leaves a note about travelling, and slips from the radar. We did some stuff on it, but it never went anywhere.'

Jake yawns. He can hear the clattering of unsober people entering the kitchen, glasses being slammed down, the record being noisily changed, laughter and shushing and the shunting of furniture. 'Another reach, Al, surely.'

Aletheia is unmoved. 'I don't think so. The disappearance looks at least questionable, and there's been a file started on it somewhere by someone who thinks all is not well.'

'And hold tight there, Jakey boy.' Jo is still moving, restless and pantherish. 'I remember another detail about her. We had her in the paper when she first came to the area, before she decided to downsize. You can imagine: a "Local woman made good" boreathon. And check this: her passion was archaeology and tracing ancestry; she was an active member of all sorts of clubs and societies.'

'As was Jordan, of course.'

Jake is about to concede the point when Livia bursts in, clutching a pile of thick towels so high they obscure all but the wavering coils of hair on her head.

'Enough chat, my lovely friends. We're heading to the sauna and then a dip, if any of you dare. Wrap yourself up tightly though, I don't want to see anybody's dangly bits in any circumstance. This is not an orgy.' She chuckles as she speaks.

Jake looks at Jo. 'This was your idea; you can't chicken out now.'

'OK, but provided the dangly bit rule is strictly followed at all times.'

They follow Livia to the kitchen, which is lurid and bright after the library's soothing gloom. Lily is already wrapped in a towel, which trails down almost to her feet, freckles sprinkled across her collarbone. Rose is asleep in the chair by the stove, a single shoe and sock lying forlorn at his feet. He snores and twitches.

Aletheia takes a towel and heads to her bedroom. 'I'll do this, but I'm keeping my knickers on. You country folk are too depraved for this city girl, you know.'

Chapter Twenty-One

The church at St Frideswide's

The sauna was a suitably chaste affair, Jake reflects the next morning, especially with Rose out of action. There was definitely something between him and Aletheia, though, something warm and curious, but it might be friendship, the sort of kinetic joyfulness that comes when genuine opposites discover things they have in common. Nothing happened last night as a result of it, he was sure of that.

Jake is the first up and out of bed, the early dawn a shimmering hint of a pleasant day to come. Livia had rolled over as he rose, bare brown leg out of the covers, putting an old T-shirt over her face to obscure the light creeping around the curtains. As he heads off on his normal jogging route, lungs opening up, toxins disappearing in his sweat, he catches a glimpse of Aletheia, clad in purple lycra, heading towards the lake. On his homeward path, the lake now on his right, he sees her again, rowing hard, eyes half-closed, muscles writhing like eels beneath her skin.

They had lasted probably no more than twenty minutes in the sauna before the heat drove them outside, childishly urging each other on to jump in the lake. They separated along the reedy shoreline, each person invisible in the black, the white of their towels occasionally caught by the moonlight. Jake and Livia together, holding hands, as they dropped their coverings and plunged in. Shrieks and guffaws and swear words in the night. Ten minutes later they were sober, drinking cocoa in the kitchen and then calling it a night. Rose, who had not moved from his kitchen chair the whole time, was chivvied into one bed, Aletheia into another, Lily into a third, as Jake walked Jo back to her car, confident she could make it home with due caution.

Jake is back to the house before Aletheia comes off the lake. He showers quickly outside and begins the process of tidying up after the night before. When Aletheia returns, eyes reddened with perspiration, chest heaving, he goes inside to give her privacy in the shower. It is odd to live in a home where the only place to wash is in the courtyard outside, and he sees how it presents an abnormal situation for guests staying over. Aletheia rolls her eyes when he hands her a towel and withdraws.

Diana wakes up soon after and joins him, with a little reluctance, in the tidying operation. They open all the windows – apart from the dark, fuggy bedrooms where the adults still slumber – and let the healthful breath of morning into the house, drifting down the corridors, circulating within like a gift from nature. It reminds Jake of *The Wind in the Willows*, the book he is reading with Diana at the moment: Mole doing his spring-cleaning, as the fizzing hints of life outside suggest a world of excitement beyond.

He and Diana actually have twenty minutes alone to read together, sitting at the kitchen table with glasses of water, the stove pleasantly warm near their feet. They are only a few pages in, and they get to the bit about the food in Ratty's hamper, all that generosity and tastiness, that 'cold tongue cold ham cold beef pickled gherkins salad french rolls cress sandwiches potted meat ginger beer lemonade soda water' described in a breathless rush, and it makes them both smile. Food in books is always a matter to savour, Jake thinks, an imaginary tang on the palate, a memorable detail to roll around your mind.

While Aletheia dresses inside, the two of them walk down to Agatha Wood. It is a perfect day for a ramble, the weather innocent and fresh, clouds drifting, the sun warming, ducks fussing and dabbling in the shiny waters beside them. Diana skips and springs, every movement an unconscious delight, filling the air with prattle and song, occasionally stepping close enough to put her hand in Jake's. He treasures that sensation, that fleeting connection: he can feel it in his palm when she runs off, and it reminds him – not without a tug of fear or regret – of his desire for more family, for more moments like this.

She scrambles up the ladder to the treehouse he has built for her, and he hears the hum and squealing delight as she comes down a minute later on the zip wire. It is dark in the wood, clean and cool, lances of sunlight inching further along the mulchy ground with every passing second. He wanders, idly casting pine cones at tree trunks, weighing up the case at hand. He would need to chase down the Janet Sanders line, he thinks, if only to rule it out, and do the same with the church vandals. Meanwhile, Aletheia could take another look at Jordan's background, to see if anything loomed unduly there, and then the backgrounds of the others on the dig too. Was Brian as jovial as he seemed? Were the two lovers, Matt and Elaine, united simply by their passion for each other and archaeology? Was there anything to be concluded from the illicit relationship between Amy and Zach, or was it to be dismissed as sweet or cloying or distasteful, his bumpy, bony figure scraping unromantically against her matronly softness? Jake smiles at the conceit. Whatever else, they need to work out how to get at Wulfnoth directly – who is he, and how can he be lured into the open?

He lets his mind refocus on Diana, the pleasure of an idle Sunday morning like this. She leaps to the ground once more, breathless and moss-stained, and they spend some time by the old brook that trickles down to the lake, where she had once seen frogspawn frothing and catching against the old slate stones. To their delight, after a little patience, they catch a glimpse of an actual frog, sombre and impassive, its chest throbbing, its muddy green colour almost blending into the weeds that emerge from the water.

The faint sound of a gong interrupts them, its reverberations disturbing the rustic peace. Livia had bought it at a house sale, as a joke, formerly the property of an old country mansion fallen into unmoneyed disuse. She used it whenever Jake and Diana rambled negligently past mealtimes, and it tells him that breakfast is ready.

By the time they return, feet sopping from the dewy grass, the sun no longer young in the sky but bright and almost hot, Livia has relaid the outdoor table and is serving a huge mound of scrambled eggs, yellow as corn, taken from their own chickens, a platter of well-done bacon, some early asparagus sitting in pools of melting butter, and a pile of thick, fluffy muffins (these especially for Diana). A large ewer of coffee stands at the table, welcoming, its roasted scents rich in the air.

Everyone is now up, Rose clearly under some protest. He is still wearing his clothes from the night before, and is sipping coffee cautiously, as if he were defusing a grenade. Lily is far brighter, and has the look of someone heading off to work, bag at her feet, long, frizzy brown hair brushed and shining in the morning light. Aletheia has a plate of eggs in front of her, tucking in with the relish of someone who feels she has earned it.

They talk delicately of this and that, before Jake brings up his plans. Livia is taking Diana to riding club, and then offers to accompany him to St Frideswide's. Aletheia intends to call Martha, and look more closely at the family who made allegations against Jordan, and the background of Janet Sanders. Lily is off to the dig – encumbered by warnings on all sides to take care – while Rose's ambitions extend no further than a sedate return homeward and a healing sleep in a shady hammock.

Two hours later, Jake and Livia are in the hamlet near St Frideswide's church. There is an old vicarage, dominating a street that twists and turns, barely wide enough for traffic in one direction. They knock at the door, but nobody answers. The place seems well-inhabited, the flesh-pink roses climbing up the porch evidently well-tended, and Livia strolls around the corner where the back garden looks out towards a small green. There, a woman of middle years is kneeling on the ground, attacking recalcitrant weeds with some gusto, green flecks in a soil that has been recently turned over and is almost black.

Before Livia approaches, she nods Jake towards the

church itself, and he takes the hint. She obviously has the sense that she might make a more immediate connection on her own. The church is – like so many Jake has encountered, admired, sat near and wondered at in his time in the countryside – old and distinguished, this one sandy and bleached with age, its stained-glass windows dark blotches against the stone. It is empty, the wooden door locked, as it would never have been in a past when the building meant more, had given life to the village that grew up around it.

Jake circles it happily enough, reading gravestones, idly imagining the lives of those now mouldering beneath the heathery sods of earth and untended thickets of wildflowers. A family taken within six months of one another in the 1780s, an accident perhaps, or a virus, a devastating and inexplicable incursion that now could be cured with a pill and without a fuss. A small headstone for a baby, half the height of the others in the graveyard, which is strange when Jake thinks about it, as if the size of the body should affect the scale of the memorial. Why? Wasn't the loss of a toddler even more of a cosmic blow, a shattering event of incomprehensible force that required some form of greater ritual response, not less?

He leans against the war memorial, which is in the top corner by a shambling old wall held together by lichen. It has more names than a small village should possibly provide, some of whom had their own relations in the older tombs he had been wandering past. There is nothing that testifies to life's futility, he glumly considers, so much as a collection of graves in the middle of nowhere. As he philosophizes, he looks up at the church, and sees where the damage had been done a few years before. Two of the windows have not been replaced, but left boarded up, an act of real neglect in such a beautiful spot. There are faint marks on the pale stone too, red paint not quite scrubbed to extinction. Jake half-closes his eyes and thinks he can make out an unflattering word, 'nonce', though he cannot be sure.

He kicks some dandelion clocks, watches the blurry filaments scatter, then catches sight of Livia heading for the village green. He vaults the wall and joins her, finding a bench in the full warming glare of the sun.

'How did that go?'

'She was a prickly one. Didn't like police much, so I said I was trying to make sense of the death of a friend of mine, John Jordan. She knew him: her husband is the vicar round here, and they were quite friendly colleagues.'

'Why didn't she like the police? I'd have thought she'd have welcomed the forces of law and order, given what happened to the church. I saw the damage, by the way. And what looked like the word "nonce" scrawled on the wall.'

'I think that's the problem. Her husband had been accused, not openly, but in that quiet, villagey, pernicious sort of way, of lusting after some of the local youth, and she thinks they should have gone after the gossip-mongers more harshly.'

'Because they might have been connected to the people who bashed the warden's head in?'

'I don't think she much cared about that bit.'

'It's interesting that the behaviour of her husband links to Jordan's. Maybe.'

Livia thrusts her hands in her pockets. She is wearing a light, cherry-coloured cardigan and brown cords indented with thick grooves. Her fringe is dancing in the breeze. 'This was seemingly more serious than the rumours about Jordan. It essentially finished his career. Even now this church is more or less closed down, and he is only clinging on because he covers other parishes, and no charges were ever brought against him.'

'Did she mention the alleged victims?'

'She talked about "local harridans" but wouldn't be drawn.'

There is a pause. Two geese fly overhead, prospecting for better landing grounds. Their honks sound like distant traffic. Jake exhales, scratches his beard. 'I don't know. This feels a long way from poisoned pen letters and murder in a dig site.'

'That's the problem when you go hunting for connections. Everything is a potential link, or nothing is.'

'OK, Confucius. This is no time to become a guru.' She smiles and their hands touch, a familiar spark of electricity. Jake nods at the church. 'It explains why the windows were never fixed. Odd, really. It's a nice spot. Though I got a bit maudlin around those graves, especially the children.'

Livia clenches her fingers around his. 'You are a softie, for a hardboiled detective.'

He leans over, kisses her smooth, firm cheek, which tastes faintly of liquorice. 'I had a lovely time with Di this morning. And then I felt sad that we might not experience that with our little one.'

'Don't give up hope yet, Jake. We have an awful lot of trying to do before we have to worry.' She sighs wistfully. Looks at the liquid blue sky, which is deep and endless and mysterious. The spire of the church points upwards towards it, as if in acknowledgement of its fathomless expanse. 'I don't know, lovey, I feel it in my bones that we'll have a baby. I just believe it. But, as I told you, I don't need it to be fulfilled to have joy.'

They walk back towards the street. A car suddenly revs loudly, an obscenity in the calm, and shoots away from them. They see nothing more than a dark smear as it passes. Was someone watching them all this time? Jake can feel Livia's pulse throbbing in her wrist as they cling closer, get in their own car and head back to the sanctity of Little Sky.

Chapter Twenty-Two

The thriller library, Little Sky

Livia drops Jake at the turn of the river so he can walk the rest of the way home. She has some work to do, and will bring Diana back to Little Sky later. He stops at the Jolly Nook for a bite to eat – a pork belly sandwich, part crisped and flaky, part unctuous with fat, topped with watercress and a thick smear of eye-watering mustard – and to gossip with Sarah. She also hands him a package from Jo, a cuttings search of the cases they had discussed. There is a message atop the pile of documents, her journalist scrawl on a piece of paper torn from a child's notebook, a small stencil of a football in the corner:

> All we have on those things we discussed, including some profiles of J. Sanders. Not sure how this connects to your dead vicar, but what do I know, I'm just a grubby hack. My feller also had a book of

local history; lots of Wulfnoth in the index. I know you like lots to read, Jakey, so have at it. Love and luck etc xxxx

He takes it with him homeward, another sandwich wrapped in greased paper for Aletheia. He follows the undulating fields up to his house, hot and suddenly foot-sore, looking forward to a quiet afternoon. Sitting by the vegetable garden he sees McAllister, in earnest conversation with Aletheia, glasses of water by their feet.

She rises to meet him. 'Jake, I hoped you'd be back. I was telling the chief about some of our thoughts.'

McAllister gets up stiffly, suit rumpled, face a little flushed in the unaccustomed sun. He shakes Jake's hand; his is damp, Jake can feel the moisture on the wiry hairs of his knuckles. 'It's been a very useful half hour, Jake. I could do with employing you all as consultants.'

Jake hands Aletheia a sandwich, which she offers to split with McAllister. He declines. They are quiet while Jake gets himself a glass of cold milk from the fridge, lets it soothe his dusty throat.

McAllister is chewing a piece of mint, green leaf clinging wetly to his tongue. 'We got nothing from the dig when it came to the slab that fell on Daisy. No useful forensics at all. The twine you found was used by everybody. Aletheia here tells me the day was misty, and certainly nobody seems to have seen anything. So I don't know what lesson to draw other than that there's a connection between Jordan and you, and then you both with her.'

Jake stretches out his tired legs, feels the knots in his calves throb and then relax. 'Unless it's more than one person acting for more than one reason.'

'I know. But I can't do much with that. Mebbe better to think about what links Jordan and Daisy, and leave you to one side as the annoying copper who got in the way.'

Aletheia nods. 'Jake and I have gone through this. There are two possible links as we see it: the general dig – both vics are significantly involved in that – and then the horde itself, because both discovered it. Either way, maybe the most interested parties are Amy and Zach. Have you questioned them, chief?'

'Yes, in broad terms. Neither has a solid alibi for any of the attacks, by the way. They were either nearby or couldn't prove they were elsewhere. As we know, they were probably off shacking up together on the quiet.'

Jake raises an eyebrow. 'So you know about the torrid affair?'

'I didn't know it was torrid, but yes. And with Jordan and Daisy out of the way, they would stand to inherit a fair old amount of cash, once the treasure was bought. We can't ignore that.'

'I wonder if either of them are desperate for money. We have a contact who might help us with that.'

McAllister raises his hands defensively. 'Don't tell me how you find anything out unless I need to know.'

'And we still don't know the other character in this, the landowner, who's maybe set to inherit millions of quid.' This is Aletheia, who is taking small bites of her sandwich, chewing them carefully before speaking.

'I might need your help on that as well. It's not on any records that I can see. Mebbe you could keep on being helpful, and get some hard evidence on the dealings around the land.'

Jake looks over at his friend. 'Al's the best person in the country at that sort of thing, and that's before she involves her contacts.'

Aletheia grins. 'Flattery will get you everywhere. Oh, all right then. And our contact will want to help too. Well she'll want to harangue us and solve a puzzle, which amounts to the same thing.'

McAllister makes a note in a small leather book. 'Meanwhile, after what you've been telling me, I'm going to go over the files of the church vandals, that old assault case, and the missing person, see if anything moves at our end.' He clears his throat, waves at a fly that has been trying to land on his reddening nose. 'I've one other bit of news: the acid that killed Jordan was brought on site; it was much stronger than the one used by the diggers there. So the thing *was* premeditated – someone came there with it to harm Jordan.'

He stays a little longer, admires the bursts of growth in the vegetable patch, the flurries of greens and yellows and purples contrasted against the deep brown of the earth. Then he walks off, a little stooped, like he has shared a burden but still has been left with much to carry.

A few hours later, Aletheia is making dinner while Jake sits in a corner, reading the material Jo has left him. Martha is set to call in a few minutes, and Jake wants to have examined as much as he can by then. He admits to feeling more intrigued by Janet Sanders, and he reads out extracts of the profile to Aletheia as she chops and fries and seasons. She is making curry with the leftover goat, from a recipe of her mother's that she has adapted to fit the ingredients in Jake's cupboards and things she could wheedle from Sarah in the Nook. It smells delicious, puttering on the stove, red-brown and meaty, the warmth of the spices filling the nostrils.

Janet is now interesting to Jake because you can make some sort of theoretical link between her and the dig, even if he couldn't yet prove that she had been there much in the past. She was writing a book on the greatest archaeological sites in Britain, a 'biography of geography' she called it: the tales of people who owned the land, what they did with it and what happened to them. St Giles was more or less on her doorstep, as she acknowledged in the interview he was reading, but she admitted to saving her full investigation into it until the end, allowing her to pursue field trips further away from home first.

'So did she then get involved in writing about the dig, or not?' Aletheia is tasting the sauce experimentally, wincing at its heat.

'I think we need to find out. She may well have done, or she may have not got round to it. This piece is very mystical about her mission, her desire to – and I'm quoting – "dig deep into the fabric of our island history". She sounds fascinated by it. It's rather charming actually.'

'So what then happened to her?' Aletheia grinds pepper rhythmically, black flecks pitting the roiling red surface.

'That's the question. She's retired anyway, she runs this farm but only really in name, has folk doing the day-to-day, who are left to manage for themselves. She lives in a remote cottage at the edge of the land. One morning she leaves a letter under a rock at the side of the watercress field, and she is gone. No sign of her since.'

'And no fuss?'

'Well, she'd been talking about her desire to explore the whole country, had no nearby family, was divorced, so who was there to really call her missing? You only found out about it because she's on a database somewhere of unsolved reports. Someone must have at least raised the question, even if the answer was that nothing could be done.'

'Can I see your antennae wobbling a bit from here?'

'The tone feels right somehow. The other cases seem like explicable violence, but I don't know. I guess I think she's the sort of person a Wulfnoth-type figure would know about in the area, would come into contact with. What do you think?'

'I'd like to know more definitely. Let's see what Martha says.'

She puts the pan to one side of the stove to stay warm, bubbling lazily away, and lays out the roti – small parcels of dough, flecked with coriander – to prove a little. Together they walk to the library, which is now clean and airy, fragrant with flowers Aletheia had gathered while wandering the grounds. Tulips of poster-paint magenta and purple, fading white and yellow daffodils, the very last of the season.

They sit side by side on the sofa, Aletheia fumbling for her device, which is already flashing with Martha's call.

'Good evening, my two-legged friends.' Martha's face, big on the screen, is wry and sardonic. Her shoulders and neck have been pinked by the sun, her hair now a bleached white. She has her pipe in her hand but is not smoking, instead letting it rattle against the table as she shifts in her seat, and then spin in her restless hands while she talks. Her liveliness seems trapped inside her, Jake thinks. She is never at repose, always twitching and twisting in body and mind.

Aletheia takes her through the events since they last spoke, including the attack on Daisy. Martha's eyes flash, sardonic throughout, and she makes scrawled notes at various points in the narrative.

After Aletheia has finished, Martha takes a sip from her martini glass, filled to the brim with some no doubt strong, clear liquor. 'I've got some more information on all this to add to the party. One question: can you send me a picture of the twine you found near the Daisy incident? I'd like to take a look.'

Aletheia shrugs. 'Of course, but why?'

'You leave that to my torturous mind for now. On the other things, let me tell you what I've got. I think we can rule out the idea of a revenge attack purely on Reverend Jordan, at least insofar as it involves the girl mentioned in the letter Jake lost in his wet trousers. And nice going on preserving the evidence there, sport. Bravo. Al, you left me to look into that and it feels like nothing. First, it wasn't really a girl, it was a young woman, almost twenty, who'd discovered religion pretty hard. Her dad, this Alan Williams, objected, and wanted her outside the influence of the church. It seems like he made some pretty strong claims about all sorts of religious folk, including people like Jordan, who'd only seen her once or twice at historical society meetings. All the other allegations from Williams, the ones I could check, came to nothing.'

Jake puts a cushion under his head, pensive. 'That doesn't mean he didn't believe them and act irrationally as a result. Giving someone acid to drink is a pretty irrational thing, all in all.'

'True, but if you'd let a woman finish, you'd hear that poor Mr Williams had a heart attack a year or so later and died. Jordan seems to have signed a consolation book at the funeral, so I think he kept the letters not out of guilt but almost as a contact, a reminder to check back up on the family. The daughter by the way is now happily married.'

'How on earth did you get sight of the consolation book, you magician?'

Martha waves her hand airily, the tight muscles of her arm shapely in the light. 'Don't worry about that. Now Al sent me the details of the other cases when she got them, and I had a brief look at your Janet Sanders.'

Jake sits up, instincts alive. Martha spots this. 'Ah, the greyhound at the slips. Why the interest, Jake, do you think she's important?'

'I don't know, maybe, maybe not. I'd be happier if we could place her in actual contact with the dig somehow.'

Martha's eyes gleam as she drains her glass, a thin film of liquid on her upper lip. 'Of course you would. You've got an orderly mind like that. Well, I've been running cross references on the colourful bunch you've assembled there, and that has indeed borne fruit. First, though, on Janet, she was someone definitely on the pathway to becoming ever more reclusive – like you, my bedraggled chum. Downsizing, the rural place, the interest in the bony fragments of the past. She'd disappear – from what I understand – and do research for days and weeks on end, confiding only in the odd friend about what she was up to and where she was going, if she mentioned it at all. A happy rambler, bothering nobody, career in the big city left behind her. Then one day, as you know, she left a letter saying she was leaving, and pouf! vanished into thin air.'

Aletheia is flicking through her notebook. 'Do you have the letter, M?'

'I do, and it's winging its way electronically to you now. Plus, I now have your connection between her and the dig.

Who do we think found the letter, placed under an old Roman tile in the porch of her secluded farmhouse at the edge of the watercress field?'

'Don't make me guess.'

'The third target of the Wulfnoth attacker: your pal Daisy Sharma.'

Chapter Twenty-Three

Daisy's house, the village of Sexton Blake

It is definitely a link in a chain, though Jake cannot see what it means other than it must be worth him talking properly to Daisy, and looking more closely at the disappearance of Janet Sanders.

The three of them linger on the call for a few minutes as Martha lights her pipe, becomes a bit more expansive, lowers her guard as far as it goes. She is in the middle of writing a new novel, and struggling with a plotline, which she is charmingly self-deprecating about. Her books, as Jake now knows – indeed, he can see all of them in a row on a nearby shelf; titles in big, bouncy, jolly red – are gentle, whimsical capers in which a ragtag band of largely loveable criminals commit heists that expose the inadequacies of the British state. They allow Martha to be quietly cutting, often funny, always slick and smart, and they are much beloved by a small but devoted group of readers. She confides in them that a TV adaptation is on the cards; she wants to be offhand about it, but they can both tell the glint of satisfaction and vindication in her eyes. 'They've bought the option, have some actors lined up. I'm sure it will come to nothing, like all promising things, but you never know, you never know.'

Aletheia talks a little about her own work, their shared colleagues, her concerns about her mum, and how much of her time she spends in care of her. This last few days has been a welcome relief, a chance to be free and independent, peace that a woman of her age should really be able to take for granted. Jake silently blesses his own lack of family obligation: parents dead when he was a teenager (car crash, no lingering); the absence of siblings. His life is what he can make it, his family is his to build as far as he is able.

Jake hears the kitchen door slam, the sound of Livia and Diana – that small, precious family of his – coming home. Bags dropped, inquiring voices, the bustle of the ending day. They hang up the phone on that cue, with Martha promising more information as she gets it, especially on the landowner of the horde site. Before they head off to the kitchen for dinner, Aletheia shows Jake the final letter of Janet Sanders, which had been typed and printed from a computer:

To whom it may concern

Time for me to depart for a while, to leap once more into the tides of the past. I know I shan't be missed by many, but I am at peace with that. I will be happy digging in the cold, black earth, wandering the long, vasty hills and vales of this country, looking back at what has come before.

I don't know when I'll return, but everything should run fine without me. A salutary thought that, perhaps.

Please share with whomever is interested, however few of you there are.

Janet

'Thoughts?' she asks.

'It is more self-pitying than I imagined it would be. There's a smack of desperation that might have made me worry for her if I'd read it at the time. I wonder if that made Daisy report it. I'll go see her tomorrow, I think, see what she says. And did you notice the phrase "tides of the past"?'

'What of it?'

Jake reaches down to the floor, riffles through the papers that had been neatly stacked that morning. 'Look at Wulfnoth letter number one, it says "What once was built high and proud has been lost to the tides of the past." Also talks about "cold, dark soil", which is not that different from "cold, black earth".'

Aletheia is silent, her long, pianist fingers drumming on the arm of the couch. 'So are we saying that Wulfnoth saw this letter?'

'Or wrote it, having killed her. Or . . .' He pauses while he lets this notion settle in his mind, checking it for absurdity. 'Or Janet is Wulfnoth, for reasons we can't yet understand.'

Aletheia is about to respond when Diana bursts in, filled with her customary glee, her twig-like arms, thin and sun-burnished, encircling Aletheia. 'Come on, show me your spicy curry!' Diana loves hot food, more so than her mum or Jake; it is a source of pride to her that she can eat it. Aletheia allows herself to be raised up, and escorted into the brighter light of the kitchen, her new friend leading the way.

Later, dishes washed, goat curry duly celebrated, Jake and Livia sit by the firepit, watch the embers pulse and flare in the soft evening breeze. Livia is wrapped in a gold blanket, thick and braided; she looks ethereally beautiful, Jake thinks, regal, pharaonic even. Diana is in her bath, Aletheia is checking work messages in the library.

He strokes Livia's hand, looks at the flames reflected in her green eyes, dark as pools in the night-time. 'I've got Daisy's address, and I reckon she'll be around for a little while longer, but not too long now the shooting's done for the show. Shall we both visit tomorrow?'

Tomorrow is Monday, and Diana will be back at school. Livia nods, absently, engrossed by the flickering sight before her. The mesmerizing of fire; a constant through human history. She squeezes his hand in return. 'I'd like to know about this woman, Janet. She sounds a little like you in parts, though you'd have written a less pretentious letter. We'll see if Al wants to come too, or is that too many of us?'

'You'll have to do it without me anyway, Liv.' This is Aletheia returning to the table, her dark, tight-tailored clothes making her almost invisible in the gloaming. 'A problem's come up at the office, and I need to get back tomorrow. But I'll be on the other end of the line, and I'll make time on this when I can. And I wouldn't mind finishing my holiday later in the summer, if you'll have me.'

Jake hands her a small glass of cider. 'Of course, we've loved having you, and I'm sure Rose will welcome a return visit. Anything exciting going on back at base?' He feels the faint tug of interest, a sense of pique that he is no longer connected to any institution that might summon him urgently in the night.

'Nothing I can talk about, even to you, old man.' Much of Aletheia's job, especially in the last two years, is in the shadowy area between policing and intelligence, the hoarding and interpreting of data about people whose actions are threatening not only to individuals, but to whole areas, communities, even nations. She exhales meditatively. 'I've enjoyed the break, though, the wilds, the expanse of all this, the air in my lungs.'

Livia smiles warmly. 'And we've dragged you into a local version of your day job. What sort of holiday can this have been?'

Aletheia looks at Jake quizzically. 'You never get away from some jobs. Look at your boyfriend over here, as a straggly case in point.'

The next day they drop Aletheia at the station. Fond farewells, promises to return. Their last sight of her, standing aloof on the dusty, lonely platform, absorbed in her phone, dragged back immediately into the pressures of her real life, this rural hiatus over for now.

Livia's old Volvo rumbles off towards the village where Daisy lives, a few miles away on narrow roads bordered by hedgerows now grown boisterous with the late passing of spring, thick sprays of leaves, scattered flowers, the endless traffic of flitting insects, life writhing and unbound. They have the windows down to enjoy the air, cool at whatever speed the old car can muster, as the twistiness of their journey slows their pace to a pleasant enough crawl.

Unlike Parvum, modernity has not neglected Sexton Blake, and its visible touches seem to have marred rather than enhanced. There are some raggedy Tudor cottages, pleasantly skewed and low to the land, as if bashful, but they sit in a street alongside some more recent, poor imitations. And clearly life is more practical here than elsewhere: there is an estate agent's and a convenience store, a chemist and a hairdresser's, gaudy flourishings on an ancient street.

Daisy's house is set back from the tiny central area, with a winding drive and sheer walls to keep out the noise of passing cars. They are uninvited so proceed cautiously, crunching up the gravel right to the front door. The building is a mongrel of styles, knocked about over time, added to and reshaped, a product of centuries of work. The garden is wild and overgrown, humming with life and grassy thickness and flowers that might be weeds. A large sprawling rose bush stretches out above the main portal, its dying petals scattered by the breeze upon the ground, like the aftermath of a wedding. There is a small sign on one of the beams supporting the door, giving the name of the property: 'The Wake'.

Jake rings the bell and waits for the ponderous chimes to settle. Livia is peering around the wall to see how far the house stretches back. He shrugs at her when she returns her gaze to his. He rings again, and stands back when he hears footsteps. Daisy opens the door, wiping her hands with a towel. Her face is composed as normal, she is smartly clad in dark practical clothes, as she always is.

'Jake, how nice to see you. Livia, I saw you at that wretched cricket match, nice to see you properly.' A stiff smile. 'It's the curse of coming from an Asian family, you know, you can never get away from the bloody cricket. Come in, come in.'

They follow her through the door. Some piano music is playing, sombre and soothing. 'Chopin?' asks Jake.

'Are you an expert on classical music?'

'God no, but I knew nothing two years ago, and I've been listening to more and more since I've had more time on my hands. On vinyl, you know, so I get the smoothness and the hiss and the whole tactile thing.'

Daisy smiles, and opens the door to reveal a rather old-fashioned record player in the corner of a study, its centre spinning sedately. 'Snap. And ten points for identifying Chopin. This is from his Études, sometimes I feel I could drift away when I listen to it. Some old things are simply better, I reckon. That's why I love archaeology probably.' She closes the door and brings them into a big farmhouse kitchen, stone-flagged and cool. In the corner, by an empty fireplace, there is a couch and armchair, to which she directs them while she goes off to make coffee.

'It's lovely to see you both,' Daisy calls over her shoulder as she clinks mugs and boils water on the range. 'I was doing a bit of cleaning. I'm back to the city next week, and might not be around for a while, especially given all that's happened. I only hope Amy gets a quiet summer now, even if she can't do much work.'

Livia accepts a steaming mug, and puts it down gently on the floor. Jake does the same. She beams warmly at Daisy. 'And will your TV programme go ahead?'

'I'm not sure, it'll only be partially my decision. It depends how this all ends up; we could dedicate the final episode to Reverend Jordan, or maybe the whole thing'll be in bad taste. I've got a meeting next week to discuss it.'

'Will you be all right, if it gets cancelled?'

Daisy is brisk. 'Oh gosh, yes. They'll still have to pay for it, and I have other projects and my life is, you know, fairly inexpensive. This house, it's big and old and lovely, but it was my parents', and so I keep it out of love and loyalty.'

Jake senses that it is best for Livia to lead on all this, and settles back to listen, ready to interject if the need arises.

Livia is looking at Daisy, her green eyes big and inviting. 'So you grew up here? How was that?'

There is a pause. Outside a songbird gives a plaintive cry, which is answered by another, its partner perhaps, aloft and invisible on the branch of a tree. Daisy's tone is cautious, but her eyes are bright, and Jake can see suppressed emotion, a seething under her skin.

'It had its moments. I was the only Asian kid in the school, and it was mostly OK, but not always, never perfectly so. You know: jokes about curry, and names and corner-shop references. The staples of television comics back then, I suppose. My parents were both doctors, their grandparents had come here with nothing, scraped by, started their children in the process of getting educated. We were a success story, and pretty proud of it. Rich by most people's standards: big garden, a patch of land, clever daughter at a posh school, a school that took me from my family for every night during the week, no less. We had this house and I had friends, but I was always different, never quite welcomed. What's your heritage, Livia? You may know what I'm talking about.'

Livia leans forward. 'My mum was from Trinidad, she came over when she was a little girl, to nothing, like your family. They shared a tiny place in the city, and just about got by. She didn't talk about it much, but I know it wasn't easy. Couldn't have been. I often wondered what the family had given up back home: there must've been opportunity here and the chance for money and all that, but they must've lost something too. The trade-off nobody talks about much for immigrants. Lucky to come to a rich and busy country, you know, consider all the jobs and the bustle and the chances for your kids – no thought about the comforts you might be leaving behind, the beauty, the warmth, the simplicity. English winter must have felt very cold and drab and unconsoling.'

Daisy stretches briefly like a cat. 'I'm sure it got easier for them, then it got easier for us. But it's not nothing, however much you want to say it is, and people want you to believe it. Being different. My grandparents were from a rich family in India, long roots there, but the family had stopped prospering sometime before Independence. That's why they came. You know my grandpa was walking down the street in Meryton – this would be back in the late eighties – and someone shouted at him, called him a terrible name I'll never put in my mouth, harassed and jostled him. He had a heart attack; it literally broke his heart. There on the street. On the floor, gasping like a gaffed fish. He was taken to hospital, came back all grey-faced and weak, dribbling out the corner of his mouth. Two years in front of the TV, my granny cleaning around him, serving him. Always the cricket on. The wretched bloody cricket. I hated it.' She smiles bleakly, her throat hoarsening. 'He never recovered. Dead at sixty-four.' She picks at some fluff from the armchair, tries to brighten. 'Now how did we get onto this?'

Livia reaches over and pats her hand, a gesture Jake has seen a hundred times. 'Family memories. You must have them whenever you come back here.'

Daisy regains control of herself, looks a little embarrassed over her display of emotion. 'Well I'm sure *you* didn't come here for them. It's nice to have you as guests, but why are you here, actually?' A coolness has come between them, despite the shared confidence, or perhaps because of it, her sense of regret that she had displayed such weakness.

Livia looks back to Jake. He puts his coffee mug down. 'You know we're helping the police on what happened at the dig. A name has come up of someone who might be connected. She might not have anything to do with it, of course. But you seem to be the person who'd know. Janet Sanders, do you remember her?'

Daisy pauses and then her face brightens, though the underlying austerity never leaves it. It never would, Jake thinks; she has a tremendous ceramic quality, of hardness, of strength beneath the surface. 'Janet, of course. I knew her – know her, I guess, though I've not seen her for a good bit. She's a friend of the site, of Amy and Brian, and I met her several times during our various filmings. She was also sort of, I don't know, flitty. She'd be around for a whole week, in the trenches, all muddy knees, telling the students her latest theory about Anglo-Saxon wine-culture or whatever. Then she'd be gone for the rest of the summer, ploughing her own furrow, exploring somewhere, tracing down some tiny piece of history. Come back months later, brown as a berry, with some stories to tell. I don't want to make her sound too eccentric, though. She was her own person, very much that. I saw her as a mentor at the beginning, really. She knew the business as well as she knew history.' The record – the music that has been fluttering in the background, sombre and meandering, merging with the birdsong outside – ends, the final chord clinging on, replaced by a barely audible hiss.

'What do you think happened to her?'

'Now that's a real mystery, not a historical one. I found a note, which you might know about, I guess?' Jake nods. 'Like I said, it wasn't rare for her to go wandering, but this one felt valedictory somehow. And then there was no sign of her. The farm was more or less run completely by others at that point, and so there was no pressure on her to come back. So we waited for a bit. Then I brought the letter to the site and showed the team there, and we agreed we should at least mention it to the police. I did that, and they said they could do very little. That was more than a year ago.'

'After the treasure was found?'

'Maybe three or four months after. But I never saw the connection. Have I been terribly dim?'

She looks flustered for a second, as if – for her entire life – she has sought to avoid error, to avoid being thought of as weak or fallible, and is now concerned that someone will judge her to have been mistaken. Jake raises a reassuring hand. 'Not at all. Nobody seems to have made any connections about her disappearance, and there may be none. Didn't her final letter remind you of the Wulfnoth threats?'

Daisy places her head to one side, thick black hair piling, woven and glinting like serpent skin. 'Not really. I mean not at all. Hers was in character really. As I said, valedictory but not a total surprise. A few lines dashed off and then a disappearance. We never took Wulfnoth seriously at that point, if you remember.'

'And yet you were concerned enough about Janet to go to the police?'

'That was Amy's idea and I agreed. You see, we all thought maybe we were being too romantic, accepting her decision to up sticks and head off into the sunset. That's why we decided in the end to report it.'

Jake lets the quiet build while he thinks. Janet's letter had clearly been seen by countless people, which could have included Wulfnoth, whoever he was. Indeed, it probably did include him, if you accepted that he was somehow connected to the dig. The existence of the similar phrases hadn't narrowed the field much at all. He frowns. The stove ticks and grumbles. More chirruping outside. A gust of wind blows some late-flowering cherry blossom against the window, a sudden patch of fleshy pink.

Livia asks the question. 'What do you think happened to her, Daisy?'

Daisy weighs her words carefully. 'I think she went off somewhere, and has found work to occupy her. At least, I hope so. And I tell myself so. It's a bigger country than we all think, you know.'

'People must have tried calling, looked for bank activity?'

'That's more your area than mine, Jake. But there's been no real search that I know of. And she didn't have a mobile phone: she wanted to get away from that sort of thing.' Her eyes soften as she looks at Jake. 'You know the feeling, don't you?'

He nods. Janet the downsizer, the escape-artist, the fleer of responsibility and bustle and obligation. 'Aren't you worried?'

'I was, and I suppose I still am. But I also try to respect people's decisions if I can. I have an abhorrence of meddlers too, Jake. Busybodies and interferers, they can be a problem, especially in little villages like this one, especially if you're the "exotic" one. That's a curse too. Janet didn't talk about herself all that much, you see, she was always so interested in ideas and mysteries. But she loved the idea of escape and independence. Getting away from things. All that wasn't some sort of aberrant notion to her.'

A big grandfather clock chimes, intruding upon their combined sense of puzzlement. An awkwardness follows, broken by Livia standing and smoothing down her trousers. 'Daisy, it was lovely to see you, and your lovely home.' She touches her on the shoulder. 'And I'm glad we learned a bit about your family.'

Jake has risen too and they start heading for the front door, Daisy ushering them from behind. 'What are you going to do about Janet then?'

Jake turns so he can see her face, wreathed as it is in concern and faint disquiet. 'We'll get some people to see if they can find her, or at least where she went, if she's been spending money, making herself visible anywhere. And we can see if there's anything that links her to Wulfnoth or what happened at the site.'

They have reached the door, and Daisy lifts the heavy latch. It swings open noisily, scents of crushed rose in the air. Her voice sounds uncertain for a second, childish almost. 'Do you think it'll be safe to get back to St Giles? I'm no coward, but I keep getting visions of that slab falling on me, and I'm not sure there's much that will get me back there, unless you catch the man who did this.'

Jake suddenly sees her, small in the big old doorway, in the vast, unpeopled house, and feels a throb of pity. Who did she really have to talk all this through with? Impulsively, likely inspired by a similar thought, Livia hugs Daisy, presses a cheek against hers, eyes briefly tight shut. Jake lets the moment pass. 'We'll do what we can. I've had my own little brush with Wulfnoth to settle too, remember? We'll be in touch either here or back in the city, and you can call us if you think of anything. Call, Liv, at least.'

Daisy squeezes out a chuckle. 'I know, no phone. A fellow escape-artist. I hope you get to meet Janet someday to compare notes.'

They get in the car. Livia performs a laborious turn and they crunch their way down the drive. As they pass the house, Jake looks back. Daisy is silhouetted through a small window. She has her head in her hands, and she looks like she might be weeping.

Chapter Twenty-Four

Morse field, Little Sky

A few weeks pass. Spring firms into summer. Dawn breaks sooner, the dew lifts quicker, the days grow long and warm, fragrant with flower and hot dirt. The coroner's inquest into the death of Jordan is opened and adjourned. Martha and Aletheia – busy with other things – snatch a little time to help Jake track the movements of Janet Sanders and the complicated land history of the site next to the fort. Jake visits the dig – in its modest, circumscribed state – at least once a week. It feels quiet there, remote and windblown and raised up, bleached pale and lifeless by the unheeding sun, as if the drama of the past, both recent and ancient, is best left in the valley below.

Lily is always pleased to see him, and seems to be enjoying the lack of activity. As one of the four graduate students left there, she has been given responsibility for maintaining some of the prominent features: managing the risk to them, limiting the damage from sun and sudden rain upon the walls and floors that have lain unexposed for millennia, hitherto sheltered by the gentle earth. There is cataloguing to do as well, and Jake sometimes finds her in the Keep, hair pulled back tight, gloves and glasses on, her expression untypically severe, as she patiently cleans and records. She has shown him how she uses thorns to remove corrosion from coins discovered in the trenches. They are taken from a particular plant, the barberry, which Amy has planted in the shade of the office. Jake had noticed it flowering, its leaves shifting from blood-red to wine-purple, and is amazed that it has such a practical use. The long thorns are sharp enough to dislodge rust, but not strong enough to dent ancient metal. Jake has an autodidact love for accumulating information, and spends many happy hours listening and learning.

    He comes to know the other students well, too. Matt, with his wispy goatee, pungent cigarettes, an accent somehow pitched between Paris and New York. He calls Jake 'man', shaking his hand enthusiastically when they meet, and trades tales of digs he has been on in return for Jake's hard-bitten police stories. There is little warmth behind his eyes though, as if his friendliness is learned rather than deeply felt, part of an attempt to fit in. Perhaps that is ever the fate of the outsider, Jake thinks, grasping for the words and gestures that best make it seem like you belong. Now he is looking for it, Jake senses Matt's frustration with Amy and the management of the site. His eyes roll whenever her name is mentioned, he has a clumsy infelicity when he jokes about her – his not quite perfect English incapable of concealing enmity within humour. Elaine sits with them, hand often intertwined with Matt's, but is more distant, or at least more understated, a quiet acolyte of the same beliefs. When she does speak, it is with precision, the faint lilt of the south-west smoothed with a touch that suggests a private education somewhere more urban. When Jake asks for her reasons for staying, she is evasive, unwilling to talk about her own past at all.

Brian is also ever-present, his shorts shrinking as the temperature rises, until Jake feels unduly well-acquainted with the freckling upon his thighs. He encourages Matt's dissent, in a careful and unobtrusive way. But he appears kind to Jake too: waving his trowel like a manic conductor, as he leaps in and out of trenches, showing where walls and towers would have been, drawing inferences from changes in soil colour, seeing edges and lines where Jake sees nothing but muck. He seems to be filling a void left by Amy, who is present but withdrawn, friendly enough, but definitely somehow lacking. Damaged by disappointment, perhaps. Jake sees her go off with Zach at the end of the day sometimes, the secret facade of their relationship abandoned, as the rest of the team cluster around a firepit with cider and song. Matt, inevitably, has an acoustic guitar, and a small repertoire involving Dylan and Cohen.

Jake is there plenty, with pleasure, enjoying the sensation of space and age and bountiful nature. He knows that he is using it as a distraction, a focus to work his mind upon to stop it dwelling on his own fears and worries. The case itself – who murdered Jordan, and attacked him and Daisy – is paused, obdurate in its refusal to provide a solid lead to follow, the sense of peril in abeyance but not entirely absent. And Livia is resolutely unpregnant, the topic a silent, smouldering presence amid their apparent happiness.

One morning, the unstated fear rises sharp to the surface. Jake is gathering up the rubbish at Little Sky, an infrequent job because they use so little packaging and recycle most things, refilling bottles with milk and cider, composting food waste, turning over the fertile soil with used coffee grounds. What lingering refuse they have is stored in the basement, and Jake then takes it to the tip every few months.

On this occasion, he is alone down there, sorting things into boxes. It is cool and gloomy, a pleasing contrast to a day already starting to broil outside. A record is playing, some cello by Bach, and he is happily immersed in the preoccupying drudgery of it all.

A small sandwich bag falls to the ground, thick with what looks like wadded tissue. As he picks it up, he snags it against an old nail he has been meaning to hammer flat in one of the wooden columns. He drops the bag once more, and the tissue falls out, as does a small plastic oblong, tapered at both ends. It is a pregnancy test, and it shows two blue lines, clear and unambiguous. He stares at it in silence, the moment frozen in his mind.

Livia is not there, out on her rounds, and he doesn't know what to do or think. His heart is racing, his hands suddenly damp. This section of rubbish has been there for a while, and so must the test have been. So is she pregnant, was this a false alarm, has anything changed since? He has to know. He throws on a vest, pulls on some flip-flops, and heads off, blind really as to his destination, because Livia could be at any of the myriad farms nestled remotely in the area.

When he gets to Morse field, he sees her, resting her bike against the old drystone wall, as she pauses for breath. She drinks some water, that songbird throat pulsing, and then spots him. Face wreathed in smiles, cheery wave. It takes him back to the first time he met her, right here on this same scrubby patch of grass, this blithely beautiful woman, friendly and self-assured, as generous as the landscape she simply fitted within. She can tell he is deeply affected as she approaches, and he hands her the test, saying nothing.

'Oh, Jake. Come sit here out of the heat and let's talk.'

The day is indeed hot, the sky a deep blue going white at the edges from the glare of an angry sun. She takes him by the hand, her fingers cool and faintly calloused, a tiny detail he often noticed and loved, part of the very fabric of her, texture caused by the heavy lifting she sometimes did in her job. They sit in the shade of the wall, the thick grass cool and soft, the stone unyielding against their backs.

'Why didn't you tell me?' He wishes he didn't sound so plaintive, but he can't help it. He knows immediately that she is no longer carrying a child.

'Jake, I wanted to be really sure before I told you. So I kept testing for a week, and then I got a really heavy period, and I wasn't pregnant any more. I didn't want to cause you pain, I never want to cause you pain.'

He cannot but think of his experience with his former wife, Faye. The surges of hope and elation, the positive tests, her changing body, the signs of life within her that they meticulously dwelt upon and celebrated. And then the hammer-blows of disaster, violent and brutal, bloody and final.

Livia is stroking his wrist, her voice firm and confident. 'This is not like what happened before with you. This means nothing, lovey. I was pregnant for an instant, but no more than that. I knew, I think, at some level, that it hadn't . . . it hadn't, I don't know taken or whatever. And so I packed it away in my mind, and left you in the dark. Was that the wrong thing to do?'

She has turned to face him, tears soft in her eyes, the colour of the ground beneath them. He kisses one away, salty. 'I don't want you to bear any burdens like this on your own.'

'But I don't carry a burden. What burdens there are – they're somehow yours, not mine. You think you're trapped in a sort of nightmare; I know that things just happen, you know, biologically; that nature is fickle, and that our future is still free and full of hope.'

He feels the opposite of hope: visceral, tugging, immovable despair. It overwhelms him, a sensation of rushing blood in his ears. He breathes through it, and it passes. The sight and sound of his surroundings return, the knuckling prod of the stone at his back, the siren squeal of a falcon circling above them, its dark wings dipping and darting against the blue, the feel of Livia's bare arms against his.

'So what does this mean?' He feels slightly pathetic as he speaks, childish in a need for reassurance.

'It means nothing, my perfect man. It means we're having unprotected sex, and that's a beautifully imprecise, messy, unpredictable way of making a baby. And we might have a few moments of uncertainty along the way.'

He stretches his legs out, looks critically at a bruise on one of his shins, which he can't remember acquiring. The tug in his guts is there, but maybe a slowly growing feeling of reassurance. The soothing of sharing. 'I think you have to trust me, Liv, enough to tell me things. Though I'm not showing off brilliantly that I can handle it.'

She laughs, grabs his hair playfully, pulls him to her, then pushes him downwards. 'You do all right, you know. And I agree, full disclosure of every little gynaecological detail from now, every little change in scent and feel and . . .' She is now clambering over him, as he writhes and shifts and pushes her away. Her face is pressed against his ear. 'And discharge!' she bellows triumphantly as he falls to the side, laughing despite himself.

Later, after they have made love under the beech tree beside the house, where a blanket on heathery grass is as soft as a mattress, she traces her finger on the short hairs at the base of his stomach and they talk of nothing, the big subjects left behind for a while.

It frees him to concentrate on the case at St Giles more readily, with greater energy and determination, and the joyful nothing of their conversation finally becomes something. As he holds Livia, her head resting on the crook of his arm, a pleasant pressure, they talk about ideas for moving things forward. Livia is, like him, concerned that a killer has thus far gone free, and keen for him – and her – to find a way of fixing it.

He decides to check on Martha's progress by visiting her in person, though he knows she will need plenty of warning, as she guards her privacy even more carefully than he does his. He also thinks he can be more active in tracing the ownership of the land where the horde was found, as well as the final movements of Janet Sanders, if he makes a short trip to the city. He and Livia discuss the logistics of his journey, and then she looks at her watch – the only thing she is currently wearing – and swears exuberantly. She wriggles into knickers and jeans, pulls on her light sweater, which had been hanging, forlorn and discarded, on a lower branch of the tree, and hastens to leave for an appointment. As she kisses his nose, they inhale the same breath for an instant, eyes closed, remembering the accord they had struck about the future. And then she is gone, wheeling her old bike along a crooked path, lost to the landscape that embraces her fast.

Chapter Twenty-Five

Martha's house, the village of Mount Peel

Jake goes to the library to sort through his papers once more, more patient now for some connections to reveal themselves. After a while he feels stuffy, the dustiness of being inside when the weather beyond is so good. So he takes a pile of them out to the bench by the lake, where he can read in the citrus light of the early evening, the hot sun a little kindlier to the touch than before. He also brings the book Jo had sent him, which is a history of the local area.

    He flicks back to the index, and dips into the various passages that mention Wulfnoth. For all the common use of the name over centuries, there is clearly one historical figure around whom most stories seem to circle. He was a native Anglo-Saxon whose family had risen up in the unrecorded past to dominate much of the area, and whose life was the subject of a hagiography by a local monk, suppressed for years and then rediscovered. Wulfnoth was, it was clear, part noble, part folk hero, a mythologized man who came to symbolize resistance against the Norman aggressor. He paid no fealty to William the Conqueror, and held out for as long as possible against the invader's attempts to impose structure upon the land. Rear-guard fighting at night, full of bravado and risk, followed by refuge in a marshy land that only natives could cross with confidence. It was because of Wulfnoth that a new castle was built some distance from St Giles, as an impenetrable structure from which to dominate the surroundings. His life, in that sense, brought about the decay of the entire site, the end of its role as centrepoint to the community, the beginning of its existence as a relic of the past.

Wulfnoth's fate after that was unconfirmed, but it was clear enough that he had been eventually deposed from authority, and killed, perhaps on an evening ride in the woods, 'snuffed out like a winter candle', in the words of one of the chronicles. He had been buried 'upon the hill where his ancestors strode', in other words the site of the dig, and Jake wonders whether his grave had ever been properly identified. He presumes someone would have said if so, but resolves to chase it down nonetheless. The main point he takes is that Wulfnoth is an obvious alter-ego, a genius of the place itself, an easy reach for someone with a bit of knowledge of the area.

He idly flicks through the acknowledgements of the book, and sees that the author was grateful for help from 'the archaeological team at St Giles', and 'to Janet Sanders, for all her digging and delving on my behalf'. Another link in the chain between the site and this woman whose life seems to have simply stopped. Where is she, he wonders, as he stares out across the lake, the dipping sun pinking the water, turning the trees on the horizon into darker outlines, their vernal green gone from sight for one more day.

For the next couple of days, he works on the garden and addresses the multiplying issues arising from his own land at this period of nature bursting forth. He tends to the trees in Wolfe Orchard, where the seasonal drop of the small fruit is happening, and there is pruning and staking to be done. The very early cherries need collecting and preserving in stewing pots, where they bubble down into the sweet, jammy compote that he'll use in the autumn with cheese, and crispy pork, and even ice cream. Young strawberries are also coming, and he picks a bushel and gives them to Diana to take to school. There is also the messy job of clearing out some of the reeds at the side of the lake that have gone foul and stagnant, which involves him wading in, naked, pulling up old roots with his hands, the water muddying around his thighs, but cool in the afternoon heat.

He relishes the solitary moments, even the uncomfortable ones, where he is lost amid the expanse of it all. Some are both hard and peaceful: like cutting firewood for the winter in the soft shade of the copse, surrounded by coolness and plenty, the hum of ongoing existence. He exercises too, running and swimming, pushing himself despite all of the other activity, boxing beneath the beech tree until his arms turn rubbery and his sweat makes his eyes red.

On a late Thursday afternoon, he packs a small bag (bottle of water, trail mix, an omnibus collection of the novels of Ngaio Marsh, a writer he'd previously neglected, and is now rather enjoying) and spends the night at Livia's, enjoying the contrast between self-reliant loneliness and the messy comfort of family life.

The next morning he is off early, the night still clinging on, greying shadows and puffs of feeble breeze. His bus is late, and he is waiting at the isolated stop, long grass whispering in endless chorus behind him, when Amy drives past in a big Ford estate. She pulls to a dramatic stop when she sees him, easily done on an empty road, and puts the window down, gesturing cheerfully.

'Can I give you a lift, Jake? I've got too little to do, as you know.'

He leans forward, resting his forearms on the door. The car looks well-used, the home from home for someone who works outside in all weathers, dried mud fragmenting in the footwells, books and old clothes piled in the back.

'That's kind of you, but I'm off to the city. I know I've been useless so far, but I've not given up entirely.'

'Do you have a lead, if people still say that?'

'I'm actually looking into the disappearance of Janet Sanders, who I know you know. I've half an idea she might be caught up in all of this.'

Amy's brow furrows in thought. Her skin is battling with the summer weather, pinking on the top of her ears and the skin above her collarbone, but she looks robust and healthful. She is dressed for the warmth in shorts and a vest, and strokes her arm as it leans on the wheel. Tiny filaments of copper-bleached hair.

'Of course I know Janet, but I don't know where she is. Foraging about the place, if we go by past behaviour. Impossible to tie down.'

'Didn't you agree with contacting the police about her, when she went away last year?'

'I can't really remember. We definitely all talked about it. Daisy's always been more of a worrier than me, though.

Least said, and all that, is my philosophy. I reckon Janet will resurface when she wants to.'

'Did she fall out with you about the dig ever? I know she was interested in it.'

'God no, she was as enthusiastic as Jordan, always at the place.' She pauses. 'Dear me, do you think she might have been killed like him?'

Her surprise seems genuine to Jake. She goes on, her words more of a flurry and fluster now. 'I was getting used to the quiet of this summer. I'd hate to think there were other things still going on. You think we're safe now, don't you, Jake?'

A car passes, veering to the right. Its windows are darkened and they can't see the driver.

Jake scratches his beard. 'It seems to have settled down, sure enough. I don't know. I'll get in touch if I find anything when I get back.'

She rests her hand on his for a second. 'I'm grateful you still care. I'll tell Daisy you're still hard at it too. It's her last day today. In fact, I better get moving, so I can catch her.'

Jake steps back, and she moves off, exhaust huffing in her wake. Jake returns to his book and his solitude. When the bus comes, he is its only passenger as it winds down through the valley, passing St Giles on one side with its looming hill and its piebald curiosity of a church. He has to wait for another bus, then another, patiently reading and thinking, letting the swelter of the day pass over him. Martha lives beyond the suburbs of the city on the other side, in a place which is typically and, he feels, deliberately inconvenient to reach. By the time he gets there, much of the day is gone, and shadows have lengthened along the path to her house. It is big and broad and ugly, an affront to the surrounding countryside, which is pleasantly bosky and peaceful.

Jake rings the doorbell, and Martha appears, wheeling herself effortlessly down her wide hallway. She gives him a wink and beckons him in, before swivelling back towards the library, which is the one great open-plan room of this part of the house.

She talks over her shoulder. 'Jake, I won't say "welcome" because you're not. I know I said you could come if you had to, but surely even someone as bumpkin as you could have read between the lines.'

Jake smiles, and is almost entirely positive she is joking. He is more reassured when he catches up with her, and sees she has prepared a jug of what look like martinis, beaded with ice, smoking in the warmth of the afternoon. She motions to a chair.

'If you're going to hang out with me, that does mean heavy drinking in the afternoon, to warn you.'

'Did you treat Aletheia like this?'

Martha is pouring. 'No, I *like* Aletheia. She's pure in a way that even I respect. You're far too earthy to be polite to.'

'Well let me take the opportunity to say what a fucking ugly house you live in.'

She hands him a glass. 'Cheers to that. It's ugly and functional, like me. I can't bear all your twee Tudor cottages with their low beams, their winding little corridors, their uneven floors. Nope, I need modern, practical precision; none of your romantic guff.'

Jake takes a sip and winces. The martini is cold and appetizing but very strong. A couple more sips – Martha already replenishing her own glass – and he relaxes, as they talk about the case. She swivels to her computer, clicks on a file, starts scrolling down with her thumb.

'I've looked at Janet's movements right up until her disappearance, insofar as I can trace them by following her bank activity. She is pretty independent and isolated, a bit like you, but less hairy. She doesn't use her card much, but likes spending cash mainly, which she takes out every few months.'

Jake leans forward, puts his glass on a coaster that has the word 'DEFY' written across it in black letters. 'What's she up to, could it be paying off someone?'

'It's possible, but as likely that she's simply hoarding money and spending it only when she needs to. Someone who loves cash, distrusts the banking system, you get a lot of them around here actually. It makes tracking her difficult, whatever the reason, but I did my best. As you see, the last time she went into a bank, she took out two thousand, not an unusual amount.' She fiddles with the mouse and the screen cuts to inside a bank, CCTV footage, and they watch a middle-aged woman enter, well-dressed and brisk, face bright and devoid of conspiracy. The transaction is straightforward, and she puts the thick wad of cash in her bag before walking off.

Martha clicks it off. 'That was six days before her letter was found. It wasn't reported, as you know, for a few weeks afterwards. The police asked a few questions, but there wasn't much to go on. There've been a couple of requests for her whereabouts on social media, but nothing doing.'

'And nothing since?' Jake feels buoyant with the booze,

though he knows he will pay for it with a similarly deep drop at some point.

'No more card activity anywhere. No car for me to trace on CCTV. Nothing.' Martha is tapping her hands on the chair, staring curiously at Jake. He smiles back.

'So we think she's dead?'

'She might be.'

'Could she be Wulfnoth?'

She turns back to the desk, face animated, twitching the screen back into life. 'I knew I could rely on you to ask that. It's a neatish thought. I've looked at her farewell letter, and compared it against the others, and there's definitely some lights flashing here. You'll remember you noticed the use of similar phrases, like "tides of the past", and "the cold, dark soil" and it reminded you of Wulfnoth. Which could imply Janet was him, or had read his work. I lean to the latter theory, with one caveat. And brace yourself, my bearded friend, because this is fucking cool.'

Jake has pulled up his chair and sits close to her. He can smell the soap on her skin, which is wholesome and lavendery, sweetened at the top edge by the alcohol on her breath. He looks down at her legs, then reflexively makes himself look up. She notices, of course.

'Jake, it's OK to look. I had my legs shot off from under me. It's interesting and shocking by anybody's standards. And I know you've seen it before, but it doesn't get less interesting.' He realizes that, despite their shared experience of last winter, he has not spent long in close proximity with her. To him she is a friend and a force of nature, but mainly a presence on a screen, a sardonic voice criticizing his literary judgement.

Today she is in purple shorts, which cover most of her upper thighs; the tanned and freckled flesh above where her knee joint should be is smooth and rounded off. It stops where it shouldn't, an abrupt termination, an unnatural shaping, and it is impossible not to view it without pity mingled with curiosity.

He looks her in the eye with affection. 'I know, but I don't want to gawp.'

'I honestly would rather that than you kept your head raised to avoid noticing anything below my waist. You're like a Victorian vicar when you do that.'

'Fair enough.' He smiles, the effects of the early evening booze, and gives her an affectionate nudge, which she reciprocates, before her face stills and she focuses on the matter at hand.

'Now listen, gawper. We agree that the Janet Sanders note has superficial similarities with that first Wulfnoth letter, but look, I've had all the letters analysed, both for their physical and textual properties. Don't ask me how I justified it, you can pay me later.' She is showing a stream of tables, analytics that Jake doesn't really understand.

'This isn't your area, so you're going to have to trust me when I say: the first Wulfnoth letters were written by one person, but the last couple AND the Sanders letter were written by someone else.'

She slaps the table dramatically and leans back. Jake's head feels fuzzy, and he wishes he'd started the conversation before the martinis. He marshals his thoughts, and finds that his own intuition had been tending that way. 'So we're saying that there was a general crank, sending letters in the name of Wulfnoth. And then someone different got involved, people started getting harmed, and they used the same Wulfnoth cover for it in two letters: the letter before Jordan was killed, and the one after I took my Roman bath. And, separately, the farewell letter from Janet Sanders.'

Martha's eyes are alive. 'Wild, isn't it?'

'And how solid is the science on this?'

'Pretty solid. I got some good people on it. First, there's the paper stock, which is faintly different on the first set, as is the computer ink. They look similar, which would fit with someone pretending to be the original author. Then there's the textual stuff, the use of certain words, syllables and so on.'

Jake is nodding. 'I think I picked up on that. The later letters were simpler, bolder, I don't know, more blatant somehow. Even the biblical quotes were different.'

Martha is searching an email. 'You do have a talent for this, dear heart. Yes, you'd make a good detective. My text guy mentioned the use of Job references in the first letters, which were used mystically for dramatic effect. In the penultimate letter, we got instead famous biblical lines, the wages of sin one, and the vengeance one, unattributed to any book, as if they had been googled perhaps, or added to sound mystical without meaning it.'

Jake slaps his thighs with a thud, as he looks at the page on which the quotes are identified. 'And the last one, which came from Numbers in the Bible – I remember where I've seen it before. It was etched on one of the crosses discovered in the horde. It's part of the treasure itself. I read the papers again last night, and saw the translation in one of the footnotes. I hadn't made the connection, but there it is. So, not taken from Bible study at all.'

Martha pours another drink. 'This is good stuff. So we

think that there is another person, interested in the treasure and the dig, who killed Jordan, tried to knock you and Daisy off, and is using the original Wulfnoth as cover.'

'And where does Janet fit in?'

'The simplest answer is that she is the killer Wulfnoth, not least because the farewell note is in her name. But she could be his victim, and the real killer faked the note. Either way she's mixed up in all this.'

'We need to bring McAllister in, I guess. Let the police do some of the hard work to bottom it all out.'

'Hard work, you say, sipping your martini. This wasn't cream cheese for me, you know. But OK, you're right. You brief him when you get back, and start looking more closely at the Sanders property as a possible crime scene.'

Jake gives Martha a hug, feels the strength of her body, sinewy as a wild animal, in his arms. 'Great work, my friend. What else have you been up to?'

She wriggles free. 'We can talk about that later. I've now drunk enough to want to eat, so let's get some food in.'

Evening is creeping closer, and they sit in Martha's disordered garden, with pizza, drinking more martinis than Jake can reasonably count. Martha is playing blues music from her computer, muddy guitars and thick-throated laments. At one point, as the night turns black, and the moon hovers above them sterile and disapproving, Jake rolls a joint, which they share, their laughter brash and loud and unstinting, raucous in the rural peace. The night ends back inside, arguments about books they have read and loved and hated, their own stories of violence and justice, deaths avenged and criminals left uncaught. Neither of them say it, but it reminds them of the camaraderie of their old work, the feeling of people coming together in a team for the greater good. A pleasure they miss without admitting it. The last thing Jake remembers before passing out on a couch is grasping Martha by the hand in mutual consolation over chances lost and choices made. And then narcotic oblivion.

Chapter Twenty-Six

The National Archives, a riverside suburb of the city

Bright light rouses Jake rather later than normal, pouring in unfiltered through the windows, arrowing behind his eyes and adding to the pain in his head. He is sprawled on the couch, trousers askew on the floor, only in his boxer shorts. His hair lies matted across his face, his mouth dry and sour-tasting. He can hear someone singing softly in the room next door.

    He drags himself up, and walks to the window, shrugging his shoulders, which give off a disconcerting, cereal crackle. There is a half-empty glass of booze on the table, whisky he thinks when he sniffs it and feels the bile rising up in his throat. Outside, all is peaceful, the honeyed lustre of the morning sun lingering on the greens of Martha's wild garden. A thrush is bobbing on a nearby branch, curve-bellied and proud, its throaty whistle pitched somewhere between a pleasure and a pain to his sore head.

He turns as Martha enters the room. She looks fresh and unruffled as the bird outside.

'He wakes! How's the head, soldier?'

She hands him a big mug of thick, sweet black coffee, which he sips gratefully.

'Bacon sandwiches OK? They normally see me right in the morning.'

He nods, then winces as his head throbs. She throws him his trousers. 'The shower's through there. Get yourself cleaned up and we'll eat outside. And, yes, my shower is actually *within* my house, so that'll be a sophisticated touch for you.'

He takes his bag into the bathroom, which is big as all the rooms have been, easy for Martha to navigate, and clean and expensive-looking. He showers and brushes his teeth and stretches, and emerges feeling almost renewed. Only his red eyes, and the bags beneath, suggest the previous night's excess.

Outside, they return to their seats from the night before. Jake packs away the old pizza boxes, empties the ashtrays, carries the martini glasses back inside, holding them at arm's length like they might explode. As they eat, they talk about future plans to find the real Wulfnoth.

Martha is first to finish, putting her plate back on the table, crusts piled up neatly. 'I was up early, while you, you fragile bastard, were still snoozing away, and I emailed Al all our findings, and asked how she was doing on the land deeds for the site of the treasure. She thinks this is still a relevant bit to sort out. It looks like the land has been generally assumed to be owned by the church, but it's based on a rather confused assessment of the parish boundaries, not a straightforward deed, and has not been tested properly.'

Jake swallows carefully. His headache is receding and he is starting to think. The thrush has been joined by a companion, and they chirrup ebulliently at one another.

'So you're saying there's no direct document confirming it unequivocally?'

'Exactly. It's never really been an issue, because it's scrubland next to a historic site. Nobody would bother claiming it in most circumstances, and there is no clear person in the frame who's tried to.'

'And it only became valuable when treasure was found in it. But wouldn't the owner, if there is one, come forward?'

'They might not know, or they might be waiting to see what happens, or be waiting for some of the folk who found it to be knocked off by a lively relic of the early medieval period. Remember the landowner has to split the money with the finders.'

'It's all a bit vague.'

'That's why you need to do some actual detecting for once; clear it up. What are your plans now – please tell me you're not going to hang around here all day, are you?'

Another joke, he knows. But there is always with Martha an element of humour as defence too; she is expert at the art of self-armour when it comes to her attitude to the world, and people in it. He wonders whether she is completely happy. He has his Livia to dilute the loneliness, to bring life and challenge and company; Martha has nobody so close that he knows of. Maybe she doesn't need it. They both enjoyed themselves last night, at least; he is willing to bet on that. Certainly, the aches in his body feel like payment rendered for past pleasure, and are the more tolerable for it.

'Yeah, I thought I'd stick around your house for a few days, really go deep into the case, give myself a break from Livia and Little Sky.' He sees the flicker of surprise across her face, and grins. 'Kidding. No, I'm heading into the city as soon as I can face the day properly. I thought I'd go to the archives and try to look into the land records there.' He has another notion in his mind too, which he doesn't really want to bring up: Faye, his former wife, is now a property lawyer and might help him understand what he should be looking for in all of these records. He had texted her cautiously the day before, as his bus was coming into Martha's village; her response was quick and friendly enough. She was happy to meet him in a few hours. Is it expertise or absolution he is seeking, a sense of where her life is going, as his is heading towards a possible change? He is not sure of the answer himself.

'I'm going to leave you my Ngaio Marsh omnibus, give you a book to lose yourself in in the sun.' Martha, a self-professed aficionado of crime books, had never read anything by that author, and Jake delights in providing a recommendation and exposing her ignorance.

'Fine, but it better not be too fucking twee. Inspector Pinchbottle finds the murderer in the tea garden. I know you and your poor tastes.'

'All right, Raymond Chandler, calm down. Some would say you're a bit of a cosy author yourself.'

'Not to my face, and not more than once.' He laughs again, his voice less scratchy, becoming clear of last night's toxins. She grins too. 'You can take a Rex Stout book with you. I'm going to crack you in the end with him, I promise.

Plus, you remind me a bit of Archie Goodwin in it: tall, in love with yourself, useless unless you're guided by someone with a bigger brain.'

'That makes you the morbidly obese mastermind does it? Maybe you shouldn't drink so much.' She throws a cushion at him, which is as good an impetus as any for him to get going. Half an hour later, he is back on another trundling bus, this time heading for the centre of the city, a novel called *Champagne for One* nestling in his lap, ignored for the moment, as he watches the urban sprawl infiltrate the landscape beyond the smudged glass, substituting greys and browns for greens and yellows, jagged edges and concrete smears for the happy interwovenness of trees and fields.

He changes bus for underground train, happy to read to distract himself as the carriage fills up around him. Women in summer dresses, flushed and wafting air across their face, men with damp temples in T-shirts with sweat patches spreading insidiously out. The dense smell of summer in the city.

He has arranged to meet Faye at the gate of the park they used to walk in, ten minutes from their old house. He is a little late, and can see her waiting, hugging the meagre line of shade provided by an old horse chestnut whose branches overhang the park's brick wall from the inside. She is in a white cotton dress, her burnt copper hair bright and long, her legs rangy and tanned. She doesn't look much different from the last time he had seen her, when they signed their divorce papers a year ago; maybe a little fuller of figure, but strong and healthful. She smiles when she spies him, her teeth white and straight apart from the slightly crooked one on the top left that she always felt self-conscious about. They hug, hot bodies and recalled smells, of perfume and shampoo and the hint of perspiration, the sensory memory you never lose after you've spent years in a relationship together, a physical reminder that however far you go, however long you remain apart, you always cling to a little particle of past connection.

She pats his stomach with offhand – and, she might say, hard-earned – familiarity. 'You're looking good, Jake. The wild life still suiting you.'

There is no resentment in her voice, or attraction. He hopes his sounds as neutral as he thinks he feels. There is no flutter in his stomach anyhow, no lingering desire, no manifest regret. 'Right back at you, though you manage it in a city, so you must be doing something special.'

She approaches the park's entrance and they come close again as they pass through the double gates, black iron railings sloughing their paint to reveal the rust beneath. 'I'm looking after myself, definitely. I work from home a lot more now, get to go to the gym, do some Pilates in the park. I still swim in the river twice a week, which is nothing to you, I know.'

Jake had used to gently mock her wild swimming, her regular morning trips to the river with her friends, which always carried the aura of some mystical ceremony, an act of communion somehow denied to him as a male outsider. His mind flits briefly to the spring at St Giles, another place of water and ritual, and recalls what happened there.

'I think doing it in your own lake is less intrepid somehow.'

She shakes her head, and the bronze tresses bounce. 'Your own lake. Goodness me, Jake, everything really has changed for us.' She squats in the shade of a huge oak tree, the ground hard and unyielding, then settles back, her legs straight, her upper body propped up on taut arms. There must have been no rain here for several weeks, the parkland is already browning all around them, a parched and scrubby expanse. Jake eases himself down a few feet away, noting the stubborn scattering of cigarette butts, shed without thought like leaves from the tree.

They share perfunctory news, Jake not too willing to give much detail of his life. Faye had read a little about his adventures – the capture of the rapist, the breaking-up of the criminal conspiracy No Taboo – and did not seem over-eager to explore his triumphs. There is a pause and then she looks him in the eye, as if unsure of herself. 'Jake, I need to tell you: I'm pregnant. Just over fourteen weeks.'

He tries to process his feelings. He sees in her pale grey eyes joy and fear and hope. And over twelve weeks is significant, a happy milestone, though they had lost pregnancies twice after that point. He touches her hand, hot and sticky all of a sudden, a prickliness across his body. He swallows with a dry mouth.

'Faye, I'm happy for you.' A simple statement that could conceal falseness, but does not. He is happy, or at least supportive. He is envious too, the pangs of worry lurking that a healthy pregnancy for her means the fault for the previous failures must be his alone.

'The doctors are keeping a close eye on me, and they say all is well.' She pauses. 'It's a girl.' Her voice cracks with emotion and pride, a touch of melancholy perhaps over what might have been. Her eyes are damp. He leans forward and hugs her, feels new meaning in her softness, the gentle expansion of a body making a home for another.

They talk a little about her plans, to move somewhere

more suburban, what she will do for work. Out of courtesy, they mention her partner little – a lawyer himself whom Jake has never met – except when she says, 'of course, we're getting married before the birth.' A faint surprise to Jake, he doesn't see her as someone bound by convention, but he mouths the expected platitudes.

Faye seems more relaxed now her news is broken, and she moves the subject towards the legal advice Jake is seeking. He reaches for his notebook, where he has jotted some questions he needs answering, and starts the lengthy process of telling the story of his investigation. The park is filling up a little. Ahead of them two women arrive noisily, tinny Europop emerging from one of their phones. They spread a vibrantly pink picnic blanket, strip to their bras, hoick their skirts and prostrate themselves in the searing hot sun, light glinting on milk-white skin. To their left, two men, topless and lean, are practising some martial art, delighted at the sweaty motion of their own muscled bodies. Out of sight someone is playing a guitar, 'Wonderwall' inevitably, the words recognizable even if out of proper earshot. A gaggle of teenagers walk past, over-dressed in the heat, hoodies and low-slung trousers, laughing excessively over jokes they don't really find funny.

Faye is generous with her expertise, and as articulate and intelligent as Jake remembered. They had met when she was a newly qualified criminal solicitor and he was a fast-tracked policeman, but she had eventually decided to move into the more sedate and remunerative field of commercial law. She explains clearly how conveyancing works, the use of title deeds, and their ordinary simplicity. 'In most cases, you have the deeds, they get preserved by solicitors and passed on each time the property or land is sold. Most places have had some form of transaction involving them in the last fifty years or so, and that means ownership is pretty visible and undisputed.'

'The bit of land I'm interested in is unbuilt upon and pretty featureless. It's never been ploughed up, from what I can see, which is why the horde lay undisturbed for so long.'

'So deeds for land like that, especially when the land is close to religious sites, may be sitting somewhere in the archives, especially if the conveyancing was last done in the nineteenth century or earlier. Churches got granted plots all the time, basically as sops to consciences in the wills of the rich and guilty.'

'From what we can tell, the church has had a casual claim on this bit, but based only on local assumption, and old parish maps that seem to accept it as part of the overall enclosure.'

Faye picks at a piece of grass which is dry and dusty. 'That might be all there is. But you should go to the archive. There may be a copy of a document called a final concord, a proof of sale, perhaps to the church or from the church. That's recognized in law, and would act as a very solid piece of evidence in support of ownership.'

'And if I had that, I could claim the land as mine.'

'Yes, and to answer your obvious follow-up, that would then enable you to claim your share of the proceeds of the treasure.'

Jake lets this percolate. He can't quite see how this connects all the way to a motive for murder, unless the records decisively tip the scale in a straightforward dispute between two claimants. The silence is filled by the chatter of people all around them, and the never-ending thrum of traffic and aeroplane noise. The sunbathing women have flipped over, prone, their paperbacks folded down, their heads lolling to the side. A family cricket match has begun despite the heat, excited appeals and lusty swings.

They talk for a few more minutes, Jake asking questions and continuing to make notes. Faye checks her watch and starts to stand. Her skin is mottled pink where she has been sitting on the hardness of the ground, and she brushes herself down briskly. They follow the path to a different exit, walking companionably, hot glare of light after the sanctity of the shade. He looks sidelong at her as they go, recognizes the details he has seen so many times, that catalogue of repetitive intimacy: the downy hair on her arms, gold-red in the sun, the tilt of her cheek, the blue-green veins running down her neck hummocking beneath her skin, the plumpness of her lips. He can tell she is anatomizing him in return. They laugh.

'It *is* nice to see you, Jake. We'll always have a good solid thing to remember about us, you know, even as we both change and move on.' They reach the gate. He is heading off in another direction, still through the park, to the old police building. They hug, a lingering grasp of affection and nostalgia. Faye clutches his arms and leans back to survey his features once more. 'And I want you to be happy. I know we've not talked much about your relationship, but I can sense it's given you peace, makes you contented. I want nothing but good things for you, you know – and that means a family we could never have.'

'I feel the same, I really do.' His voice is choked slightly. They press close once more, and then she is gone, swallowed by the bustle of the city that stops at the wall of the park, like the last ebb of an unruly tide.

Jake hurries, sweat trickling down his back, so he has a few moments to catch up with Aletheia at her office. They talk, compare notes, and trade amused complaints about Martha. Everything feels a bit surface to him, though, as if his meeting with Faye has touched him on a deeper level and he needs time to work out the appropriate response. To be content or jealous, relieved or sad, pulled back to the past or pushed onward to the future. He is unsure of himself, and that troubles him. He has to be quick with Aletheia anyway, because the archive building stays open only for a few more hours and he wants to be back at Little Sky tonight if he can. Whatever he feels about Faye, he knows the city is now irrevocably lost to the past, a foreign country of noise and dirt and heat that can't be escaped or softened, the churlish, grating throb of people and concrete and metal.

The archive library is cool at least. He gets there as the day begins to dwindle, the train to the suburbs busy with office workers heading home, uncomfortable in jackets and dresses, looking forward to shucking their professional wardrobe as soon as they get through the door. They cross the river over an old metal bridge, rusty and solid, the water beneath a sullen brown, turbid with old mud.

Jake would have liked the archive to have been Victorian, red-brick with ornate shelves and massed banks of documents, Dickensian clerks flitting about in pale shirtsleeves, like scraps of paper in the breeze. But it is a modern, glass-and-chrome building, the reading rooms as bland and anonymous as any office in the city, upholstered in a pondy blue-green that makes it feel like you are vaguely underwater, the documents stored somewhere no doubt temperature-controlled and appropriate but lacking in anything approaching romance. He has emailed ahead, misusing Aletheia's authority, and a middle manager is there to greet him, fuss-potting in an ill-fitting suit, his skin carrying the pallor of the permanently indoor. Some contrast to Jake, whose outfit makes the archivist wince, dressed as he is in loose, navy cotton trousers and a soft white T-shirt, his skin darkened by the constant companionship of the sun, his beard and hair unruly, brown fading into light-bleached blond.

Jake is escorted to a small cubicle on the edge of the main room, the closest thing there is to a private space in this age of open-plan democracy. There is a large box on the table, the lid removed, a canvas receptacle within, the leather brindled and stained with age.

Jake's escort, Mike, is stern and formal. 'Normally we do not move documents of this age from the central filing room, but we have been made to understand.' He allows himself a certain insubordinate inflection to the word 'made'. 'We have been made to understand that this might be critical to a murder investigation, and you have the delegated authority of a senior figure in law enforcement. My superiors assure me the paperwork is in order.' His raised eyebrows suggest scepticism that a man looking like Jake might be allowed within feet of his precious and perishable material.

Jake claps him on the shoulder, more boisterous than he needs to be. 'Great work, Mike. I appreciate you. Any tips on how to handle this?'

A grimace, showing tombstone teeth, each one yellowing at its borders, unappetizing. He hands Jake some surgical gloves. 'My "tip" is to handle everything as little as possible. I shall remove all the documents and lay them on the table. You can then examine them and make notes. I shall be in my office over there for you to indicate when you have finished. I must remind you that we close at seven today, and I'm not instructed to keep things open beyond our allotted time.'

The man's Pooterish approach is annoying, but Jake swallows any satirical response. He needs to look at this and leave; there is no point in any complicating wrangle. He keeps his patience, standing bouncing on his toes in the corner, while Mike lays out the documents. Most of the other occupants of the vast room are packing up ready to go home. One or two are still lost in their research: an owlish young man frantically taking notes, pushing his glasses up on his nose every few seconds; a black woman of middle age, almost concealed behind a tottering stack of files, whispering inaudibly to herself; two students, scuffed bags at their feet, leaning over what looks like a map, searching for a grid reference.

Mike is finished. As he walks stiffly out, he points to the emptied box. 'I've left the register in the base; that's the list of all who have accessed this in the last hundred years. Before that, we do not know, I'm afraid.'

Jake walks to the table, flexing his fingers, stretching the latex that clings offputtingly to his skin. The neat label on the box refers to 'The parish of St Giles and surrounding area, 1542—', with no end date. Faye had explained that many records like this began around the dissolution of the monasteries at the time of Henry VIII, when old deeds were destroyed and land peremptorily reassigned from religious houses to private individuals or sometimes the local church.

This seemed to be the case here. There are not many documents, and most are hard for him to read. Each is still enclosed in a plastic folder, but Jake gets an immediate and pleasant sense of their age, the elegant penmanship, black ink in whorls and curlicues, stroked into words that linger physically but with meanings fading inescapably into anachronism. He leans forward and sniffs, a sort of dried decay in his nostrils, like autumn leaves as a fire begins to smoulder. The folders have been labelled, in more legible modern handwriting, which acts as a helpful primer for him. They show that the hill site itself was given formally to the church from the sixteenth century onwards, together with all of the structures and holdings upon it, 'though they be in much disrepair'.

There is a beautiful hand-drawing of the area, dated from sometime in the eighteenth century, which confirmed the area owned by the church, and was tantalizingly ambiguous about the fields beneath the hill. After that a couple more documents that related to the village itself, when the church began to sell off property in the nineteenth century, and then a folder with nothing at all inside. Jake's interest begins to rise: the title label states 'assorted farmland in the St Giles area, 1912', which sounds innocuous enough, but clearly has been removed by someone at some point thereafter and not replaced.

There is nothing more of interest from what he can see, and Jake exhales thoughtfully, discovers he has been holding his breath. The room behind him has more or less emptied, a big circular clock above the central pillar indicating that it is not far from seven o'clock. He can see Mike still peering at his computer screen, skin bathed blueish in the glare.

Jake moves quickly to the box, and pulls out the register. He sees his own name transcribed at the bottom with the day's date. Above that is a record of the two other occasions where the file has been requested, both in the last year or so, both by the same person: Janet Sanders. The second time, Jake can tell immediately, was almost a week after she was supposed to have gone missing.

Chapter Twenty-Seven

Livia's garden, Caelum Parvum

It is very late by the time he gets back to Little Sky, the night hot and breathless and still. A series of trains and buses, with long, isolated waits between each, had lulled Jake into a stuporous state; a hamburger and Coke at the final station left his mouth sour-tasting, as if the unhealthful city were clinging to him inside. The walk back – across silent fields, soft and bounteous, lit strangely by a blood moon stained reddish around the edges – restored his circulation and awakened his senses, now alive to the restless manoeuvrings of nature all around him.

Long summer nights are not made for sleep. Dawn is never far away, the sky always seemingly on the turn greywards, as if the light of the day has been merely trapped and cannot but seep back out again. Jake likes being outside in few clothes at times like this, comfortable with the air gentle on his skin, moths fluttering against the lamps, the neighbourly owl hooting progress reports of its nocturnal hunt.

He leans back and smokes a small joint, trying to settle the emotional roiling within, the after-effects of his talk with Faye. A record is playing through the open windows of the house: the *Concierto de Aranjuez* by Joaquin Rodrigo, perfect summer fare, lustrous guitar amid the pomp of the strings. Jake wonders when he will finish making his own guitar, whether it will produce the right sounds when he does. And then he'll have to teach himself how to play somehow; the never-ending work of the autodidact.

Detective work is a pleasing distraction, so he hunkers down under the arbour light, a piece of paper against a book on his knees, trying to fix a timeline for all that has happened. He divides the Wulfnoth character into 'A' and 'B' based on the belief – and Martha's insight – that two separate people have been at work.

> First five years: dig begins, Wulfnoth A starts writing letters. Four received.
> 27 March: horde discovered by Jordan, Daisy, Amy and Zach.
> 13 April: fifth letter from Wulfnoth A.
> 14 May: final use of Janet's credit card.
> 19 May: file last accessed in archive; subsequently missing.
> 20 May: Janet's letter discovered.
> 18 June: Janet reported missing.
>
> NOTHING FURTHER FOR THE SUMMER
>
> 27 April: first Wulfnoth B letter.
> 1 May: Jordan murdered.
> 2 May: attack on Jake.

3 May: second Wulfnoth B letter.
4 May: attack on Daisy.
?

Jake wonders why he has seen no evidence of another letter after the Daisy incident, a message of warning or gloating. Wulfnoth B seemed to like to reinforce action with prose, but had not done so on this occasion, and that was over a month ago. He notes the thought carefully. He also makes a note to speak to McAllister, explain his own recent investigations, see whether any further official progress has been made.

No further ideas present themselves, other than the nagging feeling that the missing archive document must be crucial. Presumably, it assigned ownership of the land beneath the hill to someone, and thereby disadvantaged someone else. But who? And was it worth attacking three people over? He puts the paper down and wanders to the lakeshore, listens to the slip-slop of the water, watches clouds pass in front of the moon, dark and aimless wisps, the red tint unnerving. He wonders whether he will see Faye again, whether he would like to. At least here in Little Sky he is spared the constant torrent of their shared social media, the glib and mendacious updates of friends about their lives. He wouldn't be able to cope well with unsolicited photos of an increasingly pregnant Faye, followed by the coy announcement of the birth, the dad, bleary-eyed and self-conscious and proud, clutching the white-wrapped package filled with wriggling, mewling, successful life, then the forthcoming tales of family adventures captured in pixel-perfect instants, birthdays and holidays, brothers and sisters. Life as progress.

That might still be his own lot, of course, whatever doubts are gnawing at his insides. And even without it there is love and family in his future, peace and joy amid all this generous gift of the surrounding land. He sighs, loud in the black, and heads off to capture some sleep if he can. It will be another day dawning soon.

Light comes and, after a few hours of restless doze, he gets up to exercise, his penance for his couple of days off, and the excess of his night with Martha. The morning is warm and sticky, the prospect of the clear spell breaking, and the cold water of the lake is delicious and cleansing after his run. He swims hard, feeling each muscle in his arms and back throb with health, rising himself up on two legs at the far beach, his feet smothered by the silky, silty mud, letting the water, luminescent with sun, pour off him. Things move all around him, tiny fish the size of tadpoles at his knees, shoaling according to some unseen pattern, bees and butterflies in the hedgerow beyond, scraps of living colour.

At the bottom end of his run, he had come close enough to Sherlock Beech and seen Livia's magenta nightgown, drooping, forlorn, in the windless air. Their signal, still a thrill, to meet. He doesn't linger but swims back and showers, and walks down the sun-firmed pathway towards Parvum.

Livia answers the door urgently to his knock, mouth pressed against his, pulling him in with a welcome savagery. She draws her head back and grins, cat-eyed and splendid.

'I missed you,' she says.

He kisses her in return. 'Well, it's nice to be missed. Did you hang your nightie on the tree because you couldn't wait for my sinewy body?'

She is deftly removing her clothes as she knees the heavy door closed. 'Less talking, more stripping. I'm ovulating right at this very minute, and my temperature is perfect.' Soon she is naked, and Jake cannot see or think of anything else.

Afterwards, they compose themselves and drink coffee in the back garden. Livia is now languid in her movements, all urgency dissipated. 'It wasn't *only* for that I wanted to see you, actually.'

Jake shifts position, uncomfortable on the iron patio furniture that Livia has never got round to improving. 'How hurtful.'

'Don't be silly, I got a call from Daisy. She's planning on coming back to see Amy and the dig, and has got cold feet about it. She wants us to check her house out first, make sure all is secure. I said of course we would, if you're free.' She pats her forehead in mock dismay. 'Sorry, I forgot, you're always free.'

He sips his drink and tells her everything that happened while he was away. They had previously discussed the prospect of him consulting Faye, so she is not completely taken aback by that part of the story. But he can sense her stiffening a little when he talks about it. Nobody, howsoever secure, likes to hear about intimate moments between ex-partners. But she can also sense the sadness within him, knows how his mind will be fixating upon the likelihood of his own biological failure, him being the reason for all those tragedies with Faye, foreshadowing helplessly more tragedies to come, worse even (if such things can get worse), with her.

They hold hands in companionable silence, and both decide to leave the subject to one side. Livia puts her feet onto the rickety white table, turned a sort of dirty cream by age and weather and disuse, and talks about Janet Sanders. 'So is she Wulfnoth, is she dead, is she in the middle of nowhere unaware that this is all happening?'

'I have to think it's option one or two, surely. And why did she remove the deed from the archive?'

'That's obvious. It must have contained information that incriminated her somehow.'

'And that would be . . .?'

'Stop leading me, Jake. You've been working through this in that big old brain of yours for longer than I have. It could've shown that she owned the land, or one of her grandparents or whatever did. And if she did that, that could make her Wulfnoth.'

'But why hide her ownership, and why try to kill people for it? She could have claimed her share of the money anyway. Maybe the document showed that she didn't own the land, and she had to get rid of it.'

'Could someone else have removed it?'

Jake stares out across the rape fields that sit in the dip of the land behind the garden, heading off towards the hazy horizon, bright yellow as English mustard. 'There's no sign of anyone. Nothing quite definite, as with everything in this. You know, there does feel like the shape of an answer is there, though it's not quite graspable. God it's annoying.'

Livia picks up their empty mugs. 'For a second I was afraid you were about to wax lyrical about the power of story and narrative, and the endless search for meaning by the detective. You've done it before.'

He swats amiably at her bottom as she passes, but concedes the point. You can get mystical when you live in the middle of beautiful nowhere, and think constantly about the patterns of life and death and crime.

'Come on, Inspector Alleyn.' Livia had been reading Ngaio Marsh too. 'Let's have a quick look at Daisy's place, so I can reassure her.'

They drive, windows down, to Sexton Blake, speaking of Diana and the prospect of her response to a baby if one ever came. She had overheard them talking about it a week ago and burst into tears, saying – with commendable honesty – that she didn't want to share attention with anybody. In Jake's absence, she had been a bit surly and uncooperative, and Livia had come close to losing her temper entirely. She was worried that they had lived alone together for so long that another child might drastically unsettle her.

They are debating the likelihood of this getting worse as Livia inches the car up the driveway, gravel pinging rhythmically on the car's chassis, when their conversation is ended abruptly. Daisy's house, rising up out of the garden wilderness, is there, but damaged, defaced: all the windows at the front smashed, the wall by the door smeared with orange paint; thick, dripping letters spelling two words: 'GO HOME'.

Chapter Twenty-Eight

Daisy's house, the village of Sexton Blake

Livia stops the car and they rush out, Jake disappearing down the pathway at the side to check the full perimeter of the building. He can see from the dryness of the paint that this attack had not taken place in the last few hours, so there is no reason to suspect the perpetrator is still around. He shouts over his shoulder for Livia to be careful, though, and notices, when he looks back, that she has picked up a wrench from the back of the car, and is hefting it in her hand thoughtfully.

The back of the property, which looks out onto a large, little-tended lawn, high-walled at the end, is untouched, as are both of its sides. It must have been a frontal assault and no more. Jake takes the opportunity of peering into each window he passes, and can see nothing much altered within. The poignant neatness of an abandoned house.

Livia is looking through one of the broken windows at the front when he returns, her weapon resting on the bench by the door. A lacy curtain flutters inside, moved by the wind that is now starting to pick up. There is the smell of rain in the air, the sense of change afoot in the sky, cloud thickening in menacing clods above them.

Livia reports what she can see. 'It's not rained at least since this happened. Inside isn't much damaged, apart from the big stones that went through the glass, and the shards of the stuff everywhere. Some leaves have blown in too.'

Jake examines the front door, making sure not to touch anything. 'It doesn't look like anybody has got in. Do you feel up to checking inside? She told you where the spare key was, didn't she?'

Livia nods, and goes to the bench. Underneath one of its legs lies the key, cobwebbed deep into the dusty earth. She picks it up, and the wrench too, her face a picture of determination. Jake's laugh breaks the tension for a second. 'Shitting hell, Liv, I'd hate to come through a door and have you waiting for me with that in hand.'

She grins fiercely, but does not let it go. Jake takes the key and turns it in the lock, using his thigh to shunt the door open. They step in. The thick silence of a deserted building, no hint of the hubbub of occupation, the radio or music or the chunter of a washing machine. On the mat beyond the door there is piled-up post: flyers, a copy of the *Shire Gazette*, and poking out innocuously from beneath it, the folded cream paper of what can only be a letter from Wulfnoth.

Jake motions for Livia not to touch it, though she knows that already. His voice is soft, but clear in the silence of the house. 'When's the paper delivered? That might help us work out when this happened.'

'Fridays, I think. I'll ask Jo. What shall we do, get out and call Daisy?'

'You do that, and McAllister too. I'll have a brief look-see around the place, but it doesn't seem like our person came inside.' Livia lets herself out, bunching her sleeves around her hand so she leaves no fingerprints. Jake can hear her talking briskly to the policeman. He pads the whole place carefully, his steps absorbed by thick old carpet. Daisy had clearly packed up for a while, everything was neat and clean, put away and controlled, he thinks, like the owner herself. There is little sign of visible comfort here: all the books in the study are hardbacks, lots on history and archaeology, no guilty secrets, no novels of romance or mystery, no old favourites with cracked spines or bloated by bathwater. There are a few photographs too, just one in the living room, sepia and faded, an old family portrait that looks to have come from India. No sign of a boyfriend, nothing recognizably male anywhere.

Jake feels he is coming close to prying, so moves back to the front door, and out. Livia is sitting on the bench, frowning in thought, faint lines that disappear on his arrival.

'Cops are coming, McAllister himself, he says. He wants to see if this has any connection to the dig.'

Jake settles next to her, hand resting on the cool skin of her wrist. Thunder grumbles overhead. 'And Daisy?'

'She sounded awful, choked. She's on her way; I said we'd wait for her. She'll want to fix up these windows before she stays here. If she wants to stay, that is.'

He is quiet for a moment, feels the press of warm air against his skin. 'What do you make of her really?'

'I feel sorry for her. This house, the wildness outside, the sterile order inside. It's all so tense. She's so buttoned up, you worry about her coping. But I do like her. I think. She's successful, strong, capable somehow.'

'No boyfriend I can see.'

She pinches him softly. 'Men aren't everything, you terrible old sexist. I reckon she'd be quite a hard person to get cosy with – can you see her romping in the living room, or having a giggle in the kitchen?'

The ridiculous thought hangs in the air because McAllister's car crunches up, a clean, maroon Honda estate, a richer, more attractive cousin of Livia's shabby old thing which it parks behind. He is typically neat and formal, grey suit, clean white shirt, his thick black hair not moving in the breeze.

Jake fills him in on what they have found. He rolls his eyes when Jake mentions their brief foray inside, but Jake forestalls complaint by reminding him that it was he who asked for their assistance in the first place, not the other way round. McAllister is equable as ever, and takes the point. He surveys the outside carefully, sniffing the paint, tracing the outlines of the holes in the windows, his movements precise and careful. Then he walks back to the bench.

'So nobody inside, no forced entry. I wonder if anyone heard anything, though the house is well set back from the road, I suppose. I'll get someone to take a plod around and ask. And do we think Wulfnoth did this, or merely left the note?'

'Maybe the note will tell us.' This is Jake, weighing up the same thing.

'So we better have a wee look then.' McAllister snaps on some gloves, opens the door and retrieves the letter, taking his time to memorize its position within the pile of correspondence inside. He squats down and opens it, holding it up so all three of them can read it at the same time.

You don't belong here, the land is not yours.
I could not have been clearer, or fairer in my warnings, could I? After the policeman manqué, there had to be a reckoning for the nosy film-maker, only interested in cheapening all that has gone before you, merely for a few moments of empty entertainment.
I watched you linger, nosing, snuffling the site, an unwelcome presence. And I willed the wall to fall upon you. You are lucky it did not drive you permanently into the earth that you regularly defile.
'And they conspired against him, and stoned him with stones at the commandment of the king in the court of the house of the LORD.'
2 Chronicles 24:21
I have driven you from the field, I will drive all from the field. You know in your heart you don't belong here. Get out while your heart still beats.
Wulfnoth

McAllister stands, wincing as his knees creak. 'Thoughts?'

Jake looks back at the house, the windows crazed with damaged glass, the vile message on the wall. 'I'd like to know when all this happened, and whether the note came after the damage or before it.'

'After, surely?' This is Livia. 'The note carries the same message as the graffiti – "you don't belong here" is the same as "go home". Our Wulfnoth comes along, smashes the place up, scrawls the message and then posts the letter.'

McAllister purses his lips. 'I see what you mean. But the letter makes no reference to breaking things up, does it? It's in our chap's character to talk about what he's done in these letters, tell us it outright. He only talks about the physical attack on Daisy.'

'The stoning reference could be about the windows as well as the wall falling on her.'

Jake nods. 'That's true. But we keep coming back to the same question: why bother doing all this in the first place? Can he really be that angry about people digging about in some old field? And why wait a month after trying to kill Daisy before getting in touch? The note is definitely recent; it was nearly on top of the pile. Chief, what sort of forensics can we get here?'

'I think you know the answer to that. Not much. We can dust the door for fingerprints, and the rocks maybe. That's about it.'

'Can you scrape some of the paint and send it to Aletheia? She may be able to do some magic on it, if she gets the chance.'

'Of course, but why?'

'I'm interested in timings and chronology and also the idea of letters being sent versus words being scrawled on a wall. Why do both? It's an odd change of pace.'

Spots of rain, thick and glutinous, begin to fall around them, puffs of dust on the ground, sounds of gravelly clatter on the old tiles of the roof. McAllister decides to marshal his forces from back at the station, and leaves Jake and Livia to wait for Daisy.

They sit in contemplative silence. The bench is under

the eaves, so they can observe what soon becomes an unremitting downpour with comfortable dispassion. Talking is difficult now in any event, such is the noisy ferocity, the flood of water pounding down upon them, as if the entire sky has released its pent-up fury with everything below. The wind drops at least, so little rain is blown into the house, and the temperature starts to fall, Livia shivering and wrapping herself in a cardigan. There is no sun, gun-coloured clouds, oppressive and immovable.

It must make the sight of the house all the more bleak for Daisy, who pulls up half an hour later in a black BMW. She gets out, heedless of the rain that soaks her immediately, pasting her hair against her head, making her clothes sag sadly. They hear the wail that emerges from her lips, a cry of despair and anger, and Jake hurries out to take her by the hand and bring her to cover.

She stares unblinking at him, face still distorted, her body stiff, until Livia inveigles herself between them, kindly and soothing. Daisy dissolves into tears, that careful rigour of her outward personality impossible to maintain in the face of it all.

Inside, cups of tea made by Jake, the kitchen cold and sterile but a refuge from the water runnelling down the windows. McAllister has called to say that forensics and other police representatives will be there shortly, so there is time to talk. Jake shows Daisy the Wulfnoth letter, which he has left open on the hall table, so nobody needs to touch it.

Daisy is philosophical, introspective. She shudders as she talks about being told to 'go home', a relic of abuse thrown out so regularly, and with such impunity, in her eighties childhood.

'My name's not Daisy, you know.' She is addressing Livia directly, Jake a cautious presence in the background. 'It's Harmeet, which means "friend of God". But my parents decided that we needed to fit in, have names that people could understand and find acceptable, even pretty. So Daisy I became. A little English flower.'

'Does that bother you now?'

'A bit. I mean, I'm part of this country whatever my name, however brown I am. I see why they did it, but what good did it do, I'm still being told to go home, aren't I?' There is a dry sob in her throat.

The rain continues to hammer petulantly amid the pauses. Daisy gets up to pour more tea. Jake sees the opportunity to get practical before they are hurried off by the pestering formalities of the police.

'When do you think this happened, Daisy? Have you been back here since you left a few weeks ago?'

Daisy sits down, shaking her head. 'No, I saw you, finished packing, said my farewells at the dig, and have been in the city the whole time since. I was coming back next week, as I said to Livia. I don't know what I'll do now.' Her hands are worrying at a handkerchief, her fingernails pale and almond-shaped.

'Do you have anyone checking up on the place?'

'I had a cleaner come and do a once-over maybe two weeks ago, I can check the date. All was well then.'

'Strange how Wulfnoth waited all this time before writing to you.'

'None of this makes sense to me, Jake.'

'That's it. It doesn't make sense to me either. Where does all this anger come from, about archaeology for God's sake?'

A wan smile. 'Archaeology is all about unearthing the long-buried, maybe that stops it being ordered and rational.'

Livia pats her warmly. 'Maybe. Anyway, this could be the end of it. The dig is barely functioning, you're moving on, let's make sure you get this cleared up, and get on with things.'

Daisy is bitter in her response, a flash of passion. 'Could you move on, could you put up with being attacked in your home, called a foreigner in the place where you come from? Could you?'

Livia doesn't answer, nods sympathetically. The question hovers there. And before it can be answered there is a loud knocking at the door, stern and official. Soon the kitchen is filled with the bustle of police, polite and clunking and intrusive, and Jake and Livia decide to withdraw.

Daisy walks them out, arm linked with Livia, the cloud of dismay passed from her features. 'I'm sorry I was so abrupt, Livia. You've both been very kind. But I feel so angry, violated even.'

'What will you do?'

'What can I do? Fix the windows, brush myself off, and get on with life. I need to talk to Amy about our plans for the future, so I guess I'll get off to the city tonight, and come back as planned in a few days. I've no desire to stay around here for the next week, brooding and starting at shadows.'

They stand at the door, watching the rain continue to fall. Daisy presses their hands warmly, and they run for the car, the thrill of the cold water on their necks, the childlike sprint for shelter.

Chapter Twenty-Nine

The horde trench, beneath the hill at the St Giles site

Two days of dreary rain, an unleashing of water, often in unremitting torrent, making the river overrun its banks in places, turning fields into shallow lagoons, trees like shipwrecks surrounded by muddy grey expanses. Jake hunkers down in his workshop, fitting together the body of his new guitar, which all slots neatly into place, like some sort of minor miracle. He is content inside, the air cool enough for a fire, heady smells of wood shavings and glue, some piano music rising out of the noise of the rain. But he feels oppressed if he does nothing other than shelter from the weather, so he carries on his routine of running and swimming, and long walks in the woods, where the dense trees turn the rain into an insinuating mist, making the place feel like one big bank of dampness.

Swimming in the lake in these conditions is glorious. The rain is warmer than the main body of water, and it feels nice to shift between the two, diving down so the pattering drops are no more than tiny freckles on the surface. The storm-dark gloom all around contrasts with the narrow plane of light above, which you can surge towards and then burst through, back to the world of downpour and colour and noise.

The next afternoon he is walking carefully around the flooded extent of the riverbank, his normal route blocked by the overflow, splashing through the puddles in his shorts and a thin running top. It is raining once more after a respite in the morning, the sky merely sullen, water-gravid, before the downpour returned with new vigour. He has worked out that the fewer clothes in the rain the better; water runs off his legs with no discomfort, his feet are bare in a pair of hardy flip-flops. He could be on an Australian beach as much as the landlocked interior of the English countryside.

But being this wet is still too wet, he thinks, and he knocks on Livia's door, hoping for a towel and coffee. She emerges, expecting him, with both, and a message from Lily.

'She called an hour ago. Apparently she wants to see you at the site. She's worried about Amy, wouldn't say anything else.'

'Can you give me a lift?'

She is pulling on a pair of waterproof leggings – not subscribing to Jake's minimal clothing theory – her smooth brown legs disappearing within the crumpled blue material. Her hair is tight in a bun, a single desultory curl dangling by her mouth. 'If we go now. I've an appointment with a stable of horses, but you're not so much out of my way if I get going.'

He swigs down his coffee, scalding his throat, rubs his

hair with a towel, and pulls on a spare T-shirt, then his damp coat. 'Ready as always.'

The car crawls in the weather, dimness descending into the valley, thick and misty, the landscape a greeny-brown blur through steamy windows. They slow when they approach the hill, Livia looks across and strokes his damp beard. 'Take care, lovey. I hope everything's all right. Come home and wait for me once you know.'

He leans over and kisses her lips, which are warm and familiar, not quite sweet. 'I'll be OK, and I'll see you at home. You stay dry if you can.'

Easier said than done for him, as he opens the door to a blustery huff of wind, spraying water all the way across his front. The clouds do seem to be thinning, though, and the thrum of the rain on the puddled ground is lessening slightly. He watches Livia's car as it moves off, solid beams of headlights leading, making the afternoon seem unduly like evening, before he makes the climb up the hill, mud streaking his feet and legs as he walks.

Lily is waiting for him at the top, shifting restlessly from side to side. She is engulfed in a giant green windcheater, from which her bare legs emerge into black, tattered boots. There is warmth as ever in her hug, then she leads Jake to the office. It is empty, and he can see nobody on the plateau itself, no cagoule-clad enthusiasts digging in the murk. They shuck their top layers, and sit down in the kitchen, which is messy and cold, the sterile light above them jaundicing their appearance, making Lily look strained.

'Where is everybody?'

'Off. When we saw the weather system coming, Amy told us to take the three days as holiday. We're on such minimal duties anyway. Matt and Elaine took off for a jaunt in Paris, I'm not sure about the others. We were all going to meet up again tomorrow morning.'

'That sounds reasonable.'

'And then yesterday I got a message from Amy asking to meet me this lunchtime. I showed up and nobody was here. I've tried calling her, tried calling Zach, and nothing.'

'From what you've said, couldn't the two of them be off, screwing each other's brains out somewhere?'

'Lovely thought, and one which obviously popped into my mind. But she sent another message that's been bothering me. When I agreed to meet, she sent this—' Lily gets out her phone, which is old and bulky, with a leopard-skin casing that has been smeared with mud. She shows him the text exchange. This is the final message from Amy:

> I'm going to meet Wulfnoth first. I'll explain when I see you.

Jake can see Lily's responses, all unanswered, which began with a series of question marks, and then continued with further queries as her concern rose. He scrolls back to the beginning of the exchange.

'You were supposed to meet her at the horde trench down below. Any reason why?'

'None that I can think of. She could have as easily suggested here, or the gate, or the parking spot down below.'

'And no sign of her?'

'Nothing. Brian says he's heard nothing either. When I got here I waited in the trench in the sodding rain, then came here to fret a bit. After a while I thought I'd call you. I mean the Wulfnoth thing could be a joke, but that's not her way really. She's nice, Amy, you know, a little bit motherly to me, but not really a ton of fun. I'm worried, Jake, can you help?'

He feels a twinge of concern, as he has more than once in this whole confusing episode. 'Let's have a poke around before we call the police. I'm sure McAllister will help, but we should try to work out what we're asking him to do. We should start at the trench and go from there.'

The rain has finally stopped, and the ground is spongy with mud, making them slither as they come down the hill. At one point Jake slips, and Lily catches his arm. 'Flip-flops on a dig site, you're such a city boy.' He laughs even louder when she slips herself and he grabs hold of her elbow to steady her in return.

'Oh, shut up.'

They get to the bottom where Livia dropped him off, and follow the track – now little more than a smear of mud and crushed grass, smelling of the must of wet earth – curving around the base of the hill. The stream that follows the edge of the field is high, charged with rainwater, and bustling noisily towards the river, spilling over at points to fill dips of the land with its murky superfluity.

The trench itself is sodden inside, the soft soil turned glutinous and sticky. And there is nothing obvious to see within. It was well excavated in the past, and little has changed. The sun pokes out from behind a cloud, uncertain, casting watery light upon them that is not quite warming. It glints on some metallic object in the distance. Jake pulls himself out of the trench, hands making the damp turf squelch as it takes his weight. He walks over the rise and sees a car, stopped incongruously in the middle of the field. He calls out to Lily and they walk towards it. He needs no help in identifying it, he's seen it before: the big blue Ford estate owned by Amy.

It's empty when they get there. Jake is brisk in his assessment: the engine is cold, the ground beneath a bit drier than beyond, as if the car had been parked before the most recent set of downpours. When he looks through the windows, the interior seems the same as he recalled it from the accidental meeting at the bus stop: messy, practical, an extra room for a busy outdoors woman.

Lily blows some hair from her face, scowls thoughtfully. 'So she came here. Where the fuck is she then?'

'Would it be normal to park here? Why not go to the usual stop beneath the gate?'

'No idea. What do we do now?'

Jake is thinking. 'I guess we know she got here, so we should at least check the site itself to try and find her, and if nothing then contact the cops.'

Lily pauses, then folds her arms, wrestling with her emotions. She looks young all of a sudden, and fearful. 'If she's here and OK, we'd know, right? I've been noisy enough. You mean check the site for a body, don't you? Oh God.'

Jake gives her the most encouraging smile he can muster. 'Let's not get ahead of anything. It's a big site. She could be at one end, sheltering from all that rain. It would have covered up all our noise, I should think.'

Lily looks unconvinced, and abruptly sets off back to the path up to the gate, moving at a determined pace. Every few steps she calls for Amy, her voice loud and piercing. When they reach the path, she starts to jog, an awkward, rolling gait, her big boots sticking in the heavy ground. Her breaths heave, her voice becomes frenetic. Jake follows her, watching her disappear over the brow of the hill with some concern. When he gets there, she is out of breath, chest heaving, panic writ large across her usually sardonic features. She grabs at him, buries her head in his shoulders. 'Jake, what's going on?'

He sees she is struggling to maintain control, and recognizes she needs a task to focus on. 'All right, stay calm, let's come up with a plan. I want you to get to the office and call your brother, get him here to help us. Then call McAllister – his number is on the desk – and tell him what's going on. See if you can find out where the whole remaining dig team is, keep on calling their phones until you get through, and write down anything you learn about where they are and the last time they saw Amy. I'll start going around the site; come find me when you've done everything, or send Rose after me if he gets here quickly.'

Lily bites her lip, and nods. 'Roger that, captain. Sorry to go all wobbly. But I've got a bad feeling about this.'

'I know exactly what you mean. You get started and so will I, and let's put a stop to all this worrying.'

She enters the office with a clatter, and he is alone on the plateau, clouds glowering above him, the air damp, the patch of land a vast mosaic of brown and green and grey. It is comfortless and bleak, as wild a vision as it must ever have been over the last several centuries. He heads to the furthest side of the site, and walks inward, looking for flashes of colour and movement. A couple of magpies flutter on to a half-collapsed wall, a flash of black and white and imperial purple, startling him with their stutterings and cacklings. He reaches the tower and looks inside, where all is wet and dark, the old stones looming up impassively over his head. There is a stampede of varying footsteps in the mud, but they could have been made at any time recently.

He is glad to emerge into the air. Evening is coming apace, the sun abandoning its attempt to creep out from its heavy cover, greyness descending upon the hilltop like a shroud. Jake calls Amy's name once more, but gets nothing. He pushes on, criss-crossing the site twice more, halting at the spring, which roils and belches but appears to hide nothing.

Behind that, he walks to the first room of the Roman villa, the home of the hypocausts where Daisy had been attacked. There was some half-hearted tape cordoning off the room, fluttering disconsolately in the breeze that is starting to rise. Jake feels it as a chill, penetrating his damp clothing, making him shiver uneasily. There is no place of concealment here, nothing to see apart from the pillars and buttresses of history. No Amy.

Jake knows from the plan that the excavation continues further into what would have been the main living quarters of the ancient home: the baths that connected to the spring, the workshop, the kitchens and the bedrooms for family and also for slaves. He can see Amy's sketched plan in his mind, and follows it as he enters each new area, some parts of which have been dug down right to the old floor, others mere suggestions of rooms, a collapsed cornice here, a rubbly patch of earth denoting a doorway there. The mess of the dig, the half-churned earth, the trampled grass.

The slave quarters are a hundred yards further back, a design decision to keep the help away from the quality, he supposes. He makes for it now. There is a tumbledown wall, stones pale in the half-light, and the remains of an old archway. Beyond that are steps down into an excavated room, now cast in shadow. He feels his skin prickle as he approaches, makes himself move forward quietly. His steps dislodge some stones, fragmentary and shapeless reminders of the bygone, a texture under his feet that he will recall without reason afterwards when his mind keeps restlessly returning to the scene.

Down he goes into a small enclosure, the walls now higher than his head. Inside, dirt and damp, a stone niche that may or may not have been a bed. And lying upon it on her side, clothes in disarray, scraps of flesh a lurid pink among the greys, is Amy, eyes lolling, dead to the world. Passed away, passed over, the same past tense as everything within this unfortunate place.

Chapter Thirty

The slave bedroom of the Roman villa, St Giles site

Jake had been steeling himself subconsciously for this, but the image that fixes itself in his brain is no less shocking. He can feel acid rise in his throat, that strange commingled emotion of pity and anger and fear. He stays at the edge of the room, not wishing to contaminate the scene. Amy is, beyond all doubt, dead, her face vacant, her limbs composed in an obscene tangle, her body – cow-heavy, without life – half sliding from the stone surface. Unnatural stillness. Blood that must have pulsed crimson around her body is now pooling behind her head, a terrible hue of black, faint sheen upon it like oil. There is no sign of the murder weapon, just its irrevocable impact on her matted skull.

Jake hears a noise behind, and he turns, walking straight into someone, who grips him tightly. It is Rose, looking for him, and Jake pushes him backwards, out of that place and up the steps into what is left of the light. The wind is up again, sending ripples across the pools of water lying flat upon the grassy land. Jake keeps hold of Rose's jacket, looks him in his startled eyes.

'Don't go in there. We need to stop anyone going in. Fuck.'

Rose is calm, even tender. 'Is she dead?'

Jake nods, looks over Rose's shoulder and sees in shadowy outline Lily standing with someone by the tower. 'Are the cops here?'

'One is. That new Scotch lad everyone seems to like. He wasn't far from here and came when Lily called.'

'Go get him. I'll stand watch.'

Rose doesn't argue, but heads off across the plain, head bowed, the sky purpled above him as the sun finally sets unnoticed behind a bank of cloud. It will be dark in less than an hour, the moon unlikely to peek through. Jake feels the cold in his bones, his clothes too thin all of a sudden, the sense of chill seeping out upon him from the wet ground and dank stones. He moves back to the doorway and waits for McAllister.

He comes at a jog, pausing to grip Jake by the arm, a gesture of recognition and empathy, then steps down into the quarters. He emerges five minutes later, face set, those hairy paws of his clenching and unclenching.

'Oof, what a mess. You never lose that feeling, the blow to the gut when you see it, do you.' He gives a lugubrious sigh. 'What do we think's gone on here?'

'Looks like a blow to the head, she's half-dressed, which makes you think sex or rape, I suppose. This was a place she'd been known to meet her assistant.'

'Why was she here at all? This is no evening for romance.'

Jake explains all he knows about the day, based on what

he had learned from Lily. McAllister nods as he checks his phone and sends a flurry of messages, the signal intermittent, but good enough to begin the process of establishing the crime scene. When he is finished, he peers at Jake. 'You and I'll stay here until we lock this all down, then we better have a longer conversation about where we are with all this. No way will it be a quiet one – the press will, right enough, link it to Jordan and the TV show and we'll have a carnival. I'd like to have your involvement as my trump card, so let's keep that on the down-low, but I can see I'll be chasing my tail for a while in the meantime.'

Jake has been mulling. 'You don't need me to suggest finding Zach, Amy's boyfriend or whatever he is. He has to be suspect number one: first as a sexual partner; second as one of those who found the treasure.'

'And the only one of that merry band not yet attacked by anyone.'

'The thought did occur to me. And we should find out now, this evening, where everybody in any way connected to the dig is, and where they've been all day. How long do you think she's been lying there?'

'Not overnight, I wouldn't have thought. The blood hasn't congealed.'

'And her car looked like it had been in place for a few hours, not much more; the ground beneath was dry.'

Tacitly, they have walked back to the edge of the room. It is almost in total shadow now, Amy's white top, her ghostly skin – her breasts and the tops of her thighs left cruelly exposed – glimmer in the twilit softness. McAllister sighs. 'Mebbe we could have got ahead of this and stopped it. There must have been a way we could've known more.'

'There's always more to be done, more you could have

done, more you missed. That's the job.' Jake is right, but he knows it is scant consolation to Amy. He feels a deep throb of guilt, as well as sympathy for her, and is glad when two uniformed police officers emerge from the dark to relieve them, their fluorescent jackets bright like fox eyes. He and McAllister plod back to the entrance of the site. An ambulance is waiting at the bottom of the hill, a necessary but futile formality, and Lily is seated under a light outside the office, drizzle glinting like fireflies in its yellowing beam, as Rose whispers consolation in her ear. She has finished giving her initial statement, and a nearby policewoman is making notes, sheltering under an overhang from the roof.

Jake shakes McAllister's hand, and agrees to meet the next day. He then lets Rose drop him off in Parvum, the journey silent and sad, Rose's normal trance music silenced for once. After the car disappears into the black, Jake pauses outside Livia's cottage, brain flashing through possibilities, ideas rising and ebbing, a nameless suspicion starting to take shape, if only he could find the evidence to solidify it, make it stand up as true.

Chapter Thirty-One

Mortuary, Kings Markham Hospital

The day dawns bright and clear upon a deluged landscape. Water everywhere you look: the river, coursing high and loud, frothing along its sides with impatience; the road, black with wet, pools glinting in its dips and recesses; the thick grass and tangled plants of the hedgerow all bejewelled with droplets, sparkling inanely as if all were well in the world. Summer turned upside down for the moment.

Jake had waited until Diana had gone safely to bed, a picture of pyjamaed innocence, before opening some brandy and talking to Livia. She patched through – after some complication – a video call with Aletheia and Martha, who formed an attentive, stoic, hard-bitten audience.

Martha had spoken first. 'That lad Zach looks in trouble first and foremost, doesn't he? We shouldn't overthink this in the first instance. A spurned lover takes his bloody revenge. That's your boy ninety per cent of the time.'

'But is he really Wulfnoth?' This was Livia, who sat quietly sipping her drink, the emerald ring on her forefinger softly striking the balloon glass in her left hand.

'That's a different question. We've got to tackle the most recent murder on its merits first up. If it connects with everything else, we go from there.'

Jake stretched. 'Christ, it must do that, it must connect. A death we feared could happen has happened. I'm open-minded on Zach. It could be him as our killer, and our Wulfnoth. They need to find him quick, whatever. What do we do in the meantime?'

Aletheia had answered this. 'I'm coming down. This is a big enough case now, and McAllister said he would welcome some assistance, so I can get involved a bit more formally. As a consultant. I can be there tomorrow afternoon once I clear the chain of command issue. I'll email him now to warn him. Martha, can you start looking at the dig crew again, check the alibis as they come in? Then I suggest we let McAllister work the scene, and we go in on the Janet Sanders angle. She's still the most underdeveloped part of the case. And if it turns out Zach killed his boss stroke mistress and this is all a big coincidence, then so be it.'

Nobody believed that, least of all Jake. But he was glad to have Aletheia's urgency and presence and that calm brain power which had helped him so often in the past. It gave him a feeling of confidence to sit alongside the anger in his stomach. The brandy had tasted sour in his mouth, and he had never been a consolation drinker, so he soon brought the conversation to a close and allowed Livia to take him to bed.

Now he is up early, before Livia or Diana, up with the light of the day, and appreciating the quiet. The sun is rising warm, and he lets it sink deep into his bones like a balm. A coffee steams beneath his feet as he sits in a patch that catches the nascent glare of the morning, bare toes stretching out against the coolness of the muddied ground. He hears a car approach from some distance, the purr of its engine loud in the peace of the dawn, merely the dripping of leaves and the cautious cooing of the morning chorus for it to overcome.

It is McAllister, driving slowly past the house. He waves at Jake, who has come to lean against the fence. He stops and gets out. He is freshly shaved, his chin smooth, the hint of blue-black hair impossible for any razor to remove entirely.

'I hoped you'd be up. A bit of news. The coroner has agreed to an urgent autopsy, given the importance of the case. Can you be at the hospital by eleven? Should be over by then. And lover-boy Zach has been spotted, packing his bags and looking for a bus about an hour ago. We've got him picked up, and I was going to question him afterwards. You could tag along to that too. Our boy has some answers to give.'

Jake looks at McAllister, the light striking his face and making him look young for a second. 'You're very generous with your cooperation.'

McAllister is suddenly serious. 'I appreciate your skills, Jake. Really. And I'm glad to have you, and your old oppo Aletheia when she comes. I also appreciate results, bad guys behind bars. I'm old-fashioned like that.' He yawns, takes a glance at Jake's coffee, and steals a sip, then smiles and drains it to the dregs. 'I needed that. So, Kings Markham Hospital at eleven? See you then. Regards to Livia.'

He putters off, and Jake heads inside for another coffee.

Livia and Diana are up, still in their nightclothes and not talking. Another row had taken place, which must have been brief and immediate, still based on that underlying tension over the question of their family expanding. Jake shakes his head: amazing, he thinks, so much potential grief based on a result that he might not physically be able to achieve, however much he wanted it. Diana is rolling her eyes and folding her arms, and Livia walks out of the kitchen to avoid an explosion.

Jake sits down next to her. 'What's the problem, donkey?' A nickname from somewhere early in their relationship, possibly based on the film *Shrek*, though neither can truly remember.

'I told Mum that I don't want a baby in the house, and she went mad. Again.'

Diana is swirling her spoon in her cereal bowl, making it clink, semi-defiant. Jake leans back, speaks softly. 'Who's to say we'll even have one? But tell me, do you know what it's like to be a big sister?' Shake of the head.

'Me neither, I never had a brother or a sister myself. But I wanted one. I was really jealous of the other kids who had them. Think of all the things you can do with a little one: you can teach them stuff, you can look after them, you can be the grown-up that they most want to be like. And, you know what? We can pick the best bits for you. Because you and me don't know how to be a sister or a brother, we can make up how we want to do it as we go along. You can leave all the disgusting bits to us, the screaming and the waking and all the pooing. Everywhere. All over the place. You did that, you know, when you were little.'

Diana snorts her milk. 'Don't be gross, Jake.'

'I'm serious. You can be the fun sister, and when you get

sick of the baby, you can leave 'em to us, and go back to being brilliant Diana. I can't see what's so wrong with that myself.'

'But I don't want to share *attention* with anybody.' She must have read that somewhere, he thinks, or seen it on one of the wide-eyed, gauche American sitcoms that stream freely on her device. There is a faint transatlantic tilt to her pronunciation of it that must come from the screen.

'You say attention. Let me tell you a secret.' She leans her head next to his as he whispers. 'You won't always want attention. There'll be times you'll want a break from Mum and me, will be bored by hanging out with us.'

'Never, I promise.' She mock pouts, eyes laughing.

'You will, and then you'll be pleased there's somebody else in the family to focus on. Then you'll get older and be more embarrassed of your old mum, and her boyfriend who looks like a tramp, and you'll feel it even more. Look.' He slumps in his chair to meet her eye-level. 'Serious point now. You're the luckiest and loveliest girl in the world, you have an amazing mum, and all this happiness. Imagine if we could add another bit, make it happier, make it crazier, more fun, give you someone extra to love, wouldn't that be worth it?' He pokes at her waist, and she fidgets and giggles. So he does it again. 'I think you're in the best position, really. We may never have a baby, in which case things stay great, or we may have one, in which case they get even greater. What do you reck?'

Diana is silent, then smiles fondly. 'Maybe that is acceptable.' A word she had learned early, and still used with a winning formality, her expression regal, her bottle-green eyes wide and calm. 'But why don't you know if you can have a baby or not? I thought it's a thing you grown-ups did.'

Jake senses a trap here, is suddenly aware of Livia snorting behind the door. 'That's maybe a topic to talk about another day. But can we be cool with Mum in the meantime?'

'I'm always cool, dude.'

'Glad to hear it.'

He hears Livia move off, clumping about noisily. And, with that, the rhythm of the morning increases pace, the frenetic process necessary to get Diana out of the door and into her lift to school, a question of logistics that always seems to have to be learned anew each day: rushing and bumping and squalling, the hunt for lost socks, and water bottles, reminders of after-school groups, money for some charitable drive. There is fluster and frenzy before the door slams shut and the rural peace intrudes once more.

Livia is still in a rush, about to make her rounds on her bike, which leaves the car for Jake to use later. She heads out of the back door while he straightens the kitchen a little, before rushing back in unannounced to throw her arms around his neck, bury her face in his chest. 'Thank you for being so nice, lovey. You're going to be such a good dad.' A big plop of a kiss, and then she is gone, the fruit smell of her shampoo lingering in her wake.

Perhaps, he thinks. *Perhaps never*. The knot within his stomach tightens before he pushes the idea from his mind once more.

Two hours later he is parking Livia's Volvo by the back door to the mortuary, which is tucked away in a corner of the hospital. He'd been here before, last winter, when he had pretended to be a workflow consultant for the NHS Trust, using the name Rex Stout and an identity card faked by Martha, to find out where a body had been hidden. It had proved successful too, not least because the attendant was working there only under sufferance and was not especially interested in security questions.

It had been bitterly cold back then, the middle of the worst snowstorm in decades, the wind knifing across the open spaces with cruel intent. A caressing breeze tickles Jake's beard instead as he emerges from the car, but the good weather hardly renders the scene much less bleak. Hospital car parks are desolate places, with their industrial waste bins, the never-ending parade of shuffling patients or bowed-down relatives, bile-coloured dressing gowns incongruously out in the open, no happy chatter or laughter, the faint smell of bleach and mortality seeping from the buildings. And those buildings, he thinks, are always ugly, with their damp brickwork, failing concrete, shabby glass mostly occluded by milky-blue drapes, lurid signs everywhere pointing to various departments suggesting torment and misfortune: burns, oncology, radiology and – of course – this crowning jewel, the mortuary.

He pushes open the door, and enters a place that is, despite the brightness of the day, saturated with appropriate gloom. He can recall the same pot plants in the corner, in a state of sympathetic decay, the battleship grey of all the walls, the complete absence of life and liveliness.

Sitting at the desk is the same man as before too, whose name Jake has forgotten. He is short, overweight, with thinning, honey-coloured hair. At present, he has his eyes closed and is exploring, with a relish approaching rapture, one of his ears with a straightened paper clip, excavating deeply, moaning under his breath. He waits a few seconds before acknowledging Jake when he comes up to the desk, then a few more before removing the paper clip, setting it to one side with every appearance of delicacy.

Jake is friendly. 'I'm here to meet Chief Inspector McAllister, who's attending a post-mortem, I believe.'

'You don't remember me, do you?'

'I certainly do. We spoke a few months ago, when I came in.'

'So what's my name?' His beady eyes bore in at Jake, beetle-black, magnified by his thick spectacles; his dignity very much on parade, poised, even eager to take offence.

Jake cannot think of what he's called. He half-remembers that the guy had a surname that sounded like a first name, but can dredge up nothing further. Apart from one other fact. 'I'm sorry, I can't remember. But I do remember that you were writing a novel, which was really exciting. What was it? That's right, a futuristic spy story. Orwell meets Le Carré – it sounded great. How's it going?'

The man's face relaxes, his chest – such as it is – puffs up noticeably. 'That's exactly right. I knew it was a memorable idea. Look.' He turns his screen to the side so Jake can see lines of ordered prose, littered with exclamation marks. 'I've written fifty-nine thousand nine hundred and forty words of it. Motoring along now. I'm John, John Dennis, by the way.'

'I'm Rod, Rod Alleyn.' Jake can't help devilling him slightly.

He sees a slightly querulous look appear, as if Dennis is trying himself to remember the name Jake had previously given, but it is replaced by his more urgent pride in perusing his own text. 'I'm at a good bit now, actually. My spy thinks he's been blown, so he and his secretary, who's also his lover – and also, unbeknownst to him, an agent herself, who's only half-turned against the establishment – are on a train hurtling through a flooded landscape. They're debating whether to sleep together.' A wolfish leer. 'I'm fairly confident they're going to say yes.'

'What's the book called again?'

'You'll like this, Rod. It's called *Two Legs Bad*, a bit of a nod to old Orwell there. It's because enemies of the state in this book lose all individual identity and are known as Two Legs.'

Jake is nodding along, uncertain how to end the conversation, when he hears movement through the double doors behind Dennis's desk. A head pokes out, hair dark and thick, a badger from a burrow. It's McAllister.

'Ah, come on through. I'm sure chappy here will let you in. He was more interested in staring at online porn when I came in an hour or so ago.'

Dennis refuses to be cowed by this, looks defiantly back at McAllister. Jake can see various tabs at the bottom of the screen, beneath the novel text, with labels like 'Asian' and 'MILF' and 'hot tub'.

'Good luck with the book.' He passes the desk to where McAllister is holding the doors open for him.

'Appreciate that, Rod. Maybe you could read it when it's done.'

Jake is through the entrance before he has to come up with a polite response to that one. They are in the anteroom to the main post-mortem suite, brightly lit in garish yellow, cold and unwelcoming. McAllister nods at a further set of doors. 'We shouldn't have long to wait.'

Jake can see two people through the glass, in medical robes and masks, moving around a central table. On it lies

Amy's body, arms by her sides as if in repose, but nothing else suggestive of rest or sleep: the ugly greying tint of her skin, the open wound in her stomach and chest – for her viscera to be emptied and prodded and measured – the sense of nothing more than her animal weight, a carcass of fat and bone and muscle, with all life drained from it. The smell of bleach is a high note in his nostrils.

'You never get used to all this, do you?' Jake recognizes he is more or less repeating what McAllister had said when he first saw Amy's body yesterday.

McAllister hands him a file, wincing in sympathy. 'Here's what we've got, while they're tidying up in there.' A common enough verb for a policeman to use about an autopsy, but it still jars: nothing tidy about the fleshy mess within, nothing neat or in its proper place. Jake makes himself flick through the notes in front of him, McAllister providing an expert commentary, his soft, feathery voice never rising or falling.

'She died as a result of more than one blow to the head with a heavy object. Perhaps a stone. The first strike would have knocked her out, then two maybe three more to finish her off.' He is miming descending blows. 'Her attacker was strong, but not especially so. She must have been facing away at the time. I've got some folk hunting the stone, but, you know, finding a stone in a dig full of stones won't be easy.'

Jake's voice is oddly thick as he speaks, it sounds unrecognizable to him. 'Her clothes – they were disordered when we saw her, weren't they?'

'She'd had sex in the hours before her death, with someone wearing a condom. Nothing to suggest rape. When we discovered her, her bra had been removed, and her top pulled up, her trousers and underwear partially down. So one theory is that the murder came at the conclusion of the sex act, perhaps with her vulnerable and facing away. But there's no direct way of linking the two purely by forensics.'

'Where was her bra?'

McAllister grabs a notebook from his inside pocket, looks through it. 'We've not got a record of finding it yet. I'll chase that one up.'

'It's pointing towards Zach, isn't it, chief?'

'I think we probably don't have quite enough to charge him already, but more than enough for me to have a good go at him. You buy him as the killer of Amy and Jordan?'

Jake weighs it up, his head bobbing from side to side. 'I don't know him well enough. I didn't warm to him, I'll say that, but that doesn't mean anything. A crime of passion' – the cliché comes easily to his lips – 'like this is different to coolly supplying someone with acid to drink, though. And yet, whoever did this, we probably have to suspect of both crimes. I don't know, if I was going to murder my lover, would I do it like this: leave her in my place of work with her trousers pulled down, looking for all the world like I'd been the last person to be with her?'

'Unless it was passion, or rage, and he stopped thinking clearly.'

'Then is he our letter-writing figure, plotting away for weeks on end?'

'All interesting questions. I guess we'll have to ask him some of them. You'll come with me to watch through the glass?'

Jake nods. 'I'll follow you there.'

'You'd best park around the back. There's lots of other news around, thankfully, but we've one or two of our friends in the press circling, and I don't want to over-excite them. We should also have notes on where the other members of the dig were yesterday to look at when we get there. I'm not sure we'll find out much more here.' He waves through the glass, and the pathologist backs out through the doors, mask hanging uselessly around his neck. His gloves are spattered with dark liquid.

'I don't think there's anything else I can tell you. Death was around eleven or twelve yesterday morning. The deceased had a couple of glasses of champagne in her stomach, alongside some grapes and some sort of pastry. Romantic fare, it pains me to say. And, as I have noted, sex around a similar time.'

Jake asks the question. 'So is this evidence consistent with a champagne breakfast with sex thrown in shortly before she was killed?'

The pathologist inclines his head, hairless, the light reflecting off the curve of his skull. 'That seems perfectly reasonable.'

'Were there signs of the sex being outdoors, dirt on the knees or hands, bruises, bits of gravel?' Jake thinks back to the site of the slave quarters, thinks of how any such assignation might have been possible there.

'There are marks on her knees and elbows – pressure marks, you understand, where she may have been supporting her body – but they could have come from sex in any location. Her body had been drenched from exposure in the rain, and there was some mud on her clothing, a small amount on her lower back where her top had slipped.'

'But not her hands, the front of her clothes, or anywhere else?'

The doctor takes the file and flips through his notes.

'No, everything as described. Gentlemen, I've got another appointment to go to, thankfully a little happier than this one. As ever, you have my every hope that you'll find the person responsible for this. She was a strong, healthy woman in every other respect; had a long future in front of her. She was ripped from the world with no regard or respect.' He bows his head once more and withdraws.

Chapter Thirty-Two

Interview Room A, Meryton police station

Police stations are not much better-looking than hospitals, but Jake always warms to them more, probably from force of habit. Custom always brings comfort eventually. In turn, doctors might be intimidated by a police station, but happy in their own sterile places of noise, and smell and human misery. All institutions are somehow intimidating to the non-initiated. Visit a school out of hours, or an office block, or an army barracks, and see if you feel at home there. You can't.

Jake parks at the back as instructed, in a small enclosed space with only one other car, a pale green Vauxhall Astra, which looks to have been there a while. He knocks smartly on an anonymous door, opened by a heavy-set constable in uniform, who gives him a friendly smile. His brown hair is cropped short, but already thinning at the front.

'Nice to meet you, sir. The chief told me to welcome

you, make you one of our obscenely bad cups of coffee and see you to the right room.'

'I appreciate that, Constable . . .?'

'Stevens, sir. John Stevens.'

Jake thrusts out a hand, which is swamped by a meaty palm and pumped vigorously. 'I'm Jake. No longer a copper, so just Jake.'

'Right you are, sir, right you are. But so as you know: in this building, we remember what you did with that rapist, and those child snatchers, as well as our old boss on the make. And let's say, you need anything doing, anyone sorting, you only need to say the word. We've got your back.'

He reinforces this literally with a respectful swat on Jake's shoulder, and then leads him down the corridor, as dreary and functional as the mortuary had been. They pass various office doors, a bulletin board carrying faded photographs with captions biro'd on them, in-jokes for the small group of people who spend most of their lives in these cheerless confines. A sober injunction to take care of your physical and mental health is pinned in the corner, and Jake wonders how often it is heeded. Certainly Stevens here looked a little on the bulky side for any of the more active aspects of the job.

Through some double doors they go, and Stevens pauses to pour Jake a coffee in a chipped white mug. There are three officers in here, a young blonde woman on the phone, two others – an older woman and a man of similar age, greying at their temples, not in the finest of shapes themselves – sprawling without any apparent interest in their surroundings. They do stiffen when they see Jake, and acknowledge his presence with respectful nods. He can hear them whispering as Stevens ushers him through the door into a darkened room to their left.

This is familiar territory too for Jake. He'd sat in galleries such as this before, perched against a table or upon an uncomfortable seat, staring through double glass at an interview room. Looking for signs of guilt, stray phrases, accidental admissions, gulps and gestures, suppressed panic or swaggering bravado. This one smells like they all do, of coffee, sour notes of body odour, of whiteboard pens and industrial cleaner.

Stevens gives him another pat. 'Make yourself at home, sir. We'll be bringing in the suspect shortly. Looks a wrong'un to me, he's been curled up in a corner since we brought him in. But you'll have your view, I know.'

The door closes, and Jake sees a swivel chair in the corner, which he drags around so he is in front of the centre of the glass. The stuffing is coming out, but it is comfortable enough. He stretches his legs out and sniffs the scalding coffee with some apprehension before putting it down beside him. The interview room before him is characterless and drab, deliberately so. Nothing more than a table welded to the floor, two chairs on one side, two on the other, bright lights bouncing off walls painted an unappetizing, cheddary colour.

It has been designed to intimidate in its sheer facelessness, its brusque utility; it screams out the reality that, if you've been brought here, you are within a process that cares nothing for your comfort or your desires or your life. Hard cases would ignore it, familiarity lessening its sting, but to those whose existences had hitherto had no connection with crime or police, it would be shocking, almost brutal.

Jake remembers when he was sixteen and had been beaten up in a park. Unlucky, because he had stood in the wrong place, looked at the wrong girl; naïve because he imagined that a lack of intent or awareness on his part would have protected him from four teenagers who simply fancied the opportunity to show some swagger and superiority. Before he knew it, he'd been on the ground, foetal, protecting his head as the blows rained down. Eventually, his assailants had scarpered, to be later tracked down by bored officers, and Jake had been brought to a station to give a statement. There, he had been led through a waiting room filled with the family of the arrested lads, hostile and sneering and intimidating, and brought to a room exactly like this. It had terrified him. A sergeant – listless, chewing gum throughout, mouth half-open so Jake could see it being bounced around his chipped and yellowed teeth, like a sock in an old tumble dryer – had taken down what had happened, made him lie on the scuffed floor to re-enact precisely his experience. All the while he could hear the derisive jeers and hoots and complaints of the relatives outside, who couldn't believe their beloveds had been accused by this 'fucking queer-looking' figure of contempt.

He squirms in his chair, remembers how emasculated he felt. Was that why he had wanted to become a copper, be on the other side of the table? Not only to do a better job, but be aligned with forces of strength not weakness, a chance to shut out the ugly faces of those who had dismissed him so readily? A sobering thought, and Jake is glad to leave it, as Zach is escorted in and pushed heavily into his seat. Behind him is a tired-looking woman in a business suit, grey skirt and jacket, maroon blouse, shoes with scuff marks on the heels. His solicitor, Jake thinks, probably the one provided by the police.

They speak softly to one another for a few minutes, heads almost touching, before McAllister walks in, confident and breezy, brandishing a brick-coloured file in his hands. He presses a switch in the table to begin the recording and spends a few minutes going through the formalities. Midway through, Stevens comes in and sits down heavily, notebook in hand, chair pulled back a yard behind McAllister, as if in deference to his superior officer.

It gives Jake the chance to observe Zach closely. He is in dark clothes as normal, a black T-shirt and jeans, his arms ghostly pale in contrast, the colour of bone, and thin, scrawny. His hair is thick and hanging near his eyes, which are darting around like he is a cornered animal. He keeps rubbing a finger along his pencil moustache, before realizing he is doing it and forcing his hands upon his thighs once more.

McAllister concludes his peroration. 'So, Mr Hunter, you see, we know you'd been at the site with Amy, we know that you'd had sex with her, and we know that she got her head bashed in soon after.'

Zach flinches at the term, but says nothing.

'Tell us what happened.'

His solicitor tries to speak, but Zach waves her silent, tries to dredge up some dignity, the pomp of the well-educated man. His voice is higher pitched than normal. 'I know I don't need to say anything, but I'm not going to allow you to make assumptions about me or Amy. Of course, I admit to seeing her. We did that a lot, especially when the site was quiet. We had a late breakfast there.'

'Champagne?'

'It wasn't exactly Pol Roger, Mr McAllister. But we were celebrating the fact that we'd decided to move in together, no more skulking around, the chance to be a proper couple. We were in love.' A sob is trapped, a bubble in his throat. 'You must believe that. So we drank some champagne, talked over some plans, and then, well, made love right there on her desk.' His eyes blaze defiant, a thrill stiffening his slender shoulders, as if he were proud to defend Amy's honour.

'What then?'

'We tidied ourselves up a bit. And I went back to my shared flat. Amy said she had a meeting so would wait around and do some work. I wasn't going to see her for a couple of days because I was going to my parents' house to get some things to help me move in.' A pause, throbbing with tension. 'And I never saw her again.'

'And you didn't "make love", as you coyly put it, anywhere else other than her desk?' Zach is shaking his head. McAllister has now changed from his normal, placid, ironical self, Jake notices; he is swelling with aggression, his voice hardening, an aspect emerging redolent of the Glaswegian streets, uncompromising.

Jake has seen this technique before, and understands why McAllister would think it might work. Zach is not used to being under this sort of pressure, being regarded as suspicious or dangerous or deviant. He probably has never met anybody willing to speak to him in such tones. He wants to object, to complain, to appeal to a higher authority. But there is none. McAllister becomes relentless, trying to rattle Zach, who indeed looks rattled. 'So you're telling me you didn't take her outside to those slave quarters, half-strip her and do her on that stone bed?' McAllister lets the pause build. The soft light in his eyes is entirely gone. 'You kinky, Zach? You like having sex with a woman and treating her like a slave? She was your boss in real life, but you mebbe liked to play the boss in the bedroom, did you, big man? Do you like that sort of thing, Zach?'

He pauses again, merciless for the moment. 'Look at me. Stop snivelling and look at me. We know you liked doing it in the slave quarters. You've done it there before, champ, haven't you?'

Zach looks embarrassed at his solicitor, but answers. 'Yes, we did have sex there once. A beautiful summer evening, not some rainy affair like yesterday, and we weren't excited about the slave bit, just the idea of being in a bed that had last been slept in so long ago.'

'Yes, yes, you can dress it all up as much as you like in front of an under-educated prole like me, but it was a place that you liked to take your mistress, no more, no less. Maybe this time the affair was coming to an end, maybe it was a farewell screw, maybe she was showing you some bit of the dig because she wanted you to focus on your job for a change, and you forced yourself on her, and swung at her after you'd finished yourself off.'

'NOOOOO!' Zach's voice is now a scream, a wail, his body looks febrile, shivering with rackety sobs. His solicitor is calm, shakes her head. 'Mr McAllister, you've conceded already that there is no evidence of sexual assault. And you've admitted the deceased had drunk champagne. Your scenario here is wild, implausible and has now been forcefully denied.'

McAllister changes tack, lets his aggression subside, so it lingers beneath the surface; still there, threatening, almost tangible, ready to rise and swell once more if needed. 'Let's talk about this Wulfnoth chappy.'

The door to Jake's room opens, and the blonde officer walks in with a file. She hands it to him, with a warm expression on her face. 'The chief wanted you to see this. What we found at the site, and what we know about the whereabouts of the others.' Jake flicks through it as he half-listens to McAllister patiently probing about the letters and what Zach knew about them.

The first half of the file is a very basic forensic account of the site, with some close-up digital photographs that have been printed out, of the body, the quarters, the whole surrounding area. The crime scene had been compromised to an extent by the downpour, washing over most of the marks left there, and there wasn't too much to go on. Simply a corpse, eyes vacant, clothes disordered, skin cold and clammy in the rain. Jake looks carefully at the mud around the body, sees a couple of faint lines one or two inches across. Could be nothing, could be important. Drag marks, perhaps? The irony is manifest, him acting as an archaeologist staring hard at a silent earth reluctant to reveal its secrets. He scribbles a note in his book.

There is also a brief itemization of what was found in the office. A half-empty bottle of champagne in the sink, some grease-stained wrappers in the bin. A magenta bra, matching Amy's knickers, pushed down between the cushions of the stained and weathered sofa. A whole panoply of scuffed footprints, as you'd expect from a place that had been regularly visited in the previous week. It all seems to reinforce Zach's initial statement: a romantic rendezvous amid all that muddied clutter, urgent sex in the workplace, some sort of minor celebration and nothing much more.

Jake skips to the section in which contact had been logged with various members of the dig team since the body was discovered. Matt and Elaine had taken a while to answer their phones, had eventually responded to voice messages. They called back together on Matt's phone, with ambient noises suggestive of a rail station. If they had been abroad as they had told Lily, they were certainly back in the country by the time of their call. They expressed surprise at the news and confirmed they were returning later today. There was no especial emotion in their voices at all.

Brian had been uncontactable until this morning. He said his phone had been turned off so he could concentrate on his garden. He had no other alibi for the time of the murder. Lily had given a full statement of her contact with Amy, and what had happened that afternoon, including her involvement with Jake. But she was at home, alone, in the morning when the murder had happened, mainly asleep in bed. As with Zach, there was nobody to account for her presence at the critical time.

McAllister is making that point to Zach now. 'So you're saying you had your little dalliance, and you pulled up your pants and went home to sleep. And nobody saw you.'

Zach nods, eyes now glassy, some of the fight knocked out of him, winded by events.

'You're the last feller to see Amy alive then?'

He rallies a little. 'Apart from the killer, Mr McAllister. I'm no killer. And you can fulminate and rail at me, but nothing will change that.'

McAllister lets the silence hang. Then he stands abruptly and nods Constable Stevens out, before following him through the door. After five minutes, he comes in to see Jake, who is frowning thoughtfully.

'Initial reaction, Jake?'

'I don't love him for it. The physical evidence suggests that he had a nice breakfast with the woman he was going to move in with, followed by consensual sex that led to her bra being removed in the office. An hour later, she's half-dressed and sprawled in a different location a few hundred yards away. I'm not sure the two connect brilliantly.'

'I wish I disagreed. He's a slimy wee thing, but there's no law against that. We got a warrant to go through his home, which I have people doing right now. That might turn something up.'

Jake scratches his beard. 'I'm working on a theory. If I'm right, I think it *will* turn something up. Can you call them and ask them to check any sheltered bit outside his flat: a shed, or a place for a bike, or a container for bins? A place accessible from the front. Get them to look now.'

McAllister looks at him strangely. 'I trust you, Jake, but could you give me a hint?'

'You have to allow your amateur consultants some leeway. Ask 'em now.'

McAllister departs, muttering no doubt dire Gaelic curses under his breath. Jake stands, nose pressed against the glass, each breath fogging the surface. Zach's solicitor has given up counselling him, and he is sitting with his head in his hands, black hair falling forward, stomach hunched, the tendons of his narrow arms visible as he pushes his fingers against his temples in frustration or pain or self-punishment.

Some more time elapses, and nobody moves. The solicitor starts to shuffle her papers, eyeing the clock imploringly.

McAllister half-kicks the door to Jake's office open. His eyes are agleam. 'We found a can of orange paint, in a bike shed, sitting there. Looks like a match for the scrawl on Daisy's house. How on earth could you have predicted that?'

Chapter Thirty-Three

Janet Sanders's farmhouse, near the village of Tillingford

Jake lets the question hang in the air. He is not surprised by the revelation, and enjoys for an ignoble second the conjuror's delight of pulling off a trick that startles the crowd, all the while knowing that the humdrum explanation is likely to disappoint them when they hear it.

'Educated guess, chief. I think Zach is more or less what he says he is: the lover of Amy, who last saw her in that office for a romantic celebration. If we take that as true for a moment, what follows? Either an entirely different person then met her, had consensual sex with her in the rain an hour later on an ancient stone bed – not impossible, but we might agree unlikely – or someone killed her, moved her to the quarters, and then made it look like a crime of passion and sex. If it's the second one, then they were doing it to point the finger of blame at Zach. As he'd admitted, they'd been there for sex before.'

'Lily told you that, didn't she? I wonder if anybody else knew.'

'I would guess everybody in a small, gossipy community knew. Lily told us all at dinner for the devilment of it. I can't believe she kept it to herself all the while before that. But we should ask. Anyway, my point's that some sort of fix against Zach is in. I reckoned that more evidence against him was likely to appear at his property, in a place accessible without breaking in, to screw him down further.'

'Did you predict the paint?'

'It was a possibility, though we didn't know for sure that the graffiti was part of the same set of crimes. It's now more or less certain that it is. That requires some further thinking about. I was hoping for a murder weapon – perhaps that would have been too obvious, perhaps the murderer didn't like to be carrying a bloodied stone around with them.'

'And what of poor wee Zach now?'

'I think you could let him go, but keep him scared and co-operative. He might know something he doesn't realize; he could've seen something at the site. Plus, I could be totally wrong and he's your man after all, but I'm not sure that there's enough to charge him here.'

McAllister thinks things through, mouth pursed. 'I'm going to go after him on the paint, first of all. He could've been the vandal but not the murderer, and that would be useful to know, because it undermines the theory that you've unleashed upon me.' He grins bitterly.

Jake always liked it when ideas were being tested in the middle of a case, arguments made and rebuffed. The 'endless dialectic of policing' was how one of his early sergeants had put it, a moustachioed former communist, who liked to read political tracts through the long night-shifts and give Jake tortuous lessons in the theory of investigation, and the sins of capitalism. Jake smiles at the memory, then shakes McAllister's hand. 'Fair enough, chief. I'm heading back to the ranch to see Aletheia, hopefully. Why don't we meet to compare notes tomorrow?'

They agree a time and location, then McAllister ushers him out towards the corridor leading to the back door. Before he leaves, McAllister hands him a bundle of files, joined together with a giant elastic band. 'That's all we have on Jordan and on Amy, plus the work that's been done on Daisy's house. Not much, but it might become more relevant now. Show it to your pal, and we'll catch up when any of us have had some bright ideas.' Jake takes it and waves farewell, deep in thought once more.

Outside, the thick air hits him, balmy and sweet after all the scents of stress within, that feeling of an animal cornered and at bay. It is a welcome reminder of the expansive world outside.

It is early afternoon, and warm now, the sun's heat making the wet land steam all around him in a summery fug. The waters are receding from their flood peak, too, and as he pootles along the empty lanes homeward, Jake sees the various brooks that course through the area return to their prior routes, high and fast but remaining within the bounds of their banks. He stops at Livia's house, and is pleased to see over the fence the sight of Aletheia sitting with her in the garden, drinking lemonade and talking animatedly.

Jake walks through the kitchen, depositing the file bundle carefully on the desk, before grabbing himself a drink from the jug, the ice inside rattling alluringly. Aletheia leaps up and hugs him. She is dressed for the city, in dark jeans and a black silk shirt, her cardigan already discarded in the heat. Livia holds out a languid hand and grasps his waist affectionately.

'Jake, I have to go see a man about a horse in ten minutes. So give us the summary of what's new, and I can think about it while I go about my healing business.'

He obliges, recounting all that has happened from mortuary to police station. When he finishes, Livia and Aletheia are quiet. Two barn swallows swoop in the field beyond, dipping close to the pools of water that are slowly seeping away into the earth, harvesting unseen insects with blithe efficiency. They twist and turn, as if shocked by invisible wires, their pale chests like flecks of cloud, forked C-shaped tails visible for an instant before they dip away once more. Agitated chirruping fills the air, like squeaks on an old trolley wheel.

Aletheia is first to speak. 'I think we need to look again, then, at the attack on Daisy, which is clearly even more relevant now. Plus, I want us not to forget Janet. The police have done virtually nothing on her, and I feel we have to fill that gap.'

'Why don't we go and look at her place now? If Liv can let us have the car?'

'Let's take mine, give Liv some freedom. One thing before we go, I'm going to scan all that police information to Martha, and she can review it for us. She's calling us tonight at ten. I tried for a more seasonable hour, but you know Martha.'

Livia soon bustles off, and Aletheia goes inside to copy the files. Jake sits and waits, mind flitting like the swallows above his head, as the shadows start to lengthen, and the temperature falls in a welcome swoon. There is real heat coming tomorrow, he thinks, now that the storm is passed.

Aletheia's car, parked down the road in a lay-by, is an incongruous sight: maroon and slim and sporty, it looks like a spacecraft dropped into the medieval period. Inside it is dim and air-conditioned, smells clean and little used.

'This is flash. Aren't you some sort of spy, though?'

'Hush yourself, Jake. I earn a lot of money and I don't have that much to spend it on because I spend most of my time chasing after bad guys, or helping you out of baffling cases. So let me have this one thing.'

'I'll let you have it, all right. It'll be nice to be driven around in luxury for once.'

The car purrs off with scarcely a sound. Jake stretches his long legs out, feels the sweat freeze-dry to his body. He is wearing dark cotton trousers and a thin shirt, opened at the front, with a white vest beneath. He had buttoned it up for the hospital and police visit, which had been his only nod to formality.

'Do you know where we're going?'

'I'm always prepared, you know that. Janet owned this watercress farm of all things, but didn't really work there properly.' She points to a screen on the dashboard. 'See that mass of green? That's the farm. She had an old cottage at one end, with a bit of scrubland around it. The farmhouse proper is all the way on the other side. She wanted to be left alone – like you, Jake.'

'And yet here we are.'

'And where is she?'

It is a good question. 'Do you think we'll find a body there?'

'I haven't worked out what I think about our Janet. She

could be a violent criminal, acting in secret from a motive we don't know. Or she's Wulfnoth's first victim, and nobody has ever found her.'

Jake privately thinks the latter is more likely, but struggles to piece all the information together. 'We know that she was still alive when she visited the archive, and that was five days after she went off the grid. Where did she go in between? The day after the archive visit, her letter is discovered, which is either a fraud, or a farewell, or a suicide note.'

'I'm hopeful Martha will have stayed sober long enough to look into her more closely.' She is joking, really. Martha's ability to function while high, or soused in pain-killing booze, is well-known to them, a skill that carries its own sense of sadness. Martha's life, for all her bravado and brilliance, is ever coupled with pain, which she can numb or sedate but never truly escape.

The radio is playing softly on a classical music station, a movement from Haydn's Symphony 104, jaunty and vernal, suggestive of new beginnings and ideas. Aletheia looks across to Jake and gives him a wink. 'You've got me listening to this stuff now.'

For the last year, Jake has been keeping a list of composers he likes, those he struggles with, those who have become important to him. He knows that he has become increasingly sentimental, romantic even, and he tends to lean towards that in his musical choices: long brassy strains, plangent motifs, lushness in musical form.

'This is Haydn. Bit upbeat for my melancholic tastes.'
'Show-off.'

They reach an old gate, mossed and blistered with rain and age, grass growing truantly up its hinges. They leave the car on the short track that leads up to it. Aletheia slips some gum in her mouth, chews it contemplatively. 'Not a lot of traffic down here in the last year.'

She vaults the gate, her movements smooth and controlled. Jake follows in similar vein. There is a flattened pathway up to a cottage, weathered into the landscape, its stone facings washed-out and grey. Beyond it, the land rises slowly, first grassy plains, odd-shaped and empty, before becoming more regular in the distance, the land divided into a series of vast beds, linked by ditches filled with water, the outpourings from an unseen spring that eventually connect in bubbling network with the river itself. They are pondy and green, the plants sitting atop the surface like Monet's lilies. There is a briskness in the air, filled with peppery and enlivening scents.

The cottage is quiet, its emptiness proclaimed silently to all the world, the late afternoon sun on the wane but warming the smooth flanks of its exterior. Inside all is gloomy and hard to make out, but Jake sees signs of some disorder: a chair overturned, a chest of drawers pulled out and empty. Aletheia is wielding a skeleton key, furtively prodding and twisting, before the back door opens, swinging noisily on its old hinge. 'Don't you dare say anything,' she says over her shoulder as she walks in.

The place has been searched, there is no doubt about it, and at some length. While there is mess, visible signs of the intruder's passage through the house, it has not been absolutely ransacked or damaged. All this happened some time ago, too: there is dust on top of the pulled-out drawers, which lie askew on the floor like broken teeth, a big gaping maw above them.

Aletheia throws a pair of sterile gloves to Jake, and they

both put them on. They pad around carefully. The kitchen is cool and empty, no ticking of the stove, the fridge empty of all but a jar of mustard, some tomato paste and a half-empty bottle of vodka.

'She clearly had no intention of sticking around and eating well.' This is Jake, closing the fridge door, so its buzz subsides.

'No smug-married judgement of independent single women, thank you very much.'

They go into a study, which is booklined and would have been cosy and welcoming except for the disruption, a few books strewn on the floor, the mahogany desk – rich-toned and polished – shifted sideways with all of its drawers removed and dropped to the floor.

'This hasn't been done by a pro. It looks like it's been turned over by someone with interest, anger maybe, but no rigour. Look.' Aletheia points to the bookcases. 'They started going through the books looking for letters or papers, then they stopped, presumably because it was too much of a faff.'

'Or they found what they were looking for and left.'

'I don't think so. This room is the first off the corridor, and others have been searched too. See, they even tried picking some random books in the middle of the shelf over there, then dropped them on the floor. I read this as someone unsure of where to look, doing their best to be thorough.'

'What were they looking for?'

'We should probably try to find out.' Jake is running his finger over each book on the shelf near him, the comforting touch of paper, the sense of row upon row of thoughts made real and tactile.

Aletheia has her device in her hand. 'We can get some police out here to go through it closely, see if they can turn up anything. I'll send some photos through to Martha – she'll love the extra work.'

Meanwhile, she hands him an old notebook, empty of writing, but containing a sheaf of old photographs. Jake looks through them, getting an immediate sense of Janet's wanderlust, her love of the land. There are pictures of lush green forested plains, purple-hued mountains, lakes silhouetted against cloud-strewn, louring skies. And also Janet herself at various digs around the country, including of her at St Giles. Janet at the spring. Janet as part of a team in a trench. Janet arm-in-arm with Matt, the grad student. Matt, topless, clutching his guitar. Matt leaping, startlingly naked, into a stream, lean and sallow, head turned back exultant, staring straight into the camera.

Jake pushes these last few photos towards Aletheia, who eyes them critically. 'We didn't know about this, did we? A love-triangle with an older woman, perhaps.'

Jake shrugs. 'Worth a few questions, surely. Matt and Elaine are always around, aren't they? Effacing themselves somehow, but never absent. Did we ever get anything more on their background?'

'Nothing that leapt out to Martha or me. Their education was pretty eccentrically religious, you know super-Catholic. That always unsettles me, but that could be my own prejudices talking.'

'He's not too religious to put it about a bit, evidently.'

Jake is now moving along each shelf, looking at titles, which are mostly books of medieval British history, some about Roman Britain. They have been half-heartedly alphabetized, and near the end he gets to a slim text from an obscure university press: *Vita Wulfnothi. The Life of Wulfnoth*. His senses tingling, he picks it up, and a folded piece of paper falls to the floor.

Aletheia is faster than he is, scoops it up, and opens it, eyes agleam. She reads aloud from the first line, which – Jake can already tell – follows a familiar style.

'"To the desecrators, I repeat my warning." Jake, it looks like we might have found our Wulfnoth. It was Janet all along.'

Chapter Thirty-Four

The thriller library, Little Sky

'So that's it then. Case closed. Drinks all round. Cheers.'

Martha sips her martini and rolls her eyes. It feels late, the night warm and humid, scarcely a whisper of wind coming through the open windows of the library. They are sitting around the main table, Jake, Livia and Aletheia, whose screen has been propped up against a pile of books, topped by an old P. D. James hardback. On it, Martha has been holding forth, glass in hand, her pale arms taut with tension and the heat, a pale vein in one of her biceps faintly pulsing.

Jake and Aletheia had waited at the Sanders farmhouse for McAllister and his constables, who had arrived as the sun began to dip, turning from pale yellow to egg-yolk orange. McAllister agreed to seal the place off, and do a proper search in the morning, along with some forensics, though nobody was optimistic about meaningful fingerprints. He had also taken ownership of the letter, which looked either like a discarded draft or an incomplete beginning that had been put aside and never returned to. There was no date on it. Aletheia had photographed it and sent it to Martha, and then they returned to Little Sky, picking up Livia and Diana along the way.

After a late swim full of shrieks and joy, followed by a barbecue, Diana was in bed, and they had convened their meeting. The four of them plotting together, not for the first time. It is hot and they each have cool drinks: Livia stretched out limply over two chairs, hair pulled up away from her neck, in shorts and a vest, her long brown limbs gleaming in the flickering lamplight; Jake dressed similarly, but less delicately, his big lumpy arms and legs emerging from his damp clothes, hot and mithered; Aletheia, more restrained, less exposed, in a silk robe she had been given by a Japanese acquaintance. Delicate piano sounds are emerging from the record player, early Debussy, melodic and soothing.

In the middle of the table is Jake's timeline, to which they keep referring. He has updated it since the afternoon.

First five years: dig begins, Wulfnoth A starts writing letters. Four received.
27 March: horde discovered by Jordan, Daisy, Amy and Zach.
13 April: fifth letter from Wulfnoth A.
14 May: final use of Janet's credit card.
19 May: file last accessed in archive; subsequently missing.
20 May: Janet's letter discovered.
18 June: Janet reported missing.

?June?: Janet's house ransacked. Sixth Wulfnoth letter (begun but not sent)?
NOTHING FURTHER FOR THE SUMMER
27 April: first Wulfnoth B letter.
1 May: Jordan murdered.
2 May: attack on Jake.
3 May: second Wulfnoth B letter.
4 May: attack on Daisy.
16 June: Daisy's house discovered vandalized; third Wulfnoth B letter.
19 June: Amy discovered murdered.

Aletheia makes the central point in response to Martha. 'This all comes back to the idea that there are two Wulfnoths. I think we can make a case – at least we have to argue this – that Janet was Wulfnoth A, busily writing threatening letters over the course of five years for reasons that we don't entirely know. She gets forcibly stopped sometime in June last year. At which point Wulfnoth B comes on the scene. And that's where the violence starts.'

Livia shifts uncomfortably. 'So Wulfnoth B is a killer, which means that he might have killed Janet first. Why, and where's the body?'

'Two good questions.'

Martha's eyes gleam in triumph. 'Here's a better question, which, being me, I've got an absolutely brilliant answer to: if Janet is the first Wulfnoth, why is her farewell letter in the same style as the second Wulfnoth letters, from Wulfnoth B, and different to the first, from Wulfnoth A?'

Livia swats irritably at an unseen fly, drinks deep from her beer bottle. 'Back up, back up. You have to go slow for the scientists in the room.'

Martha flashes a smile. 'It's kinda complicated but not if Auntie Martha explains it to you. You see I've been looking at the draft letter you discovered earlier this afternoon in Janet's house. Here's how I see it. Janet is Wulfnoth A. She wrote the first five letters, and indeed the sixth that was half-finished and discarded. She obviously enjoyed the mischief of terrorizing the dig folk, and probably did nothing more than that. I had someone take a hurried look at the draft you found in her house, and it ties exactly into the earlier letters. But, but, but: somebody different, Wulfnoth B, wrote the later letters and – crucially – *Janet's farewell letter as well.*'

There is quiet. An owl hoots outside. A smaller body flits in the dark, silhouetted for a second against the brooding moon that has emerged from behind the wisps of cloud. A bat perhaps, with its tiny whirligig energy.

Aletheia is nodding vigorously. 'That's how I read it. The one letter in Janet's name is actually one she didn't write, but was left to be found after her death by her killer, who wanted it to look like she had decided to disappear. Wulfnoth B is our killer, and killed Janet first, then Jordan, then tried you and Daisy, then managed with Amy.'

'Which is another point in wee Zach's favour.' This is Jake momentarily slipping into McAllister's studied drawl. 'Otherwise, he looks like the only one of the treasure hunters not targeted, and we might think he was the one doing the targeting. The killer also plants the paint at his house to aim us at him even more.'

Livia is pointed. 'Which brings us back to who is Wulfnoth B, and why kill Janet?'

Martha nods. She is filling her pipe with green buds

taken from a plastic bag. She lights it, puffing lustily. 'Why was Janet Wulfnoth A for that matter, you might ask?'

'That's the line we need to draw, however you look at it.' Jake stands and paces as he talks, bouncing an old tennis ball he has picked up from the side of the sofa. 'Janet clearly had some dispute with the dig, starts sending letters, including after the horde was discovered. She is killed, her death concealed, a letter faked. A year later, the other attacks happen with more faked letters, culminating with Amy the other day. So why? And why the wait?'

Martha puts down her pipe. Her voice is as steady as ever, but Jake can see in her dilated pupils that part of her is now absenting itself from them. Lost in the land of pain. She frowns at him, as if she can sense he is thinking of her sympathetically.

He uses the pause to suggest a break for them all, a chance for Martha to recover herself. She takes it. She pushes herself out of vision with a wink, but her teeth are set in a suppressed grimace. The three of them in the library stand and awkwardly peel off clinging areas of fabric that have lain rucked against their hot skin for too long.

Livia gives a wicked grin. 'Excuse me for a moment, Al, if you don't mind.' She pads out, and Jake hears the outside door close. He moves to the window, which looks out down towards the lake. The night is still, the natural world drugged, stuporous with heat; the moonlight has become a threatening glow. He suddenly sees a streak of brown skin, paled in the glimmer, the bewitching wobble of bare flesh. Livia runs towards the lake and jumps in with a joyful clamour, a squeal back up to the moon. Jake smiles. He hears the splashing in the distance.

When he turns back, Aletheia is reading quietly, the heat

scarcely bothering her. Five minutes later, Livia returns, towel in her hair, a thin playsuit on her body, which glistens with damp.

'I needed that.'

'Totally normal thing to do. It's how most police conferences finish up. Were you inspired by that picture we showed you of young Matt?'

She slides back in her place, nonchalant. 'A good idea is a good idea, wherever it comes from. I'm getting ready for the second half. And we still don't have a plan, do we.' She leans forward and sips her beer, gives Jake a wink that he feels, as ever, in his stomach.

'Our watery layabout is absolutely right. We don't have a plan. And we fucking need one.' Martha has returned, pupils dilated, but a determined expression back upon her face. She takes the lead, the pain within buried deep, the focus on the case all-encompassing once more.

Chapter Thirty-Five

The moonlit edge of Chandler Lake

'On Janet, I've done a bit of digging. I managed to get access to some of her internet records. She had no phone, which is weird – and yes, I am looking at you, Jake – but she did use her computer.'

He looks across at Aletheia, who shakes her head. 'I didn't see one in the house.'

'I'm sure that's because it contained some incriminating information about Wulfnoth B on it. See if the flatfoots find anything tomorrow, but I bet they won't. From what I can tell, Janet was interested in the land all around St Giles, and slightly beyond, and not for archaeological reasons alone. Her family came from the area, you know, going back several generations. Not rich, but stubborn, survivors: labourers who dragged themselves upwards over the years. Her dad was a local surveyor, actually. Anyway, at some point she believed that a big chunk of that land had been willed to her family, away from the church.'

'But why did she care? Why does anybody care about all of these patches of ground. That's been bothering me for the last few months.' Livia's voice is less idle than before. Her nose wrinkles charmingly in her indignation.

Aletheia's response is gentle and considered. 'Ah, we're in the realm of belonging here, Liv. You know, you've got a rare gift of belonging, without seeming to reach for it. I've often thought that. You're here, and somehow everything fits. If Janet's family felt they were excluded, cheated, not allowed to possess the land they worked on, land they felt was actually part of them, maybe it gnawed at them, a sort of relentless psychosis they passed down the family line.'

'Are you talking from experience here, Al?' This from Martha, sardonic expression removed from her face for the moment.

Aletheia looks a little flustered, sips from a beer she has been nursing inexpertly all night. 'I suppose so. My family had their roots in a place not far from Cape Coast, in Ghana; land was taken from them, and so I am here. What's that phrase? "I'm here because they were there." So where do I belong really?' There is a pause. 'When people talk about landlessness, it has meaning, wherever you're from.'

Livia reaches out a damp palm, and squeezes her with affection. 'You belong with us, thank God. But I see your point. Daisy said a similar thing.'

'Did she?' Martha has a pen in her hand and scribbles a note.

'Yeah, she talked to Jake and me about not fitting in, not feeling at home. And of course Wulfnoth seemed to know all that somehow – hence that horrible vandalism. I wonder if there is a connection between Janet and Daisy as victims in that sense.'

Jake sits back down, looks benignly upon his friends, and Livia. 'M, do we know *when* the Daisy vandalism fits into all of this?'

She is puffing away again, smoke hanging in the hot night air, thick and creamy as frothed milk. Her left hand twitches the mouse, moving a file up on her second screen.

'Let's work that out. I've gone through the police file. They've done some pretty half-arsed canvassing, and uncovered one delivery driver who was working the area in the week before you found the mess. He remembers peering over the fence to look for a street number, and seeing no vandalism. That was a Thursday. Livia here has let me know that the *Shire Gazette*, ridiculous local newspaper though it may be, is delivered according to a strict timetable. That would've been pushed through the door on Friday morning, and the paperboy would've surely said if he'd seen anything amiss. You showed up, having been asked to check the place, on Sunday morning. So we are looking at that period from Friday lunchtime to when the crime could have occurred – call it mainly Saturday, June 15th. We need to check alibis for that period, I think.'

'Should we waste resources on a minor crime though?'

She exhales. 'Jake, I know you only ask questions like that to stimulate the argument. If we think Wulfnoth B did this, we stand as good a chance of catching him here as anywhere else. Better, in fact, because killers tend to be more careful when they're doing their killing than when they're up to a bit of minor destruction of property. This might not convict him of a murder, but it might help us get a chief suspect.'

Jake's beer is warm and stale in his mouth. He goes to the fridge, which has been built beneath the lowest shelf of one of the bookcases, a glass panel at its front about a foot high and six feet across, a lovely touch his uncle had obviously commissioned especially. In it, stacked in rows, a tessellation of bright caps that glint out in the dim room, are countless chilled bottles of beer and wine, together with a few cans of root beer that Jake drinks when he cannot face the booze. He grabs one now and cracks it open, medicinal-tasting and fizzy, a pleasant sugar jolt to the system. He asks Aletheia if she can arrange the alibis to be checked. She nods. She is making careful notes, a big black fountain pen in one hand. Her writing, Jake sees, is neat and girlish, the tails of her letters in whale-blue ink curling extravagantly beneath the lines. He reaches over and updates his timeline, his own handwriting cramped and scruffy.

He leans back. 'So what about Livia's idea that Janet and Daisy are somehow victims of landlessness, or rather are interested in land recovery or justice, and therefore have become the target of our killer for that reason?'

Martha yawns, silent and feline for a second. 'Yep, it would definitely be worth talking to Daisy some more. I've also looked at Janet's search activity in the archives, which is weirdly hard to access. In fact, and I hate to confess this in the presence of such august company, but I had to fracture the odd government regulation to find anything at all.'

Aletheia shakes her head wryly, but says nothing. Martha takes a small sip of her dwindling drink and continues. 'She was interested in land ownership in the whole region, especially owned by the church. There's a myriad of searches about what has been owned by the parish of St Giles, and searches of the land records relating to everybody on that dig, including Reverend Jordan. She only looked at one file in the archives, which Jake saw, and she did it twice, once after she disappeared, and that now has a whole section missing from it.'

'I have a thought.'

'Calm down, Jake, I'd hate for that woolly head of yours to get over-heated.'

'How do we know it was Janet who took the file out? Especially the second time? We know from her records that she seemed to go dark the week before. If she'd gone to the city, hunted up a file, she'd have had to use transport, buy food, maybe stay somewhere. How come there's no card activity? I know she liked cash, and that's why we've held out so long the prospect of her being alive somewhere. But what if she was killed, the letter planted, and then someone took her ID and headed off to the archive?'

Martha's head is bouncing vigorously. Livia remains harder to rouse. 'But why?'

Martha intervenes before he can answer. 'Because Wulfnoth B thought Janet had found information that compromised him in some way, maybe a title deed that proved or disproved what he owned. It all follows a pattern of behaviour, really. Wulfnoth B assumes her identity, writes that letter, steals her computer, and then starts to clean up whatever entanglement she had got into.'

Aletheia's pen is scratching along smoothly. 'This is all making some sense to me, but does it give us a suspect?'

Martha scratches her nose with her empty glass. 'I've got a vague thought, but nothing I'd want to hang my hat on.'

A longer pause. The clock ticks ponderously. The air hangs heavy as wet cloth. Livia has her eyes closed and is breathing heavily. Jake puts down his drink. 'Let's get some more information before we start naming names. I'm pretty sure we've done all we can for tonight. Martha, is there CCTV around the archives, so we can look at that visitor?'

'I can check, but I'm not sure they'd keep it that long. I'm going digging – pun very much intended – into the lives of all the remaining site team, see what moves. You keep talking to that Glaswegian copper of yours. Whatever his faults, he at least isn't a member of an evil conspiracy.'

'I'll pass on the compliment. Let's speak in a day or so. You get anywhere with my Marsh book, by the way?'

Martha reaches down to the floor and waves it at him. 'On the second novel already. It's a bit twee for my tastes, but I do like the hero – Alleyn, isn't it? Well-read and clever and charming. A bit like you, apart from the clever and charming bit. Over and out, pals.'

She leans forward and with a blip she is gone. Aletheia is yawning, and they agree to return to all this again the next day. She heads off to her room, laying a tender hand on Livia's shoulder as she goes. Livia is now fast asleep, her skin hot and twitchy, a copper coil of hair bouncing with each of her steady breaths. Jake leans forward and picks her up, firm and lean in his arms. He kisses her forehead, and she shifts and grumps but refuses to awaken. Moving carefully among the evening's detritus on the floor, he carries her to their room, the window wide open, the moon pouring silky liquid light upon the bed. He lays her down gently, and looks at her with great affection: her hair shining like brittle glass, her body long and curved and smooth.

Jake is too wired to sleep. He goes outside to sit by the lake, listen to the muted hum of night-time existence, the restlessness of the water that whispers and ripples, the reeds all around it that sigh. He wants to ponder and plot. And he has a plan building in his brain, a suspect he feels has been staring him in the face since the beginning. Not taunting him exactly, but aloof and confident in how unknowable all of their crimes have been.

Chapter Thirty-Six

The garden of the Jolly Nook, Caelum Parvum

Jake sleeps long for him, the morning's heat waking him from sticky slumber, the sun already risen up out of the horizon line, now paling in a shimmery haze. Livia has left a note.

> Aletheia is taking Di and me off to school, before she goes to police station. Thanks for putting me to bed. Can't wait until the next time we're both naked, awake even, when you do it. xxxxx

He grins, and screws it up. His mouth is dry, his body tacky and uncomfortable. The swim, when it comes, is glorious, the water cool against the day's torpor, dark blues and purples deep within a soothing contrast to the lurid light that bejewels its surface. He feels strong in his body, his mind abuzz, an idea of how to bring this whole case to a conclusion starting to form. One question nags at him: where is Janet's body, where was she killed?

After he has swum the length of the lake and back, he pulls himself out and lies upon the pier, the old wood soft and gnarly on his back, his chest heaving, each limb, firmed by the cold water, now slowly loosening as it warms under the sun's rays. He watches the rivulets trickle off his chest, beading against his hairs. He cannot linger long, though he wants to – eyes closed, the blankness beneath his closed lids turned crimson in the glare; the quiet enveloping his busy thoughts – because he has an appointment with McAllister, who may have news for him.

He does, in fact. An hour later they meet in the garden of the Nook, Sarah tacitly offering it as a private place to discuss matters, making it comfortable without being asked, with two cushioned chairs, a pitcher of elderflower cordial and some madeleines from the oven which scent the heavy air with vanilla and brown sugar.

McAllister winks at her as she puts the plate down. 'I could get used to this. I'd generally be getting my elevenses from a newsagent in the rain back in God's country, and damn the consequences.' He pats his stomach, which is firm enough. Sarah has clearly been charmed by him. 'Nonsense, you need feeding up with good food, like Jake here.' When Sarah talks about 'feeding you up', Jake thinks, you know she's on your side.

They wait until she bustles away, the bell suggesting a new customer. McAllister bites into a madeleine, a look of unalloyed pleasure upon his face for a second, before he returns to his customary briskness.

'Some updates for you, Jake. And don't think I don't accept how much you and Aletheia have brought to the table here. She's charmed everyone back at the station, you know, so much so that she's got her own wee desk now, and is beavering away as we speak. I think we're moving things along at least, though I have to confess I still don't have a true line on who did this.'

'Did she explain our theory of two Wulfnoths?'

'She did, and I'm buying it. But let's not get ahead of ourselves. Some news from me first. One, we have the murder weapon for Amy.'

Jake puts his glass down into a patch of shade, the ice in it already disappeared. 'Go on.'

'When the waters started to subside in the fields beneath the hill, there was a rock, about the size of a hardback book, heavy but, you know, manageable, sitting there. You could see the red that had not quite washed clear, and we've matched the blood with Amy's.'

'Was it near the horde trench?'

'Next to it. Why?'

'A lot of things point to the treasure in all this, and I wonder if it's deliberate.'

'Care to expand on that?'

'No, you're updating me at this point, chief. I don't want to interrupt.'

'How considerate.' He eats another madeleine, in two hasty gulps, catching the crumbs in one hand. 'You better move that plate away before I debase myself too far.' Jake stays still. 'Anyway, here's an interesting thing. I'm calling it a rock, but it's more like a relic dug up as part of the dig: an old piece of masonry, a piece of, you know, historical substance. I'm getting it confirmed with Brian, who's now more or less in charge, I suppose, but we've been told it's early medieval and it wasn't there in situ on our murder site. Which means the killer fetched it from somewhere.'

'And maybe had access to the excavated material.'

'Exactly. I'm going back to the hill to check in a moment.' His hand hovers over another cake, and self-control wins on this occasion. 'Elsewhere, we've been searching Janet's house since dawn. Excellent to get a bit of good old-fashioned Presbyterian work ethic into my folk, you know. No computer anywhere, Aletheia's already asked about that. But we found a diary of sorts, not a journal you understand, no outpouring of personal thoughts, more an appointments book. Here it is. No interesting fingerprints, so you can touch it. In fact, I'd be glad of you looking through it while I go off to speak to Brian. See if anything jumps out. I can pick it back up on my way through again.' He hands Jake a small red book, leather-covered and expensive.

'Do you think our ransacker saw this?'

McAllister shakes his head. 'Almost certainly not. It was in the far corner of one of the shelves which hadn't been much disturbed, and had fallen a bit into the back. Good effort from young Stevens, actually, to find it.'

'Anything else before you go?'

'Only that the piled-up post suggests that Janet was gone after May fifteenth and never came back. Her TV shows she was watching a programme on the fourteenth, and didn't return to it. I think that's when the murder occurred. If she has been murdered, of course.'

McAllister checks his watch. 'And one other thing. I stopped off myself this morning to talk to that young French lad, Matt. He said he had a fling with Janet three summers ago, before he met his current lady friend, Elaine. She was nearby when we spoke, looking daggers. He was gallant enough, despite Elaine being there, told me that Janet was somewhat eccentric in her views on life and sex and archaeology, and no supporter of the St Giles gig, which she thought was being extravagantly managed.'

'Sounds like the first Wulfnoth to me.'

'And her relationship with Matt puts him more in the picture – the new girlfriend too, maybe, though I'm not sure I see them as killers.' He pauses meditatively. 'Anyhoo, as they say, I better be off. Let me know if you find anything.' They shake hands and McAllister heads towards the gate and his car. Five minutes later he walks stiffly back, bashful grin on his face. He picks up two madeleines and thrusts them into his jacket pocket. 'I never could resist temptation, dammit,' he says and departs as swiftly as he had returned.

Jake has turned to the May section of the appointments book. The week around 14 May had been blocked out carefully in black pen. There is a note on the top of the page: ST GILES FINDINGS EXAMINATION, WK AVAILABLE. The first three days had been ticked off, including 14 May, but 15 May is blank. There are no later entries at all. Jake looks back through the diary, and sees Janet's habit of ticking off days with planned activities where they had been completed. She clearly did it each evening, maybe when she got home.

He sits back, looks over the lawn to the elm trees. He idly watches the leaves move in the breeze, their shadows stippling the still muddied ground. If her last appointment was at the dig, he wonders, did something happen there to her? Did Janet never come home again?

He puts the book into the waistband of his shorts, tucks his shirt over the top, and decides to walk over to the site.

It's a long trek of course, especially as the day gets hotter, the clouds burned away, the sky a piercing, fathomless blue. He takes off his shirt at one point, wraps it around his waist, and keeps going, perversely relishing the hardship, the burn in his legs, the hostile sting of the sun on his skin.

It is a languorous sort of afternoon by now, close and dense, when even the hum of the insects seems muted. He has cut across the fields away from the roads, and nothing seems to be moving all around him. The wind dies, his sweat clings to him. After a while he can see the plateau in the distance, a shimmer of dark green, the tower poking up, slate-coloured and straight, a man-made line stark against the natural dips and curves all around. It all looks as imposing as always, a place of life and death, hard-earned survival and desperate pain, over the previous thousands of years.

He shrugs on his shirt when he gets near, and nods to the policeman standing guard at the entrance. McAllister is talking to Brian near the office, carefully standing in the welcome shade it has cast over them. Jake doesn't have a brilliant read on Brian, he thinks; this gregarious, jolly – maybe even too jolly – figure, always near the centre of things but never quite at their true heart.

Brian's eyes light up when Jake approaches, though he appears to recognize the sobriety of the overall scene, his boss dead these last couple of days, the entire project cast into doubt.

'Nice to see you, Jake, though not in the best of circumstances. The chief inspector here was showing me what he thinks killed poor Amy. Breaks your heart to think about it really.'

'Do you know where it came from?'

Brian allows himself the ghost of a smile. 'You know he asked me the very same question. There must be a thing they teach all you bobbies when you join up.' Jake hadn't heard the term 'bobbies' for years, not since his gran, who had never been much of a fan of them.

'And the answer is . . .?' McAllister's voice is patient, but Jake can see the heat and Brian's prevarication are wearing his patience thin. A bead of sweat trickles down from his temple, across the bluish skin of cheek, a fresh afternoon crop of stubble already poking through.

'The answer, Chief Inspector, is yes, I do. It's definitely medieval, probably the best half of the side of a chimney pot. We dug it out last year, near the tower. Probably from the midden ditch we discovered.' He pauses, as if waiting to be asked. '"Midden" being an archaeological term of some vintage meaning rubbish dump. When things got broken back in the day, and they couldn't fix them, they tended to chuck them in a big 'ole of varying filthiness. Eventually it gets filled in, and then we digging folk come along a thousand years later and poke our noses into it.'

'And where was it kept?' McAllister's voice is remaining almost even. He swats at an insistent fly clamouring for attention around his nose.

'Oh, in the Keep, along with most of the non-high-value finds.'

Jake intercedes. The sun is hot on his face, but to get into the meagre shade would involve him standing pelvis-to-pelvis on Brian's boots. 'I meant to ask – did you keep all the treasure in the Keep?'

'Only at the beginning, while we catalogued it and gave it a rough clean. Then it was shipped off to the museum in the city for safekeeping. We have some nice bits that are still being worked on, but we don't keep everything there. Some pottery, some bones and the like. Plus, of course, the big tombs themselves: we got them out three years ago, and have left everything within more or less in situ. They're too solid to shift about.'

McAllister is about to speak, but Jake asks one further question. 'Are they easy to open? I mean, if I were interested, could I look?'

Brian mops his brow with a handkerchief emblazoned with miniature trowels. 'You could, but I wouldn't encourage it. We haven't opened them in two years, though I don't suppose the actual lid is too heavy. They're lead-lined you see, not that common for the period, so they're pretty unwieldy apart from that.'

McAllister glares Jake into silence. 'If we may return to the murder weapon that killed your boss.' Brian offers a respectful dip of the head. 'Was it accessible in the Keep?'

'Oh aye, it was. Probably recently cleaned up, stored in one of containers, you could go straight in and grab it.'

'Who would have the key?'

Brian pats the pockets of his denim shorts, which are so tight, Jake can see the outline of a key ring nestled close to an outline of a shape he would rather not dwell upon. 'Well I do. Amy did, God rest her soul, so did Zach. And we kept a spare in the bottom of the desk drawer.'

'Is it there?'

'Is it where?'

McAllister's attempts to keep the calm in his voice are now verging on the Herculean. The vein on his neck is bulging; that ineffectual swatting of the fly, his wrist a stiff pendulum of motion, is increasing in tempo. 'The key. Is it in the desk still?'

Brian removes his wide-brimmed fishing hat, and looks to the sky for inspiration. 'You know, I haven't checked for some time.'

'Could you go and do it now?'

He beams. 'Of course. Be right back in a jiffy.'

Brian strides off, all pale legs and high socks, skin mottling in the warmth. McAllister nods to his junior colleague to follow him into the office. Jake gives his friend a few seconds to regain his composure. He soon does. 'Jake, I have to admit to finding the heat a little trying. This latitude is not good for my blood, I can tell you.' He exhales. 'I'm fine. What brings you here, so quick?'

Jake waves the appointments book, which he has removed – damp and clammy – from his waistband. 'This has Janet on the site the day she went off the grid. I wonder if she never made it out alive.'

Meanwhile, Brian has returned, hat pushed back firmly on his head, his hair, its colour shifting in the light from a sort of copper through to pale straw to whiteish grey, all sticking out in curling clumps. 'Yep, Chief Inspector.'

'Yep, what?'

'Yep, the keys aren't there. Not there at all.' His expression is annoyingly beatific. 'Someone must have picked them up,' he adds sagely.

'Of course. Why should I have expected anything else?' McAllister's twitching hand is returning, so Jake asks the question he had walked all this way to get answered. 'Brian, do you remember Janet Sanders coming here to look at the findings last year?'

'I do indeed. The lovely Janet. She was here for three or four days, very nice woman, knew her onions too when it came to the medieval period.'

'Her notes say "WK" on them. Is that Wulfnoth's Keep, do you think?'

'I should say so. She spent most of her time down there. Writing a book, you know. It's never come out, least not that I've seen. In fact, someone said she'd done a runner. She's not been around all summer.'

Jake wonders if Brian is as bluff and naïve as he appears; he is too ingenuous, too much comfortably ensconced in kindly character, for his tastes. But perhaps that is cynicism, the refusal to accept that childlike enthusiasm is a real trait among the lucky few.

'What are your plans, now, Brian?' McAllister seems to have recovered his poise, right at the point a cloud has shifted in front of the sun, casting the whole area into a welcoming dimness.

'I'm at your service, sir. And then at some point, we have to decide what to do with this cursed dig. But I'll be sorry to leave it all, sure enough.'

'Is that the plan?' asks Jake.

'Has to be. We won't be able to get the staff, not for this year at any rate. Yon Lily and the other graduates are all that's left, and we can't keep them on with a killer in the neighbourhood.' He gestures at a group sitting, backs against an old, rough-hewn wall, looking rather despondent. Jake sees Lily among them, picking up handfuls of grass and watching them fall to the ground, unlimbered by the breezeless air. 'In fact, I better get them home now, to be honest. Do you need us, Chief Inspector, for the rest of the day?'

'You get yourselves home. We can find you if we need to.' They watch as Brian approaches them, avuncular concern etched in his weather-beaten features. Matt and Elaine scowl back in Jake's direction, perhaps nothing more than the sun in their faces, but their previous connection with him seems a little tempered. Nobody likes old relationships exposed to the critical eyes of strangers.

McAllister then turns to Jake. 'Hard to see how any of them benefit much from all of this. You've told me they were no fans of the direction of the dig, but now they're left with nothing.'

'With nothing this year. Who knows if the dig won't resume under new management next year, this time with Wulfnoth silent on the subject? It might be an opportunity for all of them.'

'So one or more of them have been going after the site bigwigs to make it happen – it's not impossible, is it? Anyway, I can see some other cogs turning in that scruffy head of yours. Care to share your thoughts?'

Jake's mind is indeed preoccupied, and he doesn't immediately answer. His plan, a little shapeless that morning, is becoming ever clearer in his mind, the tightening of focus upon a once-blurry image.

'Jake?'

'Chief, I'd like to talk a little more to Aletheia and our colleague Martha. And then I'd like to find a way of drawing out our killer, if I can. Can you give me a little room to move, and then I'll tell you everything?'

'I don't know about that, Jake. I've been open with you, and I'd appreciate a bit of reciprocation.'

'I understand. But you can't act on my hunches, and I haven't got proof. But I have the beginnings of an idea, and as soon it becomes solid, you will.'

McAllister weighs this up in silence. There is a singsong twittering of an unknown bird nearby. He sighs. 'I suppose I have to tolerate that, without liking it a great deal. Do you need anything in the meantime, any help?'

Jake shakes his head. 'No. I might mosey around here, now that everyone's going home.' The archaeologists are packing up their bags, hoisting them onto their shoulders. 'You've got a copper here all the time, haven't you? So I should be safe.'

'For tonight and tomorrow until it gets dark. And then we're done with the crime scene, and we'll have to leave it to the wilds. This evening you should be fine, right enough. I'd stay and play Sherlock with you, but I've folk to answer to back at base. So you take care, and don't get too mysterious on me, OK?'

Jake claps his shoulder, the material hot and damp and heavy to the touch. 'I promise I'll be good.' He watches McAllister walk down the hill, followed by Lily and Matt and Elaine. He then forestalls Brian's departure to borrow the keys from him. In ten minutes, the plateau is empty, bar the policeman at the gate, who is now sitting down, drinking greedily from a canteen, looking like he wishes he were elsewhere.

It remains a magnificent vision, though, as the afternoon heads inexorably into evening, the heat clinging to the air like an unwelcome intruder. Clouds are thickening in front of the sun, which loses all shape behind them, its light diffused and orangey. An angry sky, a sullen sky.

Jake spends the remaining hours of visibility wisely, striding the site, his body as energized as his active mind. He revisits all the relevant scenes, the places of once-ancient activity where life and death had returned in such dramatic fashion: the trench where Jordan had drunk the acid; the bubbling spring where he had been attacked;

the patch where the stone had nearly flattened Daisy; and finally the tumbledown room where Amy had been found. He looks at sight lines, paces distances between locations; he fossicks and forages. In the hypocaust room he picks up another piece of twine from the floor; in the slave quarters he takes a careful look at the stone bed.

Before the sun sets, the sky now pinkish red, livid like a fresh-raised welt, he goes into Wulfnoth's Keep, the air down there naturally cooled, a refuge from the swampiness of the day. He looks into boxes, imagines Janet here, immersed in her research, bewitched by the spoils of history before her. The two cylindrical tombs still dominate the centre, and he spends ten minutes examining them carefully, wondering whether fingerprints would have ever clung to that stone. Then he flexes his arms, and lifts one of the lids.

It is a determined and thoughtful Jake who emerges from the Keep half an hour later, into the softness and the warmth of the evening, his mind scarcely registering yet more hidden notes of a bird, a nightingale this time perhaps, its song ranging high and low, querulous and unstinting, a burble at the edge of his perception. There is work to do, he thinks, and wonders how ready he is to do it.

Chapter Thirty-Seven

The thriller library, Little Sky

It is deep twilight when Jake gets home, the world estranged by shades of grey, shapes looming unrecognizable as he plods his weary path. Livia meets him at the kitchen door, face unreadable, takes him by the hand, and leads him through to the library.

He can see the vein throbbing in the tilt of her neck as she walks in front of him, a sign of suppressed emotion. His heart sinks for a second. When they get to the sofa, she turns, arms across his shoulders, pulling him towards her. He can smell her hair conditioner, the honey in the moisturizer she has put on while she was waiting for him, which makes her skin cool and sheeny.

Her eyes are in front of his, that dark riverbank green, and they are alive with news.

'I asked Aletheia to take Di for a torch-lit walk. Jake, I want to talk to you, and you must promise to keep calm. Can you do that?'

He shakes his head dumbly.

'I'm going to trust you anyway. Jake, I'm definitely pregnant, I've done four tests. Look.' She pulls one from her pocket; the two lines are bold and clear.

Jake can say nothing. He squeezes her, helplessly expressing through his touch the depth of his feeling, his joy and his fear, his need to take a grasp of her body in all its tactile reality, to hold tight all that promise of the future to come.

She carries on speaking, her voice gentle in his ear, an effortful calmness suggestive of what is roiling beneath. 'It's so early. I didn't want to tell you, but I wanted more than anything for you to know.'

'How long?' His words are a croak, his mouth dry.

'Six weeks, probably. So a long way to go. But it's there, and I'm not saying I feel it, but I feel somehow different.'

She is returning his hug now. All around them is still, the air not moving, the ordinary bustle of the world outside paused for a moment. He says nothing, not trusting his words to do justice to his feelings.

The moment has to end, and it does. Sounds come flooding back, a bird outside, the distant bark of an animal, perhaps a deer or a fox, and at the far range of his hearing Diana's lilting laugh at some joke or thought or sight. A miraculous sound, a child's unbridled laughter. Families come with stress and pain and apprehension, he thinks; they fail and they hurt, but what everyone seeks is right there in that noise, the sound of unselfconscious pleasure in a life you have given, a life you are responsible for.

He and Livia fall together onto the sofa, her face now wreathed in smiles. 'Please speak, Jake. You've got to convince me I was right to tell you, that you can handle this.'

'I can handle this, I think. I'm so pleased. And worried, Liv, of course I'm worried, but I'm going to try not to be mental, I really am. Do you need anything, are you OK?'

She squeezes his hand. 'Jake, I'm fine, I'm great even. You know I thought things were different when I woke up yesterday with this urge to decorate the house. I even got the paints out. The nesting impulse, you see it all the time with animals. That's when I took the test. Then I bought three more to be sure. It's going to be OK, you know. I feel it. We're going to have a baby together. Get used to it.' She leans forward, a whisper of kiss against his cheek.

Through the window Jake can see torch beams bobbing, can hear Aletheia and Diana talking about the sighting of a fox as they approach the house. Livia tightens her grip on his hand. 'We won't say anything to anyone, will we? Especially Di. I want to get to twelve weeks first.'

'Absolutely. We can have that long worrying by ourselves to enjoy. Did you tell Al?'

'Not openly, but I reckon she knows. Let's still say nothing though. I want this to be ours for a while, a joy we can talk about and hold onto between ourselves.'

She finishes speaking as Diana irrupts into the room, a pell-mell run and jump into the middle of their hug. Aletheia follows more sedately, carefully blank expression upon her face, the barest hint in her eyes that she comprehends the situation.

They busy themselves with a late supper of bread, cheese and apples, an easy meal for the warm night. Then there is the bustle of Diana's bedtime, the preparations for a conference with Martha. Jake feels disembodied, nursing the news close within him, so he can weigh out and shape and prod it like clay, solid, an idea that now subsists within him whatever else is happening. He is distracted, but happily so, a half-smile forming at his lips whenever they are still. And he relishes stolen glimpses of Livia as the evening progresses, hot and beautiful and now teeming with secret life. He reappraises the curve of her bare stomach when her vest rises up as she shifts position, the twist of her hips, the soft lines of her breasts, all that magnificent force somehow held within her flesh.

But he has to drag his mind away from selfish preoccupations, and that becomes a little easier as he focuses on what needs to be done with the murder case. They are back in the library, the night well advanced, the heat of the day still buried in the ground and the building, so the room swelters and hums with it. They take their now accustomed spots, Livia the most reclined, hand complacently on her middle.

Jake holds the floor to announce his plan, while on-screen Martha observes smokily, eyebrow in permanent mid-rise, ready to comment.

'I'm sure two of you are familiar with the concept of "barium meal". It's a spy term, Liv. I got it once from a CIA novel called *The Company*, which is over there somewhere.' He waves vaguely at the espionage section of the library. 'Though I think it's taken from real life. Anyway, it's a complicated way of describing an obvious thing: the idea is that you give out deliberately doctored information and you find out who your enemies are by seeing how each person responds to it.'

'The best example, if I may, Jake', this is Martha, in a laconic drawl, 'is – if you're trying to find a mole in your organization – you send the same message to each different suspect, but alter it slightly each time. When you see one specific version passed on, you know the source and have caught your mole. It's secretly radioactive, you see, like the barium they used to use in X-rays. But we're not looking for a mole, are we, Jake?'

'No, Professor, we're not. But we know we have a suspect desperate to continue the cover-up. A cover-up, by the way, that's been maintained for more than a year. I'm going to suggest to all those we think could be involved that we have uncovered some critical evidence in the Keep that will point the finger at the murderer, and that we're about to collect it. That should force our man out into the open.'

Aletheia has laid her pen down. 'What if they know you're bluffing?'

'That's the crucial part. I'm not really bluffing. When I went into the Keep today, I opened up one of the tombs, and I saw evidence of Janet's body there. Maybe the whole thing. Maybe only clothes, evidence hurriedly concealed. But there was a modern boot squished under the main shroud, poking out, and a bit further up some remnants of a dress that have no place in an Anglo-Saxon grave. I didn't want to open it all up, and leave it exposed before I could try this properly, but something is definitely there. My bluff is, you see, also the truth. My barium meal is not false material, but accurate information: and only the killer will be disturbed by it.'

He sits back and stretches, his muscles dancing a little in the flickering light. Martha is the first to speak. 'You know how sceptical I am of ideas I don't come up with myself, but this makes sense to me. From all I can see, in terms of recorded activity, Janet's last visible visit was to the site. That's if we discount the final trip to the archives, which we now think is probably someone else. And if she were killed there, the obvious place to conceal evidence of it is a room filled with things once owned by dead people.'

Jake turns towards Aletheia, who has her eyes closed, her brow furrowed. 'Al, does this make sense to you?'

'It does, but why not tell McAllister and see what's actually there first. That's the proper thing to do.'

'I know you have to say that, and you may want to disown this conversation at some point. But say we do this all openly, tell McAllister, what happens next? The best-case scenario is that we find a body, and we can forensic it. That doesn't give us our killer. We need to lure them in, and I'm not sure the police can agree to a sting like this.'

Aletheia nods in acknowledgement. Jake knows that her ambiguous status here, as a serving officer and consultant, means that she has to be cautious. He looks at Livia, whose hands are gripping her thighs so tight you can see the tendons taut beneath her thin skin. She acknowledges his look wanly.

Her voice is more of a gasp for a second. 'So how do you deliver the barium meal?'

'We tell all the interested parties that I'll be excavating in the Keep tomorrow night. Brian, Zach, Daisy, Lily, the two grads Matt and Elaine. The police have a presence there until early evening, and so anyone with an interest in getting at the evidence will have to make a move that night. And we'll see who bites.'

'And if they do?' Martha is brisk, but with delight in her eyes at the prospect of action.

'We get enough out of them to nail them.'

'Tough talk, Jake, but not without danger. This Wulfnoth has killed three times, and tried to off you and Daisy. And as you say, has dodged all of us until now.'

'I know, so we'll have to come up with some precautions.'

'What if Wulfnoth is not one of those people we've come into contact with?' This is Livia, prodding at the concept carefully, cautious as normal, her voice stronger than before.

'Wulfnoth is clearly connected to the site in some way. We have to assume that if it's widely known what I'm doing, and when the site will be free from police, then he'll hear about it from the folk we do tell.'

They spend the next half hour working on logistics. They agree that Aletheia should back Jake up in person, by concealing herself in the office. She can wire the Keep in advance so that any evidence will be recorded, and also to ensure she can listen in and pick up any threat to Jake. The idea is that Jake releases the barium meal during the next day, with the proposal that the excavation – part bluff, part real – will take place during that night.

It feels late, and that a momentous point has been reached, so further discussion is abandoned until the morning. Martha blips away with an ironic salute and Aletheia, sensing the silent communion between Jake and Livia, heads off to bed. They tidy in desultory fashion, washing cups and straightening chairs. Jake trying not to fuss in too close a proximity to her. The night draws them outside, where the air is – albeit faintly – fresher, the breeze off the lake a mere hint at their faces, still heavy with the fertile rot of a warm, wet summer.

They can hear the garbled croaks of a frog, maybe several, nestled in an invisible corner somewhere, a sound that contrasts with the gentle susurration of the leaves and plants. Livia is holding Jake's hand. When she speaks, she does not turn her head, so it seems as if she is addressing the presiding spirit of the lake, like some sort of druidical figure from ages past.

'Do you really need to do this, Jake?'

'I think so. They asked for our help, and this will give it to them.'

'I shouldn't say this but I feel a bit hateful that I can't do much to help you because I'm somehow disqualified by pregnancy and I don't want to risk my body at all. Like I'm being forced to sit on the bench with the girl on her period, and the fat, wheezy one with the note from Matron. Maybe it's a sign pregnancy is going to be a disaster.' A tear runs down her cheek, a filigree of silver in the moonlight. 'Look at me, I was oozing optimism before, now I'm like this. I'm nervy, and every twinge in my body I'm suddenly suspicious of. I had a pain in the library there, and wanted to shriek, then it passed like the indigestion it was. Late-night cheese is never a good idea. I'm sorry, Jake, I'm all over the place, hormonal.' She laughs and it comes out like a sob.

Jake holds her in his arms. 'Liv, I can admit that I'm going to be over-protective and annoying when it comes to a baby, but I'm not sure anyone would think it wrong to keep a pregnant, non-police woman like you from this sort of thing.'

'I don't want to get in a scrap with a killer, but you know I'm not one to accept being pushed in a corner.' More teary laughter. 'God, I hate being this emotional.'

Jake feels nothing but overweening love for this woman. 'Why don't you keep an eye on things with Martha, and you can liaise with McAllister as needed? He likes and trusts you; he might need a bit of time to appreciate her.'

Livia wipes her eyes. 'It's a non-job, but I'll take it. And you' – she turns and thumps his chest with playful force – 'better fucking take care, because if you get hurt I'll never forgive you.'

A chilling thought, and they both push it to one side as they stand next to each other, the long dim vista of night before them, the lake seething in the heat, the violence of that summer an unignorable presence, as real as the scuttles and shuffles of the life all around.

Chapter Thirty-Eight

Diverse locations in the area beyond Caelum Parvum

Jake plans to visit Rose's house as the first stop next morning. He doesn't want to believe that Lily is a three-time killer who has insinuated herself into their lives with a sort of bluff ease, but he cannot deny that she has been present at all the critical moments, and he is committed to testing everybody relevant in this sprawling, complex case. Plus, one of the first rules of policing is to embrace doubt as a creative spur, to understand you can never really know anybody's inner mind with total certainty. 'If you're one hundred per cent positive, you've miscounted somewhere,' as the communist sergeant used to say – and he was right.

Livia leaves early with Diana and Aletheia, the latter to put in a stint with McAllister before breaking into the Keep that afternoon to fit it for sound. It is another hot day, too hot, the mutterings of thunder already there muted in the background, the air steamy and unforgiving. Jake has run and swum, and is showering when he sees someone coming up the path by the lake, dressed in black, crow-like against the pastel colours of the landscape. Daisy.

When she sees the shower running, she stops, uncertain and bashful, clearly uncomfortable at the thought of intruding. She turns away and sits on the bench, fretting the long sleeves of her shirt, her neck stiff, a vision of self-control even at this distance.

Jake grabs a towel and hops inside, quickly shrugs on shorts and a vest, pours two mugs of coffee and goes to join her. She makes careful space on the bench, accepts the drink gingerly.

Jake waits for her to speak, then fills the silence. 'I didn't know you were back.'

'I came back last night. The house was fixed up and there was no reason not to. I was supposed to be seeing Amy this week, though of course that won't happen now.' Her voice falters, her pale nails tap against the ceramic. 'I felt a bit lonely and empty in that place this morning, rattling round like an old skeleton, so I thought I'd come to see you and Livia, at least to say goodbye. I'm not sure I'm going to stick around here much longer. The TV show is done now, we won't be back after all this, and I can't think of the place without thinking of all the horror.'

Jake sips his drink, waits for her to continue. She leans forward, black hair with a gleam like a bird's plumage, that crow again, her cheekbones taut. 'Did you see Amy's body, did you see what happened to her?'

'I did. She was hit in the head, and left, part-stripped to make it look like she'd been killed by a lover.'

'How did she look?' Daisy's face is strange, and fearful.

'Dead. Helpless. Like someone she knew had betrayed her.'

'You don't think Zach did it then? I heard somewhere that he'd been arrested.'

'He was spoken to, but I'm not sure he'll be charged. Unless I've misread it all, of course; it's not impossible he killed Amy, the woman he was seeing in secret. But why would he do it?'

'Why does anybody do anything? Passion, perhaps, thwarted desire, rage at our own impotence.'

'Does that sound likely with Zach?'

'Not likely. But none of this is likely. I look at everyone on the dig with suspicious eyes now. How much do we really know about them, about what they think, even the younger ones? That couple, Matt and Elaine, I never quite saw why they kept coming back each year, why they've stayed. I've heard them digging together, grumbling about Amy, about their lives there, sounding like zealots when it comes to what they believe. God-bothering, desperate in their search for some sort of meaning.' She exhales, seems to want to shake off her negative thoughts. 'Not that makes them especially suspicious, I suppose.' She rubs her hand along her thigh; he can see her swallowing, her smooth neck rising and falling. 'God it's selfish, Jake, but I keep thinking it could've been me. I could've been lying there in the rain.' She turns her eyes, wide and dark, upon him. 'And would anyone really have cared?'

He thinks for a moment. The heron, which has been standing sage and sentinel in the reeds, flies upward with a complacent swipe of its broad wings. 'In my experience,' he says carefully, 'people always care. People notice the little things about you, care what you do, who you are. I don't think you should underestimate yourself. You've made a big impact wherever you've gone.'

'That's kind of you. But you've always seemed a kind and perceptive man.' Her stare is searching. 'And has this perceptive man got a theory of what happened to Amy, and Jordan, and to me and you for that matter?'

Jake stretches his legs, speaks casually. 'I think I've found evidence that Janet Sanders was murdered, and it's there to be gathered up as soon as possible. It's been stored in the Keep all this time. I've arranged an excavation of sorts by ten tonight.'

'What sort of evidence?'

'Physical material that's been hidden there, or moved there. Her body even. Likely DNA evidence of our killer. Anyway, my grand theory is that the same person killed Janet and Jordan and Amy.'

'The same person as attacked you and me.'

'Exactly.'

'So will there be justice?'

'I hope so. I believe so.'

'Oh, Jake, that would be worth waiting for.' She flings her arms around him. He can feel her heart thundering against his chest, her breaths quick and urgent. She pulls back, composure suddenly returned, like a door slammed shut. 'You must think me very odd. Coming here unannounced, an emotional wreck like this.'

'I think you've had a hard time, and you're entitled to be emotional. Once this is all over, are you sure you wouldn't like to stick around? It's so peaceful really.' He gestures with his hand at a landscape that basks in the morning glow. In the distance, you can hear the clucking of chickens, busy amidst the soporific heat.

'God knows. I came here this morning to make my goodbyes, because I feel I've come to the end of the road. Maybe that's still true once all is said and done; maybe there's a future to be plotted here. I don't know. All I've ever craved is peace, but that's not always been possible.'

She stands up to leave, smoothing the velvet material of her trousers. She is immaculately dressed as normal, precise and contained. 'Will you let me know if you get your man? When you get your man. And will you pass my very best to Livia? You've both been so kind.'

She holds out her hand, formal once more, the tendons of her wrist like bird bones, a single bangle hanging forlornly down. Jake takes it, the fingers slender and strong. 'Daisy, you know it's OK to let go sometimes. Nothing to be ashamed of.'

'It's too late for advice like that, Jake. I am who I am. But I'm glad to have seen you.'

With that she leaves, walking carefully, small steps, her hair spread back behind her like a banner in the breeze. Jake watches her until she disappears, a speck absorbed by the dip and rise of the land.

Daisy's visit had saved a call, and he knows he has to get around everybody else by the end of the day. He makes himself a cheese-and-mustard sandwich, sharp and tart in his nostrils, and eats it as he makes his way to Parvum, now dressed for night-time manoeuvres, in dark, loose trousers and a shirt.

Livia has left the car for him, and he drives to Rose's house, which is big and tucked away, not quite as old as its warped beams are meant to suggest. It emerges at the end of a long drive, and is surrounded defensively by banks of trees, like a fort. As Jake pulls up, he sees Lily and Rose lying in the garden on towels, absorbing the sun that is struggling its way through the haze. Rose is in old swim shorts, his body tanned, wiry arms but with a stomach that now has a little give in it. Lily is in a bright blue bikini, long-limbed and coltish, lying on her stomach, novel in hand.

She looks over her shoulder and gives Jake a friendly wave, while nudging her brother in the small of his back. 'Jake, nice to see you. Come sit down, have a drink. We're having sangria.' She motions with her book to a large jug half-full of cartoonishly purple liquid. Jake sees she is reading *Murder in Mesopotamia* by Agatha Christie.

Rose's eyes have flickered open, and he removes his earphones. 'Ah Jake, do you want some sangria?'

'I've asked him, but I reckon he was about to say no. Am I right, Jake? You look all serious. Are you playing Poirot today?'

Jake sits down on an old wooden chair. 'Near enough. I've had a bit of a breakthrough in the case.'

Lily wraps the towel around her waist, beneath a red jewel that winks from her belly button. She fills her glass and Rose's, tucks her feet beneath her, and squats back upon the grass. 'I'm glad to hear it. I keep thinking about Amy lying there. Poor thing. She wasn't the warmest, but I hate to think of her so cold like that. Do you think Zach did her in?'

'Do you?'

She inclines her head to one side. 'I wouldn't rule it out. But then I wouldn't have picked him as someone who'd be involved in a crime of passion.'

'I'm not sure I would either. But I don't think this was a crime of passion. I think Amy's death is linked to the others, including Janet Sanders, who was writing a book about the area. She was last seen at the dig, and never reappeared.'

Lily nods thoughtfully. 'I knew she was missing. I never knew she was dead.'

Rose has propped himself up on his arms, a thin fatty fold across his middle, which bulges a little as he moves. 'You think she was killed there as well, do you? Her, Jordan and Amy. God, Lily, I'm glad they're closing it down, aren't you?' She ignores the question.

Jake continues. 'I think there's evidence in the Keep that will point direct to the killer. I'm going there tonight to uncover it.'

Rose's eyes narrow. 'Why not leave all that to your man, what's he called, McAllister?'

Jake lies easily. 'Let's say he's not as convinced as I am about it, and I'm free to act and he's not. He's even letting the police presence slip by dusk today, which gives me a proper shot at it.'

Rose sips his drink. 'And Livia has blessed this bit of freelancing?'

'She wants this settled as much as you both do. And I hope by ten tonight I'll have evidence McAllister can't ignore.'

Rose's brow remains furrowed. 'What does Aletheia make of this?'

Jake is keen to avoid this line of questioning, so responds with a barb of his own: 'And why are you so concerned about Aletheia?'

'Yes, big brother, why so concerned? I think he likes her, Jake. And maybe he's a little embarrassed about falling asleep blind drunk at your place, when he could have taken her for a romantic moonlit walk.' Lily settles herself contentedly as Rose blusters and squirms.

'I don't like her like that. I like talking to her, that's all.

Nothing wrong with it. Anyway, she told me she was back in Parvum, so I guess she's working with you. I thought I'd meet up with her at the Nook later.'

'You guess away, and I don't care what you do with Aletheia. Talk yourself out.'

Rose gets up, pulling his shorts out from between his legs where they have got rucked in the heat. 'Glad to have your blessing, anyway. Are you sticking around?'

'No, I've got to go, do a couple more things before tonight.'

Rose purses his lips, his eyes hooded. He scratches his chest reflectively, hairs a mongrel mixture of black and grey. 'Came this way for a brief chat, did you? Well, we'll be seeing you.' Lily has already resumed her book, and waves casually as Jake sets off.

The seats of the car are hot to the touch, the sun-baked interior smelling of dried mud, the relicts of the farmyard. He has two more appointments to make before the afternoon lengthens into evening, and he needs to get moving.

He stops off at Livia's house on the way, where Aletheia has left him a note, detailing the locations of the other members of the dig. None are at work, the site now clearly deserted. Zach's flat is the closest and he drives there, windows down, watching the clouds cluster and thicken, the ozone smell of storm in his nostrils.

Zach lives in a basement flat on the edge of Meryton, the lower part of a small semi-detached house. There is a scrubby sort of patio out front, with a tumbledown bike shed pushed incongruously into a corner, the wood peeling, a dirty window half-obscured by old tar paper. Jake goes down a flight of scuffed stairs, knocks on the front door and waits. Nothing seems to stir. He can feel the sweat sliding down his back. He knocks again, and hears the sound of movement inside.

The door is cautiously opened, and Zach's face emerges, flushed in the heat, a clammy film of sweat upon his forehead. He looks wretched.

Jake puts as much authority as he can in his voice. 'Can we speak?'

Zach looks unable to decide, his eyes wide and glassy with apprehension. Jake gently eases past him into the flat. It is airless, smells of decay, the rankness of the enclosed male, but is clean enough. Jake guesses that Zach was normally a tidy housekeeper, but has done little since his arrest other than brood and mope and worry.

He is wearing an old pair of tracksuit bottoms, his pale upper body thin and hairless, collarbone jutting forth like the prow of a shipwreck. There is a can of cider on the floor, already turning cloying in the heat.

Zach shrugs his bony shoulders. 'I was trying to drown my sorrows, but I can't even do that properly. Maybe it's hemlock not cider I need.'

'How did you leave things with the cops?'

'Don't pretend you're separate from them. You're a policeman in all but name.'

Jake sits down on an old suede sofa, finding a spot between a book manuscript and a pile of archaeological journals. 'I am and I'm not. I'm helping them, but I'm also free to think my own thoughts, pursue my own leads. And can I be frank with you, Zach? I don't think you killed anybody. I think this goes beyond you and Amy. That's one of the reasons I came to see you.'

'*Timeo Danaos et dona ferentes.*'

'Excuse me?'

'I'm wary of Greeks bearing gifts.'

'You can be as wary as you like, and you can hide behind as many Latin tags as you like. Or Greek ones for that matter. You were sleeping with a murder victim, and she was found half undressed in a place you were last seen; orange paint was found in that shed out there, which matches stuff scrawled on a wall of an Indian woman who you also worked with. She was attacked at the dig where you worked too, as was Reverend Jordan, who was killed. Oh, and all three of them had recently found treasure with you, potentially worth millions of pounds. You're one of two people still alive to claim it. So, you'll forgive me for bearing the gift of refusing to believe what many would say is blindingly obvious: you killed Amy in a moment of passion, and others besides.'

Zach is shrinking back into his chair, his arms curved around him, creamy white, like twisted bedsheets. He says nothing.

Jake takes that as acquiescence of sorts. 'What do you know about Janet Sanders?'

Zach looks surprised, pushes his hair from his eyes. 'Not much really. Amateur historian, used to be around the place a lot, bit batty maybe. Had a bit of wildness in her eyes. She knew Amy and Brian pretty well, and Daisy too. What's she got to do with this?'

Jake leans forward, measuring the impact of his words. 'She's dead, Zach. Killed a year ago, I think. And the evidence of her death is in the Keep, and I'm going to try to find it tonight. The police will be gone by six this evening, so I can get a free shot at it.'

'In the old tombs down there, I guess.'

'Why do you think that?'

'Because that's where I'd hide anything I wanted to stay hidden. We're keeping them sealed, and they have a sturdy lead lining which makes them very secure. I can remember all the problems we had shifting them. If you could open them, and you were desperate, why wouldn't you?'

'And did you?'

'Of course not. Why would I mention it if I did? God, are you trying to trap me? I can't cope with this stuff, it's too much.' There is anguish in his face, his body tense as if there is a shock running through it, tautening the sinews and tendons visible beneath his papery skin. He grabs his hair and pulls it, keening all the while. 'Amy's gone, and all anyone thinks is that I did it.'

Jake reaches out and touches him; he recoils as if scalded, skittish like a cornered animal. 'Zach, if anything, I'm trying to help you.'

Zach turns away from him, averts his eyes. 'I think you should go.' He sits there, immobile, shut down, refusing to acknowledge anything further. Jake looks pityingly upon him, and is glad to climb the stairs back to ground level, where the humid, turbid air that meets him feels if anything like a balm.

Jake mentally tosses up between Brian and the two graduates for his next visit, opting for the former almost at random. Which turns out to be a good decision, because, when he eases his car to the side of the road twenty minutes later, he can see all three of them together, sitting around an old wooden table in the corner of a field by Brian's house.

Brian's welcome is typically effusive. 'Come down, Jake, we're drowning our sorrows and talking history. I reckon we've got about an hour before the heavens open up on us, too.'

Jake leaps a stile and follows the well-worn track towards the cottage, which is small and slate-coloured, the hedgerow to his left a contrasting collage of dog roses and late-blooming violets, simpering pinks merging into deep purples. Brian hands him a beer from a cooler by his feet. Matt and Elaine smile and shake hands, but their eyes are suspicious.

They talk about the dig, and its geography, the hill and the stream, the lonely plateau beneath its never-ending sky, the human interventions of fort and villa. The presence of murder left unstated for a while, as if each wanted to remind themselves of what had originally drawn them there.

Jake then brings the conversation around to Amy, and things become more stilted. Brian's attempts to be jovial fall upon stony ground, and Matt and Elaine initially seem unwilling to venture reflections or opinions.

Matt is smoking a rolled-up cigarette, which hangs heavy in the still air. 'I hate to speak poorly of the dead, but she was never inspiring.' Brian's hands rise in mild protest. 'No, Brian, she wasn't. I'm sure she was a nice person, to you at least, but I do not want to mislead and pretend that I'll miss her. She didn't run the dig well, was too distracted by her little Zach.' The full Gallic disdain there in those final syllables. 'And we were always running late, not following the lessons of the land. Brian, you and I have often spoken of this. You told me always you could be doing a better job.'

Brian looks uneasily towards Jake. 'I wouldn't go that far. Professional disagreements, you understand, perfectly normal.'

Matt resumes his thoughts. 'Perhaps. But we were not

going to get funding next year, I don't think, so whatever happened our time there was going to come to an end. Even Amy told me she thought that. We were in too many parts of the site, discovering too little. You know this.'

He turns to Elaine for support, who nods, and intertwines her fingers with his. 'It was all too much summery hi-jinks, bucket and spades in the sun, not serious archaeology.' Her voice is cold. 'We didn't mind, I suppose, but we weren't going to get rich on it as a job.'

'Unlike those who discovered the treasure,' Jake says quietly.

She drums her fingers on the table. 'Well quite. And if the area beneath the hill had been judged part of the dig, nobody else would have got rich either. I'm sure you know, Jake, that you don't get a reward for treasure found on a recognized site. They were lucky that bit had never been designated, or at least nobody knew if it had. And, you know, treasure hunters give all archaeologists a bad name, in my opinion. It's all rather distasteful, seeking profit from the past. No skill or love in holding on to a metal detector. Any moron can do that.' She offers a theatrical shudder. 'I don't think professionals should be doing it.'

'Was Janet Sanders interested in that sort of detecting?'

Brian's face, which had been rather gloomy, brightens. He doesn't appear to notice the tension in his two companions at the mention of her name. 'She knew, or wanted to know, every blade of grass in that whole area. She was more of an expert than me, than Amy. Book-clever, like Daisy. They got on ever so well, of course. That's why Daisy kicked up all that fuss when Janet went missing. We expected Janet to come and go, a free spirit you understand, but our Daisy she insisted summat was untoward.'

Jake takes a small sip of his beer, which is cold, American and tastes of nothing. 'She was right, I think. I've got some evidence that Janet was murdered on site, as Amy was, and there's proof of it hidden there in the Keep. I've got the permission of the police to search it tonight; they're coming off the site anyway in a couple of hours.'

Brian looks surprised, Elaine is twitchily as hard to read as ever. Matt offers a forced grin and lights another cigarette. 'Christ, this place, eh? The twists keep on coming.'

Jake meets his eyes, does not break the stare. 'Aren't you concerned that Janet might be dead, Matt? You had a relationship with her, didn't you?'

He expels a plume of smoke defiantly. 'Man, you make it sound so old-fashioned. I had a thing with her, sure. She was nice, especially for an older lady. I was single, it was summer.' He looks across at Elaine briefly. 'But that was it, a little fun and nothing more. She had no claims on me, and I had none on her. She was a free spirit. I hope she's not dead. She's more likely to be . . .' He struggles to seek out the English word. 'You know, hiding off away somewhere, like she often did, and that would make me happy.' He squeezes Elaine's hand. She does not reciprocate.

Jake lets the awkwardness linger. 'Two others dead, Daisy nearly killed – I'm not sure how confident I'd be about her hiding in secret, as you say. But I want to bring the twists to an end tonight if I can. I should have it done by ten. I hope I'm wrong about Janet, but I'll let you know either way.' He rises to leave, his bottle, beaded with condensation, mostly untouched.

Brian accompanies Jake halfway back up towards the car. He takes him by the arm, and whispers fiercely in his ear. 'Anything I can do to help you find the bastard doing this, you only need to say.' He is strong, he has strangler's fingers drawn tight at Jake's elbow, leaving the outline of a faint bruise when he withdraws.

Jake nods in agreement, and heads to the road. He pauses at the stile and looks down to the table where Brian has seated himself once more. The three of them appear strained and silent, the sky above them now black with storm-hungry cloud, the only real sound the hum of bees and insects, a blur of frenzied activity, as if they know a big outburst is, inexorably, on its way.

Chapter Thirty-Nine

Wulfnoth's Keep, St Giles site

The rain comes before Jake can get to the site, heavy and relentless, an outpouring that pounds the roof of the car loud like the shifting of an anchor chain. The road in front of him is a blue mist, dark shapes looming on either side in a sodden blur. He slows down and parks the car at the base of the hill, which has never looked more desolate, the grey in the clouds pressing down upon the plateau as a dampening drape.

When he gets out, he is wet to his very core in seconds, as if he has been upended in a barrel, his hair plastered down across his neck. He runs to the office, where Aletheia lets him in after an agreed knock. She wordlessly hands him a towel, and he strips off his top and dries himself before cautiously slipping it back around his shoulders.

'Nice day for it, Jake.'
'How's it gone here?'
'Good. The main body of the Keep is not so far down

that I can't create a proper signal, and I put in a booster between there and here, luckily before the deluge came. I've got no pictures, only sound, but it's up and working. The constable left an hour or so ago, no action so far.' She points to her laptop, which is open on a blank screen, an audio symbol showing. 'And look at our expert panel, who'll hear everything.' She clicks a button and the screen splits between Martha's and Livia's homes. One side shows a cluttered desk, covered by old books and cannabis detritus; the other catches Livia walking past. She waves, and sits down, speaking into her microphone.

'Hello, lovey. We have to talk about you stripping off your top in front of other women, though.'

'She's lucky I didn't have to take it all off. I nearly swam here.'

Aletheia is pretending to cover her ears in horror. Jake leans forward and speaks quietly. 'Are you OK, my love?'

'I'm fine. And I'll be around tonight when it all goes down. Di's with Jo for the evening. She's demanded that you give her the inside track afterwards, of course, as payment.'

'She can't admit to being a nice person, can she?'

Livia shakes her head, the curled tips of her hair brazen in the light of the room. She waves and moves out of vision. Jake turns back to Aletheia.

'So we know the plan. I'm going to go and see once and for all what's in that tomb; the idea being it's all laid out when our suspect arrives. I've told them I'd be working around 10 p.m.; that gives them time to sneak in, now that the copper has gone.'

'I don't love the set-up, Jake. You'll be on your own in there.'

'If you came too, we'd never get them talking. They'd run or clam up. I'll be very quiet while I wait, even talking to you. By the time they've come through the door to see me, they'll have revealed themselves. Then we shall see. They do know me, they want to talk to me, I think. This is a killer who communicates, after all. They *want* to make their argument.'

'Once we have them, I'll call McAllister and then come and help you directly. Then we hold the place down until the cavalry comes.'

'Have you told him what's going on?'

Aletheia looks wry in return. 'I've hinted at it. He knows we're on manoeuvres tonight and is ready. I only hope we can give him a result. I saw Rose for coffee too.' She looks almost embarrassed. 'He's definitely suspicious you're up to no good.' Jake checks the clock on the wall – cheap and plastic, ticking inaudibly given the roar from the rain – and decides they need to get moving.

It is now early evening, but as dark as night outside; the sallow office lights a paltry beacon in the murk. He switches them off, and the room is cast into gloom, the only glow coming from the computer, faintly blue and ghostly.

Jake hands Aletheia a document he'd prepared that morning. 'This is all we know so far, and what we have in terms of evidence. It will be better coming to the police here from you, especially if anything happens.'

Aletheia casts her eyes down it, sees the name of Jake's chief suspect. 'As ever, old man, we're in total agreement.' She pats his chest briskly. 'Time to stop talking and get into position. Our guest could be early.'

Five minutes later, shirt buttoned up against the chill, the damp material no especial comfort, Jake uses the keys and opens the door to the Keep, shutting it behind him softly. Immediately the noise of the weather dips, a welcome relief, and he is in the quiet corridor that runs down into the main room. A faint thrum is all he can hear, distant, the world shut out for the while.

He enters the main room, and says quietly, 'I'm in.' His voice oddly loud in the cushioned dimness, like a blurt in a library. Everything is in place, as it was before. The sword winking beneath its lamp, the keenness of its blade visible and threatening.

Jake puts on his gloves and walks up to the first of the tombs. He knows precisely what he is looking for, and he gets straight to work. The lid is old and heavy, covered with mystical runes, etched painfully into the stubborn stone. He can move it sideways with some effort, but then it slips from his hands and crashes down to the ground, sounding like a bomb going off. Dust puffs up from the floor, and the echo rebounds around the room.

Jake can feel his muscles quivering at the shock. His voice is a croak when it comes. 'All well, Al, only me being clumsy.' He can imagine her sitting at the desk, as she had done so many times working with him over the years, eerie screen-glow bathing her face, which is screwed up tightly in concentration. He can see her smiling at his clumsiness.

The overhead light is shining upon the inhabitant of the tomb, a skeleton from another millennium, complete, the skull empty-eyed and grinning, a huge hole in its back. Apart from that, everything looks intact, perhaps too neat if anything, arranged as if in an anatomy lesson. It is lying on what looks like a stretcher of sorts, made from animal skin, which is brown and faded, but still solid. Emerging from the side, beneath it, are the things he had seen briefly before: a modern boot at one end, a piece of a purple cotton sleeve at the other.

He finds if he stands parallel to the side of the tomb, he can insert both hands on either side of the stretcher. Mouthing a silent apology for the desecration – and thinking ironically of the complaints raised by the original Wulfnoth – he lifts. There is movement, dust that tastes chalky and acrid in his mouth, and he realizes he is inhaling the final remnants of a once living person. He closes his lips tightly.

As he pulls, the bones shift. They are loose, the connective tissue long gone, they collapse together into the dip in the material he has created. The whole thing is not too heavy, though, and in a few seconds he has deposited the stretcher on the ground. The skull has lolled obscenely round, the yellow, sharp-pointed teeth now visible. He spends a moment roughly rearranging the bones, which are smooth and dry, weak-feeling and friable. He knows he is wasting time as he does it, delaying the inevitable, the confrontation with the reality of the case, so he makes himself stand, his own bones feeling old in sympathy for a moment, and returns to the tomb. Lying there, twisted, waxy blackened palms upward, is the dead body of a woman Jake knows to be Janet Sanders.

An unpleasant scent fills the air, sweetish and sharp, like the top note of vomit, death right there in his nostrils, the rottenness of it all, the inarguable tang of life ending – as it must – in decay. The coffin has preserved the body better than it would have done in the ground, the lead lining doing its work, the dry air in the Keep helping. Jake can see the living Janet there in the shambles beneath him, though: her blond hair, thinned almost to nothing but a few strands clinging on, her skin stretched taut like medieval parchment, still covering some of the dirty-coloured bones beneath. Jake opens the tattered remains of her coat, and reaches for where the pockets should be. There is a small purse there and he removes it carefully. It opens with a puckering pop, the only noise that has been made in the last five minutes. Jake realizes he has been hardly breathing, realizes that Aletheia is sitting there waiting for him to tell her what is going on.

He plucks a credit card from the purse, reading out loud 'Janet Sanders. There we go. It's her, Al, stuck beneath the original bones. Half-decomposed, she looks like she died about a year ago, at the time we thought she did.'

He circles the tomb, looking for signs of violence. He doesn't want to disturb it too much, or damage any evidence ahead of the eventual post-mortem, so is careful in his movements. At the head-end, he cautiously lifts some of the straw-like hair; it disintegrates in his hand, falling to the base of the coffin like crop stubble. Amid the gooey residue beneath, he thinks he can see the site of an old wound, the skull cracked open. Another irony, he thinks: two bodies a millennium apart, made to share a resting place, and killed perhaps in the same violent way. He whispers what he can see to the invisible Aletheia, and resumes his pacing.

He feels the familiar lurch in his stomach as he does so, the sensation of pity and fear, the disgust – it is definitely that as well – at the wasteful messiness of it all. He can feel the blood, the contrasting life force deep within him, pumping loud in his ears. His eyes rove the human wreckage, which draws his entire focus, his concentration complete.

Which is why, perhaps, he hears no other sound in the

room, including the door swinging open, the soft footsteps behind him, until, too late, they are only a metre away. He turns, surprised, to see Lily, her face twisted and angry and determined, her arm already moving, a blow about to fall and now impossible to avoid.

Chapter Forty

Wulfnoth's Keep, St Giles site

It is a slap across his face, sudden and stinging. He reels back, on his heels, before stepping forward to avoid another, catching it on his forearm, and using his momentum to push Lily to the ground.

She half-sprawls, propping herself up with one hand, her dark eyes fierce, rage blazing across her features. She tries to push herself forward, but gives up the effort almost immediately, as he stands aggressively above her.

Her defiance remains, though. 'Jake, I'm so angry I could spit.' Jake can see that, but also that she seems faintly chastened by her fall, her desire to fight a little cooled.

'What the fuck are you doing here, swinging away like that?'

'I'm here because I don't like being tricked. And I sure as hell don't like being sneakily accused of being a killer. I came to your house, man, my brother looks at you like one of the family.' She subsides once more and he can see the flush of emotion rising from her chest to her chin.

'What are you even talking about?'

The fire flares up again, like breath upon an ember. 'Don't keep treating me like a fool. I know what you've been up to. Going around telling folk that you've got this important evidence, and you'll be here tonight getting it ready. A trap. A trap to catch a murderer. Maybe me. Which means you think I could be a murderer. Jesus.'

Jake grabs her roughly by the wrist and drags her, resistant, her body suddenly inert, over to the tomb. He pushes her forward so her head is above the centre, brown curls orange in the light. 'Look at that, Lily. That's a woman who a year ago was standing in this room, living and breathing. Now she's that. Two other people have died as well, and I'm not going to apologize for doing whatever I can to find out who did it. Even if it means, even if it means upsetting your delicate sensibilities. Or Rose's, for that matter. Look at her.'

But she cannot. She has wrenched herself away, and is now retching in the corner, hands on her knees, her back to him. She is wearing a thin summer coat, marshmallow pink, and it is dripping softly onto the ground. He watches her heaving body, his own anger – such as it was – dissipating. He thinks that this is probably the first real dead body, rather than dry bones in an archaeological dig, Lily has ever seen.

When she turns there is contrition in her face. She walks towards him, but seems held back by an invisible field emanating from the tomb. She also notices the skeleton on the stretcher for the first time, and steps leerily around it. Her voice is shaky, rather quiet.

'Jake, all right, I shouldn't have slapped you. But I think you might have trusted me, and Rose.'

Jake moves past the forcefield and stands alongside her. 'If it makes you feel better, I did trust you. Aletheia's in the office, listening to everything, and she has a name on a piece of paper identifying our suspect. It's not you. But we're playing here for high stakes, and I had to be thorough. I didn't want to draw you in, but I couldn't leave anything undone.' He raises his voice slightly. 'By the way, I wonder if Rose wheedled info out of Aletheia when they met earlier.'

Lily giggles softly, an incongruous noise in that room, especially after the last ten minutes. 'I think she implied to him that you were testing a theory, and he got a bit huffy on my behalf. He doesn't know I'm here. I think he respects you too much to interfere himself.'

'But you don't.'

'Let's say that neither of us know each other well enough to be totally sure. But we will in future, please God it never happens again.' She runs a casual finger along a container of potsherds, uses her other hand to push her damp hair from her eyes.

'What time is it, by the way?'

Lily looks at her phone, which brightens up, showing a close-up photograph of her gurning in a nightclub, wearing a giant pair of fluorescent yellow sunglasses. 'Not quite nine.'

'You need to go. There's a genuine suspect coming, at least I hope there is, and I don't want you caught up in it. Can you get home safely?'

She chucks him under his chin, ironically. 'Half an hour ago he wants to make sure I'm not a killer, now he wants me to get home safely. No, I borrowed big brother's car, and I'm all set. This rain has to slow down soon. Will you be OK?'

Jake massages his cheek, which still feels hot. 'My face may not recover quickly, seeing as you ask. But no, I think I'll be all right.' He raises his voice. 'Aletheia will see you into your car.' He then speaks more quietly. 'I'm sorry you had to see Janet lying there like that.'

Lily's voice is also soft, sorrowful even. 'I'm sad that she's ended up like that. You thought it was going to be her lying there, didn't you? Rose always said you were good at this. Well, good luck.' She lingers, awkward, before skipping close and giving him a hug, and a brief kiss on his cheek. 'You take care of yourself.'

Jake watches her leave, contemplating the ridiculousness of the situation. A slap and a kiss on the same location, ten minutes apart, while a newly discovered corpse moulders in the corner. How did he end up here?

He sits on a chair at the edge of the room, next to a desk cluttered with stony debris. He thinks of his last couple of years at Little Sky; before that, his flight from the city, and his job, and Faye. Faye with her new man, her new baby on the way. A baby like his. His baby, growing unseen and parlous and much doted-upon inside his Livia. A thing precious he cannot touch or hold on to. He rubs his cheek, tries to focus his mind.

He clears his throat delicately. 'I hope you enjoyed all that, Al. And don't think I don't blame you for being indiscreet with Rose. I blame you entirely.' He can't keep the amusement from his voice. 'I don't know: you used to be a law machine, a robot, now you're as weak as the rest of us.' His words ring out into the nothingness. The room is quiet once more: him alone with all these remains, both ancient and recent.

Jake gets up and returns to Janet's body. He delicately lifts her legs, half-rotted and spongy as they are, his mind as still and clear as possible, seeking to maintain an emotional distance from the carnal reality before him. His approach over the years when dealing with the horrors of a crime scene was always to somehow render himself in the third person, to see himself removed from the grim reality at the same time as experiencing it, as if he were both camera and subject, implicated and aloof.

It doesn't work entirely. The reek of death is there in his nostrils, the turning in his stomach as he contemplates what once was living and vital and now is in the midst of its final disintegration. As if to prove his point, when he shifts one of Janet's boots, her fibula pokes through the shoddy vellum that is her skin. He swears softly to himself. But he keeps going, because he can see that her handbag has been squeezed beneath her feet.

He pulls it out and carries it over to a lit table. He removes each item out patiently in turn, itemizing them softly for Aletheia's benefit. Glasses case. Hairbrush. Tampon. Keys. Notebook. This is the most interesting thing there, and he turns the pages carefully. It is mainly jottings for her planned book, the different sites she has visited, beautiful pen drawings of archaeological discoveries: pre-Saxon crosses, the bottom half of a Roman shield, the cover of a medieval book of hours, the elongated, perspectiveless figures, the complex curlicues of its writing, all beautifully rendered. It reminds him of the work of a monastic figure of a past age, someone lonely and eccentric and fixated, in thrall to the beauty of the past.

Jake turns to a page headed 'St Giles site' and sees it swiftly becomes notes for an investigation into the land-ownership of the plateau, and the treasure site. Janet uses not quite a code but abbreviations for her own benefit, yet Jake begins to see what she is getting at: the connection between what lies beneath and upon the hill. The point strikes him forcibly: Janet had discovered that the whole site did actually extend down to, and encompassed, the field below the plateau. He is half-expecting this, and the two conclusions that follow: the treasure should have been considered part of the overall dig, and so could never be subject to purchase at all; the church is likely still to own both parts of the land anyway. For both reasons, the treasure-finders would not become millionaires. He reads the conclusions out for Aletheia, and then sits, lost in thought, for a few minutes.

His back is to the door, but he hears it open this time. He puts the notebook down carefully, making sure not to crease any of its valuable pages. He does not turn his head, even as he feels the presence in the room, the soft breaths of someone nervous and expectant, even dangerous.

He speaks calmly. 'I'm so glad you decided to come. It's time we finished this once and for all. We can't keep letting you get away with murder, Daisy.'

Now he turns, and she is there, all in black against the sandy light for a second. Black trousers, black shirt, her dark hair up to reveal the fullness of her face, black eyes glinting. As is the black barrel of the gun now pointing directly at him.

Chapter Forty-One

Wulfnoth's Keep, St Giles site

A second later, she has flicked a switch, turning the room into mostly darkness, apart from the islands of light around the desks. Her voice, when it comes, is harsh and brittle. 'You might've predicted this, but you can wipe that smug expression from your face, Jake. You've underestimated me, like everyone does. You thought I'd come in, all innocent, self-effacing, the modest woman seeking the reassurances from the big strong man.' She laughs, a glassy sound. 'And I might've done; I might've played that role for a bit. But I was nosing around the office, and heard you reading out the notebook, and knew I'd better act more drastically. I'm getting better at drastic action, Jake. You see the dark patch at the end of the gun. I'm afraid that's blood from your colleague's head. She was keen to – let's say – deter me from taking further action, and I was forced to take steps. I'm actually becoming rather adept at violent blows to the skull – a talent I simply never knew I had.'

She removes her other hand from behind her back, and drops Aletheia's computer on the floor, where it lands with a sharp cracking noise. 'Whoops.'

Jake makes an instinctive move towards her, but she waves the gun in immediate admonishment. 'Ah, ah, Jake. You can stay seated, if you don't mind. A shot down here would get swallowed by these old walls. Nobody would hear a thing, and I'd have all evening to hide your body, maybe luridly in some place of historical interest, maybe at the bottom of one of these tombs. I'd then have plenty of time to make my escape. That's the problem with these sort of sites, Jake, the history of them all gets into your blood somehow, or into your brain, it fills you with a sense of romance.'

'Romance is hardly the word I'd use.'

'Yes, but it's the word I'm choosing. And the thing is, my words, my actions are what count now. I'm tired of being passive, you know, the little girl that people shout names at, the girl from the family that had their land taken off them back in India, and then again when they struggled to make good in this country. The victim. The target. "Paki, go home."'

Jake watches her shift her weight from side to side. She is a ball of nervous energy, but she is barely remaining in control of the situation. The tip of the gun weaves in tantalizing fashion, though he is too far away to make a leap for it. He needs to talk his way into an opportunity to get closer. His mind flashes immediately to Aletheia, and the hope she is OK, before dismissing the thought as unhelpful for the moment.

When he speaks, he puts as much authority into his voice as he can muster. 'I can actually understand, to a point, Daisy. You as the killer always made sense to me.'

She frowns. 'How so? You can tell me, Jake. It's not

likely that we're both walking out of this ridiculous folly, is it? Unless you can come up with some solution that doesn't involve you joining poor Janet, I fear we're approaching end times, as it were.'

'I think the identification between you and Wulfnoth was always right there. A rebel who lost his land, like your family did. And your house, The Wake, I looked into that. It's named after another famous rebel – old Hereward the Wake – who tried to fight against the ruling classes who were determined to steal from him, keep him down. I saw a book about him in your house. And you told us about the ruining of your family back in India, and I understand how that could have got into your head.'

'You. Could. Never. Understand.' Her words are sibilant, spat at him. The barrel of the gun pushed forward. 'You might fancy yourself a modern empathetic man, Jake. But you've no idea what it's like to come to this country because your family lost everything, and then to fight for whatever you can get when you're here. Your colleague up there might know what I'm talking about, or Livia even. I always felt she understood what I've been feeling.'

'But all that would've happened before you were even born.'

'Look around you, Jake. History is never the past, it never stays buried. It's just the beginning of the story – and, like all beginnings, it dictates its own end.' She kicks at a chair and manoeuvres it across the floor, its wheels squeaking, so she can sit down in front of him, six feet away, gun now in two hands. 'Forgive me, though. I was waxing philosophical, when instead I wanted to hear about the brilliance of your deductions.'

'I was hardly brilliant. I was slow. But I did think that the treasure was always key to all of this. It's a lot of money to turn anyone's head, and also the chance to own part of history, be in charge of it, benefit from it. Get paid for what you deserve. I'm guessing you felt you had a claim to the land, and Janet's investigations were going to harm you. Because she'd uncovered an earlier deed that trumped yours, because she'd established that the treasure site was part of the fort and so the horde could not be claimed as treasure at all. She was here one night, working on her book, and talked to you, confronted you even. And only one of you walked out.'

Daisy's heart is visibly racing, he can see the rise and fall of her chest, the simple silver band of her necklace winking as it moves in the light. She cocks her head to one side. 'I had no intention, really, of killing her, but her face as she lectured me. It' – she exhales slowly, self-soothingly – 'it infuriated me, Jake. This privileged white woman who could've taken away land and money and worth from me with a scratch of her pen. You see, I'd managed to prove that my family had a late claim to that patch of ground beneath the hill. That deed she'd found was a catastrophe for me. She could certainly have proved that the lower land where we found the horde was part of the same patch of land as the dig site, so the treasure was worth nothing to any of us. It was no more than archaeological material owned by the government. And that deed also showed that my family had never owned the land in the first place; their rights to it were meaningless. She took our claims and turned them to dust.' She breathes in, nostrils flaring with anger. 'And she couldn't see the harm she was doing. Even as she wagged her finger at me, she underestimated me, thought I was weak and submissive. She turned her back on me, for God's sake, like I was some wretched servant! And

I felt this anger, this passion rise in me. I'm not a passionate woman, Jake. You've probably found that. I've never had what you have with Livia, you know. I've always been coiled up, restrained, fearful of showing myself or acting up. Making a fuss, my dad used to say. "Daisy must never make a fuss." This was a man so keen to avoid making a fuss he changed my name to the blandest, most boring English flower you can think of. But I obviously felt passion deep, because when she turned, I let it surge right through me. I picked up an old bit of pottery, and felt power as well as passion. And you know what followed.'

'And you were lucky. Janet's lifestyle meant that she could be disappeared without too much fuss or attention. You had a ready-made tomb here that would last for years. You wrote her farewell letter, and I wonder if it was then that the idea of becoming Wulfnoth occurred to you.'

'When I was sorting through her stuff, I discovered she had been Wulfnoth, writing those crazy letters. Some of it was because she liked the pranking, I think. She was a strange fish in some respects. But she had her own ideas about the land and history: she thought parts around here belonged to her family, not to me, and not to anyone else. She didn't like the church much, but she seemed to have proved that the church was still in control here, still owned the land without earning it. I think some event may have happened in her past that refused to lie still. Maybe some holy predator fiddling away at her, maybe some taint on her family caused by a priest. Sadly we never got the chance to speak about it. But, yes, with the first Wulfnoth gone, I had the opportunity to slip into his shoes. I even took the trouble of using a phrase or two from her original letter.'

There is silence. The rain outside must have stopped;

there is no noise at all, except perhaps the merest hint of a wind, a high note almost out of all hearing. Jake's chair creaks. He leans forward. 'With Janet gone, you could keep hold of your claim to the land, and make sure it was classed as separate from the main dig. That's why after she was dead you borrowed her ID and went to the archives to steal the deed she'd found. And I presume you wanted to keep all the money for yourself, so you developed the plan to go after your fellow treasure-finders too, but not straight away.'

'No, I thought I'd leave it, make sure Janet's disappearance went unnoticed. Which it did, even when I asked the police about it. But this was never about simply money.'

'In my experience, that's what greedy people always say to themselves, when they do things for money.'

'Take caution, Jake. I'm extremely sensitive to being disrespected. I felt that way about Reverend Jordan with his clumsy hands, or even hapless Amy, all pale and squishy, letting herself be fondled and fingered by that overgrown student of hers.'

'Did Jordan grope you?'

There is more rustling quiet, a faint hissing sound, like a record whirling without sound. 'He didn't assault me, Jake. But his hands lingered, those stubby dirty fingers of his, on my shoulder, brushing against my bottom. And he made jokes about me, called me a "dusky maiden", other things too.'

'So you killed him?'

'Let's say I negligently left the acid in the wrong place and fate intervened. He was also – as I'm being frank with you – interested in the history of the land, and could've picked up Janet's trail at any point. He was the biggest risk to me, and my well-being, and my entitlement.'

'And Amy?'

'Amy always felt I was a figure to be ignored and patronized. Don't make me feel like that now, or it will go hard with you. You know she had her own theory about me being Wulfnoth, right at the end? She told me about that the other morning, in her superior way. I had been toying with not killing her, letting things lie, and sharing the money; it was more than enough for me. But when she tried to probe me about the letters and Jordan, I could tell she had to go. Killing her then was as much about self-defence as anything. So you should can the pop-psychology; instead, you should carry on explaining how you found me.'

'We knew Jordan's killer had to be close to the dig. And then when you were attacked here, it looked like all the treasure folk were being knocked off, perhaps leaving one at the end who would scoop the pot. It was a good touch, that. Portraying yourself as one of the victims. Ironic, given that you seem to regard victim status as so demeaning.'

'Avoid irony and stick to facts, Jake. I won't warn you again. The last time I thought you were a danger to me, you ended up half-drowning with a broken scalp.'

Jake grins wolfishly. 'Another sign of our killer being close to the dig: only someone connected would've even known I was there. And the stone that hit me seems to have given you the idea about faking your own accident. I noticed the possible train of thought. And then the blue twine that came off the stone that hit you – that felt wrong. Why was it there in an otherwise clean trench? Could be an accident, or it could have been wrapped around the stone, so you could pull it down on yourself. An attack that was colourful and visible, but not really that harmful. And which relied on a change in the weather that couldn't be predicted, something a real killer wouldn't have risked.

All nagging details to bear in mind, certainly. Then there was the vandalism on your house. Another nice touch. But why was the note from Wulfnoth *beneath* the local paper, if the attack had happened after the paper had been delivered? Surely it implied that someone had entered the house after the vandalism and placed it there, probably without thinking too much. The only person who could have done that was the owner. You.'

'There was a spare key, as you know. Someone else could have done that.'

'That key hadn't been moved in months; it was dusty as hell when we lifted the bench. No, that was an elaboration too far. As was the attempt to frame Zach. Amy's body left as if straight after sex, braless and exposed. But sex out there wasn't plausible, in the cold and the rain, it wasn't likely. I guess sex has never been your speciality, actually.' Daisy gulps but says nothing. 'And Amy's bra was in the office anyway. The place where she was most likely to have made love that day. No sign of outdoor sex on the body, no dirt, no grit. The only physical evidence those marks where the body was dragged there after death. Oh, the set-up made sense, theoretically, logically. And you are, it strikes me, a deeply logical person. But it felt too baroque, too stagey. If Zach hadn't killed her in the act of making love, then someone was trying to make us *think* that he did, and that someone was beginning to identify herself. I have a colleague who can trace licence plates and the movement of cars – not around here, but in certain places where there are cameras, and yours was in all the right places at all the right times. Even following me and Livia to that church at one point. No, by the end, it could only be you, I'm afraid. And here we both are. I actually feel a little sorry for you.'

'No! Do not pity me.' Daisy's voice is pitched somewhere between a curse and a wail, high and angry and sad. The gun rises up again, threatening.

'But I do. I think you probably have been badly used in your life. And although I'm no expert, I can see how your family have been abused over generations. That graffiti, so out of character for Wulfnoth when you stop to think about it, so far removed from the pattern, it was a real cry of anguish. Go home. Because people always wanted you to, and there was no home for you to go to.'

'I said no more fucking cheap psychology, Jake. I don't want to be explained away by you, a man desperate to be wise and neat and patronizing. But I do accept you've done better than I thought when it comes to looking at evidence. I had wondered whether you might still not have enough for your police friends to come for me. Which would have at least given me the chance to let you go. Your word against mine, and no proof against poor, lonely Daisy. But my word is not going to be enough. I see that. And of course it never would've been. I'll always be a second-class citizen here.'

Jake is concerned she is winding things up, talking herself into definitive action. He needs to break the momentum. 'Did you really kill Amy, then, to save yourself?'

When she answers, her voice has gone soft again. 'Partly. Partly to stop her getting the money, I suppose. Partly to put attention on Zach, get the final treasure-seeker out of the way. And partly out of, I don't know, disgust. You see, I'd been watching them, and let me tell you there's not much dignified about a middle-aged woman and a student doing that to one another. All that flesh. His scrawny pale flanks and buttocks, like a child's; her degrading herself, on her knees, on her back, bosomy and matronly, letting him smear himself against her body.' The tone hardens once more, disdain written across her features. 'There were lots of reasons to do it. I could then have waited a few years, made my claim to the land, got the money and started again.'

'Where would you have gone?'

'Maybe to somewhere like Goa, somewhere rural and vast and shapeless. Hot enough to burn away the past. I could have lived like a princess there with all that cash. A figure to be admired and respected and feared.'

'Instead, you're talking to me, thinking about making a huge mistake, in the depths of a man-made hole in the depths of the English countryside.'

'Jake, you have, genuinely, been kind to me. And if I could conceive of a way out, perhaps I would. But one more death means little to me now, and now I have to clear up this mess. What's that *Macbeth* line? "I am in blood / Stepped in so far, that, should I wade no more / Returning were as tedious as go o'er." You know I never understood the word "tedious" in that scene before. The idea that killing someone could be tiresome, fatiguing. But it is. I feel I could fire this gun, watch it obliterate your features, make your blood well up and pour itself away, and feel not much more than a shrug. Go off and sleep for a month.'

'I don't accept that.'

'What do you mean?'

'You're a thinking, feeling person, Daisy. All sorts of things have conspired to bring you here, some of them happened before you were born. But you're not a bored, psychopathic murderer. You're someone with a heart. I believe that.'

A croaking noise in her throat. 'Nice try, Jake. Appease the mad, bad old bat and maybe you'll get out of here alive.

No, we've reached the end, I'm afraid. I'll try to make sure the lovely Livia isn't the one to find your body.'

She raises the gun. Jake swallows. And then out of the darkness a shaft of metal appears from nowhere, its sharpened point pressed against Daisy's throat so firmly that a thin line of red-black blood trickles down.

Livia's voice. 'I can't let you do that, Daisy. And I'm not lovely. I'm someone who would rip your heart out to protect Jake, and not even think twice about it. Drop the gun now.'

At the same time, the lights flicker on. Daisy gasps and turns towards another presence. It's Lily, coming swiftly from the side of the room, only three steps away, reaching forward and knocking the gun from Daisy's hand. Her body stiffens as she turns back towards Livia. Jake sees the desperation in her eyes, her recognition of being checked, controlled by the situation. With a lunge of her head she tries to impale herself against the point of the sword, driving her neck towards it so it can cut through her buttery flesh. An act of self-harm, a need for the clarity of sharp pain, or because she simply wanted to bring an end to it all. She is sobbing as she does it. Whether Livia predicted this, or was lucky in her reactions, Jake can't tell, but she pulls back immediately, in time, and Daisy falls to the ground. Jake picks the gun up and holds it to her head.

'Move, and I won't kill you; I'll just knock you out.'

Daisy looks beaten, but Jake does not trust her, has renewed faith in her desperation, her powers to propel herself forwards to terrible effect. He motions to Lily, who throws across some blue twine from one of the tables, and he quickly trusses her hands tight behind her back.

Then he grabs Livia in a hug that shudders him down to

his boots, mouthing words of gratitude and love into her ears. He can faintly hear the noise of sirens in the distance as he does so.

He pulls back and searches her face. 'What about Aletheia?'

Livia's voice is grave. 'She's unconscious upstairs. When genius here knocked her out and closed the computer, she thought it would've switched everything off. But it kept broadcasting enough for us to know there'd been a problem. Martha got the cavalry coming, by the sounds of it. In the meantime, I knew you needed me. When I got here, Lily was outside fuming, and then was rather keen to help.'

Jake stretches out a hand and clasps Lily's shoulder. 'I won't forget that. Your family has a habit of being in the right place at the right time, you know.'

He checks Daisy's bonds once more, and heaves her up, ignoring her quiet sobs, and they move out of the Keep. Outside the rain has stopped, and the air is fresh and cool, the world bathed and cleaned and renewed. Below the plateau, Jake can see the blue lights flashing, hear the sounds of people scrambling up the incline.

He pushes the office door open, and throws Daisy forward into the sofa. Lying on the floor behind it is Aletheia, dark stain behind her head. She is not moving.

Lily swears under her breath. 'Don't worry, Jake. The ambulance is on the way.' He falls to his knees and reaches for her neck. There's a thready pulse, weak but undeniable. He looks up with a smile, which turns immediately to rictus. Livia is leaning against the doorway, gasping. There is blood trickling down her leg.

Chapter Forty-Two

Various parts of Kings Markham Hospital

That sight of blood, so familiar and frightening. The lurch in his stomach like a sudden kick. His urgent desire to get her help. He half-carries Livia down the hill, her breath coming in short bursts, her hand gripping his, as if clinging on to life itself. Behind them, he hears the paramedic crew, who had rushed past him as if in a dream, some sort of carnivalesque parade of green-clad strangers, bristling with equipment. They are clustering around Aletheia, fussing her into a stretcher, shouts of 'one, two, three, now!'

He and Livia pass McAllister on the way up, who is hurried but still poised. He claps Jake swiftly on the shoulder and whispers: 'Martha's been in my ear. I know what's gone on. Go look after her.' Jake grunts, and hopes beyond hope that he can.

At the bottom of the hill, they wait in the unforgiving light emerging from the ambulance's interior, a painful hiatus, him murmuring platitudes that sound hollow even to his own ears. Livia, not in pain, but with visceral, vivid fear painted across her features. Aletheia is ferried past them into the vehicle, stock still, corpse-like. Jake agrees with one of the paramedics that he will take Livia in a following car, and he bustles her as gently as he can into her seat.

The journey is an extension of the nightmare, seemingly interminable. One hand on the steering wheel, the other touching Livia's arm, his brain fraught and empty, the black landscape passing by, silent and unflinching, the obscene blue glint of the ambulance ahead of him.

At the hospital, Aletheia is wheeled off without a word, and Jake and Livia are shunted to a different part of the building, into a room where others sit with vacant stares, hopeless expressions, waiting for help.

A doctor – a middle-aged Asian man – comes out to see them, tie askew and tired eyes, and has Livia brought to an examination room. A nurse briskly removes her shorts, wipes the trickled marks of blood from her legs with antiseptic solution.

'You must not worry,' the doctor says. Jake almost laughs, as he feels the vomit acrid against the back of his throat. 'I have seen plenty of things that look bad and mean nothing.'

He is speaking as he squeezes gel upon Livia's stomach, a sonogram in his hand. 'That's it – breathe in and out, in and out.' His voice hypnotic. Jake looks at the ground, imprinting the patternless scuff marks on his brain, not praying but *willing*, as if by sheer force of mind he can make everything be OK.

That pause lasts a lifetime. And then the doctor speaks. 'Do look up, Dad. There we have, ever so tiny, the beginnings of a baby.' He gestures at a screen filled with what looks to Jake like meaningless static. The doctor turns a dial, a thudding noise fills the room, fast and unremitting. 'And that, Mum and Dad, is the sound we love to hear, isn't it? The pitter-patter of life. Unmistakable.'

Jake can't move, tears sticky on his face, hand squeezing Livia's for all it is worth. They stare silently into each other's eyes.

The doctor, unseen, continues to speak. 'Now, I must be stern for a moment. Stress is not good for mum or baby. Running into hospital is not good for mum or baby. So you must be calm, rest, keep out of stressful situations. You understand me?' The ludicrousness of it hits them: it is good advice after all, try not to find yourself, pregnant, holding a sword to a murderer's throat to stop her killing the father of your child. If you can possibly help it.

Livia laughs, a gasping sound. Jake is crying quietly, bright lights blurred in his eyes like a city seen through a rainy window. Smears of colour. The doctor withdraws with tact, and they cling tight to one another. He can feel Livia's heartbeat, a slower echo of what else he now knows is beating within her, indestructible for the moment, the life to come asserting itself amid the panic of life as it is now. Minutes pass, and they slowly rise, Jake refusing to let go of Livia as they leave the hospital, hand in hand, survivors of a near catastrophe.

Chapter Forty-Three

Still in Kings Markham Hospital

A day later, and Livia is restored to her confident self, buoyant in the sturdiness of her body, refusing to dwell on what might have been. Jake, typically, finds worry harder to shake. But his concern is now with Aletheia. He stands in another waiting room, in another part of the hospital, being studiously ignored by doctors and nurses alike.

He watches a door swing open and closed, and in the swift instant gets a glimpse of her face, skin greying in the harsh lights, beneath a swathe of bandages that merge into the pillow. He walks through and stands beside her. There is nobody else in the room, nothing more than an empty bed in the corner. She is asleep or unconscious, he cannot really tell which. He stands for a few moments, watching her breathe, listening to the minor-key bleeps of a machine. There is a pad and pen in the corner, and he writes a note, expressing his worry and his hope and his care for her. He tucks it under a plastic drinks bottle on the tacky tray connected to the side of her bed, and makes his way softly out.

Rose is waiting outside, bashful and awkward, his feet set at odd angles, as he seeks to avoid the notice of the hospital staff. Jake greets him, and surprises himself with hugging him tight. 'She'll be OK, you know. Tough as anything.'

Rose shrugs. He looks awkward in formal institutions, like he doesn't quite fit in, which indeed he does not. He has always liked to work angles, to slide through life avoiding too much meddlesome intrusion, to be in control of his own modest destiny. Jake feels a lot of sympathy with that approach. But neither of them can do that now. When things go wrong, when you have to rely on others, when officialdom is forced to take notice of you, such independence disappears, indeed seems futile. No amount of cunning will help Aletheia as she lies inert in a bed before them.

The next day, hope has dwindled slightly. Aletheia looks strong, but is unresponsive, eyes closed, head swaddled in thick white. Jake only leaves the hospital to check on Livia, Rose seems scarcely to leave at all. But he is seldom long in the room with her, instead moving resolutely outside in the grounds, sitting glass-eyed on benches, feet scuffing at cigarette butts and dusty topsoil where the grass has been kicked away, restless amid the languor of the patients around him.

Another day passes. Next morning, Jake and Rose together in the room by chance, quiet, well beyond the need for conversation. Aletheia wakes. She smiles weakly. 'Jake, Rose, how lovely to see you.'

It becomes clear that she knows where she is and how

she got there. Doctors come in, examine charts, preach caution, but Jake hopes, believes that once more life's essential sturdiness has reasserted itself. Rose gives a wan gesture of relief, strokes her hand briefly, and walks away, not looking back even for a second.

Epilogue

A week later, Jake's hopes have been largely proved right. Aletheia, out of hospital, is now spending some time at Little Sky, stretched out on the grass by the lake, walking the land, regaining her strength. Livia is doing the same, under Jake's more watchful eye, her own body visibly robust, her skin and hair sleek and shining, copper and gold in the hot sun; a sense of something being minted like a treasure within.

He feels he can let much of the case go now. McAllister has neatly tied it all up. Daisy made a full confession. She had to, given the physical evidence, and the recordings made within the Keep. And a voice inside her wanted to give a reckoning, to testify, to make sense of what she had done. Janet's body was disinterred from its unwelcome resting place, and buried properly. All work on the dig has been formally suspended for the year, but there is hope that Brian will be allowed to resume operations next spring, with Lily and perhaps even Matt and Elaine with him. Zach has disappeared back home to his parents, shattered.

The future of the horde remains a matter of legal dispute, and it is most likely it will be appropriated by the state without anybody getting rich from it. The deed, first discovered by Janet and stolen by Daisy, has been recovered. It showed that the horde's location was indeed part of the original dig site, the land most likely belonging to the church. It was easy to say it was not worth dying for, but – in Jake's experience – that meant nothing in the aftermath of murder.

A month later, Jake still likes to walk to the plateau near St Giles when he can. When home feels too close, too cramped, too bustling with familial concerns: Livia's health, Diana's potential relationship with a baby, his own prospects as a father, how they will live, how they will cope. He enjoys standing, back to the tower, at dusk: the sky a swirl of peach and pink and orange, bruise colours; the hill as lonely and as desolate as it must ever have been; its history sleeping beneath the soil, half-exposed but still protective of its secrets.

The past is always there, he thinks, especially when you go looking for it. What happens next under a brand-new sky, though, is still to be decided.

Playlist

I listen to music when I write – it's part of the way I take my mind into the world of Little Sky – and it permeates the novel in the form of records that Jake puts on while detecting, or pottering. In case you like reading with music on, here is the playlist of the songs mentioned in the book. I've also put the list up on Spotify.

Guitar Concerto in D Major by Antonio Vivaldi

On the Nature of Daylight from *The Blue Notebooks* by Max Richter

Papillons, Op 2 by Robert Schumann

Violin Sonata in A Major by Cesar Franck

Parce Mihi Domine from *Officium* by Jan Garbarek

Rhapsody in Blue by George Gershwin

The Girl from Ipanema by Stan Getz featuring Astrud Gilberto, composed by Antônio Carlos Jobim with English lyrics by Norman Gimbel

Etudes Op. 10, No 6 in E-Flat Minor by Frederic Chopin

Cello Suite No. 1 in G Major by Johann Sebastian Bach

Where Did You Sleep Last Night? by Lead Belly

Concierto De Aranjuez, 2. Adagio by Joaquin Rodrigo

Symphony 104 in D Major, 4. Finale by Joseph Haydn

Acknowledgements

Here's a sentence you don't always read: I'd like first to pay tribute to my mother-in-law. Jeanette Sanders (known in the family as Baba) is a member of the Windrush generation, who came over to the UK from Trinidad as a young girl. Her family made something of themselves in this country through hard work and stoicism and spirit, sometimes in the face of shameful cruelty and intolerance. The parts of this novel that feature the issue of racism – and some of the experiences that are described – are based very much on my conversations with Baba, and I dedicate the book to her, and to her beloved father Wilfred Eugene Sankarsingh (1926-1994). Whatever else, their journey here ultimately brought my wife to me, and I'll always be grateful for that.

This is the third Jake Jackson book, and it has given me as much joy to write as the others, if not more. Although, as the publicity team keep telling me, I should also make clear to people that it is a standalone novel as well as part of a series. Elizabeth Dawson and Maud Davies are great PR people, wonderful to hang with, and I probably should listen to their advice more. HarperCollins is generally a magnificent publisher, and I am lucky to have in Kathryn Cheshire a supportive and clever editor. Julia Wisdom, who runs the imprint, is the crime-fiction badass to end all badasses. The book was copyedited brilliantly by Anne O'Brien, who tactfully demonstrated that I have some sort of problem with over-using the words "just", "couple of" and "something". I've taken hundreds of examples out, but feel free to note where they persist in stubborn palimpsest. And no, I've no idea what's wrong with me.

My constant companion in navigating the literary world is super-agent Cathryn Summerhayes, who is small, tough, Welsh, and all-conquering. That is, essentially, an unimprovable combination.

Family is pretty much everything to me. My parents read everything I write, and were the reason I got into reading in the first place. My dad's love of history was transmitted to me, and we spent many happy evenings watching the archaeological programme Time Team together. The debt to that wonderful example of television in this book is clear. My mum has asked me to keep writing about Jake and Livia, so I have no choice but to keep telling their stories, whatever the publishers think. My elder children Nelly and Teddy are supportive in a teenagery, I'm-not-going-to-read-your-stuff way, and I love them dearly. My little one Phoebe is my biggest fan, a prodigious writer, drawer and gluer in her own right, and a total inspiration to me.

But my biggest debt, as ever, is to my wife Nadine. Life without her is unthinkable, the bits of life that are the best are because of her entirely.